Erin had not wanted to write about the blond American TV heart-throb, Jago Miles. She expected him to be vain and empty-headed, so it was a shock to find that he was an articulate Viking who didn't want to have anything to do with *her*!

BACHELOR IN PARADISE

BY
ELIZABETH OLDFIELD

MILLS & BOON LIMITED
15–16 BROOK'S MEWS
LONDON W1A 1DR

First published in Great Britain 1986
by Mills & Boon Limited

© Elizabeth Oldfield 1986

Australian copyright 1986
Philippine copyright 1986
This edition 1986

ISBN 0 263 75463 4

Set in Times 11 on 11 pt.
01–0986 – 45460

Computer typeset by SB Datagraphics,
Colchester, Essex
Made and printed in Great Britain by
Wm. Collins Sons & Co, Glasgow

CHAPTER ONE

HE looked *ordinary*.

Yet another fantasy bites the dust, Erin thought, a wry smile inching its way across her mouth. From the start she had treated Cleo's superlatives with healthy disdain, and now she was being proved right. As with so many of his breed, the man's appeal could be attributed ten per cent to being photogenic and ninety per cent to publicity hype. The smile edged dangerously close to a giggle. This was Super Stud? Oh dear, her agent would have been disappointed.

Shading her eyes against the dazzle which came off the pool, she walked closer. The man asleep on the candy-striped lounger was muscled and tanned to be sure, yet no more muscled or tanned than any of the young men she had seen that morning during her jog. Florida must be packed with such males, and most would be a darn sight more presentable than this one.

Golden stubble glinted on his jaw. He was badly in need of a shave. Not that a shave would transform him into anything spectacular. His chin would continue to be too angular, the line of his nose too sharp and most decidedly skew-whiff. At least he was a natural blond, which was something to be said in his favour, but what had happened to that flowing tawny mane, the Jago Miles trademark? In his role of TV heart-throb he wore his hair overlong, parted in the middle. Two vital wings sprang down

across his brow; wings destined to be brushed aside
with piratical verve or run through by feminine
fingers at what seemed to be monotonous three-
minute intervals. But this morning's sleeping
position and the heat had combined to flatten his
hair damply to his head. So much for leonine
splendour!

Curiosity drew Erin round the corner of the pool.
From the slump of his long body, the creases in his
sawn-off shorts, it was obvious he had spent the
entire night there. Why? She cast a glance over her
shoulder. If the white Hollywood-style villa, with its
green tiled roof and sweeping porches, was half as
grand inside as out, there would be a king-size bed
in a king-size room waiting for His Majesty. Had an
excess of alcohol caused his collapse? Maybe high
jinks with a girl, or several girls, had rendered him
too drained to crawl up from the poolside?
Recalling the magazines she had scanned, anything
seemed possible. Jago Miles was not the type to
settle for cocoa, a good book and an early night.

Suddenly she stopped. Her sense of purpose had
begun to wobble. Waking him would be presumptuous. In any case, nine o'clock on a Sunday morning
was a little early to come calling. She had never
intended to call, but the time difference had had her
rising from her motel bed at an indecently early
hour. Itchy with an urge for action, Erin had
decided to explore. According to her guide book,
the island was an 'exotic semi-tropical wonderland
of silver beaches and tranquil lagoons, studded with
some of the most luxurious real estate on Florida's
west coast', and so she had set off. Clad in Sloppy
Joe T-shirt and short shorts, with a cotton hat as
protection against the already strong sunshine, Erin

had jogged along the beach, cut up through parkland and skirted the approach to the narrow causeway which connected the island to the mainland. Whilst on the move it had seemed sensible to check that the actor's home was situated where the motel receptionist had said it would be and, approaching along a palm-tree-lined lane, she had discovered the wrought iron gates wide open. Open gates had appeared to symbolise a welcome, but . . .

Erin whipped off her sunhat and ruffled her long dark curls. Retreating to telephone later was more civilised. She would return to the motel three miles away, shower and change, then call to fix a formal appointment. Sunday presented a golden opportunity to introduce herself and set things in motion, because if contact was not made today when would Jago Miles next be available? Involved in churning out episode after episode of the soap opera *Taro Beach*, his workload would leave little breathing space. But suppose he had taken wing by the time she phoned? As one of the show business brigade wouldn't he possess an insatiable lust for getting out and about, making contacts, being seen?

With a sigh, Erin fixed the sunhat back on her head. Why had she ever allowed herself to be pushed into featuring him? It was *her* book, after all. Originally she had chosen to profile a portrait painter, a dentist, a mountaineer and a casino boss—then her agent and publishers had brought pressure to bear. She had been advised that if one of the quartet were American the book could be brought out in the States, and if that American happened to be well known, the venture would be more profitable all round. Economics mattered.

Accordingly Erin had drawn up a tentative list of senators, business tycoons, even an astronaut, but agent and publishers had combined to promote a different idea.

'We need someone with sizzle,' Cleo had explained. 'Think back and ask yourself who was responsible for nudging your book on women into the best seller list.'

'Patrice Lanham,' she had replied gloomily, then retaliated, 'but the other three women were far more ... substantial.'

'I agree, yet it's a fact of life that an instantly recognisable household name attracts attention. Now, suppose we substitute the casino boss with Jago Miles? He's well known on both sides of the Atlantic, and as one of television's ten most eligible men has a tremendous following. I've already taken the precaution of having a word with his agent, and he says——'

'No thanks.' Erin's mouth had thinned. 'No way am I writing about a performing peacock again.'

'But he'd be perfect, and it's unreasonable to condemn an entire profession on the strength of one unfortunate incident. I know how you suffered at the hands of Patrice and co.,' Cleo had given her a sympathetic smile, 'but don't let that make you cynical. Thare's no reason to suppose Patrice and Jago Miles are two of a kind. If you include him in the book I guarantee your bank manager will smile for the next ten years. And don't tell me money's not important.'?

'I get by,' she had protested.

'Get by! Why eat mince when you're being given the chance to dine off fillet steak? Be smart.'

*   *   *

Erin scowled at the slumbering man. Cleo would award *him* top marks for being smart. Once a serious actor of promise, drawing critical acclaim for a controversial Hamlet, rave reviews for characterisations in Ibsen and Chekhov, two and a half years ago he had abruptly switched to playing the romantic lead in a soap opera. Thinking of the isolated episode of *Taro Beach* she had seen, she shuddered. How could he do it? *Taro Beach* wasn't even one of the better soaps. The answer was that it paid. For flicking back his hair and smiling a crinkle-eyed smile, he collected dollars by the truck load.

Erin sighed. The prospect of writing about a stereotype matinée idol was making her feel quite numb. All Jago Miles was likely to produce would be kiss-and-tell exposés, anecdotes geared to reveal, accidentally on purpose, what a devastating dreamboat he was. Gossip columns were the place for that kind of drivel. Patrice Lanham, whatever her personal shortcomings, had been a member of the English theatrical fraternity for more than forty years, and was dedicated to her art. This man wasn't dedicated. He didn't care.

Intent on departure, she turned, but a beer can, a full one, had been left standing at the rim of the pool and as she moved Erin knocked it with her foot. The can toppled over, rolled and fell into the water with a noisy plop.

'Oh!' she gasped, fingers flying to her lips.

The man on the lounger sat bolt upright. 'Susie? It's Susie?' he muttered, his tone fraught and strained.

'No. I'm——'

'You've come about Susie?' He blinked, struggling to awake. 'You're from——'

'The Driftwood Motel,' she supplied, when he broke off to grind two large fists into his eyes. Her bright smile was intended to be an apology for waking him. 'From England, really. I flew in last night.'

He staggered to his feet. He was taller than she had imagined, around six foot three. A hand was placed on the top of his head, as though it was whirling and needed to be steadied. The previous night must have been a hard one.

'You haven't brought news of Susie?'

Erin's smile became appropriately regretful. ' 'Fraid not.'

Ice-blue eyes, clear and deep-set, fixed on her. 'Then who the hell are you?' he demanded.

Jago Miles was not ordinary any more.

CHAPTER TWO

'MY name's Erin Page.'

'I take it I'm expected to leap up and down and shout "Wowee"?' he replied, unnerving her with a fast-freeze stare.

'Not—not really.'

He hooked his thumbs into his belt and yanked the denim shorts higher on to his hips. 'I don't know any Erin Page,' he said flatly.

'Yes, you do. Well, no, you don't.' He might be bedraggled, wearing only crumpled shorts, but of his presence there was no doubt. He emanated an energy which was impossible to ignore. His Hamlet must have been spine-tingling. 'But you remember my name? You must. Mr Steen said how much you were looking forward to meeting me.'

'Did he? Then I guess Mr Steen got carried away. It happens frequently.' His lip curled in a spasm of contempt. 'So you're one of Burt's bimbos? Hell, I thought at last I'd got it through to him that when I require feminine company I make my own arrangements. Sorry, but I'm not in the market for whatever it is you have to offer, and especially not at——' He squinted at the watch strapped to his wrist. '—— nine-o-five in the morning. What do you think I am, some kind of push-button hormonal wizard?'

'You've got it wrong, Mr——'

'No, *you've* got it wrong,' he slammed. 'So kindly report back with the message "Thanks but no

thanks." You might also add you're a shade too pale
for my taste.' A sardonic brow lifted. 'Plus you're on
the old side.'

'Old!' Indignation flushed away any nervousness.
His attitude was offensive. She had not travelled all
this way to be insulted by a lank-haired American,
even if his middle name was supposed to be Mr
Wonderful. Added to which she knew for a fact
Jago Miles had been placed on this earth thirty-six
years ago, half a dozen earlier than she had. She was
too old? He was almost a museum piece! 'Maybe
I'm not a nymphet with a suntan the colour of a
leather saddle,' Erin retorted, 'but I can assure you
that in some circles I'm——'

'In my circle——' He took a menacing step
towards her. '— you are surplus to requirements.'

She stood firm, which required an effort with him
bearing down like a barefoot gangster.

'I'm afraid you don't understand,' she said,
relieved when he stopped a yard away. He was a big
man. If he had picked her up bodily and thrown her
in to join the beer can on the bottom of the pool she
would not have been surprised.

'Damn right,' he barked, 'so why don't you
explain? For a start I'd like a full account of how
you managed to gain access to this property.'

'I came in through the front gates and—and I'm
not here at Mr Steen's request.' Erin swallowed,
unwilling to dwell on what it was the actor had
imagined she had come to offer. 'Well, that's not
quite true. Mr Steen did arrange——'

'Through the gates or over them? Or maybe you
crept up from the beach?'

'I came *through* the gates.'

Jago Miles folded muscled arms across his chest,

a chest which she had to agree came up to glamour-
boy requirements. Broad and firm, it was covered
with the requisite mat of golden hair. And from his
chest a neat vertical line of body hair ran mid-centre
down the flatness of his belly to disappear into the
denim shorts.

'You bribed Rafael? I guess that wouldn't have
been too difficult.'

'I bribed no one. Least of all because no one was
there to bribe,' Erin said, growing impatient. 'The
gates were open and I walked up the drive. I
wondered about ringing the front door bell, but then
I caught sight of you here by the pool so I——' Her
hand sketched an investigative gesture. 'I dare say I
could be accused of trespassing, but——'

'You *are* trespassing,' came the swift
condemnation.

'But I wanted to see you.'

He rubbed his jaw, scowling when the stubble
rasped against his fingers. 'You mean you're a fan?'

'Good grief, no!' She broke out laughing. Did he
expect her to produce an autograph book? Beg for a
signed photograph? 'Er—yes,' she amended, her
thoughts skidding around like balls on a pin-table.
Jago Miles was an actor and as such would possess
an outsize ego. Admitting she was not an admirer in
such a definite way could be suicide. She must not
rile him, she must calm him. The aggression she had
unwittingly sparked off was counter-productive.
How could she write an account of his life without
his co-operation? Personal preferences must be set
aside, for her book's sake she must attempt to win
his acceptance and trust. 'I watch *Taro Beach* every
week,' she gushed.

'Then what's your opinion of my car, the silver

Maserati?' he questioned, the big freeze glare
narrowing until his eyes resembled piercing blue
icicles. Privately Erin christened him the Ice Man.

'It's—it's marvellous.'

'Don't lie. I thought you reckoned to have just
come over from England, but the series lags a year
behind there. The Maserati has yet to make an
entrance.'

'I must be confused,' she blustered. 'Look, Mr
Miles——'

'Yes, you must. It's my guess you're also confused
about the gates being open. You're not a fan. Maybe
I did wake up only a moment ago, but I'm not that
dopey I can't recognise a sneak thief when I see one.
The papers said there'd been a spate of daylight
robberies.' He reached out to fasten a grip like a
steel claw around har upper arm, and before she
knew what was happening Erin found herself being
roughly bundled along the side of the pool. 'What
were you hoping to pick up—cameras, jewellery, a
wallet stuffed with hundred-dollar bills? Save it for
the cops,' he said, when she started to protest. 'I'm
going to call them right now. A patrol car'll be
round to collect you in minutes. With my troubles,
you I really need,' he muttered, propelling her
towards the house at breakneck speed. 'A sneak
thief with big brown eyes, long legs and a sassy
backside! It's true what they say, the bad guys look
suspiciously like the good guys these days.'

'I'm not a thief,' she jabbered, half tripping in her
attempt to pull free. 'I'm a writer.'

'Yeah?'

'*Yes.*'

The icicle look stabbed sideways. After a
moment indecision glimmered across his face, and

then he sighed. He appeared to believe her. This was an improvement, but only in the sense that the bow and arrow had been an improvement on the cudgel, for his expression continued to be stern, his fingers continued to bite into her arm, and his stride never faltered. Still she was being frog-marched towards the house.

'Not another goddamn journalist? I might have guessed.' Cold blue eyes scoured the smooth sweeps of grass and scarlet hibiscus bushes in the distance. 'Where's your pal with the camera? It's not like the paparazzi to miss a trick. Or has he already got what he wanted, courtesy of the long zoom lens?'

'You're mistaken,' Erin said, but was drowned out.

'Thief? Journalist? So what? You're still trespassing and I'm still calling the police.'

'Please do,' she hissed, furious at being hauled around like a common criminal. 'I don't care. I'm not a journalist, I'm a writer. There's a big difference. I write books, quality books, and you're due to be featured in one of them. It's been arranged for ages. My travel plans were finally agreed with Mr Steen a couple of weeks ago, and confirmed in writing.'

Jago Miles stopped dead. 'What the hell are you talking about?'

'You can't have forgotten.' Erin recognised he would lead a full life, but it couldn't be so full that combining with her on what was more or less a biography had slipped his mind—could it? A feeling of betrayal swamped her. Because the book absorbed her every waking moment she had automatically assumed the actor would regard his inclusion in it as—perhaps not earth-shattering, but at least worthy of consideration. Not so. 'I'm writing a factual account about four men from different walks of life,' she explained. 'Last summer discussions took place between Mr Steen and my agent, Cleo Munro. It was agreed then you'd be one of the quartet.'

The steel claw unfastened itself from her arm. 'This is news to me.'

'It can't be,' she protested.

'It is. I've seen no agreement, let alone put my signature to one.'

'No, Mr Steen said it wasn't necessary, but——'

'And I have more publicity than I can handle right now.'

'This isn't a PR thing,' Erin said earnestly. 'This is an in-depth look at contemporary people and their lives.'

'So?'

'So it's not just . . . candyfloss. Look, I've already completed the profiles on the other three men, why don't I let you read them and——'

'Pass.'

Must he be so damned arrogant? Must his refusal sound so definite? In retrospect it was clear Cleo should have insisted on some kind of formal contract. But perhaps he was just playing hard to get? Perhaps he wanted to be coaxed?

'Mr Miles,' she began, remembering how Patrice Lanham had been a glutton for flattery, no matter how thickly it was trowelled on.

'Miss Page,' he countered 'You are becoming a nuisance.'

'Mr Miles, as a man of our times the public are fascinated by your views, your opinions, your lifestyle.' Erin spoke quickly, intent on preventing an interruption. 'It's not everyone who was once called the thinking woman's Ádonis, and——'

'The what? Jeez!' He threw back his head and laughed, only to sober in double-quick time. The chill look returned. 'Nice try, but the answer remains the same. I'm not in the mood to be dissected, even if it is by a quasi-sociologist, so I'd be grateful if you'd quit hassling me and go.' He jabbed a long index finger towards the front of the house. 'Go!'

Her heart sank, her insides felt nipped. Erin could recognise a genuine rejection when she heard one. But where did that leave her? The interviews with the mountaineer had taken longer than expected, due to his habit of disappearing without notice to scale remote crags, and now the deadline for completion of her manuscript was fast approaching. Two months in Florida to assemble information and draft the profile, one month back home to finalise, her schedule was trimmed tight. And if she didn't write about Jago Miles, whom did she write about? Locating a suitable replacement at such short notice would be wellnigh impossible.

'But I've done the groundwork,' she told him, her voice straining upwards in distress.

'Go!' The ice developed a crack. 'If there's been some kind of mix-up, I'm sorry.'

'Are you? Well, it's a darn sight more than a mix-up,' Erin bit out. Why hadn't she followed her own wishes and insisted on interviewing the casino boss, come what may? Show business people were all suspect. Once before she had been the victim of the pick you up, drop you down technique, and here was Jago Miles, another supreme exponent of the art. His denial of all knowledge did not fool her. The

notion of appearing in her book must have appealed
last summer and down through each and every
month until as recently as a fortnight ago, but on a
whim he had changed his mind. Not in the mood—
how dare he! 'You and your agent are nothing but a
pair of con men,' she announced, yellow flecks
glittering in the depths of her eyes. 'What am I
expected to do? Put wasting my time and the cost of
the air fare down to experience? Strange as it may
seem, I don't appreciate experiences like that.'

'Suppose I go some way to reimbursing you?'
Jago Miles suggested, striding across the patio. He
opened sliding glass doors and directed her into a
living-room where morning sunshine gilded plush
white carpets, overstuffed leather couches in ice-
cream colours, expensive furnishings. 'How much
are you out of pocket—seven, eight hundred
dollars?'

Erin glared. 'You imagine paying me off makes
everything all right?'

'Can you suggest an alternative? Don't answer
that,' he snapped, when she started to speak. 'I
haven't time to stand and argue. There's someone I
must visit this morning. It's important.' He went to
a writing desk. 'A cheque will have to do. I don't
keep that much cash in the house.'

'To hell with your cheque,' Erin blasted. 'I'm fully
aware that standing in front of a camera like a
reciting robot and indulging in gratuitous chest-
baring has made you a wealthy man, but I wouldn't
take a single penny. Maybe on the eighth day God
was supposed to have created Jago Miles, but as far
as I'm concerned he needn't have bothered because
you are one of the most ill-mannered men I have
ever met.' Her tongue was being reckless, but she

did not care. She felt too strongly about the injustice of her situation—a situation *he* had dropped her into. 'Your initial salvo was that I'm in my dotage, next you accuse me of being a cat burglar, then you—you——'

Erin's tirade petered out. Her antagonist's attention had strayed. Head tilted, blond brows dipped in query, he was listening to the crunch of tyres on the drive. A car had arrived at the front porch.

'I wonder if this is Poll?' he muttered, and paced off through an archway to investigate.

Left alone, Erin stood and fumed. The man was not only a louse and an ignoramus, he was also committing sacrilege. What gave him the right to refuse to be featured in her book? Her other three subjects had been delighted—even honoured—to take part, acknowledging the seriousness of her work. They had had their priorities right, but not Jago Miles. Here she was, giving him the opportunity to gather kudos from appearing in an upmarket dissertation, and all he could think about was girls. Poll. Susie. Less than ten minutes in his company and his fondness for females was in high profile. Erin wrinkled her nose in disgust. Didn't he know there was more to life than sex? Much more. Through the arch he was opening the front door and she waited, expecting the arrival of a juvenile and golden-skinned sex kitten. Instead a short, dark, thickset man in his early forties erupted into the house. He wore a vibrantly floral shirt and even more vibrantly checked trousers.

'Hi there, Jagie-baby,' he carolled, eyes twinkling behind gold framed spectacles. 'You're not going to like this but, please, before you say a word, hear me out. And trust me. There's this old broad arriving

from England. My information is she's a top drawer
writer. She wants to include you in——' Bounding
through the archway, he saw Erin. 'Didn't realise
you were entertaining,' he grinned. 'I'm sure sorry if
I've burst in on a beautiful experience.'

'You haven't.' Jago's reply was verbal frostbite.
'And I suspect the old broad has arrived. Allow me
to introduce Erin Page.'

'You're Erin? Here already?' After a split second
of surprise, the newcomer bounced back. 'Gee,
forgive me. I had this dumb image of an ancient
bluestocking, but instead you're young and lovely.'
He grabbed hold of her hand and pumped it up and
down. 'Burt Steen. Great to know you.'

Faced with such an enthusiastic welcome, it
would have been ungracious not to respond. 'How
do you do,' she said stiffly.

'Get a load of that accent!' the agent exclaimed.
'Isn't it peachy?'

'Peachy.' Jago sniffed. 'Okay Burt, talk and talk
fast. I don't know what stunt you're attempting to
pull this time, but presenting me with Miss Page as
a *fait accompli* won't work. I'm not prepared to be
written up in some goddamn book. Since when did I
need that kind of ego trip?'

'But this isn't just any old book. This is to be a
prestige production, twenty-four carat class. Erin
isn't your usual hack, oh no. She's an academic. She
has a degree in history from——' Burt paused to
smile at her like a dog show judge, '— Oxford.'

'Is that my cue for wild applause?' Jago demanded, flinging her a scurrilous look. Erin flung one
back. Grudgingly she was being forced to accept
that the actor seemed innocent of any trickery, but
did that make much difference? She had still been

brought out to Florida on a wild-goose chase.
Maybe Burt Steen was the real villain of the piece,
but blaming client rather than agent felt far more
satisfactory. 'If Miss Page translates Homer for
kicks, sings madrigals and wears pince-nez, heigh
jolly ho.' Jago had lapsed into a sneering English
voice. 'But count me out.'

'Ease up. You're too tense. Your shoulders are
knotted. Aren't his shoulder muscles knotted?' Burt
appealed to Erin. He patted the actor's arm. 'I can
tell you're short on sleep, buddy, and I sympathise. I
know what you're going through. But trust me. The
bottom line is that this book's going to be a best
seller. Erin writes best sellers.'

'I've written one,' she felt compelled to point out.
Burt's persuasive tactics might be in her own
interests, but the truth remained important.

'This'll be another.' The agent spoke with the
authority of someone who had his own private
crystal ball. 'And when the book hits the top of the
pile, Jagie-baby, you'll make bucks.'

'I benefit financially?' Her antagonist swung to
her. 'You never said anything about that.'

'I didn't have much opportunity, did I?' she shot
back, then added, 'The arrangement is that in
return for your co-operation you'll receive a share of
the royalties. Mr Steen has full details, has had them
for over nine months.'

Burt's smile was blithe. Despite evidence to the
contrary it was clear that in his own mind he had
dissociated himself from any malpractice, and now
his round features radiated the desire to please.

'The deal's well worth consideration,' he assured
Jago. 'As Erin's here, why not give it a spin? This
time next year you could be kicking yourself if you

don't. Get my drift?'

'Yeah.' A look passed between the two men, and the blue eyes which travelled to Erin took on a speculative glint. 'You reckon there's a chance of this book doing well?'

'It's possible, though naturally I can't promise a surefire success. The public are unpredictable and much depends on what else is being brought out at the same time. However, my writing has achieved a certain level of respect.' Her tart tone indicated it was high time he showed her some. 'Cleo reckons the profiles I've already submitted are better than anything I've done before, so the book looks . . . hopeful.'

'How many books have you written?'

'Five. Four Edwardian biographies and the companion to this one, which featured the lives of contemporary women.'

'Didn't I tell you this chick has pedigree?' Burt chimed in.

'You look too young to have written five books,' Jago said suspiciously.

Erin dispensed a sweet smile. 'Ten minutes ago you were telling me I was too old.'

'Yes. Well.' The bramble on his chin was scratched. 'Burt, you and I need to talk. Drive Miss Page over to her motel, then come and fill me in.' He turned to Erin again. 'We'll get back to you on this.'

The Ice Man had dismissed her.

Lying on the bed, Erin stared at the ceiling. For two hours she had been anticipating Burt Steen's promised call, but there had been no contact. Now she was on the brink of lifting the telephone, requesting Cleo's number and advising her agent to expect her back on the first available plane. Why should Jago Miles be allowed to play God? She deeply resented being forced to hang around waiting for him to deign to say an icy yea or nay, and even more so when it was clear any yea would stem entirely from financial considerations. It had amazed her how his attitude had changed at the mention of cash—amazed and sickened. If he had stuck to his guns and refused to be written up come hell or high water, Erin would have granted him certain admiration, but instead he had reinforced the image of himself as a person willing to do anything for money. And much wanted more. Yet in comparison with the well documented salary he drew from *Taro Beach*, his share of the royalties would be pocket-money. Pocket-money he would doubtless drool over.

Lost in contemplating his greed, she was taken by surprise when the telephone shrilled.

'Erin-baby, we have lift off,' announced a triumphant Burt. 'Jago's ready and waiting, itching to get started. I'll collect you from the motel in fifteen minutes, okay?'

A hair's breadth away from saying, 'Nuts to Jago Miles' and slamming down the receiver, Erin remembered her deadline. Like it or not, she *needed* the man.

'Okay,' she agreed.

A quarter of an hour later she was sitting beside Burt in an electric blue Cadillac, listening as he did his best to make amends.

'Once you get to know him, you'll realise Jago's a real nice person. He might be a star, but his head hasn't been turned. The guy genuinely believes he's nothing special.'

'Fancy that,' she remarked, but her sarcasm went unnoticed.

'What you gotta remember is that Jago's living under pressure. The *Taro Beach* schedule means he's up at dawn and doesn't get home until gone eight each evening. There'll be a break in ten weeks' time, but that's way off. At the moment it's go, go, go.' He flashed her a smile. 'Isn't it understandable if occasionally he gets uptight, blows his top? Yeah. Added to which you've met him at a very stressful period because——'

'Because what?' Erin prompted, when he clammed up.

The agent braked slightly as he swung the car onto the private lane, then continued smoothly, 'Because he's experiencing some aggression from Kiel.' Kiel, it transpired, was a 'good-looking dude with ebony hair' who played Jago's long-standing enemy in *Taro Beach*. 'Problem is, on screen the guy's as lively as cardboard and he knows it. In retaliation he works out his hostility on the rest of the cast, but mainly on Jago. It bugs him that Jago gets twice the fan mail. Though he would, wouldn't he—being a legend in his own lifetime?' Burt remarked, displaying the skills of a megalomaniac public relations man.

Erin's mouth twitched. ' "See, the conquering hero comes!" ' she recited. ' "Sound the trumpets, beat the drums!" '

'Gee, is that Shakespeare?' breathed her companion.

'Thomas Morell.'

Their arrival at the entrance to the villa fore-stalled any questions as to Morell's identity, and this time the gates were indeed closed. Burt was required to sound his horn once, twice, three times, before a sleepy Hispanic teenager stumbled from the bushes to be identified as the truant Rafael. Yawning, the boy dragged open the gates and stood aside as they cruised on to the drive.

'Jago said for you to go straight in,' Burt explained, depositing her beneath the porch. He climbed back into his car and gave a genial wave. 'Have a nice day.'

'I'll try,' she muttered.

Briefcase tucked beneath her arm, Erin walked through the open door and into the entrance hall. Assuming a greeting at any moment, she stood and waited. And waited. She brushed a shiny, freshly shampooed curl from her shoulder, adjusted the belt of her navy linen dress, and coughed politely to warn of her arrival. Nothing happened. Through the archway the living-room spread itself in unoccupied splendour. All she could hear was the distant whirr of an air-conditioner. She coughed again. She had not expected Jago Miles to lay on red-carpet treatment, but she had expected him to be here. Erin waited. Still nothing. Burt's insistence that the actor was itching to get started appeared to be baloney, like so much else.

'Mr Miles?' She peeped into a dining-room, then a sleek modern kitchen. There was no sign of life. 'Mr Miles?' She stood in the middle of the hall. '*Mr Miles!*'

'Come on up,' called a far-away voice.

Her fists clenched. She could have killed him. Not only did he lack the courtesy to meet her in the

proper manner, now he expected her to go chasing
up the stairs after him. Erin took a fierce step
forward, then halted abruptly. Although he had
seemed anything but enamoured, was it possible
Jago Miles could be waiting for her in his bedroom,
like a spider luring a fly? She viewed the staircase
with wary eyes. She had no intention of walking
into a trap. Hadn't she had trouble before with a
man who, in the belief he was irresistible, had
pounced when least expected? She was weighing up
whether being too pale and too old could be
interpreted as meaning she was immune from
seduction, when a figure appeared on the landing.
As he leant over the railing she saw that the lower
half of his face was covered in creamy white foam.

'Hi. Come along up and then you can tell me what
you want,' he ordered, and promptly vanished.

Erin stood and stared at the empty space. She felt
dazed. What *she* wanted? Had the Ice Man melted
to become Santa Claus? Intrigued, and deciding
that someone smothered in shaving soap would
scarcely be milliseconds away from ripping the
clothes off her, she fixed her briefcase more securely
under her arm and mounted the stairs. A faint
rasping sound guided her to a bathroom. Through
the open door she saw Jago Miles. He was standing
before a mirror, cut-throat razor in hand, busy with
the soaping, the scraping, the pained facial expressions necessary to remove stubble from jaw. The
denim shorts had been exchanged for white drill
slacks, but the tanned chest remained bare. The
seal-like gloss of combed-back hair indicated he
had recently stepped out of the shower.

'I suspect you'd have preferred me in jacket and
tie, sat behind a desk,' he remarked laconically, in

between slicing bubbles from his face in long, smooth strokes, 'but, like I told you, I had to go visiting. It's been one hell of a rush.' The evil cutthroat glinted. 'Give me a minute and I'll be with you.'

No, the Ice Man hadn't melted, though there had been a thaw of sorts, Erin decided, as she looked at him from the doorway. When previously encountered he had been strung up tight, now he seemed more relaxed. The prospect of extra dollars must have the same effect as tranquillisers, she thought acidly.

As she waited for him to finish, a strange yearning began to creep over her. How long had it been since a man had shaved in her presence? How many years since she had listened to a baritone sing off-key in the bath? Domestic intimacies came flooding back—the balled-up socks under the bed, a jacket tossed askew, masculine paraphernalia cluttering the bathroom shelf. Mesmerised, her eyes followed each movement as Jago cropped the final whiskers in a rasp of the razor which was almost sensuous. Remnants of soap were rinsed away, he checked his jaw, reached for a towel. The final touch was aftershave. Satisfied and unselfconsciously beaming at his reflection in the mirror, he slapped the liquid on his cheeks, wincing against the tingle. Lime-lemon spiced the air. Jago straightened, his task complete. Despite the angular jaw and skew-whiff nose, on him manhood looked good. Very good.

'Go ahead,' he said, as he reached for a fresh white shirt.

'My usual approach is to first have a series of general conversations. I need a fair amount on tape

before I can decide which angle to pursue,' Erin
explained, rattling off. She was grateful to be able to
talk. Watching him, there had been a hurry in her
blood which was both unexpected and unwelcome.
'Later, more specific topics can be discussed. I've
listed your career from open-air theatre in Central
Park to *Taro Beach*, but I've little on the other areas
in your life. May I suggest we start with your
childhood and take it from there?'

'My childhood?' He sounded surprised.

'Why not?'

'No reason, except that I've never been asked
about my childhood before. Reporters restrict their
questions to my adult life.' Jago gave her a quick
glance as he buttoned his shirt. 'The emphasis being
on my love life.'

'I'm not a reporter,' Erin pointed out firmly. 'And
I'm interested in the man, not the myth.'

The crinkle-eyed smile made its first appearance.
'You reckon my love life's a myth?' He slid a large
hand into the vee of his shirt where golden hair
glistened, and massaged thoughtfully. 'As things
stand at the moment, I guess you could be right.
Okay, we'll start with my childhood.' He pursed his
lips. 'You realise I don't have much free time? How
about us sitting down together, say from nine until
ten each evening, Monday through Saturday, will
that do?'

'Is there any choice?'

'None.'

'Then it'll do.'

Jago tucked his shirt into his trousers, and
walked with her along the landing. 'I'd better make

it clear from the start that certain subjects are off-limits.'

'Like what?' she asked, immediately sensing trouble.

'I'll tell you when we come to them.' He saw her frown. 'Don't worry, we should be able to cobble together something decent.'

'Cobble something decent!' Erin stopped in her tracks. 'Mr Miles, it's obvious we're at cross-purposes here.'

'Call me Jago.'

'Jago,' she snapped. 'Well, Jago, if I'd wanted to cobble I'd have been a shoemaker. I'm not, I'm a writer. I write well-researched and factual accounts which have a beginning, a middle and an end. I have more respect for the reading public than to attempt to palm them off with something *cobbled* together.' The yellow flecks glittered in her eyes again. 'You may find this surprising, but my writing matters to me!'

'And my private life matters to me!' he shot back, then raised two placatory hands. 'Let's not fight, I think we've done enough of that for one day. As I see it, the position is this—I'm not ecstatic about being the subject of a profile, and I get the impression you're not over the moon at the prospect of writing about me. However, for various reasons we appear to be stuck with each other. I'm willing to play ball with you, if you're willing to play ball with me. Do we have a deal?'

Erin bit her lip. Not a word had been put on paper and already Jago Miles had announced his intention to call at least some of the shots. None of her other subjects, Patrice Lanham included, had thought it necessary to lay down rules beforehand.

They had trusted her. Why couldn't he trust her and simply co-operate? She was not a gutter press journalist, out for sensation. She had no wish to embarrass or cause distress. As someone who had incidents in her own life she would hate to have broadcast, she respected the privacy of the individual. That said, she was committed to writing the truth and, where possible, the whole truth. How could she interpret 'off-limits'? The term conjured up a bundle of images, all unwelcome. Was Jago Miles intending a wholesale deletion of incidents he felt might dent the Mr Wonderful image? Was his aim to trim away imperfections and nudge the facts into a more acceptable form? She could not agree to that. She had not come to Florida to script a superficial saga about a perfect person—nobody was perfect. Deep in thought, Erin walked down the stairs beside him.

'How far does this censorship of yours go?' she questioned.

'Not too far. Let me explain. One of the penalties of fame is that I'm considered to be public property and——' he grimaced, '— to a degree I accept that. What I don't accept is that the spotlight should also fall on my family. My parents are dead, but I have brothers and sisters, and protecting their privacy is important to me.'

His tone sounded eminently reasonable, and the problems Erin had visualised a moment ago receded. She gave a pert nod.

'It's a deal.'

'Good. Now, what else do you require apart from chat?'

'A glance at anything which mentions your name. Items from school, college, theatre programmes, whatever. The majority won't be used, but I'd be grateful to have the chance to select and reject.'

They had reached the living-room. Jago indicated a seat, and dropped down on the couch opposite. He reached for a packet of cigars. 'You're in luck. I have four tea chests stuffed full with papers.'

'Four!' Her biographer's spontaneous rush of delight at the prospect of such goodies was rapidly tempered. Jago Miles might be co-operating, but wasn't she being offered the collection of an egomaniac? Papers would doubtless mean reviews, though never bad ones; photographs, but never those taken from an unflattering angle; articles, buttered with calorific compliments. If he was like Patrice, he would be addicted to self-gratification. The actress's 'papers' had been arranged in a score of albums, each a visual hymn of praise of which she had never wearied. 'I'd like to take a look,' Erin said, trying her best to sound keen.

'Fine.' He pushed a hand through his hair, hair which as it dried was rapidly becoming a thick mane of burnished gold. 'Though here and now I disclaim any responsibility for you winding up cross-eyed. My mother wrote small, neither could she spell.'

'Your mother? I don't understand.'

'Ursula never threw anything away, so the tea chests contain a lifetime's collection of memorabilia, or trash—whichever you prefer. The rest of my family were all set to burn the lot after she died, but somehow I felt——' What Jago felt was left to her imagination. 'Amongst the papers are her diaries. I mention them because you said you were interested in my childhood and the diaries contain references to me. Not many though,' he warned.

'I'll read them.' Erin took a determined breath.
'And may I examine reviews, press cuttings etc?'

He lit the cigar. 'See Burt, he keeps track of such
things. Anything else?'

'Oh, er——' Such a peremptory dismissal of the
scrapbook syndrome left her stumbling. 'I'd like
permission to speak to a few people about you.'

'Elaborate,' came the request.

'The one dimensional approach has a tendency to
be flat, and I'd prefer to pep up the profile with a
quote or two from different sources—say from Mr
Steen and work colleagues. I'm not on the prowl for
gossipy titbits,' she assured him when he looked
hesitant. 'I just want snippets of additional
information.'

'Okay, but check anything Burt might say with
me.' The crinkle-eyed smile returned. 'You'll have
gathered that he's an atrocious liar.'

'Will do,' Erin grinned, delighted to see how the
Ice Man's thaw was continuing. 'Would it also be
possible for me to visit the *Taro Beach* set and watch
you at work?'

'Shouldn't be any problem. The entire team'll be
here next Sunday for a barbecue, why not join us?
You could have a word with William, our director,
and set something up.'

'Thanks.' She took her tape recorder from her
briefcase. 'Shall we make a start on your childhood
right now?'

'You're quite a whirlwind of efficiency, aren't
you?' he commented, looking amused.

'That's the way I work.' Erin pressed the
appropriate switch. 'Fire ahead.'

'I was born in Thailand on the seventh of

October, nineteen hundred and——'

'Thailand?' she queried in surprise.

He nodded. 'My parents were on a Siamese kick at the time. My father was an architect, my mother a sculptress. They'd gone out there to look for inspiration. Such trips weren't unusual. My parents, my mother especially, had a definite bent towards the nomadic. As a result I attended more schools than I have fingers and toes.' He took a pull on his cigar. 'I was the first of six children born to John and Ursula Miles, or Ursula Liden, as my mother preferred to be known. She was one of the original feminists. When you read the diaries you'll realise she was very much an independent spirit.'

'Ursula Liden?' The name rang a bell and Erin tried hard to remember. 'Swedish-American,' she declared, after a moment. 'She did a tondo which created a tremendous controversy at the time. It was commissioned by a Viennese art foundation, but when the sculpture was delivered the trustees rose up in horror and demanded it be removed. Eventually the tondo was sited on a headland near—near——'

'Rio. But how do you know this? The tondo gained its notoriety more than twenty years ago. Added to which, Ursula's press coverage was a flash in the pan. She never produced anything else of note.'

'One of the men featured in my book is a painter. We were discussing the various forms of art one afternoon and he mentioned the tondo. He said it represented a powerful pagan image.'

'Others likened it to an extremely obscene rock cake,' Jago said with a laugh. 'But we're digressing.' He had another drag at his cigar. 'From day one I lived what I suppose you could only call a pretty bohemian existence.'

Erin leant forward. The numbness had gone, adrenalin was flowing. Contrary to being a 'what you saw, was what you got' Tinsel Town product, Jago Miles had hidden depths. And the paramount purpose in her life was to plumb them.

CHAPTER THREE

THE first few days were spent becoming acclimatised and establishing a routine. Erin arrived at the sprawling white villa each morning on the dot of nine, broke for lunch at one, then worked through until six. She returned to the motel for dinner, retracing her route mid-evening when she met up with Jago for their conversations.

'Use the back bedroom as your study,' he had suggested, and so she was installed, together with typewriter, tape recorder and the four tea chests.

'Back bedroom' seemed a tame description for the sumptuous pink and white boudoir which overlooked the blue sheen of the Gulf of Mexico. As she sat at the desk attempting to decipher Ursula Liden's scribbles, so her eyes were drawn to the huge water-bed with its white satin coverlet. How many fevered couplings had taken place there? she wondered. Sinking to gossip column level she may be, but she could not help thinking that way. Burt had delivered vast files of cuttings, and although Erin had only glanced through, it had been noticeable how most included pictures of Jago with a stunning blonde or brunette draped all over him. Publicity was doubtless at the back, front and sides of some of these romances, but they could not all be make-believe. As a younger man his name had been linked with several women, and though on reaching thirty he appeared to have steadied down, there were mentions of an actress called Olivia, a live-in

lover. Yet Olivia was in the past. Since his arrival in
Florida two and a half years ago no serious
relationships had been reported. Erin was reluctant
to take his word about his love life being a myth, yet
he did live alone—and in great style.

In addition to the boudoir there were three more
bedrooms, each with bath, while downstairs the
spread included gymnasium, sauna, games room,
and a den with the largest television and stereo unit
she had ever seen. So much space for one man, so
much equipment, so much attention too, she
thought, as Maria the housekeeper bustled in with
morning coffee and cookies. Maria, aided by two
other women, kept the house pristine, while outside
three gardeners, a pool boy and the dozy Rafael
tended to multifarious needs.

'The girls and me have been thinking, hon,'
Maria announced, setting down the tray. 'We
reckon you should move into the bungalow. The
place is just sitting there doing nothing, and two
months in a motel will cost you plenty. Most of your
time is spent here already, so what's the difference?
Would it help any if I speak to Jago about it?' she
offered, sensing Erin's hesitation.

'Thanks, but no. I'm happy at the Driftwood.'

'Now hon,' Maria cajoled. 'As well as saving
dough you'd be spared all that to-ing and fro-ing
each day.'

'The Driftwood suits me fine,' Erin insisted.
'Really.'

With a smiling shrug of resignation the housekeeper departed, and Erin carried her coffee over to
the window. By looking left, beyond the garage
block, she could see the trim white bungalow sitting
in the sunshine. Fully furnished and cleaned on a

regular basis, it had been built to accommodate staff, but Maria and her cohorts went home each night. Erin sipped thoughtfully. Free lodgings would be attractive for her budget was tight, but wasn't Jago doing enough? Blighted with a mercenary streak the man might be, yet when it came to providing a work base, countless coffees, daily lunch and the use of his pool, he had shown no hesitation. Erin took another mouthful, thinking a touch sceptically that keeping her sweet was in his own interests—financial interests. He wanted her co-operation as much as she wanted his. Well, a move into the bungalow would serve *her* financial interests. Would it be presumptuous to float the idea? Why not? The Jago Miles of today was no longer the frosty Ice Man of last Sunday.

After such an ill-omened start, everything had gone surprisingly well. Maybe not so surprisingly, for Erin had done her best to make it happen that way. An advocate of positive thinking, she had made a determined effort to gain his acceptance and now—it was Friday—felt that a pat on the back was warranted. She did not claim all the credit for the way Jago had relaxed over the week—it could be that his relationship with Kiel had eased—but she had made a definite contribution. She had done her best to put his greedy *raison d'être* to the back of her mind and treat him as a committed contributor to her book. By nature she was a good listener, always fascinated by other people's experiences, so her interest in what he had to say was genuine. Jago had responded to that. Erin had 'played ball', and he had more than done his share.

At the appointed hour of nine each evening, he had sprawled in a chair with a cheroot between his fingers, a tumbler of whisky close by, and reminisced in a low American drawl which was easy on the ears. That he could work such long hours and talk informatively and coherently at the end of the day was a source of constant wonder—and thanks. Erin had seen how tired he was, detected lines of strain, yet he never complained. For his discipline, he had gained her gratitude.

It had to be admitted that at first her encouraging smiles had been underscored with suspicion. As someone with a stated lack of enthusiasm for the project was he going to shortchange her, tell half-truths, fob her off with inaccurate flashbacks which had gathered a gloss through years of repetition on the party circuit? But his reminiscences were genuine and spontaneous. Erin had conducted sufficient two-way exchanges to be able to spot the trotted out phrase, a rehearsed recital, and although on the alert had found him guilty of neither.

Coffee cup empty, she returned to work. Her scrutiny of the diaries had only just begun. Blessed—or was it cursed?—with a methodical nature, she had first felt it necessary to remove every single piece of paper from the tea chests and arrange them in some kind of order. The chore had not been simple. On her knees for hours on end, Erin had filled the dust-sheet around the desk with mountainous piles of postcards, letters, sketches and travel documents which spanned fifty years. Each had been inspected, her biographer's curiosity had insisted on that, but now she accepted she had been wasting her time. If the thirty-thousand-word profile had featured Ursula Liden the items would have been of interest, but they contained few items of information pertinent to her son.

Would the diaries be equally deficient? Jago had warned of minimal references, and the diaries she had read so far had indicated that his mother was not the type to wax lyrical in print over a child. Still, if nothing else they would confirm Jago had been where he said, when he said. Erin turned a page, and then another.

'I'm sure my eyeballs have much in common with a road map of Central London,' she said that evening, as she changed tapes in her recorder. 'Your mother's writing is diabolical.'

'Highly individualistic, like her. But after causing problems all your life, why stop just because you're dead?' Jago grinned and lit a small brown cheroot. 'India,' he murmured, 'that comes next.'

'India?'

'See how fortunate you are, having me to bring a spot of colour into your otherwise drab existence?'

'But a moment ago you were in New York. Your second sister had just been born.'

'Ah, then Ursula was beset by the urge to inspect Hindu carvings.'

Erin sat back, her eyes wide. 'So the whole family upped and went with a new baby—just like that?'

'Don't sound so scandalised. People do do these things.' Jago looked at her from beneath thick blond brows. 'Though maybe not your kind of people.'

That was very true. Erin's growing up had taken place in a cosily confined environment. The sole offspring of doting parents, she had been born and bred in a quiet English village; the same village where she lived now. As a child she had known few surprises, and also few shocks. Jago's upbringing was one long shock. How she would have coped

with the 'pretty bohemian existence' she dreaded to
think. Yet he spoke easily, uncomplainingly about
the endless upping of roots, the wandering minstrel
travels, the non-conformist mother and often
absent father. The baby in Thailand had taken its
first steps in the States, toddled through Europe,
started school in South America and at present the
boy—Jago had reached his tenth year—was back in
the States.

'No, it wasn't the whole family,' he corrected.
'My father was tied up with work, so he stayed
behind.'

'Which means your mother gaily went off alone
to India with what—four children?'

He nodded. 'My youngest brother and sister had
yet to appear. Simmer down. You should know by
now how unorthodox Ursula was.'

'Have you always called your mother Ursula?'
Erin enquired, replacing 'unorthodox' with
'madcap'.

'From being able to talk, and my father was John.
They wouldn't have it any other way. Said it broke
down barriers.'

A gleam lit his blue eyes. 'Let me guess, you called
your parents Mummy and Daddy, and still do?'

'Mum and Dad, actually.'

'Actually,' he mocked.

Erin refused to rise to the bait. Jago on a teasing
kick had an alarming knack of quickening her
blood, but she had not flown out to Florida in order
for her red and white corpuscles to be exercised. She
had flown out to write a profile, and maintaining a
detached view of her subject was essential.

'Wasn't your mother frightened one of you might
fall ill, or be allergic to the food? Wasn't she worried

about the baby falling foul of the climate?'

'Ursula's mind didn't work that way. She was a creature of impulse. Her obsession was stone, nothing else came close. If someone told her about sculptures, a mountainside, even a quarry face which had some interest, off she went. Problems arising from day to day living never entered her head.'

'She chased around all over the world, dragging young children in her wake?'

Jago grinned. 'Wasn't it fortunate we all enjoyed travelling?'

'Was India . . . fun?'

'You wouldn't have enjoyed it.' His grin widened. 'We started off in a hotel, but Ursula miscalculated the currency, so after a week we swapped to the porter's uncle's house in downtown Bombay. The whole place stank of curry, and the bugs—jeez, the cockroaches were the size of porcupines. To compound matters Ursula's sense of time was shaky, so whenever she went off we could never be certain when she'd return. She was capable of getting carried away and watching patterns on stone from dusk, through moonlight, to dawn.'

Erin was aghast. 'Your mother left you on your own all night?'

'Occasionally, but the Indian family kept an eye on us, and don't forget I was a capable ten-year-old.'

'Ten's not much,' she retorted, remembering how her parents had insisted on babysitters until she was well into her teens.

'It was only me and the other two kids, she took the baby with her,' Jago explained, as though that corrected matters. 'Ursula was feeding my sister herself, so she travelled in a sling on her back.'

'Like a load of washing.' The words slid out of her mouth, the tone inferring *dirty* washing.

'Don't get prissy.' He squinted through a cloud of blue-grey smoke. 'I suppose any infant you had would sleep undisturbed in a padded crib?'

'In a silk-lined padded crib with frills, so there! And I'm not being prissy, I'm just wondering where routine and woolly winter vests and a lullaby at bedtime fit into all this.'

'They don't, but isn't it swings and roundabouts? My brothers, sisters and I may not have had the conventional mothering, but neither did we suffer the smothering. We were treated as adults and allowed to develop free from prejudices and pressures. Keeping up with the Joneses was unknown. Also we learned young that life isn't always smooth. When the bumps come we're immensely capable of clearing them.' Jago frowned, tapping the ash from his cigar. 'How many people can say the same?'

'I can,' Erin shot back, responding to the question as though it was a challenge.

'Yes?' He raised amused eyebrows. 'What do you know of life, real life? First it was Mum and Dad, then the ivory towers of Oxford, and now Burt tells me you live in a cute little cottage in a cute little village, with a cat.'

'What's wrong with having a cat?' she demanded, annoyed to discover Cleo must have discussed her with the brash Mr Steen.

'An unmarried girl with a pussy-cat who lives deep in the English countryside and for the most part spends her time scribbling Edwardian biographies?' He was laughing. 'My God! Miss Erin Page must have taken some knocks.'

'I'm not Miss Page. I'm Mrs Stuart. I'm a widow,'
she informed him, indignant pink suns bursting on
her cheeks. 'My husband died seven years ago. I
write under my maiden name so it's simpler if I use
the Miss. Peter's death was bumpy and——' Her
mouth took on a bitter slant. 'And so was the period
which followed. But I coped. It was what is called a
"learning experience".'

Jago spread a hand. 'Then I apologise.'

'Apology accepted.'

'But you do live in a cottage?' he persisted. 'And
you do have a cat?'

She nodded an irritated agreement. What had
Cleo said? she wondered. Her agent often accused
her of having become a backwater prude, acting
like a dry as dust spinster, and this appeared to be
the message which had buzzed across the Atlantic.
Erin resented being viewed in that light. It was not
true. Or was it? Her brown eyes clouded. Still,
better to be thought of as a dry spinster and a prude
than as a—as a what? Loose woman? Sexy little
piece? How many times in the heat of passion had
Ned called her his sexy little piece? Once the phrase
had thrilled, made her feel wickedly alive and
exciting. Now it infused her with shame. How could
she have been so reckless, done such wild things?

'Have you lived alone since your husband's
death?' Jago queried, and she jolted back to the
present.

'I had a few months in London once, but let's get
back to you in Bombay,' she replied swiftly. 'How
did you deal with the cockroaches?'

'I wouldn't say we "dealt" with them, we just
yelped when they scuttled across us in the night. It
wasn't too bad,' he grinned, when Erin shuddered.

'On the whole we were adaptable kids.'

'Seems as though you had to be.'

'True. I remember once when——'

Back on the track, Jago talked about his Indian memories, and Erin gave herself a private lecture. Dwelling on her affair with Ned was degrading. It had been kept out of her head for ages and now she resolved it would stay out. Board that train of thought—Ned, lovemaking, her past abandonment, her present strait-laced control—and she was on a journey to nowhere.

'I'll call a cab,' Jago offered, when the proceedings came to a halt at ten o'clock.

The mention of transport brought to mind Maria's suggestion about the bungalow, and as he made the phone call she wondered how best to broach the subject. Back home the villagers would look askance on a young woman who suggested to a bachelor of known sexual prowess that she should live on his property, but where was the danger? Their relationship, though amiable, was a working one. The only thing they had in common was the profile.

'I seem to be becoming the taxi firm's best customer,' she remarked, when he said a cab was on its way. 'Three miles is too far to walk four times a day, so I'm back and forth, back and forth.' Her sigh slid down to her shoes. 'Pity I can't find a closer base.' Erin looked for a reply. 'Isn't it?' she prodded.

He yawned. 'What would you like, toots? A motel at the end of the drive? Try commuting between here and Miami each day like I do, then complain.'

'I'm not complaining.' She slipped her recorder into her briefcase. 'Maria tells me the bungalow's

standing empty, all shiny and clean. Do you think it
would be——'

'No, I don't. You can't,' Jago cut in, reading her
mind. A heavy wing of tawny-blond hair was
pushed from his brow. 'You can't move in because
the bungalow's already let. Poll's taking up resi-
dence there next week.'

The poolside was crowded, and the patio, and the
lawn. People sat round small tables, clustered in
gossipy knots, weaved their way through the
brightly dressed throng to return with plates piled
high. Beneath the shade of a palm a white-hatted
chef grilled steaks over glowing charcoal, while to
one side guests chose from a vast array of salads.
Waiters circulated, ensuring no one went without a
drink, be it an exotic Caribbean cocktail or Perrier
water. Conversation hummed. There was much
laughter.

How different this gathering was from Patrice
Lanham's claustrophobic 'at homes'. The actress
had packed her London drawing-room full of
supercilious snobs and bores, which meant Erin had
found herself tackling each evening like an obstacle
course. Could she avoid the Green Room freak with
the back-of-the-stalls voice? Don't trip over the
actressy actress who had once played opposite a
knight and was determined to relive the experience
ad nauseam. And woe betide her if the famous
knight himself made an entrance, he of the
wandering eyes and wandering hands. But the *Taro
Beach* team and accompanying partners grouped
together beneath the clear blue skies were a
complete contrast. Unassuming and friendly, they
had welcomed her into their midst. There were

poseurs, of course. A photographer was going the
rounds, and girls in painted-on white suede or
skimpy black ciré were taking deep breaths and
smiling letter box smiles in the hope of attracting
attention, but they were in the minority.

Erin had noticed Jago having his photograph
taken with the *femmes fatales*, and had wondered
whether Poll or Susie could be numbered amongst
their midst. Was Poll the pneumatic blonde with
pink bows in her hair? Could the redhead who
never stopped laughing be Susie? There was no
chance to find out for she was not introduced,
though Jago did introduce her to plenty of other
people. He was an attentive host, taking care she
was not left alone. In expectation of being a
member of the persecuted minority she had been
grateful, but had quickly realised that no obstacles
needed to be avoided here.

'My hips go in and out like a concertina,' sighed
the matron beside her, making eyes at a slice of
blueberry cheesecake on a nearby plate. 'I swear I
have no idea why.'

'Would you cut it out already?' ordered her
husband, a cameraman, with mock bombast. 'You
spend half your life with your goddamn head stuck
in the goddamn fridge.'

'Marvin, I don't!' she squealed.

'Ethel, you do.' He hugged her around the waist.
'That's where all those sexy inches come from, and
the more the merrier as far as I'm concerned.'

'Sexy inches?' purred a velvety male voice into
Erin's ear. 'The sexiest inches here today belong to
you.'

Unimpressed by this opening gambit, she turned
to find a young man smiling down at her. Erin had

to admit that although his words might not have impressed, his looks did. He had jet black hair, heavy-lidded dark eyes and a tan smoother than bronze. Sharply dressed in black shirt and designer trousers, with a twist of gold chains around his neck, he was a very long way from the boy next door.

'How ya doin', Kiel?' chorused Marvin and Ethel.

'Fine thanks. How are you folks?' He offered Erin a hand and a flawless white smile. 'Kiel Jennings, and you're Miss Brains and Beauty combined.' He gestured to the far side of the pool where Burt Steen was wiggling stubby fingers in a hello. 'I've been hearing all about you.'

'Don't tell me,' she groaned.

'Why not?' The dark eyes smouldered. 'Burt didn't exaggerate.'

She gave a dubious smile and, beneath the ensuing banter, took time to study the new arrival. A 'pretty dude' the agent had said, quoting a melting-pot ancestry of Sicilian-Italian and American-Indian, and there he had not been exaggerating. Kiel Jennings registered high on the breathtaking scale, though he was too perfect, too aware of the impact he made for her taste. Erin's eyes strayed through the crowd to Jago. Casual as always, he was wearing faded jeans and a shirt which had seen other summers. Laughing with friends, he unconsciously rumpled his hair, scattering blond strands across his brow. He was not classically good-looking, yet that inner force gave him ten times the charisma of the young man standing beside her. She much preferred Jago. Erin frowned. *She much preferred Jago*? Where had that thought come

from? It sounded disturbingly solid. She switched
her eyes back to the group around her, her mind
back to Kiel. It was surprising that such a
lightweight character possessed the power to make
Jago as tense as he had been last weekend. She
would have thought Jago more likely to brush off
the other actor's fits of pique.

'My will-power's having an off day.' Ethel was
ogling the cheesecake again. She linked an arm
through her husband's. 'Let's you and me go in
search of desserts.'

'Jago's laid on some wonderful food,' Erin
praised, as the older couple headed off in the
direction of the buffet table.

'Correction, Jago's laid on nothing,' she was
informed. 'He might be playing mine host, but the
television company's picking up the tab for everything today. Old skinflint Miles'd never splash out on
food and drink for damn near a hundred guests.'
Kiel's laugh removed most of the sting from the
words. Most, not all, she noted. 'This is a
promotional shindig to push *Taro Beach* in the
press. That's why the photographer's shooting
everything which moves.'

Erin shrugged, accepting she did not know the
form. 'Well, it's nice of him to open his house and
gardens to everyone.'

'Wrong again. This mansion isn't his. It belongs
to a contact of Burt's who's off on a world tour. The
guy needed someone to keep an eye on his house
and staff, and because Burt has always felt cheated
that his Numero Uno chose to live in a timber
shack, he used that silver tongue of his. Seems the
guy's wife went ape at the mention of Jago's name
and—hey presto—moving in was a formality. Mind

you, I hear Burt needed to give Jago a sharp kick in the pants to get him to agree.' Her companion's gaze fell to the cut crystal tumbler she was holding. 'Can I get you a fresh drink? What was that, gin and orange?'

'Straight orange, but I don't want another one, thanks.' Erin handed her glass to a passing waiter. 'You say Jago lived in a shack?' she enquired.

'Would you believe a rented shack? No, not a shack exactly,' Kiel adjusted, 'but not the kind of place you'd associate with a high roller who pulls in his money. But that's our Mr Miles all over. Doesn't own a house, a boat, not even a car.' Judging from his disgust, not owning a car equated with not owning a toothbrush. 'No wife, no kids, and he's avoided getting soaked for alimony like some of us. The guy has it made. A bachelor in paradise, that's him.' Her partner slid a bronzed hand into a hip pocket to withdraw an aggressively expensive leather-bound cigarette case. 'Smoke?'

'I don't,' she said vaguely, her mind fleeing around these revelations.

'You don't drink, you don't smoke. What do you do?' The dark eyes burned a path from her head to her toes. She was wearing a lavender-pink silk shirt and slacks, but might as well have been wearing cellophane. 'With a body like that I sure hope it's something two can share.'

'I spend most of my time writing. Though I do jog and swim, and things,' Erin added, too busy thinking about Jago and his finances to pay much attention.

' "Things" sound interesting.' Kiel indicated roughly-hewn stone steps at the far corner of the lawn which led down through a grove of palm trees to the ocean. 'Let's go.'

She gazed in surprise at the hand he held out to her. How had they come this far, this quickly?

'Aren't we supposed to circulate?' she stalled.

'No sweat, we can circulate later. Who's going to panic if we dodge out for a while?' He put his hand over hers, linked through his fingers and held on tight. 'I'd like to see the beach,' he said, pulling her with him across the grass. 'It's rare I visit this coast, it's rare any of us do. The studios are on the east, over a hundred miles away, so I've yet to puzzle out why Jago chooses to base himself here.'

'The island is very beautiful,' Erin pointed out.

She had decided she would go where Kiel led. So long as his talk centred on their host she was interested. Any information about Jago was grist to her mill and today she was learning a lot.

'Beautiful—pah!' her escort derided. 'All the action's in Miami. Something's happening over there twenty-four hours a day. The town's alive with nightclubs, fancy hotels, restaurants, but what you got around here?' His lip twisted. 'Not much else than the Everglades. And what's that—a goddamn swamp!'

'A swamp teeming with wildlife,' she said, picking her way down the steps in her high-heeled sandals.

'You like that kind of stuff?' Kiel demanded.

'Well, I haven't actually been, I've only read the guide books, but——'

'There you are, you haven't been and who the hell wants to? No, this coast is dullsville. Jago has to be crazy to motor across Alligator Alley twice every day. All he's done is saddle himself with a hefty chunk of unnecessary travel.'

'Alligator Alley?'

'The two-lane highway which cuts straight across the foot of Florida. Say, how about me picking you up next Sunday and taking you over to Miami?' Kiel suggested, as they walked between the palms. 'You'd get to see Alligator Alley and I could lay on some wildlife.' He grinned suggestively, squeezing her fingers. 'The personal kind. I'm a tiger when I'm aroused and that sexy sway to your hips says you are, too.'

With a sharp tug, Erin freed her hand from his grasp. A little of Kiel Jennings went a long way.

'Sorry, but I'm busy next Sunday,' she told him. 'As you probably know I'm working on a profile on Jago, and——'

'To hell with Jago. I'm asking you out, he never will. Even a beautiful English rose couldn't coax that guy to ease open the purse-strings. Jago never socialises, so don't you get any ideas about being wined and dined.' Kiel had been scowling, but now he switched on the flawless smile. 'Why are we talking about Jago when I'd rather talk about you— us?' In a feat of engineering which must have been honed through years of practice, he slid an arm around her shoulders, steered her from the path and had Erin positioned with her back against a palm tree in seconds. 'You're different,' he said, leaning over her and starting to purr. 'No plastered on goo, no false eyelashes, just a light tan and——' the dark eyes undressed her '— one helluva good body. Skip writing next Sunday,' he appealed. 'You and I can——'

As he leant forward to whisper his intentions into her ear, Erin decided it was time to depart. A speedy evaluation showed he had one hand spread

on the tree trunk above her head, the other beside
her hip. Would a firm shove be the most effective
method of escape, or a quick wriggle under and out?
She selected the wriggle, but had no time to duck for
at that moment a tall figure in faded jeans strode
into the grove.

'Cool it,' said Jago, his hand landing on Kiel's
shoulder. 'Erin isn't up for grabs.'

Surprised, the younger man spun round. When he
saw who had arrived, he bristled. 'Who says I'm
grabbing?' he demanded.

'I see you in action daily. I know your technique,'
Jago replied, in a tone which was not so much
disapproving as faintly incredulous.

Kiel adopted a fighting stance. Bronzed fists
were clenched, the shoulders beneath the black
shirt flexed. 'Do you want to fight?' he threatened.

'No, thank you. Look, there's no need for bully-
boy tactics, so just beat it. Please?'

'You try and make me.'

'Again, no thanks.' Jago sighed. 'All I'm saying is
Erin's out of bounds.'

'Since when?'

'Since now. And put your fists down—please.'

Erin's eyes moved from one man to the other.
Whilst Kiel was menacing, lips stretched back
across his teeth and all ready to fight, Jago's
behaviour was as she would have expected. He was
calm and composed. The other actor was not
upsetting him today. Yet had she decoded an
impatience? If the pseudo-heavyweight reached
back to throw a punch could it be Jago's knuckles
which struck home first?

'Violence isn't the answer to anything,' she
intervened.

Jago slung her a sideways look. 'You mean make love, not war?' Her reply was to nod feverishly. 'Toots, your wish is my command,' he replied.

His arm encircled her waist, his head came down and, to her amazement, he kissed her. Zappo. The immediate pressure of his lips was innocent, but then she felt a movement within him and his mouth parted on hers. His tongue thrust into her mouth, an erotic invader. Startled and utterly captivated, she responded, allowing the kiss to deepen. Blood stormed through her veins like a flash-flood. Dimly Erin was aware she should protest, break free, but a raw sexual need which she could not control was directing her actions. She was paralysed. How did she come to be pressed up against a lean, male body? she wondered. And *this* male body? If Kiel had laid claim minutes earlier, her evasion would have been swift, but to have her mouth plundered by a blond Viking left her clinging to him for support.

Eventually Jago raised his head. 'Well now,' he murmured.

She gazed at him, pleasure, fear, shame, all swirling topsy-turvy inside her. 'What—what do you think you're doing?' Erin managed to gasp, aware her usual decorum, her common sense had let her down miserably. Had she gone temporarily insane?

'Obeying orders.' He directed his attention to Kiel. 'Erin's out of bounds for the simple reason we're ... hot.' His male to male wink conveyed nights filled with debauchery and orgiastic activities. 'We prefer to be discreet and we'd be obliged if you could keep quiet, too.'

'Sure thing.' Because a claim had been actively

staked, Kiel understood. 'I'd never trespass on another man's territory,' he vowed, backing away. 'No hard feelings?'

'None,' he was assured benevolently.

'Thanks.' With a hand raised in farewell, he headed off towards the sounds of the distant barbecue.

'What was that all about?' demanded Erin, pushing all thoughts of *her* co-operation, *her* response, to one side. 'How come you say I'm not up for grabs and promptly grab me yourself?'

'You needed rescuing.'

'I did not!'

'You can't mean—?' Jago shifted his weight on to one leg. 'Are you as green as a fresh dollar bill?' he enquired. 'Surely you can see Kiel's a——'

'I know all about Kiel,' she cut in tartly. 'I may live in a cute little cottage in a cute little village, but I'm not Red Riding Hood. I can recognise a wolf when I see one. I can also recognise being compromised.'

'But I had to rescue you some way. Hell, I'm responsible for you, and a friendly peck on the cheek wouldn't have worked. Kiel doesn't understand subtlety. For him everything needs to be spelled out in capitals.'

'As in H O T?' The letters shot from her lips like pellets from a gun. 'You don't honestly believe he'll keep that piece of news to himself, do you?' Erin demanded. 'My guess is it's going the rounds right now.'

'Could be.'

'Could be?' she spluttered. 'Is that all you have to say? But then, what's another rumour where you're concerned? It just adds a notch to your ladykiller reputation. But what about me? I need a rumour about us—us messing around—like I need a hole in the head. One of the criteria in writing biographies——'

'I thought you were writing a profile? Jago interrupted.

'A profile, but nearly a biography,' she insisted. 'One of the criteria is that the biographer is an observer, someone who makes a detached assessment. How is anyone going to believe my account of you is detached if my name is bandied around as—as——'

'As my lover?' he queried, amusement at her fury showing in the creases at the corners of his mouth. 'Aren't you taking this whole thing much too seriously?'

'No, I'm not. My integrity's at stake here!'

His shoulders rose and fell. 'If you feel that strongly I'll find Kiel and put him straight,' he offered. 'Though it'll mean he's going to consider you are up for grabs. So whatever happens, don't disappear with him into the bushes again. Understand?'

Erin placed her hands on her hips. 'You're missing the point. I can look after myself, thank you very much. I had the situation under complete control, and as for you being responsible for me— you're not!'

Jago shook his head in disbelief. 'That guy's a compulsive chaser, Erin. He eats little girls like you for breakfast.'

'One.' She held up a tapered finger. 'I'm not a little girl, and two.' A second finger came up. 'What about your reputation?'

'Toots, by current standards I'm relatively puritan.'

'A Trappist monk?' she scoffed. 'Sorry, it won't wash. Don't forget I have access to Burt's collection of cuttings.'

'And most feature items he's made up and fed to the press. Yes. Burt insists, and to a point it's true, that for the sake of my career I must appear to be . . . adventurous. If I said I stayed home nights and built cathedrals from matchsticks nobody's going to get excited. And in my line, unfortunately, image matters.'

With a sigh she conceded the point, then added, 'But I'd be grateful if in future you'd allow me to handle my life my own way.'

'What you mean, toots, is don't kiss you again. One single kiss is what you're arguing about, isn't it?'

'No!' Erin said indignantly. 'Yes!'

Jago chuckled. 'Come along, I'll introduce you to William.'

Back at the barbecue the *Taro Beach* director, a dapper individual with silver-white hair and a goatee beard, was happy to be taken to one side. When Jago explained who she was and the favour she required, he smiled widely.

'Burt's already filled me in.'

'Don't believe a word,' Erin begged, to the accompaniment of Jago's laughter.

'I imagine after Burt's build-up you can't figure out whether to bow to Erin on bended knee or discuss Einstein's Theory of Relativity?' he teased.

The director nodded, joining in the fun. 'One thing's for sure, I realise we can't afford to miss out on her patronage.' He patted the chair beside him.

'Sit down, sweetheart, and let's you and me talk.'

'Then I'll disappear,' Jago said, glancing at her in such a way she was sorely tempted to stick out her tongue. 'I need to set Kiel right on a thing or two.'

'Why not visit us on location in a couple of weeks?' William suggested, when they were alone. 'Normally we film around the Miami-Fort Lauderdale area, but a lakeside sequence is planned for this episode. The date's not been finalised, but I'll pass on a message when it is. The location is forty miles or so south of here. You could come down with Jago in the studio limo.'

'Thanks,' Erin said happily. 'That sounds ideal.'

'It'll mean an early start,' the director warned, though not as early as usual for Jago. Damn near two hours travelling at the beginning and end of each day would flatten me. How he stands it, I don't know.' William peered through the crowd, locating their host who had been sidetracked by Ethel and Marvin. 'He's a great guy. Professional to his fingertips. Between you and me, Jago keeps *Taro Beach* alive. But he's doing too much, he needs to take things easier.'

'How? Six days a week and all that travelling make for a gruesome timetable.'

'Five days.'

Erin frowned. 'Five?'

'He never works Wednesdays. He insisted it was written into his contract from the start. Though despite turning in just five days, it's equivalent to six. You don't find Jago fluffing his lines, or complaining the lighting doesn't flatter him, or——' the director searched out Kiel '— or needing time off to comb his hair. I'd like to think Jago rested Wednesdays, but I'm sure he doesn't.'

'Then what does he do?' she enquired, her curiosity on full alert.

William grunted. 'God knows, I don't. I did ask once, but I was told to mind my own goddamn business.'

CHAPTER FOUR

JAGO not only had hidden depths, he was also
riddled with subterranean caverns. Over the days
which followed, Erin devoted far more time to
thinking about what she didn't know about him
than what she did. As a man with an inflated salary
and none of the usual outgoings, he must be piling
up riches, but for what? One explanation could be
that after such a raggle-taggle childhood he required the security of dollars in the bank. Yet Jago
did not rate his childhood as raggle-taggle, that was
strictly her view. Also he appeared steadfastly
secure in his own psyche. Next she moved on to the
mysterious Wednesdays. Maybe he was a sports
fanatic, and had insisted on a mid-week break in
order to ride surf or sail? No, that did not ring true
either.

These depths and caverns were a challenge. One
of the most intriguing aspects of writing biographies was the investigative side, and Erin felt a
frisson of excitement. What a fillip for her book if
she could reveal something totally unexpected!?

The plan must be for her to discover the truth as
far as she could and, given it was admissible,
persuade Jago to allow her to use it. In the past she
had sometimes needed to coax her subjects to agree
that certain facts should be, and could be, published, but no one had suffered. No one had
regretted being honest, divulging their secrets.
What were Jago's secrets? If only she could ask

59

outright what he did with his money and where he
went on Wednesdays; but such a frontal attack was
impossible. If he had told a long-time colleague
such as William to mind his own business, he was
not going to respond favourably to a query from her,
and Erin had no wish to upset the *status quo*. So far
Jago had co-operated in full. Nothing had been
declared off-limits, and the longer it stayed that
way, the better. The ease between them must be
consolidated. Before searching questions could be
risked, she needed to accumulate a store of good
will.

Ease? Good will? When writing the previous
profiles she had had no difficulty in stacking up
ease and good will on one side, while maintaining a
detached view on the other, but could she do this
with Jago? As an observer, her role had exper-
ienced an unfortunate blur. Erin sighed. That
damned kiss was the blur, it seemed to have put
everything ever so slightly out of focus.

'You need a man,' Cleo had once declared when
lambasting her for her subdued lifestyle. 'A big,
lusty man.'

Recalling the dither she had been reduced to in
his arms, she wondered uneasily if this could be
true. Certainly ever since, the touch of his lips, the
moist warmth of his mouth had been relived in a
manner more suited to a moonstruck teenager than
a sensible thirty-year-old. Enough, she told herself
sharply. Obliterate the kiss. It meant nothing. Erin
came to a decision. The minute this book was
finished she would take a break, a long break from
writing. If she circulated and had more contact with
the opposite sex, then surely she would be better
able to take maverick kisses in her stride? Her brow

creased. No, she wouldn't have time off after this book, it would be after the next one. Another Edwardian biography was already stewing in the back of her mind.

She returned to her current project. The pieces of Jago's life which she held in her hand did not make much sense, but wasn't that often the way? Writing a biography was a slow process, much like constructing a jigsaw. You could build and build, and not see the picture clearly until—click—one piece fitted in and made sense of all the rest. For her book's sake she was obliged to search out that vital piece which meant, she assured herself intently, it was her duty to ask questions.

'I understand Jago doesn't go into the studios on Wednesdays,' she said, when Maria appeared with the afternoon's supply of coffee. 'What does he do?'

'Don't ask me, hon. He just shoots out of here at nine in the morning, and doesn't return until after we've gone at night. I've tried quizzing him, but— zilch. He sure can be tight-lipped when he chooses.' The housekeeper settled a plump hip on the corner of the desk. 'Maybe we shouldn't have done, but the girls and me got Rafael to trail him once. Didn't work out though. The kid followed Jago across the causeway and several miles south, then he lost him. 'Course, Jago goes like the wind.'

'You've no idea where he could've been heading?'

'None. Rafael lost him before a fork in the road. The right-hand route heads towards the Everglades, the left veers inland.' Maria shrugged. 'There's nothing much inland. Farming land mostly, with a few mobile home communities, camp sites, a cemetery and a hospital.'

Wednesday evening found Erin keen-eyed and sharp-eared, looking and listening for clues. Under cover of his reminiscences—Jago had reached his adolescence—she made an inspection. Did he seem less tired, more tired? Invigorated? Depressed? Happier? Sad? Less talkative, more talkative? Frustratingly, he seemed exactly the same. She learned nothing.

But when Poll moved into the bungalow a day later, she did learn something—that it was a mistake to go for the obvious where Jago was concerned. Yes, the girl was young and brown, but she also had short, straight mousy hair, a flat chest and glasses.

'She's a nurse,' Maria reported, perching on the edge of the desk for what had now become a regular mid-afternoon chat. 'Works nights and sleeps most of the day. Doesn't say much. I gather she's moved in here because she's looking for peace and quiet. Too many kids running around in her last neighbourhood.'

'And I thought she was Jago's girlfriend!'

The housekeeper went off into peals of laughter. 'He'd hardly stick her out there if she was, would he? He'd have her in the house with him. But that skinny little Plain Jane and Jago? No, he'd need a whole lot more woman than that to satisfy him.' She giggled. 'I'd put my name forward myself if I didn't know my old man'd kick up a rumpus.'

'Has he had girls living in the house before?' Erin queried.

'Nope. There've been a couple who stayed the night, but it was only a night.' Maria's voice dropped to swapping confidences level. 'I reckon he's pining for that Olivia. They lived together for

three years, all lovey-dovey, then split up real
sudden. One minute she was there, the next she'd
gone, like she fell off the edge of the earth. Sounds
fishy to me. I tried to tackle Burt, but he got cagey.
Wouldn't meet my eyes. His version is Jago lost
interest, but the girls and me figure it must have
been the other way around. You only have to read
the magazines to know the guy was smitten. He
took Olivia everywhere, made sure she had her
share of the limelight. 'Course Burt would never
admit Jago could get dropped like a hot potato,
same as anyone else.' The housekeeper sighed.
'That Olivia must have been crazy. When she
dropped him she dropped a gorgeous fella. Hadn't
you better drink your coffee, hon? It'll be getting
cold.'

Amassed wealth? Hush-hush Wednesdays? And
now a question mark against Olivia's name. With
Jago nothing was straightforward.

Although his account of his childhood was
interesting, Erin was relieved when the end of the
week brought an end to that portion of his life. His
younger years represented the *hors d'oeuvre*, but in
his adult life she was being offered a course she
could really get her teeth into.

'So another episode begins,' Jago remarked, as
they settled down the following Monday evening.
He placed the toe of one foot against the heel of the
other and eased off a sneaker, then repeated the
process with the other shoe. 'Aren't you bored with
listening to me rattling on?'

'Aren't you bored with rattling on and me
listening?' she countered.

He smiled his crinkle-eyed smile. 'Oddly enough
I'm enjoying it—sort of. Usually I detest interviews,

all that hokum about am I involved with my leading lady.' Jago stretched out his legs and wiggled his bare toes. 'But speaking to you is—therapeutic. Like going to a shrink, but cheaper.'

This mention of finance seemed to open the door to a pertinent question.

'Did you go into acting because of the money?'

'Go into a high risk business like this for cash? Give me a break. Have you any idea of the percentage of the acting profession who are unemployed at any one time?' He rolled his eyes in horror. 'No, I went into acting by chance, and because I didn't possess qualifications to do much else. All the moving around as a kid loused up my formal education and thus my career prospects. No way could I become an attorney or an engineer. As it happened I was friendly with a guy who helped make TV commercials, and he said that with my hair he could find me work.' Jago grinned, flicking dismissively at a tawny-blond wing. 'If I go bald it's oblivion for me. I did a couple of commercials, one of which was seen by a producer. He required a Scandinavian type for a play he was setting up and before I knew it I was——' He waggled his fingers to denote quotation marks '— an actor.'

'Sounds easy.'

'It was.' His expression stilled. 'Sometimes I lie awake nights feeling guilty because I've never starved or slogged my way through drama school. But maybe I'll be forced to atone later, who knows?'

'You mean if *Taro Beach* finishes you could have difficulty in . . .'

'Why should *Taro Beach* finish?' he interjected, his tone becoming flinty. 'Soap operas go on for years.'

'Not all of them,' Erin demurred. 'And according to the newspaper I read this morning *Taro Beach* has dropped a point or two in the ratings.'

'A hiccup,' he said, and lifted a packet of cigars.

'Why did you join *Taro Beach* in the first place?'

Okay, she accepted the question was premature, but if Jago continued relating his tale at an even pace they would not reach his soap opera debut for another week, and her curiosity refused to sit in a corner and wait that long.

'Do I detect veiled criticism?' In what seemed slow motion, he selected a cheroot, lit it, inhaled, exhaled. 'I joined because the money was great, the people friendly, and the place right. Florida has a wonderful climate. It's not called the Sunshine State for nothing. I guess the accusation is I sacrificed my art for dollars, but——' the blue eyes which met hers were steady '— as a career move it made a lot of sense.'

'Did it?'

His explanation sounded reasonable, yet Erin remained unconvinced. Even if the soap opera did attract hordes of followers, it was still trash. Watching an episode at the motel, she had felt that a teenybopper scribbling on the back of an envelope would have been capable of producing a more sparkling plot. Admittedly Jago had given a good performance, at times he had even managed to lift the banal story into the realms of realism, but a good career move? She thought not. Or were her own prejudices getting in the way? If you acted well, did it really matter whether you acted before an élitist middle-class audience who had paid money to sit in a theatre, or before the masses who lounged at home in front of a flickering screen? Erin gave a mental shrug.

'But why do you live so far away from the studios?' she questioned.

'Because I prefer this coast to the other. Non-stop concrete does nothing for me. Also if I went out on the streets in Miami there's the chance I'd be mobbed, but on the island people respect my privacy. I can go around here like a normal person—almost.' Jago pulled on his cigar. 'Have you had much of a look at the island yourself?'

'Not yet.'

'You must. Why don't I take you on a tour next Sunday?' he suggested.

'Er, I was intending to type up some of our conversations then,' Erin waffled, thrown into sudden confusion.

She had presumed all future contact would be within a working environment, and was unsure of the wisdom of deviating from this pattern. Would it serve any purpose in terms of the profile? Building up good will was important, but . . . In spite of all her self-denials, the memory of his kiss continued to haunt her and she had noticed a propensity in her to be overly aware of Jago as a very attractive male.

'The excursion won't take long, the island's not that big.' A grin tugged at his mouth when he saw her reluctance. 'Doesn't all work and no play make Erin a dull girl?'

Her chin lifted. 'I'd love to come.'

'Great, I'll pick you up around two. Now, back to the grindstone. In that first play I was more or less just a spear carrier, but in the next——'

Erin changed her clothes three times before finally

settling on pale soda-pink garage mechanic-type overalls. A pink chiffon band was tied around her head, then untied then tied again. She did not want to look too studiedly dressed, yet at the same time she wanted to look a little bit special. She baulked at defining why. Maybe it was because those girls who had posed with Jago at the barbecue had been glitzy creatures, and she needed to prove she could give them a run for their money? She grimaced at herself in the mirror. With big brown eyes, short straight nose and a generous mouth, she was not bad looking herself. Add false eyelashes a foot long, and she'd be a glamour puss.

When she ventured out into the sunshine at two o'clock, there was no sign of Jago. Then a horn blared. Erin looked round to see a man on a motorbike, a beat-up old motorbike, raising a hand in salute. He was wearing an ancient white T-shirt, brown cords, a flat cap and dark glasses. She blinked and approached with cautious steps.

'It's you,' she said stupidly.

'Who else?'

'But——'

She gazed at him in dismay. Jago intended to take her a tour of the island on a motorbike? But she had never been on a motorbike before. Too late she remembered Kiel saying he didn't own a car, and at the same time Maria's comment on him 'going like the wind' reverberated.

'Do I look that bad?' he asked with a grin. 'Don't worry, I'll dispense with the disguise once we're out of town. It's just that in the vicinity of the motel there's a danger of bumping into fans, and I'd prefer not to be recognised.' He touched the peak of the cap. 'It's amazing how effective this is at changing the shape of my face.'

'I don't mind the cap, it's—it's——' Erin's eyes drank in the motorbike. It looked fearsomely big and powerful.

'Sorry my steed's short on polished chrome,' he said, continuing to pick up the wrong vibes, 'But the engine's been souped up, so it does go.' To prove his point Jago adjusted the throttle, and the bike roared like thunder.

She gave a thin smile. 'I believe you.'

'Hop on.'

At this point the sensible thing would have been to confess she was a greenhorn where motorbikes were concerned, but instead she took a deep breath and gamely swung her leg across the pillion.

'Here.' He reached back to take hold of her arms and wrap them around his waist. 'Hold on tight,' he cautioned.

Erin held on tight. Very tight. She jammed herself up against him, her breasts flattened against the solid wall of his back. The name of the game was togetherness. They shot away from the kerb with her clinging on for dear life. Her heart thumped staccato. It seemed at least a mile before she dared draw breath. At first she couldn't work out where to put her head—her chin was jammed up against his shoulderblades—then her legs caused problems.

'There's the marina,' Jago shouted over his shoulder, as a dock decorated with bobbing white boats whizzed by. 'That's the sailing club and——' he pointed '— that's a great restaurant for sea food. Their fresh stone crabs are delicious.' As he spoke his hand was waving around in emphasis. Erin wished very much he would put it back on the handlebars. 'Over there's the riding school, and in a minute or so we'll come to one of the golf courses. The island has three.'

'Nice,' she gulped, hearing her voice sound thin and wavery But at least it was a response. She had not uttered a word since they had left the motel, and Jago's running commentary was for her benefit. It was time she contributed.

'We're heading out of town, if you can call it a town,' he yelled, the words blowing back to her ears on the warm wind. 'This is where the unspoiled part of the island begins. From here on it's bays, beaches, lagoons, and most of them deserted. Great, isn't it?'

'Great,' she cried, hoping he wouldn't turn and see the strained expression on her face.

They skirted the golf course, skimmed around a lagoon, left the town behind, and in time her panic began to ease. Jago might drive fast, but as far as she could tell his handling of the bike was faultless. They made a long uphill climb, their speed reducing, then crested the peak and swept down.

'Corner ahead,' he warned.

In preparation Erin tensed her thighs and tightened her grip around his waist. He was firm and solid, she could feel hard muscles moving beneath his skin. The corner meant they tipped at an angle, but instead of being scared she was unexpectedly exhilarated. Emerging on to the straight, she wanted to chuckle. She had managed fine. Riding a motorbike was not that difficult, after all. She began to understand why Jago was so obviously an addict. To be speeding along with the hot air bombarding your body felt invigorating, adventurous, heady. Erin discovered she was enjoying herself. The wind was rippling through her

hair, the sun was warm on her back, and the power
of the machine beneath her was intoxicating.

Jago shouted something she couldn't catch, but
whatever he'd said, he was laughing. She started to
laugh, too. This was great stuff. Like a child let out
of school, she sat behind him, a grin plastered all
over her face.

There was hardly any traffic, and the island
proved to be as unspoilt as he had promised. Clean
of hamburger joints and funfairs, all she saw were
one or two people stretched out on the sand or
collecting shells. Yachts with red sails, white sails,
yellow sails, rode the waves.

'Fancy a crack at the Rally of the Pharaohs?'
Jago called.

She strained to hear. 'The what?'

'Rally of the Pharaohs.'

Erin did not know what he meant, but when he
swung off the road and on to a trail which wove its
way between desultory palm-trees towards rolling
dunes, she began to understand. Kicking up sand
and stones, they bounced along. Bump—bump—
bump. Erin's breath might be being pounded out of
her, her balance precarious, but the grin remained
in place.

'Okay?' shouted Jago.

'Okay.'

He reached round and patted her back. 'Good
girl.'

Erin laughed out loud. She hadn't had so much
fun for ages, years even. Barely aware of what she
was doing, she snuggled closer, her cheek against
his shoulder. She liked being glued to him, liked his
strength, his masculinity. He was an easy man to
lean on.

'Jago,' she said, deciding it was time he realised she was a novice rider. 'I have a confession to make.'

'Can't hear you.'

They were almost at the sand hills and now he throttled back, reducing their speed.

'I have a confession to make,' she began again, pulling back to reposition herself. As she moved, Erin's glance fell. His T-shirt had come adrift from his trousers, and she saw a strip of tanned skin—smooth skin, gleaming with health. Would he be tanned all over?

'You have a what?'

In turning his head to catch her answer Jago didn't see the stray boulder, half hidden in the sand. Donk! There was a fierce double bump. He swerved, the machine jerked, shuddered and freewheeled amongst the dunes. Somewhere along the way Erin toppled off while Jago and the bike continued on. Winded, she lay on the slope where she had fallen. She wasn't hurt, they hadn't been going fast enough for that, and when she thought how adroitly she and the bike had parted company, she wanted to giggle. She had shot off in one direction, it had kept going in another. Very neat. Very smooth. Like something out of a Twenties slapstick comedy. She lifted her head and looked around. Jago was nowhere in sight, but noises beyond the curve of sand told her he had also fallen off and was now scrambling to his feet.

'You okay, Erin?' he called. 'I'll be with you in a minute. I've lost my damn glasses and——' She heard him scuffle about. 'Got them!'

High above the sun dazzled, and Erin closed her eyes. Then a grin spread. Jago had tricked her with that kiss, but wasn't trickery a game two could play? She removed the grin, arranged herself in a suitably rag doll position, and lay still. She heard him approach. He was pushing the bike.

'Erin?' he said. It was difficult to keep her face straight, but she managed. 'Erin?' he said again, cautiously this time 'Oh my God, Erin!' The bike thudded to the sand. He dropped to his knees beside her. His shadow fell, cutting out the sun's glare.

She opened her eyes and smiled. 'Boo,' she said.

'You bitch! You silly little bitch!'

Her smile froze. Jago was leaning over her, his face contorted with rage. The joke had misfired.

'Jago, I——' she began.

'You think that's funny?' he blasted. 'You think pretending to be hurt's funny? Well, it's not. It's irresponsible and childish and downright cruel.'

She pushed herself up on to one elbow. 'I only——'

'You have a warped sense of humour, do you know that?'

His nostrils were flared, his eyes as cold as icebergs. 'Let's give Jago the fright of his life. Ha, bloody ha!'

Erin recoiled. His fury would have been comic if it had not been so real.

'I'm sorry.'

'Sorry, sorry? Is this the way you get your kicks, making other people suffer? What do you do for an encore?' he demanded. 'Splash tomato ketchup over yourself?'

'I've said I'm sorry.'

'Big deal.' Jago glared at her from beneath the peak of his cap. 'I've heard of sick jokes, but this has to be the sickest, the dumbest, the——'

'Stop it!' She sat up straight. 'And calm down. What's got into you? I was only teasing. There's no need to go on and on.'

He peeled off the cap to run a large hand through his mane of blond hair. 'No, no there's not,' he sighed, his anger collapsing. 'I guess I'm over-reacting. Forgive me. It's just——' There was a fraught pause, and when his blue eyes met hers she glimpsed a pain inside. 'It's just that the last time I saw a girl lying like that, her head to one side, her limbs disjointed, she wasn't teasing. It was for real. We'd been driving along and this fool in a pick-up truck came out of nowhere, and——' His face seized up.

'Jago.' Her hand flew to his arm, to touch and comfort. 'I had no idea. I'm terribly sorry.'

He gave an embarrassed laugh. 'It's not your fault, it's mine. I never realised how close my emotions are to the surface. I thought I'd put memories of the crash behind me, but seeing you like that triggered them off again.' He paused, tracing an aimless pattern in the sand. 'I don't know why it should. You look nothing like——'

'Like who?' Erin enquired. Her biographer's antennae had been sensitised. There was information to be had, if only she could coax it out of him.

Jago brushed the sand from his hands. 'Like no one. Let's pretend this never happened, okay?' Everything was being put back into a box and the lid firmly closed. 'What say you we leave the bike here and stroll down to the sea?'

'Sounds like a good idea, ' she agreed, having no alternative but to accept that he had eluded her. Using his arm as leverage, Erin stood up. 'On your feet,' she said, when he sat there.

Jago held up his hand and grinned. 'I'm not as agile as you. This old man needs assistance.'

'You forget, I'm the one who's too old and too pale,' she said drolly.

His eyes swept over her. 'You're developing a great tan, and as far as the age bit goes—I'd had a bad night when you woke me up and I was cranky. I'm only human,' he cajoled, adopting an air of pained innocence. 'Help me.'

'Erin obliged by grabbing hold of his wrist with both hands and pulling for all she was worth. He never budged an inch.

'Ever heard of the word "co-operate"?' she panted, her cheeks growing pink.

'Yes, and I am.'

'You're not.' She was leaning back on her full weight, her sandalled feet sinking deeper and deeper into the sand. 'You rogue, this is no contest. You must be four or five stone heavier than me.'

'Suppose I strip off, would that help?' Jago enquired, and zing, zing, zing—the air was electric. A series of neon dots flashed and twinkled, transmitting themselves from his eyes to hers.

'It wouldn't make any difference,' she replied, wishing he wouldn't look at her like that, for the blue eyes beneath the blond brows had a disturbing intensity.

'It would make a hell of a lot of difference, toots. Heave!' he encouraged.

'You heave, instead of sitting there like a great big—tondo.'

'Who's a tondo?'

'You are. Now, get up,' Erin demanded, tugging on his arm like a mad thing.

He did as he was told. He raised his backside a

few inches from the sand and hovered. They were
like people at a crucial point in a tug of war, using
his arm as the rope. She was at one end, he weighted
down the other. Erin's feet spread, dividing right
and left until she was halfway to doing the splits.
She wobbled. Jago sat down with a thud. She lost
her balance. He jerked his arm, and she wound up
sprawled on top of him.

'Shall I strip now?' he enquired, smiling into the
flushed face inches above his.

'No, thank you.' Did he know the way her blood
was racing? Could he feel the uneven bump of her
heart? 'Behave yourself,' Erin said, uncertain just
who needed the reprimand.

'Why?' His arms tightened around her waist,
binding her to him. On the bike she had been glued
to his back, now she felt as if she was glued to every
inch of him. Glued to every inch of six foot three of
male virility. Was it heaven or was it hell?
Whatever it was, it was not conducive to a detached
assessment. His smile spread. 'Kiss me,' he
requested.

'Jago!' She attempted to escape, but quickly
stopped. Squirming around on top of him was
having a disastrous effect.

'Feel what you've done to me?' he murmured.
'How could you?'

Easily, it seemed.

'Let me go.'

As a demand, it sounded suspiciously like a plea.
What had happened to the unflappable Erin Page?
For years she had been the woman in charge,
always serene, always controlled, and here she was
metamorphosed into a quivering length of flush-
faced, tumbled-haired confusion.

'Not until you've kissed me. It won't hurt.' Jago was smiling that smile which had drawn 'oohs' and 'ahs' from a million fans and which was now drawing something—she dared not think what— from her. 'You liked it last time, remember?'

'I didn't.'

'Now, Erin,' he chided. 'Credit me with some intelligence. It was obvious you found me ... *simpatico*.'

'You're wrong,' she protested, placing a hand on either side of his head and pushing up against the sand. He allowed her to rise, but only inasmuch as she hovered head and shoulders above him.

'I'm not wrong.'

'You are.' Erin strove for dignity, which was tricky, considering her position. 'I'm your biographer, not——'

'Not a would-be bedmate?' Jago cut in, grinning.

'Precisely.'

'I do love that haughty air of yours,' he chuckled. 'It's a real turn-on.'

'Jago, in my kind of writing one of the rules is that——'

'Who cares about a crummy rule? Can't you stop thinking about that book of yours for once and simply follow your instincts?' He moved one hand from her waist and brought it up to cup her breast. 'You're a beautiful, sensual woman,' he said softly, his thumb brushing across a nipple which sprang to rigidity beneath the thin pink cotton. 'You shouldn't be scared of that sensuality, Erin. It's a wonderful gift. Enjoy it.'

Enjoy her sensuality? It was a wonderful gift? She felt the beginnings of hysterical laughter. Jago had everything twisted the wrong way around.

'No I won't. I mustn't! I mean—can't we go down to the sea?' she wailed, and collapsed on top of him as her arms gave way.

'What is it that worries you?' he asked, sliding his hand out from between them. 'Me as the actor, me as the man, or sex itself? But on the bike back there you were rubbing yourself up against me and cooing, so——'

'I was not!'

'Why the hang-up? I want you. With my glands so obviously rampant there's no way I can say otherwise, so why not admit you want me? It's not a crime. We're both free and single, the sky is blue, the birds are singing, God's in his heaven, so?' Jago was watching her closely. 'Have you ever made love outdoors?'

'Don't,' she pleaded. 'Please don't.'

'Always in bed with the lights switched off? What a waste.'

'Jago, let me go.' She bucked and bristled, desperate to get free, but his arms tightened around her.

'After you've kissed me.'

What else could she do? Erin aimed for his cheek, but at the last moment he moved his head which meant her lips collided with his. A hand left her waist to mesh amongst the rich dark curls at the back of her head, and she was held in place. His kiss was dynamite. It blew her apart. His mouth opened beneath hers and Erin found herself participating in an embrace which made any other embrace seem like a pale imitation of the real thing. Her body heat soared. Jago was exploring her mouth, tasting her, then nibbling. He captured first her upper lip between his, and then the lower, again and again

until inside she felt as sweet and soft as a dewdrop.
When he finally stopped, she did not know whether
to laugh or cry.

'There,' he murmured. 'Together we could press
all the right buttons, ring all the right chimes, if you
gave us a chance. You may go now,' he said, when
she continued to lie on top of him like a beached
whale.

Erin scrambled to her feet and began a fastidious
brushing off of her clothes. Inside she squirmed. He
had been seducing her and she had loved it. Just as
she had loved Ned's seduction! Head down,
refusing to meet his eyes in case he was laughing at
her, she went with him to the water's edge. A soft
breeze teased chestnut wisps from her brow, lifted
strands of dark hair from her shoulders. Gradually
her composure seeped back.

'Talk to me,' Jago requested, as they strolled
along, leaving footprints behind them in the wet
sand.

'What about?'

'You '

'There's not much to tell.'

'Don't be evasive.'

'I'm not.' She gave him a brief résumé of her
childhood. 'See, it's all very dull compared to your
experiences.'

'It's all very secure. Go on.' Her teenage and
university years lasted until they reached a tumble
of rocks at the far end of the bay. 'If you studied
history how come you're writing books?' Jago
asked, when they turned to walk back.

'At Oxford I specialised in the Edwardian era
and one of my projects was an actor—manager,'
Erin explained. 'I went through his life with a fine-

tooth comb and discovered some facts which hadn't come to light before. When my tutor read what I'd written, he suggested he approach an agent on my behalf to see if a biography would be of interest. The agent was Cleo. She said yes. I graduated, the book was published and, much to my surprise, the critics liked it. Patrice Lanham——'

'The actress?'

'That's right. She read the biography and asked Cleo if I'd be interested in writing about her.' Erin stuck her hands in her pockets and paced along. 'I wasn't. I'd already had an idea for a book on contemporary women, but they were intended to be women in the street. Writing froth to boost someone's ego held no appeal. However, Cleo has a flair at twisting arms and Patrice was included. The profile on her was——' she pulled a face '— okay. Some froth but also a chunk of information about her work in the theatre. Mind you, if I wrote it again it would be very different,' Erin muttered, then, wary of having sounded vengeful, added with a smile, 'There are always things I want to change when my work appears in print and it's too late.'

'That's the way it goes. When I see myself on the screen I invariably kick myself for not having done better.' Jago frowned, rubbing his chin. 'From what you've said, I take it the book on women was written several years back?'

She nodded. 'I've done three Edwardian biographies since.'

'But why the gap? Why wasn't this book on men a straight follow on? Given a success, the usual procedure is to take advantage and deliver more of the same.'

Erin inspected the horizon. 'Well, I didn't.'

'You mean after the women book you promptly turned tail, retreated from the real world and buried yourself in history again?'

His words were random, yet he had described what she had done with eerie exactitude. She knew there had to be a way of rebuffing what sounded almost a condemnation, but for the moment it escaped her. Then she remembered a snatch of something he had said.

'As a career move it made a lot of sense,' she retaliated.

Hearing his own words thrown back at him, Jago's eyes hardened. If she hadn't fully believed his justification, it was clear he also did not believe hers. He seemed ready to protest, then thought better of it. An awkward silence fell between them.

'What about your marriage?' he asked abruptly.

Erin sighed. 'It was short and sweet, and now it almost seems as though it happened to someone else. Peter and I were married a year or so after I came down from Oxford. Everyone in the village came to our wedding, the little church was packed. It was packed again nine months later—for Peter's funeral. He had leukaemia.'

'That was rough,' Jago murmured, his fingers fleetingly touching her arm.

His sympathy brought an unexpected mist to her eyes, and she blinked.

'Yes. We'd known each other all our lives, yet our actual time together was over in the blink of an eye.' She stared into space.

'Who has there been since? I know you live alone, but I can't believe you've been left alone. A host of young hopefuls are bound to have beaten a path to your door.' He cast her a glance. 'Who?'

Erin went still inside. Somehow this 'talk to me' had turned into a full scale investigation. She felt herself under siege. Jago was expecting names to be named. And why not? she thought contrarily. A name wasn't much. It wouldn't mean anything to him.

'Ned, and—and one or two others,' she said. She had striven to sound offhand, but it didn't work. She knew it didn't work. Terrified he might look into her face and see the whole sordid story written there, she gabbled off in a totally different direction. 'Has a date been set for shooting the lakeside sequence of *Taro Beach*? William said he'd give due warning, but I haven't heard a word.'

'Damn, I'm sorry. I clean forgot.' Jago bounced a palm off his brow in punishment. 'He asked me to tell you it's been fixed for next Tuesday. I also forgot to say I'm flying to New York on Wednesday. I'll be away eight full days. A shoot up there has been off and on for ages, but the guys who control the budget suddenly sanctioned it. I know it'll mess up your schedule and I apologise, but——'

'I am flexible,' she smiled.

'Good.' He paused. 'About the——'

'Race you to the bike,' Erin challenged suddenly, fearful he was restarting his questions about the men in her life.

She leapt forward as if from starting blocks and galloped across the sand. Surprise gave her the advantage, and for the first fifty yards or so she was in the clear, then Jago drew level. He overtook her, went way beyond, using easy, loping strides. He shouted back, laughing, telling her not to be a tortoise, then disappeared from sight into the dunes. When she panted up she found him beside the bike, ostentatiously patting away a yawn.

'Never mentioned my Olympic gold medal for the sprint, did I?' he drawled.

'Must have slipped your mind,' Erin gulped, catching her breath. 'I have to admit that for an old man you can still move.'

He thwacked her on the backside. 'Less lip, junior. you'd be surprised what this old man can still do.' He raised his eyebrows, as if to allow time for the thought to sink in, then began feeling in his pockets.

'If you're looking for your spectacles, you put them in that pannier thing,' she told him.

'Did I? Thanks.' Jago started to unbuckle the worn leatherette container. 'Talking about the Lanham woman, which we aren't but we were, I remember some guy once told Olivia she reminded him of a young Patrice.'

'Was she flattered?' Erin enquired drily.

He grinned. 'Thrilled to bits. Treated the remark as a prophecy she'd become a beldame of the theatre.'

'With regard to Olivia,' she said, deciding this mention of his girlfriend was too good an opportunity to be missed. 'With regard——' She stopped, uncertain how to proceed. Discussing Jago's childhood and career was one thing, discussing a live-in lover was another. 'Er—did the two of you ever join up on stage?'

He had found the spectacles and now he slid them on to his nose. 'No.'

'Why not? Was the idea never mooted?'

Jago rammed on his cap, jerking the peak down over his eyes. 'On the subject of Olivia, I'm not prepared to talk. She's a closed chapter. You may use what's already appeared in print, but understand I'm adding nothing.'

Erin gazed at him. 'You don't mean—you can't mean you're not going to talk about her *at all*?'

'Not a word. I did say certain subjects were off-limits and you agreed it was a deal,' he reminded her.

'I never expected this kind of a veto to be slapped down,' she snorted. 'You and Olivia were together for three years. That's a long time. You can't pretend she never happened.' Erin saw what had promised to be a wonderful profile begin to slide away from her. 'You have to give me something,' she insisted.

'I don't have to give anything.'

'Yes, you do. I'm writing——'

'You're writing a book that's all, not the damned Declaration of Independence.' His voice was clipped. The eyes behind the dark lenses had built a barrier to hold her off. 'A book which'll keep the reader amused for an hour or two, not change the axis the world spins on.'

Erin glared. How dare he talk of her work in such a feckless fashion? Why must he make it sound so—trivial?

'You can't expect me to slap a dollop of recycled material from gossip columns bang in the middle of a first-hand account. That's ridiculous.' Her voice had shrilled, and she needed to make a conscious effort to lower it. 'The entire profile would be rendered null and void.'

'Nonsense.'

'It's not!' she flared. 'Can't you understand how important it is the profile should be authentic?'

'It will be authentic,' Jago replied irritably.

'How, if a portion's just stuff which has been laundered? I think you're being unrealistic.'

He thrust her an icy look. 'And I think you're being too damned pushy. I said no Olivia and I meant no Olivia, so I'd be obliged if you would kindly get off my back and stay off!'

CHAPTER FIVE

ERIN glanced from between thick black lashes. It was early Tuesday morning, and she and Jago were in the rear of a plush limousine, being driven southwards at speed. Her companion's head was resting back and his eyes were closed. He appeared to be asleep. It was a pretence. In reality he was shutting her out, putting space between them as he had done since their argument two days ago—and the reason was Olivia.

After such a promising collaboration everything had been thrust back to square one. Ease? Good will? They seemed vain hopes. Although Jago had talked the previous evening he had been stilted; his dislike of interviews and interviewers resurrected. And in response Erin once more floundered amongst her original misgivings. She had suspected 'off-limits' could be translated as 'problems'. She had suspected correctly. Accuse her of being pushy he might, but didn't her profile give her the right to press for facts? Yes. Why couldn't he see that? Erin chewed at her lip. She supposed there was one consolation in this upheaval, that he would not be kissing her again. Yet as a silver lining it seemed oddly tarnished.

Adding two and two together, it had not been difficult to deduce that Olivia must be dead. She had been the girl lying with limbs disjointed after their car had crashed. Erin could understand why

Jago blenched from talking about her and sympathised, but wasn't he being too extreme? Although the
cuttings had contained no report of any accident,
she had pinpointed Olivia's demise at more than
two and a half years ago, when all mention of her
had ceased. Surely after such a span of time he
should have come to terms?

She gazed through the tinted window. Sunday's
veto had prompted her to read and re-read every
word she could find on the actress. Erin had been
searching, though for what she did not know. Did a
common denominator exist between Olivia, the
mysterious Wednesdays and Jago hoarding his
money? If so, it was not to be found amongst the
press cuttings, though a couple of interesting facts
did emerge.

The first was that Jago had devoted considerable
effort to promoting his girlfriend's career—and to
no avail. Indeed, several snide comments indicated
he would have used his time more profitably if he'd
gone fishing. Erin could only agree. Admittedly the
girl was decorative, in a starlet kind of way, but in
talent she must have been sorely lacking, for despite
Jago's help all she had achieved were walk-on parts,
infrequent ones at that. A future beldame of the
theatre? Not in a million years.

The second fact which shone clear was that when
Olivia had been around Jago had socialised in
plenty. His hot little hand had not clutched the
purse-strings tight in those days. There were
photographs of them at the kind of expensive
restaurants where celebrities congregate, together
at first nights, patronising trendy nightclubs; all
with his girlfriend smiling brightly into the camera.

She had had no inhibitions about being caught as the shutter clicked, nor in providing a comment for the press, which made Jago's stonewall silence all the more frustrating.

Recalling his response to her playing dead at the beach, Erin's stomach churned. She felt dreadful. Yet if nothing else the incident had made her aware of the hurt which he allowed to fester deep inside. Such a private hurt was an unhealthy hurt. A self-destructive hurt. She did not expect him to forget Olivia—she had not forgotten Peter and never would—but Jago needed to cauterise his wound. Two and a half years was long enough to bleed, and until the bleeding stopped he would never be able to build a new life. He urgently needed to work through his feelings, bring them out into the open. Erin frowned, thinking how he had said talking to her was therapeutic. What better therapy could there be than talking about Olivia? And why not face his loss square-on by agreeing to it being mentioned—fleetingly, sensitively—in the profile? How she wished she could persuade him, but that veto had sounded so *final*.

Her brown eyes clouded. There was always the possibility she might be on the wrong track altogether. Maybe Jago's silence could be attributed more to career reasons than to emotional ones? Could the motivation in keeping quiet about Olivia be coldbloodedly a fear of his image being spoiled? Jago had been in the car at the time of the crash, so the chances were his hands had been on the wheel. The driver of the pick-up truck sounded to have been solely at fault, but even so was he afraid of his popularity plummeting if his involvement in Olivia's death became common knowledge? The public could be fickle with their heroes. Uncharacteristic though it seemed, did self-interest reign supreme? Erin shivered, unhappy with her thoughts. Was that why all mention of the crash had been kept out of the newspapers? She turned to frown. What went on inside Jago's head and inside his heart?

He must have sensed her look, for he opened his eyes and spoke. 'Another twenty minutes and we'll be there. The road splits just ahead. We keep right, but if you went left you'd be en route for the area where I lived when I first came to Florida. It's peaceful down there.'

As he closed his eyes, Erin undertook some rapid computations. The fork must be the one Maria had mentioned, and now she would have bet money on Jago having headed left. Cogs turned. Think, girl, think. He had been returning to familiar ground because . . . because there was a cemetery? Because Olivia lay buried in that cemetery? Was it possible Jago had set one day a week aside in order to kneel at the grave of his beloved? Icy fingers clutched at her heart. What a poignant vigil. No, what a *morbid* vigil. Jago was too young to spend the rest of his life looking over his shoulder, constantly grieving.

She must be wrong. Or was it that she wanted to be wrong? Could her own feelings be obscuring the issue? If only she had remained a step removed she would have been able to see Jago in a cool, clear light, but those kisses, those *shared* kisses, had added an extra dimension. Because she found the idea of him being so tightly bound to Olivia unwelcome, that did not mean it could not be true. People do do these things, he had once said. And people did devote themselves to the dead. Hadn't the Emperor Shah Jehan built the magnificent Taj Mahal in remembrance of his wife, Mumtaz Mahal? The icy fingers bit deeper. Jago had been to India, and at an impressionable age. Had he visited the white marble mausoleum? Was his money being used to keep Olivia's memory alive? Not in the building of a tomb, but maybe in some other way?

The idea was too bizarre. However much he bled, Olivia was not an obsession. Proof lay in his interest in other women, his interest in *her*. But was that proof? Men had a different make-up from women, and could involve themselves in physical intimacy whilst remaining emotionally unmoved. Could his attraction to her be physical, full stop?

The thought caught at her throat, made it difficult to breathe. That all she represented to Jago was a female shape equipped with the necessary curves and fissures made Erin feel wretched, yet why not? Ned had viewed her in that way. He hadn't given a damn about the woman who lived inside the body. And if Jago's attraction was similar, then his affections could continue to belong to his dead lover.

The driver turned off the main road. They sped along a track which led into a flat green landscape. On both sides were shallow lakes, where saw-grass sprouted in tufts. Despite the sun above and the blue sky reflected in the water, the Everglades had a desolate air, and the cypress trees which rose from the swamp like bald grey posts emphasised this melancholy.

'If you go exploring, stick to the boardwalk,' Jago warned, coming awake. 'And watch out for alligators. The Seminole Indians do wrestle them barehanded, but——' he arched a brow '— it is a knack.'

'Are there many alligators?' Erin asked, looking warily out at the marsh.

'Ten thousand or so, but as the Everglades cover over a million acres they're thinly spread. I believe there are also five hundred crocodiles, but they prefer sandy beaches and salt water so there shouldn't be any around here.'

'Which means if a jaw fastens itself on my arm I can rest assured it'll belong to an alligator?'

'If a jaw fastens itself on your arm you can rest assured it'll belong to a mosquito,' Jago replied. 'Don't go anywhere until I've rounded up repellent.'

A picnic ground had been requisitioned for the day and here, beside a lake of grass, the limousine came to rest. The people of the *Taro Beach* unit were already gearing themselves up for action, and Erin looked around, fascinated by the clutter of cameras, cables, lights and people. To one side stood a large trailer which was to do duty as dressing-room and make-up booth, and Jago vanished inside. When he re-emerged, he was brandishing a can of insect spray. Her legs were covered in scarlet pants, but a skimpy white cotton top left her arms bare and vulnerable. Not for long, for Jago set to work, painting her down like a subway wall.?

'You should be okay now,' he said, pushing the cap back on to the can. 'William reckons it'll be another half hour before we're ready, so if you want to reconnoitre now's your chance. But keep your eyes open.'

Erin touched her brow. 'Yes, sir.'

A boardwalk led from the picnic ground into the marsh, and she set off. She did keep her eyes open, and when she stopped to peer down between the wooden slats, she was rewarded. Shoals of silver fish glided in patches of clear water, a frog croaked on a submerged log. She did not see any reptiles, but she did take note of what, according to her guidebook, could only be an anhinga, a bird-type creature which swam under water with its snake-like neck protruding. Up in the air, silhouetted against the china blue of the sky, an egret, or was it a heron? fluttered. The half an hour disappeared in no time, and Erin arrived back to watch the first of the two scenes planned for the day being organised.

The action sounded simple. An airboat, a flat-bottomed contraption powered by a huge airplane propeller, was to skim across the lake towards camera and stop at a wooden jetty. Jago, Kiel and a young blonde actress were to climb out, exchange a few stormy words, then head for the waiting Maserati. Is that *all*? she thought. Child's play.

In take one the airboat overshot the jetty. In take two clouds of the blue smoke which belched from its engine drifted into the camera lens. In take three the actress stumbled. In take four someone sneezed. The airboat swooped back and forth across the water, its engine roaring at several hundred decibels. The temperature increased. Endlessly the action was stopped, started, repeated. There was an awful lot of waiting around. As the morning

meandered on, Erin undertook a drastic reassess-
ment. Her crack about 'reciting robots' had been
patently untrue. Slipping into scripted emotion for a
few seconds, only to be cut off in full spate,
demanded a high degree of professionalism. The
nervous strain had to be enormous. She noticed that
while Jago and the actress lapsed into silent
resignation at each break, Kiel was growing
increasingly rattled. He paced around, demanding
first a mirror, then a cold drink, then a cigarette,
and all the time flaunting his irritation.

'The noise of that thing's giving me a sore head,'
he complained, jerking a thumb at the airboat. 'And
it's like a furnace inside this suit.'

Both actors were wearing suits; Kiel all in white,
while Jago wore city-gent grey with a pearl-grey
shirt. He looked very different from the man who
sloped around in casual clothes and kicked off his
shoes when he talked to her. But then, Erin
recognised, he wasn't Jago Miles any more, he was
a character in *Taro Beach*. His stance was different,
his movements were different, even the angular
planes of his face looked different. Reciting robot?
Never.

'Can't we break for lunch?' grumbled Kiel, when
the scene was repeated for the umpteenth time.

'Soon,' William promised. 'Let's give this one
more try and please, go for realism, there's a good
guy.'

Kiel did. The director was satisfied. Jago
collected her and they ate a picnic lunch with the
rest of the crew. Marvin and some of the others
from the barbecue came over to talk, but it was
noticeable that Kiel could only manage an offhand

wave from the distance. And a merry Christmas to
you too! she thought. Forty minutes later William
began calling out for the second scene to be shot.

'Everything's as we rehearsed yesterday. To
recap, you——' he pointed to the actress '— climb
into the Maserati real quick to allow Jago and Kiel
to slug it out. Kiel, you grab Jago. He throws you
off, you grab again. You slam him right down across
the bonnet and lean over. Allow a pause for him to
catch his breath, then when he pushes back against
your chest, you stagger. Just a step or two. Then the
dialogue starts. Okay? And maintain the realism,'
the director added.

Kiel scowled. 'You want realism, you got
realism,' he muttered.

Everyone took their places. There was silence. A
camera began to roll. A clapper-board clapped. As
the actress disappeared inside the car, so the two
men exchanged heated words. Next came a frozen
tableau when they glared at each other. Viking
versus Italian hit-man, Erin thought, unable to keep
from comparing this confrontation with the one at
the barbecue. Yet Jago wasn't versus anyone except
her! The tableau sprang to life as Kiel gripped both
lapels of his opponent's jacket. Instantly tanned
hands chopped down to destroy his hold. He lunged
again, spinning Jago around and off balance.
Realism was one thing, but Kiel appeared to be
using the scene as free licence to release his hostility
for, with his fingers curled tight around Jago's
shoulders, he viciously smashed him down. The
Maserati was low slung, and Jago had a long
backwards fall before he hit the bonnet. A thud
rang out as his head cracked against the shiny silver

metal. Erin winced. That must have hurt. For a
moment Jago lay spreadeagled, then his hands were
raised. Inches from making contact with the other
man's chest, they fell. Kiel stepped backwards, and
the entire film crew held its breath as their romantic
lead slid slowly and unceremoniously to the ground.

'You stupid son of a bitch, Kiel!' cried William.

'It wasn't my fault,' he croaked, staring down in
horror at the prostrate grey-suited form.

'Like hell it wasn't, you——' The director let rip
with a string of highly coloured expletives. 'Bring
some water,' he called, and everyone leapt to life.

In seconds Jago was surrounded by people on
their knees, people flapping handkerchiefs, people
standing up. Erin followed the swarm, but from the
outer edge all she could see were occasional
glimpses of him being propped up in a sitting
position against the car. His arms hung limp. His
eyes were open, but he did not seem to be focusing.

'Where's that water?' demanded William.

'Give him smelling salts,' somebody called.

'He's seeing stars.'

'He's fainted.'

'He's out for the count.'

The actress lifted his hand and patted it. A
technician felt his brow.

'You fool, Kiel,' William blasted, and began a
second berating. 'Why do you have to be so
goddamn stupid? You know there's no time built
into our schedule to allow for interruptions. All
we've been allocated is this one day out here, and
now you have to go and louse it up, you no-good,
low-down——' Off went the expletives again.

'He's coming round,' said the actress, and

William ceased his curses mid-stream to bend over Jago and beam hopefully. Kiel used the diversion to slink away.

'All right, pal?' the director enquired. 'Better now? Let me give you a hand. We'll take it from the top again, but gently this time.'

Erin needed to stand on tiptoe to see what was happening. The director had slung Jago's arm around his shoulder and, with Marvin's help, was struggling to raise him. Given that he was six foot three and a dead weight, the task was not easy. When she saw how he was all slack arms and legs and vacant eyes, her Girl Guide training came back to her.

'You're not supposed to do that,' she called. 'You mustn't.' No one took any notice. 'Excuse me.' Erin began pushing forward. 'Excuse me, please.' Her request must have struck the correct note of importance, for now the people parted like the Red Sea and she ended up in the centre of the circle. 'Er, Jago'll be in shock,' she explained to William, somewhat surprised to find herself fronting the crowd. 'He shouldn't be moved. He needs to rest and—oh, he should be given a cup of hot, sweet tea.'

Marvin, his head buried beneath Jago's armpit, looked up, very impressed. 'Are you a doctor as well as a writer?' he enquired.

'Er, no.'

'You've been trained as a nurse?'

'Er, no.' Erin's cheeks flamed. All eyes were fastened expectantly upon her, and relating how she had been the leader of the Kingfisher Patrol some fifteen years previously did not seem much of a qualification. 'I have a little bit of medical know-how,' she proclaimed, trying her best to sound positive. Like anyone else, she did not relish making a fool of herself.

Jago guffawed. At least to her it sounded like a guffaw, though everyone else seemed to interpret it as a groan.

'All is not well,' he announced, in a tone which started out as ringing, but which dropped with a clang. 'I doubt some foul play.'

'Now, pal,' soothed William. 'I know Kiel was hasty, but you mustn't take this too hard.'

'I think he's quoting from *Hamlet*,' Erin intruded. 'When you're concussed you can sometimes say irrelevant things. You see, concussion's a bruising of part of the brain as the result of a blow.'

'You sure know your medicine,' praised Marvin. 'Come on, William, I guess we'd better take Erin's advice and let him rest.'

Jago was carefully lowered to the ground and propped up against the Maserati once more. There was a movement in the crowd, and someone miraculously produced a flask of tea.

'How many sugars do I give him?' William enquired.

'Four.' Even to herself Erin sounded efficient. 'And we need more space.'

'Space. Space.' Marvin took up the chant and began shooing off the onlookers as if they were troublesome pigeons. 'You heard what the lady said. Space.' People began to drift away.

'How long before he recovers?' William enquired, handing over the brimming cup.

'Hard to tell.' Jago had begun to blink, which she

took to be a sign of recovery. 'I'd say at least half an hour.'

'Okay folks, thirty minutes,' William hollered, and Marvin and the dregs of their audience ambled off to find some shade.

'It could be longer,' Erin protested. She tasted the tea to check it wasn't too hot, then knelt down. To her relief Jago sipped obediently.

'Thirty minutes maximum. *Taro Beach* is more or less an assembly line production and the machinery isn't geared to cope with delays,' the director informed her. 'In thirty minutes Jago'll be fine. Won't you, pal?'

'He might not be.'

Her patient gave an idiot's smile. 'Shall I compare thee to a summer's day?' he enquired.

William frowned. 'Say again?'

Jago moved his head and winced. He raised a slow hand to the back of his head, then brought it round to stare at his fingers. 'Blood,' he said dopily. He focused on her for a second. 'Erin, it hurts.'

'Oh, gee, don't let him get blood on his suit,' yelped the director. 'We're not carrying a spare.'

She threw him a filthy look. That Jago might be in pain came a long way down the scale. She disposed of the cup and made an examination. At the back of his head she found a patch of blond hair sticky with blood.

'The skin's broken. Jago ought to see a doctor,' she declared.

William sat back on his haunches. 'And where do you suggest we find a doctor, out here in the wilds? Nah.' He gave the bloody patch a quick look. 'It's not much. He'll be okay.'

'Okay,' slurred Jago.

'See, he's coming round,' William rejoiced. 'Take off his jacket, will you? Can't risk it getting stained. And how about his shirt?'

Erin rounded on him. 'Would you like me to take off his trousers, too?' she demanded, and Jago produced another guffaw. 'That cut should be cleaned. It may even require to be stitched.'

'Stitched!' Horror hit the director so hard he almost toppled over. 'We don't have time for stitches. Every minute our production overruns costs dollars, plenty dollars. And if Jago has stitches, then I guess they might need to shave off some of his hair. They mustn't do that'. He jumped to his feet. 'I'll fetch a cloth and some water. If you clean up the blood he'll be——'

'He needs to see a doctor,' she insisted, easing Jago's arms from his jacket.

'Sweetheart, you don't understand what's at stake here.' William dropped back and began to speak in a furtive whisper, his eyes circling to make sure no one was within earshot. 'This is a very fragile time for *Taro Beach*. We've slipped in the ratings, with our storylines I'm not surprised, and the whole shemozzle's in the melting pot. If the series folds our salaries will be sliced off——' he moved a hand '—just like that. I finalised on a waterfront condominium just a few months back, and I'm in debt up to the hilt. Now is not the time for delays in production, any extra expenses. The accountancy boys insist we run on a shoestring. You've no idea the way I had to fight for the shoot in New York. I——'

'If Jago doesn't get to see a doctor, he may not be

fit enough to travel to New York,' she said, the words sizzling out of her like steam.

'Oh hell.' The director frowned. 'The blood's not running on to his shirt collar, is it?'

'No!'

Jago blinked, stretching his eyes open wide. 'I won't let you down, William,' he murmured. 'Give me a hand.'

'Don't you dare,' Erin threatened. 'Look at him. He's giddy. There's no way he can stand, and as for acting—forget it!'

'I think that shirt should come off,' William fretted.

Her teeth scraped together. 'You,' she said through them, 'have your priorities all wrong. Jago is concussed, his head is bleeding and he requires proper medical attention.'

'But what about *Taro Beach* ?' came the wail.

'*Taro Beach* is something on celluloid, that's all. Where's the nearest hospital?'

'I don't know. I'm a stranger on this coast, like everyone else.'

Erin frowned. 'I think I know where there's one,' she said hesitantly, remembering that Maria had mentioned a hospital on the road which forked inland.

'Is it far?'

'Around fifteen, twenty miles—I think.'

William surveyed his romantic lead's helplessness, the pallor of his complexion.

'I guess you'd better take him. He's not going to be any use like this and I can't risk the New York shoot being loused up. Ask the doctors to dose him

with painkillers or something, but whatever happens don't let them shave off his hair. And honey——'
he gave a pleading smile, 'try not to let him get blood all over himself.'

The make-up girl provided a wad of paper tissues, and armed with these Erin clambered into the limousine. William and Marvin manoeuvred Jago in beside her and, with the rest of the unit watching from a respectful distance, they drove away. At the first bend her patient slumped against her, murmuring incoherently, and keeping him steady and trying to protect his wound became a full-time job.

'How far now?' asked the driver, when they arrived at the fork in the road.

'No idea. I know there's a hospital down here, but I don't know where. We'll just have to keep watch.'

Jago stirred. 'Don't want to go to hospital.'

'That cut must be looked at,' she said gently.

'No, it's fine.' With a determined effort, he pushed himself up to gaze blearily out at their surroundings. They were driving through grassland which spread for miles. 'Turn round,' he ordered the driver.

'Take no notice,' Erin countermanded. Something else she remembered from her Girl Guide days was that concussion could cause belligerence, and the scowl on Jago's face indicated he was running true to form. 'Do you have a headache?' she queried.

'A bit. No, I don't. I feel better now. I'm okay. I *am*. Let's just go back to the unit. Let's just——'

She ignored him and advised the driver to do the same. Jago muttered beneath his breath for a

minute or two then sank into a sullen silence. Erin
looked anxiously around. Fields, farms, wide open
spaces were the order of the day. Had she
misunderstood Maria? Then she saw a cluster of red
brick buildings ahead and her spirits lifted.

'Here we are,' she announced, as they passed a
'Hospital' sign.

The driver grinned at her through the mirror,
obviously as relieved as she was. He turned the car
on to a drive which led through well-tended lawns to
a porticoed entrance.

'I'll stay with Jago while you get things organised,' he suggested, when they came to a
halt.

Erin walked into a low-ceilinged foyer. Carpeted
in terracotta and filled with leafy green plants, the
atmosphere was tranquil. She approached a reception desk and began to explain the situation to a
nurse in crisp white. In response the emergency unit
were contacted.

'Mr Miles will be attended to in a moment,' the
nurse told her, then added conversationally, 'It's
quite a change for us to be dealing with him as a
patient when he's been our star visitor for so long. I
don't think he's missed one Wednesday for over two
years, and he comes most Sundays. He deserves a
medal for devoted service. He—oh, excuse me.'

Two medics had arrived with a stretcher, and the
nurse darted out to lead them to the portico. Jago
was helped from the car, his wound subjected to a
swift inspection and then, muttering protests, he
was laid on the stretcher and wheeled away.

'Mild concussion,' the nurse confirmed, as she
and Erin returned to the reception desk. 'The cut

isn't deep, so I imagine Emergency'll just bathe it in antiseptic. He shouldn't be gone long. I suppose you'd like to trot along to Room 28 while you're waiting? His young lady's always ready to chat.'

'Er——'

Everything was happening too quickly. First Jago's Wednesday rendezvous had been revealed, now she was being offered more. She needed time to think. Did she say yes? Did she say no? Erin was faced with a dilemma. She was reluctant to intrude on what was glaringly an area he wanted kept secret, and yet ... Didn't she have her profile to consider? The nurse took her silence as acquiescence and dialled a number.

'What name do I say?' she enquired.

A lip was nibbled, then, 'Erin Page.'

CHAPTER SIX

MEMORISING instructions, she set off down a wide corridor. Was she on the brink of discovering that elusive piece of jigsaw which, when fitted in, would reveal the full and clear picture of Jago's life? It seemed so. And a full and clear picture meant she could write a full and clear profile. A profile of merit. Delight added a spring to her step. Yet as she walked along delight began to waver, and in its place came apprehension. Her step slowed.

'His young lady's longing to see you,' the nurse had reported.

Erin fiddled with the strap of her shoulder bag. The person on the other end of the phone had known about her, but it was one-way traffic. She felt uncomfortable, at a disadvantage. Who waited in Room 28? The name which sprang to mind had to be Olivia's because, thinking back, she realised Jago had never said the actress was dead. Erin scolded herself for jumping to conclusions, both then and now. His young lady could be anyone. But why was she in hospital?

As Erin veered to allow free passage to a porter pushing a trolley, an agony of indecision gripped. No need to be told Room 28 and its occupant were off-limits, so should she turn right around and head back to reception? Was that the decent thing to do? She felt a pang of unease, and stood immobile for a long minute. But it wasn't as though she had made

enquiries, turned over stones, poked her nose in.
Fate was responsible for bringing her here, and who
was she to quarrel with fate? Jago couldn't blame
her for taking an opportunity which had been
dumped in her lap.

Erin frowned, starting to walk again. Yes, he
could. And he would. Verbal pyrotechnics would
burst around her head when he learnt she had
solved the puzzle of the mysterious Wednesdays.
But on reflection he must agree her profile provided
a legitimate excuse—mustn't he? He would understand how she needed to know the truth, to write the
truth, for all the proper reasons—wouldn't he?

She passed surgical wards and a physiotherapy
unit, patients in dressing gowns, hurrying nurses,
and eventually reached a door marked 28. Squaring
her shoulders, Erin knocked. Think positive, think
profile, she told herself.

'Come in,' called a voice, and she entered a room
filled with sunshine.

Decorated in corn-gold and white, with a yellow
carpet, floral curtains which lifted on the breeze, a
television set and video, the room was luxuriously
equipped. Sprays of fresh blossoms added a
fragrance, and there were baskets of fruit. Beside
the window sat a girl—in a wheelchair.

Erin's thoughts took off in a breathtaking spiral.
Blonde and in her early twenties, this was not
Olivia.

'Hi, I'm Susie. I've been dying to meet you,' she
grinned, steering forward and holding out a slender
hand.

Trying to mask her confusion, Erin murmured a

greeting. She well remembered Jago's mention of Susie, but who was she?

'For the past three weeks Jago's conversation has been peppered with references to a knock-out intellectual who's flown over from England,' the girl said, with a teasing lilt. 'And I was eager to see whether or not you do have two heads. Not that I ever imagined I would. Family and friends pass through Jago's security screen, no problem, but anyone with the faintest whiff of the media is kept well away. Take a bow. You're the first writer to receive my brother's top level clearance.'

Brother? Instantly Erin saw the resemblance. The girl was a slight, feminine version of Jago, though without the skew-whiff nose. The diaries had named the youngest of his sisters as Suzanne, a sibling he affectionately called 'the kid'. His comments about this baby of the family had been sparse, and now she began to understand why. He must have been wary of her making a connection with the girl he had demanded news about at the poolside.

'I haven't had top level clearance or any clearance,' Erin confessed. 'The only reason I'm here is because the nurse——'

'Poll?'

'No. Does Poll work at this hospital?' she asked, realising as she spoke that she would. 'We've never met. I've only seen her from a distance.'

'Poll's my night-time angel.' Susie's fine brows dipped. 'But if Jago didn't give permission and Poll isn't involved, how come you're here at all?'

Taking care to emphasise her brother's injury was slight, Erin explained. 'A few minutes ago he

was whisked off to Emergency. The nurse in
reception presumed I was a friend and suggested I
might like to see you.'

There was a giggle. 'So when Jago calls in to visit
me and discovers you've arrived first, he's liable to
flip his lid?'

'I don't think he will call in. He's in a rush to
return to the set. Every minute counts.'

Susie made a moue of protest. 'But he flies off to
New York tomorrow. I know he's already said his
goodbyes and that he'll telephone every day, but
even so——' Her face brightened. 'Say, how about
you and me hightailing it down to the emergency
unit and giving him one big surprise?'

'If you want to go and surprise him, please do. I'd
rather not.' Erin's smile was tepid. 'As you said, he
could well flip his lid when he discovers his security
screen has been breached.'

'But Jago in the full flight of fury is always worth
watching,' his sister proclaimed, laughing.

'Not when the fury's directed straight here.' Erin
flattened a hand on her chest. 'He already has a sore
head. Is it fair to make it worse?'

'I take your point. Okay, we'll leave him be.'

'Thanks.'

'I could suffer a bout of amnesia where you're
concerned,' Susie offered. 'But on one condition,
that you visit me while Jago's in New York.' She
smiled appealingly. 'I understand he's been talking
to you about his childhood. Maybe I could add to
that?'

'Done,' Erin agreed promptly. Visiting Susie
would make a refreshing break to her routine, and if
she could add another source of information to her

profile, that was a bonus. She inspected her watch. 'Another couple of minutes then it's vital I get back to reception. I'd hate your brother to miss me and launch a full-scale search.'

'Coward!' Susie gestured towards a bedside photograph which showed a smiling, dark-haired young man. 'On your next visit I'll introduce you to Robert. He's also been wondering what an Oxford graduate looks like.' She gazed adoringly at the picture. 'Robert's my boyfriend. He's paraplegic, like me. He shattered his spine falling from a horse, my accident was in a car.' She tilted her head, the blonde hair dropping down in a straight line. 'Or did you know that?'

'I—I guessed,' Erin admitted. 'Have you been here ever since?'

'No, the first six months were spent in Thailand, that's where the crash happened. Initially it was too dangerous for me to be moved, but when I grew stronger Jago chartered a plane and brought me here.'

'Why here?'

'Because he'd made enquiries and discovered that the resident surgeon, Dr Heger, is one of the finest where spinal reclamation is concerned.' Susie laughed. 'Though he charges the earth. Jago hoped I might be able to be patched up as good as new, but it's not to be. I've had a series of operations, the last was just three weeks ago.'

'On the Saturday?' Erin asked.

'That's right. How did you know?'

'I first met Jago on the Sunday morning. He was—wound up. Then when I saw him later in the day his tension had eased.'

'It figures. He came along mid-morning to check I was okay. I was. He gets far more worked up over these things than I do. Jago gives all the appearance of being laid back, but he isn't. He worries about me, and my brothers and sisters. He's saddled with a highly developed sense of responsibility. Too highly developed, Robert says. Mind you, with parents like ours it's a good thing someone was around to take charge. Oops,' her hand clamped over her mouth. 'I shouldn't have said that. Big brother objects when I criticise. His motto is "United we stand, etc."' Susie gulped in an excited breath. 'But the last operation was the final one, and now I want to be united with Robert. We're making wedding plans. In two months' time we're both due to be discharged, then——' Erin received a slightly defensive glance. 'We can manage fine, we know we can. Robert's career is in computers, so him being in a wheelchair's no problem. All we need is a house constructed to meet our requirements, plus a car each,' she added, with a toss of her fingers, 'then we'll be independent. I admit a house would be a major expense, but once we were installed Jago won't need to spend another bean. Robert insists that when we're Mr and Mrs we support ourselves. Mrs Robert Pierce,' she crooned. 'Sounds great, doesn't it?'

'Great. Jago would provide the house and the cars?'

'My brother's the most generous guy imaginable,' Susie announced gaily. 'I've done my sums and I figure a custom-built property in a prime position would cost around six months of his *Taro Beach* salary. Robert maintains we could do it much cheaper, but why should we? Jago likes me to have the best.' Her brow creased in a moment of irritation. 'Trouble is, he's holding back on us getting married and I can't understand why. He swears he likes Robert, but I have my doubts. Why else would he insist we're rushing things when we're not? I asked Jago to come with us to look over some land which was for sale, but he made excuses.' A strand of flaxen hair was twisted around a finger. 'I don't think he's convinced that Robert and me should set up home together.'

'Perhaps—well, perhaps—well, you did say a house would be a major expense,' Erin faltered. It was not her place to reveal Jago's *Taro Beach* salary might not be as automatic as Susie believed, but didn't she deserve a hint?

'Money isn't the issue. Jago has plenty.'

'Yes?' She frowned, then, remembering the time, leapt to her feet. 'I must go.' She made her farewells. 'When shall I come again?'

'Tomorrow,' Susie said decisively.

'Tomorrow it is.'

Several people were sitting around the foyer, but none of them was Jago. When Erin made enquiries at the reception desk the nurse, a different woman from the one she had spoken with earlier, made a noise of exasperation.

'You've missed him by minutes. You must be the young lady he was looking for.'

'What was the verdict on his head?' she asked anxiously.

'All clear, no stitches were needed. Emergency cleaned him up, handed over a couple of aspirin and sent him on his way.' The nurse smiled at her relief,

then continued, 'We searched everywhere for you,
but Mr Miles had to leave. Something about
production time overrunning. He said to give you
his apologies and ask if you'll follow him on. Shall I
fix a cab?'

'If you would.'

'Where do you want to go?' the nurse enquired,
lifting the receiver.

Erin looked blank. All she knew was that they
had turned off the main road on to a track and
driven for a good ten minutes before reaching the
Taro Beach unit. The track had been one of several,
all unmarked, and the Everglades had a sameness
about it.

She sighed. 'To the Driftwood Motel, please.'

Before arriving at Jago's home that evening, much
serious thought took place. Erin obliterated any
doubts about whether she had acted correctly in
going to see Susie, and instead fell back on the
conviction that fate's hand had pointed the way.
Fate had also arranged for her to be heading back
there tomorrow, plus fate had ensured Jago was
disappearing for a whole week. Everything had
been preordained with a view to her compiling the
finest and most complete profile possible.

Standing on his doorstep, she adjusted her grip on
her briefcase. Now she knew the direction the
profile would take—given Jago's agreement. His
agreement was the crunch. At present a gap existed
between what she wanted to write and what she
knew he would allow, but couldn't that gap be
bridged? If she chose exactly the right moment,
exactly the right mood, and if her argument was

persuasive enough, Jago must agree. She had no doubt fate would lend a helping hand there, too. Refusing to fret about the mechanics of gaining permission, Erin rang the doorbell. First she must listen to what Susie had to say. Second she must assemble facts pertinent to a responsible and sensitive profile. Third that profile must be drafted, and then . . .

'How are you feeling?' she enquired, when Jago greeted her. She searched his face, but the pallor had gone. He looked fit and alert, and very pleased to see her.

'The cut's sore, but my head doesn't ache any more.'

'No after-effects?'

'None,' he assured her.

Erin hovered uncertainly. 'I rang earlier to ask if you felt up to talking, but your answering machine replied. Even though you're feeling okay, I quite understand if you want an early night.'

'You think I'm crazy enough to turn away my very own Florence Nightingale?' The crinkle-eyed smile dazzled. 'But what would I do if I suffer a relapse and need you to cool my fevered brow?'

He took hold of her elbow to usher her into the house. The aloofness of the past couple of days had disappeared, it was obvious they were friends once more. Erin's first reaction was relief, but was relief appropriate? Instead of giving three cheers perhaps she should run for cover? Jago's appeal was considerable, and already the touch of his hand on her arm had speeded up her blood.

'You couldn't reach me earlier because I've only been home ten minutes,' he explained, as they sat

down in the living-room. 'William was determined
to complete the day's schedule if it killed him.'

'Or if it killed you!'

'He isn't your favourite man?'

'No way. I was under the impression directors
possessed the understanding of Freud and the
philosophical flair of Socrates, but William!' She let
out a breath. 'All he cares about is *Taro Beach*. Talk
about single-minded!'

'Aren't other people equally single-minded?'
Jago enquired, his tone lazy, his eyes not. 'About
stone, about writing books? You looked after me
today and I have a whole list of thanks prepared,' he
continued, speeding up. 'Before I start on them
though, I must apologise for leaving you stranded at
the hospital. When I couldn't make contact there
seemed no alternative but to return to the unit.' He
lifted his hips to slide his hands into his trouser
pockets. 'Where were you?' he enquired.

'Out walking.' Erin found a thread of lint on her
scarlet jeans. 'I arrived back at reception just
minutes after you'd gone, but I couldn't follow
because I didn't know the way. I took a taxi to the
motel instead.'

'So that's what happened. When you didn't
appear I presumed you'd got bored.' A grin curved
his mouth. 'I'm well aware filming can come over as
the most tedious activity ever known to man.'

'It was interesting,' she defended, then, as his
grin spread, amended, 'and tedious.' She paused in
unfastening her briefcase. 'If you came back just ten
minutes ago you won't have had dinner?'

'I don't feel like eating.'

'You must! After what's happened today you

need food. If not you might start feeling faint.'

Jago stretched back in the chair, his hands still in his pockets. With his long legs spread, the material was pulled tight across his thighs. Must he lie there looking so—male? Erin wondered, suddenly stricken by his attractiveness, his virility.

'But if I faint you'll need to give me the kiss of life. Your mouth over mine can't be bad. Okay, okay.' The blue eyes were wide with innocent repentance. 'I'll eat something later.'

'You'll eat something now.' Unable to stay still and look at him any longer, Erin surged into action. 'Let's go and see what Maria's provided. And if you don't fancy it, maybe I can rustle up something to your liking?'

'Yeah, boss,' Jago drawled, and laughed when she wrinkled her nose in reply. 'From what I hear you were also giving your orders earlier today,' he teased, following her into the kitchen. 'I have a vague recollection of you taking charge, but when I returned to the set Marvin rushed to give chapter and verse. That guy's a fully paid-up member of your fan club. He's also under the impression you dabble in brain surgery in your spare time.' His amused tone faded. 'I gather there wasn't too much milk of human kindness being splashed around until you took charge. I want to thank you for your concern.'

'My pleasure,' she replied, trying to keep things casual. Did he know that when he smiled at her like that she was tempted to move close, to touch him, to . . . Erin held out a plate she had taken from the fridge. 'Cold meat salad?' Jago's response was a shudder, so she ran her eyes over the shelves. 'How about hamburgers, or gammon and eggs, or omelette, or——'

'Omelette, with some of this.' He pointed to a slab of cheese. 'If it's not too much trouble.'

'Trouble? You're looking at a girl who makes omelettes while she pats her stomach *and* rubs her head.' To prove her point, she became hyperactive. The pan was heating on the stove, the eggs were whisked, a place was set at the pine table in minutes. 'Coffee or tea, sir?'

'Coffee, please.' Jago sat with his elbows on the table, his chin in his hands, watching as she waltzed around. 'I like you,' he murmured. 'Am I allowed to like or does that contravene the biographer's rules?'

'Liking's permissible.' Erin found that grating cheese required intense concentration. 'I trust Kiel went easy when it came to smashing you down on the Maserati a second time around?'

'He did, plus the third, fourth and fifth time.' He saw her dismay. 'Don't panic, he was gentleness itself. How dare he be anything else with William muttering threats from the sidelines?' A wry brow tweaked. 'I understand your education has been enhanced by some choice obscenities?'

Nodding, Erin slid the omelette on to a warm plate. 'My education has also been enhanced by the knowledge that *Taro Beach* could well be destined for the chop.'

'William told you?' Jago sighed. 'Okay, so I reckoned the drop in ratings was a hiccup, but the litany of show business is don't talk failure, and bad news travels like wildfire.'

'You think I'd have rushed out and shouted your confidences from the rooftops?' she rebuked.

'No, I don't but—well, I guess I have a habit of keeping things close to my chest.'

'Is there life for you after *Taro Beach*?' she enquired, setting the plate before him.

'I don't know.' Jago began to eat. There was a long stretch of time before he spoke again. 'To be honest I can't imagine anyone rushing to sign up an actor so closely identified with a soap opera, especially a failed soap opera,' he admitted. He ate on for a while, before continuing, 'For years I've itched to try my hand at directing. Once I did start to save up with the idea of financing a film of my own, just a low-budget production, but the cash wasn't there. This would have been the ideal time to have had a go. Directing would have removed me from the screen, allowed the character I play a chance to fade from the public's memory, but——' He shrugged and threw a quick glance across the table. 'You must wonder what I do with my money. This is off the record, but a couple of years back one of my sisters had a long spell in hospital abroad. At first she was in intensive care, then round-the-clock attention was required, specialist nursing, expensive drugs. In order to pay the bills I begged and borrowed all over the place, and as a result landed myself on a financial treadmill. When I joined *Taro Beach* I had a huge backlog of debts to settle, plus current outgoings, plus future demands on my earnings.' He threw her another quick glance. 'I'm not complaining. If families can't provide support when it's needed, we might as well give up. I also recognise I'm extremely fortunate to have earned the sums I have. All I'm saying is that I'm not as stinking rich as it would appear. There's invariably an account to meet, a forthcoming expense to be borne in mind. Stop it, Erin,' he ordered suddenly.

'Stop what?'

'Stop thinking about all this in terms of your goddamn profile.'

'I'm not.'

'You are. I can recognise that crusading gleam in your eye. I don't think there's ever twenty consecutive minutes go by without you thinking about your profile.' He jammed his lips together. 'You know it's scary the way you evaluate everything with your writing in mind, but if you think there's a chance of portraying Jago Miles as a good Samaritan in the gospel according to Erin Page, you can think again.'

She opened her mouth, then closed it again unable to meet his attack. She *had* been thinking about the profile, but why not? And it wasn't a case of portraying him as a good Samaritan, it was a case of portraying Jago as Jago. His generosity was an integral part of the man.

'Money apart, won't you be relieved to be free of *Taro Beach*?' she enquired hesitantly.

She received a baleful glance.

'I knew you'd get around to that. You never did believe it was a good career move, did you? This is off the record again, but yes. I badly want to return to acting and not re-acting.'

'You *do* act in *Taro Beach*,' Erin protested.

'Thanks.' He grinned, easier now. 'Yes, I try to get inside my character, but the whole series is so

over the top it's unbelievable. Given the chance I'd
like to do something multi-faceted, something that
stretches, makes me take risks.' Jago pushed aside
the empty plate. 'What the hell. I'll survive whether
I act or not. I can always dig ditches. And if your
writing ever palls, you can always find work as a
cook.' He beamed. 'That omelette was delicious.'

'Glad you approved.'

There was a timeless moment when they sat and
smiled at each other, then Erin reached to begin
clearing away.

'Don't.' His hand covered hers. 'Maria can do
that tomorrow.' He ran a finger across the back of
her wrist. 'You know what I'd like to happen now,
toots?' he enquired softly. 'I'd like us to take our
coffee through to the living-room, me to have a
cigar, us both to sip brandies. Then I could talk into
that machine of yours for a while—just to keep you
happy—and later I'd like us to wander upstairs and
make slow, easy love. It's been a long time since I've
had a woman in my bed and I suspect it's an even
longer time since you've had a man in yours.' Jago
frowned. 'No, I'm saying this badly. I don't want a
woman, I want you. And I think you want me. I
want to hold you near and kiss you, and——'

'Jago.'

'I wouldn't start exclaiming in that horrified tone
of yours if I were you,' he murmured, his finger
moving back and forth across the bones of her
hand. 'You know how amorous it makes me. But I
reckon you should have got the hang of me by now.
Have I rushed off nights to rape and pillage? Has a
stream of women flitted around my house in a state

of undress? Aren't I impressing you with my sobriety?'

She gazed at him, her brown eyes wide and troubled. 'Yes, but——'

'I'm not asking you for a one night stand, just a quick roll in the hay. In fact I'm not quite sure what I'm asking for at all—but, as Burt would say, trust me. I think you need me and I know damn well I need you. Don't you ever yearn to feel arms around you in the middle of the night, to know the wonderful release of——'

'I can't.' Erin swallowed. 'It's not that I don't like you because I do, but——'

'I'm not talking about *liking*, dammit! I'm talking about——' He broke off to glower, snatching his fingers from hers. 'What the hell does it matter what I'm talking about? Us coming together is against your professional ethics, that's why you're getting so damned uptight *again*.' His voice had gathered an icy edge. 'Tell me, is there a time scale on this? Are we allowed to fraternise once the book's published or must I wait ten years before the 'hands off' clause expires? And where will I find you in ten years' time, still stuck in your cottage with your cat, writing, writing, writing? There has to be more to life than putting words on paper.' Jago caught hold of her hand again. 'Doesn't there?'

'Yes.' The word emerged as a whisper.

'Time's passing by, Erin, and who knows what tomorrow might bring?' A cloud crossed his eyes. He was thinking of Susie, she knew he was. 'You're young, healthy, intelligent. You should be making commitments to something more than a damned manuscript!'

'Yes.' This time the word sounded stronger. Her spine straightened. 'Okay, we'll take our coffees through, have a brandy, go upstairs——'

'And?' he asked, when she hesitated.

'And I'll wash your hair. There's a stiff patch at the back where the blood was cleaned off. Jago Miles can't take New York by storm unless he's looking his best.'

'No?' His laugh was faint and dry. 'Maybe you're right.'

Coffee and brandies were drunk. Jago talked about one of the Ibsen productions he had appeared in, and time passed. It was nearly eleven o'clock by the time they reached the bathroom. A spray fitment was attached to the bath, and he stripped off his shirt and dropped down beside it.

'Be gentle with me?' he begged, grinning up.

Erin made a careful inspection. 'It's amazing how such a tiny cut produced so much blood.'

'Shows how macho I am, all that rich red stuff pouring out.'

She wetted his hair. 'You don't look macho to me, kneeling down like that with your eyes tight shut. You look like a little boy. Maybe a big little boy,' she amended, starting to lather. 'Am I hurting?'

'No.'

'Don't shake your head, dumbo, otherwise I might.' The shampoo was rinsed off, then she repeated the process and rinsed again. 'Rise, Sir Jago,' she grinned, blotting his head with a towel.

While he had been below her everything had been under control, but as he stood the perspective underwent a dramatic change. Erin was conscious of the bareness of his chest, the gleaming tanned skin, his muscular shoulders. Her heartbeat quickened. A droplet of water slid down his jaw, and she reached to dab it away. The moment she touched him, she knew her mistake. An emotion flickered in his eyes, only to be matched by an echoing flicker inside her. With his hair damp and tousled, he was a long way from the smooth Mr Wonderful of *Taro Beach*, yet he seemed infinitely more desirable. Erin's skin itched, her mouth went dry. There was an impatient yearning, a need. If he asked her now to make love, she would agree. Whatever he commanded, she would obey. She forgot about the profile, she forgot about the lessons Ned had taught her. If tomorrow she had to pay, so be it, but for tonight . . .

'Enough,' Jago said harshly. He clasped her head in both his hands and drew her to him. He kissed her roughly once, twice, and then took a deep shuddering breath. 'You must go.'

'Must I?'

'Mustn't you?'

The air throbbed.

'Yes.' Common sense had made a comeback. She had been leading with her heart and not her head, but in that direction lay disaster. 'I'll keep my fingers crossed that the New York shoot goes well and that *Taro Beach* takes an upturn.'

Jago didn't hear. He had folded his arms and was studying her. 'I don't understand you,' he frowned.

'I don't understand myself.' Erin gave a tremulous smile. 'I hope you avoid being mauled by the fans.'

'I will, if I follow your example.'

'What—what does that mean? she asked, aware

that the blueness of his gaze had backed her into a
corner, a cold corner.

'It means that if I keep my head down and devote
myself entirely to my work, I'm bound to emerge
unscathed.'

CHAPTER SEVEN

IN response to Susie's pleas her hospital visit the next day was repeated the subsequent afternoon and the following one, to become a regular event right through until the day of Jago's return. She and Susie hit it off well. The girl in the wheelchair was an appealing personality—candid, a touch spoilt perhaps, but with a bubbly spirit. Robert, who turned out to be far more pragmatic and down to earth, made the perfect partner. Holding hands as they chatted, the young couple were very much in love. They were also very keen to plan the future which, in Susie's view, hinged on being lavished with a dream house. Yet when she disappeared, wheeling off to round up soft drinks, Robert's ambivalence towards outside help became clear. He told Erin that if Jago wanted to finance a property he would be grateful, but . . .

Susie's account of the Miles family childhood made an interesting contrast to her brother's. Shared situations took on a completely new slant, reminding Erin, yet again, how the same facts can fall into different patterns when viewed from different standpoints, yet be equally valid. Whereas Jago seemed to subscribe to the theory that if you're stuck in a situation you can't change, you get on and cope, the family's baby had been content for others to cope for her. 'Others' had often meant her eldest brother. Over the days there were references to Jago bandaging scraped knees, taking her to school, even jogging Ursula's memory when a new party dress was required.

'Jago is brother, protector, friend, father—all rolled into one,' Susie affirmed fondly, 'and not just with me. You should see him in action here.' She grinned at Erin's furrowed brow. 'His Wednesdays were originally set aside to keep me from becoming lonesome,' she explained. 'Friends and family visit as often as they can—Jago's always happy to shell out for air tickets, gasoline, you name it—but when I first arrived I went through a very blue period when I was desperate not to be left alone. In time that passed. I made friends, didn't need so much support, and Jago started to take an interest in what else was happening around the spinal injuries unit. Now he goes into the gym, helps out at hydrotherapy sessions. Everyone's amazed to meet a TV star who comes across as normal.'

'He *is* normal,' Erin protested, then blushed at the fervour of her defence. 'If only I could put this into the profile,' she remarked wistfully, 'but he wouldn't agree.'

'No. His version is he's not helping anyone, they're helping him by being an antidote to the artificial world of show business.' Susie shrugged. 'The kids in particular think Jago's great, but he's always had a knack with kids. He was marvellous with me when I was young.' A strand of pale hair was picked from a shoulder. 'I've often wondered why our parents bothered to produce one child, let alone half a dozen. On the face of it you'd think six blocks of granite would have suited Ursula better.

Still, even if she was haphazard, she did love us.
Olivia's mother didn't love her.' There was a pause.
'Has Jago ever mentioned Olivia?'

'Only to say she's a closed chapter.'

'She is.' Susie's mouth pinched up. 'The one
positive aspect of the crash was that it removed
her—and good riddance!'

Erin gulped. 'You mean she's—she's dead?' she
questioned, as the harsh verdict revived her earlier
surmisings.

'Heavens, no.' Hoots of derision filled the room.
'Olivia's like a cat, always lands on her feet. The last
I heard she'd fastened her claws into some L.A. film
mogul. Once again she'll be poised to leap into the
big time. It's incredible how skilled she can be at
persuading people to open doors, then achieving
sweet nothing once she's inside.' Susie was sneering. 'Jago opened doors. He should have had more
sense.'

'But he tried to help her because he loved her,'
Erin said, using the voice of reason.

'Just shows how blind love can be! Olivia had
already spent six, seven years getting nowhere when
she met him, and even to an outsider like me it was
plain she didn't have what it takes,' Susie continued, using the same sneering tone. 'But Jago made a
point of introducing her to the right people,
directing her towards openings, and then bore the
brunt of her frustration when her career lay flat as a
pancake. She could be real vindictive at times, but
he took it all. The dummy! I know there must have
been good moments for them—why else would Jago
have been so attentive?—but from my angle it
seemed an odd affair. And it was me who

introduced them!' She heaved a sigh of regret.
'Olivia was a friend of a friend of mine, and because
she dropped such heavy hints I arranged for her to
meet Jago. She can be vivacious, good company
when she wants to be, and he was attracted. Only
attracted,' the girl in the wheelchair stressed.
'Funny thing is, it wasn't as though she'd hit him
like ten thousand volts, which makes no sense of
why they stuck together. I'd have said much of the
initial attraction was that, like any man, Jago found
it difficult to resist someone who gave such a
splendid performance of being besotted.'

'It was only a performance?'

'No,' came the grudging admission. 'I think she
genuinely did fall for him, but there were many
other threads to what she felt. There's no doubt she
derived a kick from being seen around with a well-
known actor, someone who had status, though as
the months went by there was a backlash.' Susie
turned down her mouth. 'Olivia began to resent
Jago being the one always fussed over. When she
voiced her complaints, he did his best to compen-
sate. He tried to keep an even lower profile than
usual, and pushed her forward instead. From the
start of their relationship Olivia had followed Jago
to wherever his work took him, and now she
declared she'd sacrificed her career for his. Who
was she kidding! If she'd been offered a job he
wouldn't have seen her heels for the dust.' Susie
dripped scorn. 'I told him at the time he was being
taken advantage of, but he came down on me like a
ton of bricks. Reckoned I didn't understand.'

'Greater love hath no man than this,' Erin quoted
ruefully and not altogether appropriately.

'Huh! I even approached Olivia privately and appealed for her to quit hustling him, but all she did was dissolve into tears and play "poor little me". She was a whiz when it came to pathos. She said why did I resent my brother giving her chances when so far she'd had such a raw deal out of life? Wasn't she entitled to her share of good fortune? What was wrong with reaching from the gutter for the stars? As a kid she'd had a squalid time, and she used that to great effect.'

Erin was intrigued. 'What had happened to her?'

'It was the classic case of a drunk for a father and a couldn't-care-less mother. Whereas Ursula carted the six of us around everywhere, Olivia's mom couldn't wait to be rid of her. The kid was dumped anyplace while her mother headed for the nearest bar or dance hall. As Olivia told it, she was always in the way, always neglected. She grew up grabbing love and attention wherever she could.' Susie became pensive. 'She had a great big streak of vulnerability, and I guess Jago, soft-hearted mutt that he is, responded to it. He'd have been far better off if he'd cut loose, but he was always so *concerned* about her.'

'So how did the car crash remove Olivia?'

Silence. A taut silence. Susie frowned, rubbing a finger on the arm of her wheelchair. 'I don't——'

'Forgive me, I'm being insensitive,' Erin said quickly, scolding herself for asking the question. She should have realised such memories would be everlastingly painful. If Susie spoke about the crash she must do so of her own accord, and not be prodded. 'Remember your amnesia where my visits are concerned?' she queried, hurdling her mistake.

'I've kept quiet when Jago's phoned through from New York,' Susie assured her.

'Thanks, but come Sunday the amnesia can end. All this week I've been working on a draft of my profile and although it's open-ended because I've still to hear more about Jago's career, it is taking shape. On Saturday I plan to plonk it down before him and with luck avert an explosion. You did agree I could mention you so I have, sparingly, and——'

'I don't understand how you hope to avert an explosion,' Susie interrupted. 'When Jago reads my name and realises we've met, my guess is he'll embark on a full flight of fury.'

Erin shook her head, the brown curls tumbling. 'There's no mawky sentiment, no purple prose, no drum beating. In fact there's nothing at all in the profile to which Jago can take exception.'

Susie grinned. 'You hope.'

'I *know*.'

The determination to compress as much as possible into the period of Jago's absence meant that at first she had collected up her notes and typewriter at the end of each day, and staggered back to the motel for a further session. Then Maria had made a suggestion.

'Why not work on at the house, hon? That way you won't disturb anyone with the rattle of keys. I'm sure our lord and master won't mind.' The housekeeper had smiled. 'And I can make you a bit to eat to stop you from fading away.'

Erin had given thanks and settled down in the pink and white bedroom where she was free to type, play back tapes, study notes to her heart's content.

Each evening she had worked through until ten,
when tools had been downed and she had summoned a cab. Even she had her limits.

As Wednesday presented the last opportunity for
following this régime, she was eager to make the
most of it. She said goodbye to Maria and the girls,
ate the pizza provided, and returned to her labours.
Jago had called the previous day to ask how she was
getting along and had mentioned that he was
booked on to a late flight. He would not be home
until midnight, but by then she would be long gone.

Reading through the paragraph she had just
typed, Erin smiled. Everything was flowing. Although this was only a first draft and incomplete,
she knew it was a good draft. A good draft augured
well for a good book, a very good book, a wonderful
book. With a contented sigh, she turned back to the
typewriter. Her fingers were raised to the keys when
suddenly she frowned. Erin tilted her head. Was
that a noise downstairs? She strained to listen. Yes,
there were noises. For a moment she went cold,
fearing intruders, then she relaxed. A key had been
turned in a lock, then came the sound of the front
door being opened and closed. No intruders, this
would be Jago home early.

Jago! Into action she dived, ripping the paper
from her machine, bundling up her draft and
pushing it into a folder. The folder was shoved
inside her briefcase, and the briefcase fastened.
Timing was everything. And timing meant it was
vital he didn't know about her draft until Saturday.
She dare not risk him idly lifting a page and reading
his sister's name ahead of time. If she was to gain
agreement to Susie's inclusion, then her hand must

be on the tiller, things must be steered her way. Rapidly she set a pile of press cuttings to one side of the desk and inserted a clean sheet in the typewriter.

She scanned her work base. Yes, all tracks had been covered. No one would ever guess she was currently involved in something which might be termed 'clandestine'.

Tucking her mocha silk shirt more neatly into the waistband of her slacks, Erin set off down the landing to greet him. At the top of the stairs, a welling of emotion halted her. Jago was below in the hall, his back towards her. Head bent, slightly stooped, he was in the process of patting his pockets, perhaps in search of cigars. Her eyes moved over him; lingering on the thick fair hair which curled at the nape of his neck, on the width of his shoulders beneath the pale grey jacket, on the tall familiarity of him. She had missed him. Very much. Foolish tears filled her eyes. Jago seemed so dear, so welcome, she needed to fight an impulse to rush down and throw herself into his arms. Erin blinked and began to descend. She had almost reached the foot of the staircase before she spoke.

'How was New York?'

He jumped. 'What are you doing here?' he demanded, swivelling.

'Working late. Sorry if I startled you.' She noticed a bleakness around his mouth, a tension in the angular planes of his jaw. 'What's the matter?' she enquired anxiously. 'Have you got a headache?'

'Yes—you!'

Her hand went for the banister. Erin needed its support. Anger, cold as an Arctic blast, was filling the hall, sending shivers down her spine. He knows I've met Susie, she thought, recognising the man two steps below as the Ice Man.

'I used my time in New York to think—about you and me,' Jago grated, launching into an immediate attack. He slid his hands into his trouser pockets, placed his feet apart. 'I decided I was going to tell you about Susie, about a lot of other things, too. Not for publication, of course, but because I wanted to *share*.' He hurled the word at her like a harpoon. 'It isn't often I share things. Somehow it's always been taken for granted I'm the strong man in control, and strong men aren't supposed to admit to worries, to confess they wake up in the night scared stiff and in a cold sweat. However, I decided I could talk to you. Your intelligence and stability impressed me, made me think you'd understand. I even thought you might help!'

'I'd——' Erin's throat needed to be cleared before any reasonable sound could emerge. 'I'd like to help, to share.'

'Wouldn't you just! So long as it was a three-way share—me, you and that goddamn profile. It fills your mind to the extent that nothing else matters. In its name you're perfectly happy to give the nod to a dirty trick or two, or three, or four!' His laugh was bitter and disgusted. 'Why did I ever allow Burt to persuade me you were different? Why did I ever think you could be trusted? You softened me up real good, and I fell for it. Because you looked after me, made me that omelette, washed my hair—and bloody kissed me as though you meant it!—I believed you cared. Oh, not about me as Jago Miles, an actor whose life might make an hour's agreeable reading, but cared about me as *me*. How wrong I was!' His whole body vibrated with hostility. 'Writer, journalist, what the hell? You're a shark and without ethics like most of your media buddies.'

'I'm not. I——'

He allowed no entry. 'Today filming finished sooner than expected, so I caught an earlier flight. Having been gifted with some free time I decided to go and surprise my kid sister. Guess what? *I* had the surprise.' His blue eyes scratched a frosty path over her. 'Do you receive backhanders from the C.I.A.?' he demanded. 'It wouldn't surprise me to discover you're on their payroll. My God, I've heard of snoopers in my time, but——'

'I wasn't snooping, I wasn't,' Erin broke in, desperate to state her case. 'I came across Susie by chance. The only reason I went to the hospital in the first place was because you'd hurt your head.'

'And Florence Nightingale changed into private dick mid-stream?' he sneered. 'You can do better than that.'

'But I had no idea Susie, as a patient, existed.'

'You knew the hospital existed. Marvin made it very clear it was you who insisted I went there.'

'Someone had mentioned it, and—and I remembered,' she said stiffly.

'Someone? Which someone?' He shifted his stance, like a bull pawing the ground. 'Tell me!' he thundered.

Her hand tightened on the banister. 'Maria.'

'I bet! What reason would Maria have for mentioning that particular establishment? You make a big thing out of how you tell the truth in your

writing, why not have a shot at telling the truth
now?'

'I am. And if I make a big thing out of writing the
truth, so you make an even bigger one out of
keeping secrets. Do you think no one ever wondered
about your hush-hush Wednesdays? Of course they
did, it's a natural reaction,' she continued, when he
was slow to answer. Erin frowned. The housekeeper's name had been forced from her, but Maria's
involvement ended there. She refused to incrimi-
nate her. 'Apparently a tradesman reported how
he'd seen you heading in the direction of the
hospital.'

'This news was served up along with the coffee?'

Her chin lifted. 'No, I asked. You granted
permission for me to ask questions and——'

'I didn't grant permission for you to employ the
third degree,' Jago hissed.

She felt uneasy. 'It wasn't the third degree. It was
one question. A legitimate enquiry.'

'Legitimate? Like hell!'

'How do you expect me to write an in-depth
profile when one-seventh of your life's a blank?'
Erin challenged, refusing to admit her query to
Maria had been less than justified. She executed a
rapid change of course. 'The nurse on reception was
responsible for bringing Susie and me together. She
suggested I might like to meet your young lady
while I was waiting for you to be patched up.'

'You could have said no,' he slammed back.

'But—but it was fate,' she replied, wishing he
wasn't making it sound as though she had committed a crime.

'My God, now I've heard everything.'

'It just—just happened,' she faltered, her heart thumping inside her breast like a jackhammer. She *had* done the right thing, she told herself. She *had* acted from the most worthwhile motives. There was no reason to buckle beneath his criticism. Yet the doubts which had once surfaced began to pinprick again.

'Happened? What you mean is you regarded the nurse on reception as heaven-sent. She must have been the one on duty today. She called to me as I was passing. She wanted to talk about my young lady, only this time she was referring to *you*. She said did I know how lucky I was to have found such a caring person?' He lifted his eyes to the ceiling 'Oh boy! She went on at great lengths, telling me how kind you'd been, going in to see my sister every day while I was away.'

'But I've enjoyed visiting Susie.'

'There was never any doubt about that,' he taunted. 'After all, what does Erin Page enjoy more than furthering the fortunes of her book? The unfortunate part is that although Susie knew you were interested in gathering information, she also believed you went as a friend.'

'I did!' Her voice squeaked in protest. 'I like her.'

'You like *pumping* her.'

'You're putting entirely the wrong slant on this. Yes, I did ask questions, but——'

'You sneaked in to see my sister behind my back. You arranged for your visits to be kept a secret. Your sole motivation in going to the hospital was your book!'

Her stomach churned. It was obvious Jago felt she had betrayed him, but she hadn't. Wasn't a successful book in his interests as well as hers, and ultimately in Susie's? Royalties would help finance her house. Rapidly Erin assembled a defence.

'You're wrong. For a start sneaking in sounds like I shinned up a drainpipe, but all that happened was the nurse rang through of her own volition, and Susie wanted to see me.'

'She would. When you've been stuck in a controlled environment for ages you don't turn away a new face.'

'Did you really tell her I was a knock-out intellectual?' she enquired.

'What's that apropos of?' he scowled.

'Nothing. Did you?'

'Yes. What I neglected to mention was your volatile streak! Don't sidetrack. The fact is you knew how I'd kept my visits secret, so you knew my so-called young lady was none of your goddamn business,' Jago said grimly. 'Why the hell couldn't you have stayed in reception until I came, and then asked me who she was?'

'Would you have told me?'

'Probably not.'

Erin moved a hand. 'There you are.'

'Where? Unlike you I don't subscribe to the belief that all's fair when it comes to love, war and writing books.'

'Neither do I.'

'No?'

'No.' Instead of churning, her stomach felt hollow. 'As far as keeping quiet about my visits was concerned, it was a temporary arrangement,' she said, flailing around in the hope of recapturing shreds of what was now a fast-disappearing confidence.

'I know, Susie explained. She explained *everything*. She didn't want to, but I——'

'You weren't rough on her?' Erin implored. 'Most of what she told me confirmed your account of your childhood, that's all. And in biographical terms two sources are always better than one.'

'Biographical terms?' He chewed on the phrase and spat it out. 'So we're harping on our book again, are we? It's always the damned book. Don't I remember you saying *Taro Beach* was just something on celluloid? Well, this all-consuming passion of yours is just black marks on paper, and does not excuse your actions.' His eyes signalled disgust. 'Not one iota!'

Erin felt queasy. No pinpricks, those doubts had begun to stab. Her grounds for visiting Susie had seemed so sturdy, but had she been mentally manipulating her reasons into an acceptable form? Jago's condemnation made horrible sense. Could absorption in her work have sucked her into overstepping the mark? Was she guilty of sharp practice? No. Maybe. *Yes*. It was a daunting realisation. Erin wished a crevasse would open and gobble her up. She drew a breath.

'You're right. I was wrong to have visited Susie without your permission,' she admitted. 'At the time I did wonder if I should, but——'

'So there wasn't just a blind belief that what you were doing was right?' he cut in. 'Well maybe there's hope for you yet. Where is this profile of yours?' he demanded suddenly.

From rock bottom, her spirits soared. Jago was

interested. All was not lost. Once he read what she'd written he would forgive and understand. He would agree that, on this occasion, the end did justify the means.

'It's upstairs. Come and have a look,' she offered eagerly, and when he joined her, she smiled. 'It's a first draft and incomplete, so please don't expect much. There are alterations, crossings outs, and not much polish, but you should be able to get the flavour.'

The look he flung suggested the flavour might well be cyanide. Jago accompanied her into the back bedroom, where he straddled a chair and waited impatiently as she opened her briefcase.

'I hope you like it,' Erin said, handing over the manuscript as though handing over the Crown jewels. Jago frowned down. He's not going to read it! she panicked, in a taut moment when he remained immobile. Then he began to thumb through. 'Chapter Five's the one which refers to Susie,' she burbled, relief making her loquacious. 'And if you're wondering, I haven't included Olivia.'

In response she received a steely glare.

'I don't know why I'm doing this,' he muttered.

At first his inspection was cursory, then a sentence caught his eye. Jago read a little, and in time turned to Chapter Five. A paragraph was scanned here, a comment frowned over there. Please let him like it, Erin prayed. This piecemeal scrutiny was not the long leisurely read she had planned for Saturday, yet surely he would recognise how Susie and her disability had been handled in an understated and sensible manner? The minutes dragged on. A clock ticked somewhere. No use attempting to read anything from his expression, for Jago was poker-faced. Erin felt as if she was growing into an old, old lady.

'Well?' she breathed, when finally he raised his head.

'Very good.'

She sank back. 'Thank you.'

'That doesn't mean it can be published.'

She jerked upright. 'Why ever not?'

'Erin, I've kept my sister away from the media for well over two years now,' he said heavily.

She waited for more, for a fuller explanation. Nothing came. 'That's it?' she asked.

'Isn't it enough?' She shook her head. 'Well, it's all you're getting.'

Why was he so belligerent, so guarded? This desire to protect Susie was overdone, did not make sense.

'What possible harm can a little exposure do?' she appealed. 'And it is a little.'

'No.'

'Jago, the public——'

'If you intend to quote jargon about the public having a right to know, forget it. It's rhetoric. It means nothing.'

'I was going to say that the public are not ogres,' she said tersely. 'Look, if guilt's involved in this, it shouldn't be.'

'Guilt?' he questioned.

Abruptly, she was stumbling. 'If—if you feel guilty about the crash.'

'I don't.' Jago frowned at the bundle in his hand. 'This can't go ahead as it stands.'

'But if the reference to Susie's picked up and some publicity results, she won't mind. She's said she won't. I think she'd enjoy it. That girl has spunk. She's well adjusted and——'

'No,' he bit out, his face darkening.

'You mollycoddle her far too much. Her body might not be perfect, but her mind is. She can cope, she——'

'No.'

'Any publicity would be a nine-day wonder.'

'No.'

'Can't you be something else but negative?' she flared. Erin had tried all the angles she could think of, and each time come up against a solid brick wall. 'Can't you see reason?'

'Can't you see further than your goddamn book?'

Her jaw tightened. 'You should be grateful for my goddamn book. If *Taro Beach* finishes you may well need the money it'll bring in.'

'*Taro Beach* is finishing, confirmation came through while I was in New York. So yes, I'll need the money, but not from this.' He rapped the sheaf of paper with his knuckles. 'Any royalties will be for the next profile you write—a different one—one which complies with my wishes. I've provided plenty of first-hand information, so there shouldn't be any problems. Leaving Susie out isn't going to——'

'I don't want to write a different profile.'

'Exactly. You want to write what you want to write. That's why Edwardians are tailor-made. They can't squawk if you go too far.'

'I don't go too far. I write the truth, which is what I want to do now.'

'You will.'

'The *complete* truth.'

Jago raked a hand through his hair. 'You're not a shark, you're a terrier clinging on to a bone. Sorry, but you're going to have to let go. Tomorrow you can start on a fresh profile.'

Erin glared. 'Suppose I refuse?'

'You mean it's this or nothing?'

The earth juddered beneath her feet. Juddered and went still. 'Yes,' she announced impetuously.

'Then it's nothing.' Jago flung the chair out from under him. 'Forget you ever met me, because I'm damn well going to forget I ever met you.' With the papers clutched in his hand, he headed for the door. 'The only thing to do with this is to burn it.'

'Burn? Burn my manuscript?' she spluttered, gazing at him in wide-eyed disbelief.

'Why not? It's of no use any more.'

'But you mustn't! You wouldn't! You can't!' Erin flew across the room. 'Give it to me.'

His raised his arm, holding the cargo high above his head. 'You think I'm fool enough to let you take this back to England?'

'It's *my* property.'

'It's *my* life. If I say it goes up in flames, then go up in flames it does. I don't want this kind of private information kicking around. As long as it does, how can I rest easy? For all I know you might decide to sell the story to——'

'I wouldn't! I wouldn't sell it to anyone,' Erin rejected hotly. She lunged upwards, but the papers remained tantalisingly beyond her reach. 'I'm not an opportunist.'

'No, you're not,' he agreed with a frown. 'What

the hell are you? Money and fame aren't the
motivations, so what makes Erin tick?' Jago
switched the manuscript to his other hand, thwart-
ing her. 'It's blatantly clear you use your writing as a
dumping ground for all the emotions you should be
using elsewhere, but why?'

'Give me that manuscript!'

He stepped aside to avoid her thrashing arms.
'What happens if you board the plane without it—
the world falls apart? This isn't the Holy Grail. You
aren't an emissary on a divine mission.'

'I want it.' Erin pushed brown curls back from a
forehead which had become flushed and clammy.
'*Please.*'

'No. You'll feel much better when this has gone,
when it's out of your system. You need to be
exorcised, then perhaps you can start to live again—
live properly.' He fended off her grabbing hand.
'Hell, my career's important to me, but I don't
devote my entire existence to it to the exclusion of
everything else.'

She thumped a fist on her chest. 'Give me my
manuscript.'

'It's of no use.'

'I don't care, I want it.'

Erin threw herself forward, clawing and flailing,
but was held off with infuriating ease. How could
she make him hand over *her* property? Leaping up
and down was futile, thumping at his chest wasn't
doing much good either. But the manuscript was
hers, hers, *hers*. She lifted her foot and slammed it
into his ankle as hard as she could.

'You——' Jago cringed, swore viciously, then
flicked his wrist. He sent the papers skimming

across the room to where they landed, dead centre of the water-bed. 'Wait!' he commanded before she could leap for retrieval, and the authority in his voice acted like a leash. 'Behave like a bitch, get treated like one. You sit and you stay, and you listen to me.'

He had indicated a chair behind the desk. Erin glowered. There was a moment of hesitation in which she weighed up her survival if she rebelled, but a look at his face said retribution would be swift and uncompromising. Jago in this mood was not to be treated lightly. She went and sat down. In turn Jago limped to his own chair, straddling it again. His ankle was rubbed, frowned over, then he lifted his head.

'Don't imagine you have a monopoly on determination,' he said. 'Ever since I kissed you I've wanted you. I still do, which, considering the present circumstances, seems remarkable. However, I appear to be lumbered with a libido which has a will of its own. Which means——' the blue eyes narrowed to slits '— that if you get on that bed and touch that manuscript, then I get on that bed and I touch you.'

Her stomach tightened. Erin heard a ringing in her ears. 'You—you'd rape me?' she gasped.

Slowly he shook his head. 'It wouldn't be rape, would it? Oh, maybe you'd fight a little, but you'd soon surrender. We both know that. You gave yourself away at the beach when your lips clung to mine just a moment too long, when you stayed on top of me. Would you like to lie on top of me again, with us both naked this time?' His voice had become silk and smoke. 'Would you like to feel my

mouth on your breast, know the ecstasy when I part
your thighs?'

Erin lowered her lids. 'Don't,' she begged.

'Why not allow me to introduce you to the joys of
making love on a water-bed? The drifting feeling
adds a whole new dimension to intimacy. It'll bring
out the best in both of us and your best, Erin my
sweet, could be very, very good.' He stretched out a
large hand. 'Shall we?'

'No!' she yelped. She was aroused enough with
him talking like this. Whatever happened, Jago
must not touch her.

'It would be a memorable way to say goodbye,
and especially for you. After all, you have been
leading a hellishly boring life.'

'Have I?'

'Haven't you?' he drawled. 'If I was in your shoes
I'd leap at this chance of some action.'

He was so condescending, so supremely in
charge, so inviolate, that something inside her
snapped.

'You think I haven't known much *action*?' Erin
demanded.

Jago moved wide shoulders. 'I think there's a
good chance you and your husband were virgins on
your wedding day, and that due to such a short time
together the sex never got to be too fantastic. Never
mind, I can——'

'You can what?' she interrupted, in a brittle
voice. 'Enlighten a small-town girl? Open up a
whole, new, wonderful world? Sorry to disappoint,
but you've been picking up faulty signals. My sexual
education was completed six years ago by another
actor, so I don't require extra tuition. Ned taught

me how to press all the right buttons, ring all the right chimes, and I was a fast learner. Very fast!' Her chin jutted. 'We made love night and day, and never in bed with the lights switched off. Ned had far more energy and imagination than to be content with that!' She flung Jago a caustic glance. 'So you see, I know precisely what kind of a gift my sensuality is. And yes, you're right, I would surrender because you attract me as Ned attracted me. You're both big and blond and——' she gave a strangled sob, '— bastards.'

'Erin——' He rose from his seat.

'Leave me alone!'

The shame of what had happened so long ago erupted inside her like a volcano and those tears came flooding down her face. Hot tears. Unstoppable tears. Tears which needed to be shed. Head in her hands, she sat there and sobbed while Jago looked on impotently.

'Erin, I'm not Ned,' he insisted, when the racking sobs gradually lessened.

'No, you're not.' She blew her nose, wiped her wet cheeks. She shuddered. 'I want to apologise. I should never have gone to see Susie without first clearing it with you, and I should never have bowled on and included her in the profile. I guess I knew all along my behaviour was . . . irregular.' Red-eyed and still shuddering, she struggled to compose herself. 'Somehow my writing gave me tunnel vision, and I seemed able to justify anything.' She swallowed. 'Now I'd like to wipe the slate clean and begin again. I can write a perfectly acceptable

account of your life without any reference to Susie
and, if you agree, I'll start on it tomorrow.'

Jago smiled. 'I agree. Shall we seal the bargain?'
He held out his hand. This time she took it.

CHAPTER EIGHT

SUCH a thorough shake-up left Erin bruised and battered. Tight-closed corners of her mind had been wrenched open and in consequence her lifestyle, aims, hopes; her present and her future—everything—needed to be reassessed. Now she understood that whilst her writing had provided a necessary survival kit following the trauma of Ned, over the years it had moved in and taken control. The time for her to control *it* was long overdue. Channelling all her energies, creative and otherwise, into a single stream smacked of obsession, not the dedication she had previously congratulated herself upon. When had she last gone on holiday, taken an interest in buying new furnishings for the cottage, picked flowers, even raised her eyes from her typewriter to marvel at the colours of a sunset? These were omissions which needed to be rectified, urgently.

And what about the Edwardian biography planned to come next? Maybe the idea should be scrapped and she should stick with writing about today's people, today's world? Cleo would approve, for it had been her agent's dogged determination, not her own impetus, which had lifted this current book off the ground.

'Stop vegetating in libraries, kick the habit of poring over dusty documents at home,' Cleo had implored. 'Your Edwardians will keep. I've trundled out this suggestion before—like on fifty

separate occasions!—but why not have a bash at a
sequel to your women book? From a personal
standpoint making contact with the living has to
pay dividends. And along the way try to grab some
fun, maybe even fall in love, there's a good girl.'

Fun and love, where were they? Such commod-
ities seemed to have been in short supply. Although
she had dated over the past six years, it had been
sparingly and always with men who made few
demands on both her time and her body. Erin had
not been aware of choosing escorts for these
reasons, but now she began to wonder. And where
were the husband and babies she had once
visualised? In the past she had been smug,
informing herself that whereas any dimwit could
have a family, only the sacred few were capable of
producing a book. Besides, she had plenty of time to
find someone to love. That time had dwindled. She
was thirty. Not ancient exactly, but lagging behind
her friends who were well established with husbands, plus one, two, even three children. Once her
books had seemed far superior to any husband, any
child. Now they seemed to be—just books.

Yet how did she set about restructuring her life?
Fun was no problem; in the month which followed
that solved itself—thanks to a lively nature which
was now allowed free and varied expression. And
thanks to Jago. On seeing how promptly she had
sought to set her work in a less intense context, he
had made a positive response. Over the past four
weeks they had swum together in the pool, strolled
along the seashore, whooshed around on his
motorbike—this last pastime resulting in Erin
becoming almost an addict herself. Despite these

excursions, the profile had not suffered. Jago had
fed the remainder of his career into her tape
recorder, while she had kept pace with the writing.
Erin had discovered afresh how work can be
harmoniously combined with pleasure.

On Wednesdays they had visited the hospital.
Jago had been insistent she join him and, though
apprehensive, she had agreed. Apprehension
proved superfluous. There were no recriminations.
Within seconds of her meeting Susie again, a joke
had been cracked and the three of them had
laughed. Erin could relax. The visits, like the
swimming, the strolling, the bike riding, had been
fun.

That left love. To her bewilderment, Jago had not
made a positive response there. On the contrary, the
blond Viking with a glint in his eye had switched to
being ultra-correct, ultra-proper, ultra-platonic.
There had been ample opportunities for him to give
rein to that wayward libido, but he had ignored
them all. Admittedly there were moments when
Erin wondered if—hoped that—the sparkle which
joined them might be attributed to something more
than a cheery companionship, but when he continued to keep his distance these had had to be
dismissed as figments of her imagination.

She could only assume the revelation of her affair
with Ned had brought about this change. Jago's
interest had been piqued by a woman he had
considered unschooled in the ways of love, but once
alerted to the fact she was a member of the
cognoscenti, albeit a lapsed member, his interest had
fizzled. Not that he was aloof. He was so damned
amiable Erin was tempted to lash out at his ankle

again and demand to know what he thought he was playing at. 'Brother, protector, friend, father—all rolled into one' had been Susie's description, and now it so aptly applied to his attitude towards *her*.

But she didn't want Jago as a brother or as anything else platonic. She wanted him to acknowledge her as the sensual woman he had insisted she was. She wanted him to . . . Erin sighed, conscious of the unrelenting tick of time. What did it matter what she wanted? This Sunday was her final day in Florida and already it was evening. Tomorrow, as Jago travelled to Miami to complete the penultimate episode of *Taro Beach*, she would board a plane to fly up, up and away into the wide blue sky. Chances were they would never meet again.

'You're very quiet, toots,' Jago remarked, drawing Burt's Cadillac to a halt beside the toll booth. He stretched to fiddle in his trouser pocket for coins, then tossed them into the basket. Seconds later they were heading across the causeway towards the island. 'Has the sunshine worn you out? Never mind, it's added the finishing touch to a wonderful tan.' He surveyed her, smiling. In a sleeveless pistachio-green shirt and brief shorts, Erin was a creature of honey-brown limbs. 'You'll be a sensation back home. You'll bring the traffic to a complete standstill.'

'Will I?' she said wistfully, thinking she would rather be a sensation here, bring him to a standstill. 'I am tired,' she agreed. 'It's been a busy day.'

They had started early. Commandeering Burt's air-conditioned Cadillac for the long ride in preference to the bike, they had driven north to an aquatic theme park in central Florida. There Jago had donned the requisite sunglasses and flat cap, and wandered with her incognito. The day had been a parade of delights. They had applauded performing dolphins, sea-lions, starched-front penguins. Visited aquariums, watched dancing fountains, laughed themselves silly at a water-skiing pig. They had been able to enjoy themselves like any other anonymous young couple for, in all those hours, Jago had been recognised just once. Several questioning glances had come his way, but as no one expected a TV heart-throb to mix with the *hoi polloi*, and especially dressed in last year's jeans and an unprepossessing checked shirt, those glances had skated on. Only a little girl, braces silvering her teeth, had seen through his disguise. Sidling up, she had patted his knee for attention and when he had bent down had whispered shyly into his ear, 'I love you, Jago Miles.'

A lump blocked Erin's throat. It had been a busy day. A busy day for thinking. As time ran out, minute by minute, hour by hour, her feelings had crystallised. 'I love you, Jago Miles.' Now she knew those were the words she wanted to say. But what would happen if she did? At a guess she'd be awarded a quick squeeze and have her hair tousled, like the little girl. Why must Jago choose now to manifest this old-fashioned sense of propriety? she wondered in disgust. Why couldn't he have suggested they embark on a red-hot love affair? She would not have resisted. Indeed, there was a distinct probability she would have been across the room, sitting on his knee, before he had completed the first sentence. Erin shifted in her seat. This was zigzag logic. Completely slain she might be; a lover, live-in or any other species, she was not.

'The theme park was great,' she added, careless
of the stretched pause since her last remark. 'Susie
would have loved it.'

'Yeah, especially the killer whale,' he agreed, and
began to relive the events of the day.

Water which had shimmered blue on either side
of the causeway was replaced by wafting palms;
now they were on the island. Jago continued to
reminisce, but Erin wasn't listening. All she could
think about was that in less than five minutes' time
they were destined to reach the Driftwood Motel. In
less than five minutes, they would make the
appropriate noises and say goodbye. Everything
would be over. Five minutes shrank into three, two,
and still Jago yammered on. Erin's muscles contracted. She clasped her arms across her stomach.
Whatever existed between the two of them, its
death seemed to be more than she could bear. At the
sight of the low white motel, bathed golden in the
setting sun, she cringed. Dimly she became aware
of Jago tacking a query on to a comment about the
antics of the water-skiing pig.

'How in hell's name do I finance Susie's house?'
he asked, and she shot him a look of astonishment.

The amiable distance of the past four weeks had
meant that nothing which could be remotely
described as 'personal' had ever been discussed.
Osmosis had not been needed to absorb that whilst
they might be friends, Jago remained disinclined to
share. Any problems were his, something he dealt
with alone. Yet here he was, asking a question and
looking to her for an answer.

'You don't,' she replied, sloughing off her

melancholy. 'Next time you visit the hospital you come clean about *Taro Beach* folding and explain that a custom-built property is far beyond your means.'

The speedometer needle flickered and fell. Jago swung the Cadillac on to the motel forecourt and steered into the appropriate slot outside her room.

'No,' he argued, as he cut the engine. 'No, I——'

'If you intend to borrow money and go into debt again, you're mad,' Erin informed him crisply. 'Look what happened before. In order to stay afloat you were forced to accept a role in a tacky soap opera.'

'What else could I do?' he protested, a tightness around his mouth giving clear indication that such bluntness was neither expected nor desired.

'Nothing, then. It's different now, crisis time is over. Agreed you have responsibilities towards Susie, but you also have them towards yourself. Shouldn't they be considered? You're a fine actor, Jago, yet step on that financial treadmill again and you could end up squandering your talent for ever and a day.'

'But——'

'But Susie has her heart set on a dream house and she'll be disappointed if it doesn't materialise? I know. I agree. But she'll understand. Not instantly, not like that.' Erin snapped her fingers. 'But after a while, when the first disappointment's over and everything has had a chance to be digested. Personally I think leaving her to wallow in Cloud-Cuckoo-Land is both shortsighted and unfair.' The tightness around his mouth had been joined by a scowl. She ignored them both. So often she had

been on the brink of voicing her misgivings about
the attitude he adopted with his sister and now—
well, he had asked for an opinion. If that opinion
wasn't what he wanted to hear—tough! 'Susie
deserves access to the facts,' she continued. 'Irre-
spective of whether or not she's sitting in a
wheelchair, she's an adult. Why not start treating
her like one? You do no one a favour by
pussyfooting around. The sooner she knows the true
situation, the sooner she can get to grips with it.
And it's time you realised she's interpreted your
reluctance to commit to a property as an aversion to
Robert.'

'I like the guy,' Jago retorted. 'I've told her so.'

'You can tell her until you're blue in the face, but
until she receives an honest explanation of why
you're holding back, she won't believe you. She's far
too perceptive to be fobbed off.' Erin's tone
softened. 'Listen, instead of mumbling about how
the pair of them are in too much of a hurry, why not
confess you're no longer Mr Rockefeller?'

He pulled a face. 'I guess that makes some kind of
sense,' he admitted.

'It makes *real* sense. And if being told a de luxe
villa isn't available is disappointing, it's scarcely a
major disaster. More of a setback. Both Susie and
Robert are capable of handling a setback. They
don't need to be pampered, they don't *want* to be
pampered,' she insisted, as Jago tugged at his ear.
'Leastways Robert doesn't, and in the long run
won't what agrees with him find agreement with
Susie? As it is he's dubious about receiving hand-
outs. Maybe he can't walk and he can't run, but he's
just as much a man as you are. He has his pride. And

whilst he accepts the need for some assistance, some support, he gags at the prospect of largesse being stuffed down his throat.'

'Then what would you suggest I do? Let me lay my resources on the line,' he continued, exhibiting a sudden willingness to open up. 'I have near enough seventy thousand dollars in the bank and there's also a residue of my *Taro Beach* salary yet to come. That's the good news.' Jago sighed. 'The bad news is there are some medical fees still outstanding and the possibility I could be out of work for—perpetuity.'

'So how can you assess how much is needed to support yourself for an unknown number of rainy days?' Erin was thinking aloud. 'It's tricky.'

'Suppose I split the money straight down the middle?' he suggested.

'Good idea,' she agreed. 'That would enable you to explain your predicament to Susie and Robert, and follow up with the offer of a set amount towards the purchase of a more modest house, an existing one which could be economically adapted to suit their needs. Then Robert can find the remainder of the purchase price himself. He can, he's told me he's able to raise a fairly robust loan,' she explained. 'And if he's responsible for the lion's share it'd be perfect, because then he'll rightfully be in a position to consider himself the owner!'

Jago grinned at her triumphant tone. 'So all that's needed now is for Susie to be dissuaded from setting her sights on anything too ambitious, like the White House.'

'I know she enjoys company, but guided tours marching through morning, noon and night? Come off it. If you like I could prod my publishers to see if they'll cough up an advance from your royalties,' Erin offered.

'Thanks. If those rainy days turn out to be the monsoon season I shall need all the help I can get.' Jago eased himself lower in the seat. Talk of rainy days he might, yet his grin had not been dislodged. It was the kind of grin which could have electrified if she hadn't recognised it as the infuriatingly amiable grin of a brother, protector, etc. etc. 'I know it's crazy,' he said, 'but for weeks now I've been knotted up over Susie and her goddamned house, and all of a sudden everything seems— manageable.' He reached out for Erin's hand and brought it to his mouth. 'Thanks for being such a great unraveller,' he murmured.

His tone was teasing, the look in his eyes was not. Brother *et al* flew out of the window. The pressure of his lips had Erin feeling heated and ruffled. Why decide now that I merit attention as something more than a buddy? she groaned inwardly. Now is too late.

'Pleased to be of service, sir,' she quipped, extracting her hand to administer a flippant salute. She avoided his eyes. If she wasn't careful the power in them would have her melting into a puddle. 'Is a plan of action organised for when *Taro Beach* grinds to a halt?' she asked, matter-of-factly.

'I can't see what else to do apart from hawking myself around. Unless you have a better suggestion?'

She had several. Like him coming to live in her cottage, like him allowing her to whisk him off to the kasbah, like her using him as her plaything.

' 'Fraid not,' she said.

'Oh well.'

Jago shrugged. He removed the ignition key and began to toy with it. He shifted his hips in the seat, grew restless. In contrast, Erin froze. Goodbye time, that dreaded time, had arrived. He was preparing a farewell. But how could she sit meekly and listen? No way. She lurched for the door handle. She couldn't find it. Where had the stupid thing gone? She found it and, pressing down to open the door, she turned.

'Jago——'

'Erin——' he said simultaneously. They both laughed. 'Do you have a copy of your book on women?' he asked.

'Yes, in my suitcase. Cleo insisted I bring one. I think she feels I ought to waft it around like an advertisement. Why? Would—would you like to read it?' she enquired, thinking that he left everything to the last minute.

'I already have. You didn't think I'd expose myself to you without taking the precaution of examining your credentials?' he teased, when she looked surprised. 'Enchanted with your big brown eyes and long legs I might be, but I do retain tatters of common sense. Burt obtained a copy at the very start of our collaboration.'

'Oh.' Enchanted with her eyes and her legs, was he? But it was too late, too late, too damned *late*. 'Er—did you approve?' Erin thought to enquire.

'Very much, but there's something I'd like to check.'

'I'll get the book.'

'I'll come with you.'

She dived out of the car. 'There's no need, really.'

'There's every need, really.' He shone a smile across the roof of the Cadillac. 'Or do the management have rules which state that men caught entering the rooms of unattached young ladies will be castrated?'

Erin blushed. 'The management is very good,' she said, hastily elbowing the conversation on to a less disturbing line. 'They train their staff well here. Everyone's pleasant, the service is excellent.' She unlocked her door. 'I've been very comfortable here. As you can see there's plenty of space. The air-conditioning is quiet, an electric kettle and coffee bags are provided, and——'

'Don't tell me. The towels are changed twice a day?'

In confusion she dropped to her knees and began a rapid search through the half-packed suitcase. Clothes which had been folded with care were now flung aside. She found the book, handed it up. 'What is it you want to check? she enquired.

'A name.'

'Oh.'

Yet another inane 'oh'. For a wordsmith her vocabulary was surprisingly limited. Erin rose to her feet. She longed to know which of the four profiles he was leafing through, longed to know which name he could possibly want to check, but Jago had withdrawn to a couple of yards away.

When he found the page he wanted he gave her a sombre glance.

' "But forget Lady Macbeth and Blanche in *A Streetcar Named Desire*, the role closest to Patrice's heart has always been the one of mother",' he read.

Erin was mortified. She remembered what came next, remembered only too well. Metaphorically Jago had placed his hands around her neck and was in the process of throttling her. ' "Edward, her only child, whilst not born in the proverbial trunk, did spend much of his youth in and around the theatre",' he continued. ' "This was a useful apprenticeship for now he is successfully following in his mother's footsteps." ' The book snapped closed. 'Edward Lanham,' he said, thrusting the name at her. 'He's Ned.'

The pink in her cheeks became a dull rose. 'Yes.'

'What happened?'

'I've told you.'

'No. All I learned from your outburst a month ago was that while you regard the man as your enemy now, at one time you and he were two people madly, impetuously in love.'

Erin's head went down. She stared at the carpet. Woven with a diamond pattern, each shape was outlined in dark amber, the inside a paler shade. Carpet, curtains and bedspread were all amber-hued, while the bedroom walls were white. Her eyes followed a diamond from one point, to the next, the next, the next.

'It wasn't two people,' she muttered. 'It was one. Just me.'

'What happened?' Jago repeated.

'If you don't mind, I'd——'

'I do mind. I want to know.' Tossing the book into the suitcase, he caught hold of her chin. Thumb and fingers spread, he raised her head until she was forced to meet his gaze. 'You can't keep everything bottled up inside for all time.'

'Who says I have?' she attacked.

'Erin, in six years who have you told about your affair?'

'Cleo. Well, she knows parts.' She felt agitated, fractious. 'I'm not ready to talk.'

'After six years? Come on. You're ready. You *are* ready.'

Was she? Six years of silence suddenly struck her as—obsessive. She had been obsessive about her writing, and that was wrong. Wasn't keeping quiet about Ned equally a fault? Tucking a strand of hair behind her ear, Erin decided she would talk. What did she have to lose? She knew Jago would despise her when he heard what she had to say, but it didn't really matter because in a few hours' time she would be gone.

'I met Ned through his mother, obviously,' she said, and Jago stepped back, releasing her. 'I'd gone to London and——' Erin broke off. If this was her confessional, honesty demanded she set everything very clearly in the correct time scale, no matter how shaming that time scale might be. She started again, gesturing towards the discarded book. 'I'd completed two of those profiles when Peter's illness was first diagnosed. Naturally writing fell by the wayside and after his death I couldn't seem to summon up the will to start again. Cleo left me alone for a while, then came to see me. She explained how the publishers were chary of leaving the project hanging and asked if there was a chance of me completing the book, like as of now. She pointed out that having something else to think about would be beneficial, and I had to agree. Patrice Lanham's profile was the next one scheduled, so I made contact.' Erin sank down on the bed. 'She welcomed me with open arms. It was "dahling" this and "sweetie-pie" that, and although I accepted much of it was affectation, I gained the impression she liked me. When she suggested I move into her house while we worked together, I was happy to agree.' She scowled. 'No, I wasn't happy, that's a gross understatement. I was so damned *pleased*, that when I think of it now I want to curl up and die.'

'Ned lived in the house, too?'

She nodded. 'Patrice is divorced from her third husband, so it was just the two of them. A great double act!'

'He began to pay court?'

Erin gave a bleak laugh. 'Nothing so restrained. He marched into my room one night, a week or so after I'd moved in and calmly advised me we were made for each other. He'd never believed in love at first sight, but then he'd met me. I was the half which would make him whole. This thing is bigger than both of us.' Her mouth became a harsh line. 'All the tired old phrases poured out, blah, blah, blah.'

'And?' Jago prompted, when she lapsed into a frowning silence.

'And I let him into my bed. Amazing, isn't it?' she demanded, waiting for a gasp of incredulity. None came. Instead, her companion folded his arms and rested a broad shoulder against the wall. 'I could hardly believe it myself,' Erin continued, knowing that although outwardly noncommittal, inside Jago must be shocked to the core. 'One minute I was telling him to get out of my room and protesting I hardly knew him, the next——' Disgust coarsened her voice. 'The whole thing was like a dream, now it seems like a nightmare. Peter was barely cold in his grave and there I was, kissing this stranger as though my life depended on it.'

'Perhaps it did.'

'What do you mean?' she demanded suspiciously.

'That you were raw, fragile, and in need of comfort.'

'But Peter had only been dead four months!' she cried. 'Four short months!'

'And you've whipped yourself with those months ever since?'

Her eyes blazed. 'Shouldn't I?'

'No.' Jago moved, reaching down to place his hands on her shoulders. 'Erin, you were still in shock, lost and desperately lonely. At times like that the cuddle factor is of great importance.'

She looked away. 'It wasn't cuddles, it was sex. Pure unadulterated sex!'

'It was someone holding you close, murmuring endearments, someone cherishing you when you needed to be cherished.'

A tear escaped to roll down her cheek. 'I behaved like a slut.'

'Stop being so goddamn hard on yourself,' he protested, giving her a little shake. 'If a young widow responds to solace, who can blame her?'

'Solace from a man like Ned?' she derided. 'He was on television a while back and even a two-year-old would have spotted him for a phoney. The thing is, I think I always knew that, I just never would admit it to myself.'

'But at some time in our lives all of us are drawn towards someone we know is no good for us, yet we don't—can't—pull back. This Ned offered you cherishing, plus some excitement. A walk on the wild side, if you like.'

'I did like,' she said impatiently, 'but Peter——'

'Peter was dead, Ned was alive, that's the difference. One hell of a difference. Also he sounds to have been a demon lover. Your husband wasn't a demon lover, was he?'

'N—no,' she stammered, unprepared for this directness.

'But even so he'd awakened your sexuality. When he became ill, died, that sexuality continued to grow, like a bud opening in the grass. Along gallops Ned and you're ripe for the plucking.' Jago released her shoulders. 'How did his mother react to your love affair?'

'Like a cheerleader. Patrice was always hip-hip-hooraying. "Dahling, I've never seen Ned in such a tiz-woz. It'll be so cosy when you're my daughter-in-law, sweetie-pie" ', she mimicked. 'Not that Ned proposed, but with his mother banging the tambourine, who needed a proposal? I was so blind. The two of them were in league, buttering me up so I'd produce a favourable profile, and all the time I thought——' Erin nibbled at a fingernail. 'During the period I was their guest they must have been busy cementing Ned's friendship with the daughter of a theatrical impresario, the girl he married soon after. She was money in the bank where his career was concerned, while I——' Her voice cracked. 'I was disposable. I served my purpose and was then tossed out with the trash.'

'It's not a sin to make mistakes. The Lanhams were hard-boiled sophisticates while you——'

'I was the serving wench who slept with the
young lord under the misapprehension one day he'd
make me his lady?' she taunted. 'The irony is I *loved*
sleeping with him.'

'Shouldn't you have done? Erin, sexuality is a
part of human nature,' he said, in a distinct tone of
exasperation. 'Maybe making whoopee with a
skunk like Lanham wasn't rational, but at the time
you weren't in a rational state of mind. He took
advantage of that, plus the fact you possessed a
normal, healthy appetite for sex. Yes, normal,' he
stressed. 'If the beginning of a love affair isn't hot as
in H O T,' Jago's mouth quirked, 'you can bet your
bottom dollar something's wrong.'

That quirk made her mouth quirk, too. All of a
sudden her past did not seem as dreadful as she had
imagined. 'The steam certainly came out of my
ears,' she said, and grinned. 'The day the completed
profile went forward for publication was the day I
got dumped. Ned took me out to dinner, and over
the smoked salmon explained how driving fifty
miles out into the countryside to see me could prove
inconvenient. By the steak and green salad, it had
become a distinct hitch. At the profiterole stage he
damn near paralleled the journey to a trek to the
North Pole. I retreated to my igloo, and two weeks
later read of our reluctant explorer's engagement to
the impresario's daughter.'

'Exit Mr Lanham, stage left?'

'Not quite. About a year later, when his wife was
in the final throes of pregnancy, whose Mercedes
should draw to a halt outside my garden gate but
Ned's.'

'The   North   Pole   had   suddenly   become

accessible?'

'It had become *the* place to visit,' she said drily.

'With his usual charm he explained how, of late, nostalgia had struck. He had such fond memories of our time together and he was wondering about us recreating some of our own private mayhem.' Erin lifted the rich fall of hair from the back of her neck, unconsciously arching. 'I thanked him politely for the suggestion, but advised that although once I may have possessed an altruistic bent, it did have its limits. Succouring errant husbands fell beyond them. Ned found that very hard to believe, so hard that I needed to point out a couple of his most glaring character defects before the message sank in.' She let the hair fall back to her shoulders. 'Seeing him again didn't do much for my sense of worth. I mean, if I had to behave disgracefully, why couldn't I have done so with somebody halfway decent?' She rose from the bed. 'Somebody like you.'

'I'm halfway decent?'

'All the way.' Erin took a step towards him, surprising herself with her boldness. 'Are you a demon lover?'

'Are you making a pass at me?' Jago countered, an amused brow lifting.

'Yes.' A pause. 'Do you mind?'

'Not in the least. The only reason I've been back-pedalling this past month is because I know you're in the middle of sorting yourself out, and it's something you must do without any outside influences.' He moved to meet her halfway. Reaching out long fingers, he pushed her shirt an inch or two back from her shoulder. He lowered his head, the tip of his tongue protruding. 'Tastes good,' he murmured as he licked the golden-brown flesh. 'Of sun and salt and Erin.'

'Better than tutti-frutti ice-cream?' she smiled, as her blood began its dizzy chase.

'Much better.' Jago opened his mouth and gently bit her shoulder. 'What happens next?' he asked, when she stood immobile. 'What do you want to happen next?' He pressed his lips to the faint crescents of teethmarks. 'Toots, sometimes you have to come right out and ask for what you want.'

Her heart fluttered. 'I'm—I'm scared.'

'After six years of playing safe, who wouldn't be?'

He straightened and began to rub his forehead against hers in slow motion, back and forth, back and forth. The rhythm soothed.

'I—I want a shower,' Erin got out. Eternity passed by. 'With you.'

'Then why are we wasting time?' He went to the window and closed the curtains. Coming back through the half-light he reminded her of a Nordic warrior, his hair shining like a blond helmet. 'I trust there isn't a no-nudity clause in your contract?' Jago murmured, as he eased her shirt from her shorts.

Slowly the garment was unbuttoned—slowly because kisses intervened—and then it was cast aside. Naked to the waist, Erin trembled. Yes, she was scared, but as he looked down on her that fear transformed itself into pride. She was proud the sight of her pleased him, proud their shared kisses had brought that glow to his eyes.

'You're beautiful,' Jago breathed. For a moment his eyes alone caressed her, then, as if her body held a fatal fascination, his hands joined in. Firm fingers slid up her ribcage until the silken smoothness of the underside of her breasts was being stroked. He cupped the full curves in his hands, rejoicing in their weight, their texture. 'Beautiful,' he sighed again. He had touched her tenderly, reverently, but a need was beginning to build. One hand wound into her rich dark curls. He pulled her against him and his mouth crushed down. Their tongues entwined, hotly, magically. His free hand returned to her breasts as though he *had* to feel, *had* to touch, had no choice but to roll a taut nipple urgently between the tips of his fingers until Erin gasped. The mouth on hers smiled.

Jago slid his hands down, pressing the shorts off over her hips. In like fashion lacy silk briefs were removed. Now he succumbed to an orgy of touching. His fingers moved from her shoulder-blades to her waist to the curve of her buttocks—feeling, moulding, possessing. 'Beautiful.' His hands came around, starting with her shoulders again but touring over the pout of her breasts, her stomach, across the triangle of brown moss to nudge between her thighs. Once again she gasped. Once again the mouth on hers smiled.

'It works both ways, honey,' he murmured. 'Feel what you've done to me?' Jago had said this before, but this time he took hold of her hand and steered it down between their bodies, leaving her in no doubt about his arousal.

'If it works both ways, you must be naked too,' Erin grinned, and working together they speedily removed his clothes.

Now she was free to press her fingers against the throbbing pulse, making Jago tremble, jerking back

his head in a muffled cry. He kissed her again, thick
and fast. The flames which for six years Erin had
feared, began to ignite. Vivid and orange-warm,
they licked over her body. More kisses, and her
hands began to move of their own accord, seeking
and finding pleasure in the width of his shoulders,
in the hair on his chest, returning to the hard virility
of his thighs. Jago shuddered, gave an incoherent
moan and then, their mouths still locked, steered
her across the room and into the shower.

The water's sting snatched away her breath. The
warm spray lashed down, slicking their heads to
gloss, creating rivulets which ran pell-mell over
their bodies like mountain torrents. Jago found the
soap and, as steam rose around them in white
clouds, began to massage her neck and shoulders.
The feeling was exquisite. Erin laughed, she sighed.
She kissed him fiercely, wetly, and murmured her
delight. His hands moved lower, drawn to the
luscious curves. He began soaping her breasts in
firm, sweeping movements, allowing his palms to
caress only the very tips until the pleasure was so
total she could not stand it any longer. She cried out,
buckled, fell against him, and in time recovered.

'With soapy hands, Erin began some massaging
of her own. She loved his muscular hardness, loved
the vertical line of body hair which ran from his
chest across his belly and down. She traced its path,
first with a fingertip and then with her tongue,
laughing as Jago begged, 'Further, further, further!'
He raised her to kiss her lips, and for a long time
they stayed pressed together as the water thrummed
down.

How they reached the bed, and more or less dry, Erin did not know, but there they were, tangled and kissing on white sheets. Jago clasped one breast, rounding it with his hand, pointing the peak skywards, the better to cover it with his mouth. She cried out, she whimpered, thrusting herself up. The flames burned, she exalted in their burn. Jago's hand slid to her inner thigh, and again she cried out.

'Erin!' he exclaimed, through clenched teeth. 'Erin, I love you.'

'And I love you,' she vowed.

Holding her hips firm, he entered her, shuddering. Hot as in H O T. But where her heat ended and Jago's began, she did not know. He loved her and she loved him. They were one, moving together.

Oh, the bliss, the agony, the splendour! Thrashing beneath him, Erin offered up all the love she had to give. His love joined hers, mingled, exploded, and together they reached fulfilment.

Afterwards they slept, to make love again later. Held safe in the circle of his arms, Erin nestled closer. Maybe she should cancel her flight home tomorrow? she wondered drowsily. Maybe she should move into the sprawling white house? Maybe she should . . .

'Honey, I must go.'

'No,' she murmured.

'I must. It's nearly——' Presumably he told her the time. 'And I——' Presumably he gave her reasons. Whatever they were, she was too drugged to hear. Sun and love had taken their toll. Jago's voice sounded from a distance. 'Come back when you're ready. If you get in touch with Burt he can pass a message to me wherever I am.' She felt his lips brush her cheek. 'Understand, Erin?'

'Mmm,' she murmured, and fell fast asleep.

CHAPTER NINE

THE removal men gave a blast on their horn in farewell. Erin waved until the van disappeared around a bend in the lane, then walked back indoors. Earlier that day, when curtains had framed the latticed windows, when furniture had been spread throughout the rooms, when the horse brasses pinned to the oak beams had glinted in the sunlight, her home had been cosy. Now, stripped of everything bar the carpets, the cottage felt as barren as a barn.

'Well, that's it. The end of an era,' she said jauntily, joining her mother in the kitchen.

Mrs Page paused in her final wipe round. 'Are you sure you've done the right thing?', she fretted.

'If I haven't, it's too late. There's no turning back, not with my goods and chattels on their way into store, and the new owners moving in here on Monday.'

'But selling up is such a drastic step, Erin. Everything's happened so quickly that I just wonder if you've not rushed in. And why Scotland? Why must you go so far?'

'Scotland isn't Siberia,' she protested. 'You and Dad can always jump in the car and come to see me.'

'Scotland must be five hundred miles away.'

'Four, and in any case I'm only going for six months.'

'Yes, six months in Scotland and then where?' Mrs Page clicked an exasperated tongue. 'Given your present mood it wouldn't surprise me if you *did* disappear to Siberia. Abandoning your writing when you were so nicely established, so nicely settled, makes no sense at all.'

Erin sighed. They had been through this before, several times. 'I wasn't settled, I was in a rut. Now I'm climbing out. Writing's a very solitary occupation and I've been solitary for far too long. I need to meet people.'

'You call showing tourists through a castle meeting people? You could have met people round here.'

'I know everybody round here,' she said patiently, then grinned. 'Cheer up. Maybe a rugged Scots laird will sweep me off my feet and before you know it you'll be knee deep in those grandchildren you're always hankering after.'

Mrs Page gave the tiled worktops a severe double-check, then stashed the cloth away in her shopping basket. 'Kevin asked after you yesterday,' she said, patting her grey hair into tidiness and slipping on her coat. 'Every time I see him, he asks. He's such a nice boy. You could go a long way and not find anyone as nice as Kevin.'

'As far as Scotland? But I've known Kevin since he sat behind me at junior school and pulled my pigtails, and never once felt—drawn. The chances of me walking past his butcher's shop one morning and shouting "Eureka" when I see him weighing out a pound of liver have to be remote.'

'But Kevin would be so—convenient.'

'Like Peter was convenient?'

Mrs Page drew herself up. Although she could not put her finger on it, she sensed criticism. 'We knew Peter's background, we knew he was solid and reliable. We knew his parents because they lived locally, we knew——'

'I thought you were in a hurry to go home and start preparing the dinner while I finish off here?' Erin interrupted. She kissed her mother on the cheek. 'Thanks for all your help. I could never have managed without you.'

Diverted, Mrs Page beamed. 'My pleasure, pet. Yes, I will pop off. We'll be having chicken in lemon sauce with courgettes, one of your favourites. It's lovely to think you'll be living with your father and me again, even if it is just for a few days before you head up to Scotland.' Walking into the hall, she paused. 'Isn't the gas man supposed to be coming to read the meter?'

'Yes, he is. I wonder where he's got to?' Erin checked her watch. 'If he doesn't come soon, he can go and whistle.'

When her mother departed, she plugged in the vacuum. She wanted to leave everything spotless, and all that was needed now was a final tour round with the cleaner. She set to work, tackling one room after another. Even though the cottage did feel like a barn, in reality the dimensions were small and with no furniture to hinder her progress, the task was quickly accomplished. A quarter of an hour

later, the carpets were pristine and the cleaner was
stacked up by the front door. Still the gas man had
not arrived. Where was he? Erin wandered upstairs
to perch on the window-seat in the front bedroom.
From here she could keep watch.

She drew her bejeaned knees up to her chin,
wrapped her arms around her legs, and sighed. Her
mother's worries had been fielded off with a perky
confidence, but that confidence had an annoying
tendency to flow and ebb. It was ebbing now. She
suddenly felt timid. Yanking up thirty years' worth
of roots demanded strength and resolve, and she
wondered whether she had much of both, either,
any? A job had been found and the cottage sold at
such speed, she had had little time to dwell on the
pluses and minuses, but now she began to do her
sums.

She was swapping security for insecurity, the
known for the unknown, proven success for ...
what? Erin bowed her head. Stop evading the issue,
she scolded herself. None of this matters. What
really matters is why Scotland, why not Florida?
Why wasn't she following where her heart led and
throwing in her lot with that blond Viking who, two
months ago, had said, 'Come back when you're
ready. Understand?' She did understand—now.
Initially she had floated home with her head full of
daydreams; about her and Jago on their wedding
day, going off on honeymoon, crooning over their
first baby, raising a family together. Together
meant man and wife. But as one week, two, three,
had passed without any contact between them, so

those mind pictures had altered like shapes in a kaleidoscope. The ingredients had remained constant, but . . .

She knew Jago would be leaving her alone on purpose, giving her peace in which to finish the profile, allowing her time to think through what she wanted from life, and she was grateful. Yet didn't this wide berth indicate an inherently casual approach? She did not regard him as nonconformist or unorthodox, like his parents, but he was not a person hidebound by conventionality. The more she thought about things, the more convinced Erin became that although for her the natural progression in their relationship would be marriage, it was not so for Jago. That did not mean that if she went to him he would not love her, would not commit himself to her. She believed he would, but not as a husband. Husband and wife became man and woman.

Man and woman wasn't enough. In her world love and marriage were inextricably intertwined. Love without marriage was a halfway arrangement and she was not a halfway person. Short-term maybe she could accept what her mother would denounce as 'living in sin', long-term—no. The daydreams which had suspended her in mid-air vanished, she had fallen to eerth with a bump. Facts had to be faced. In the show business sphere living together raised no eyebrows, and Jago inhabited that sphere. At thirty-six he was still a bachelor. But the crux of the matter was that he had loved Olivia, lived with her for three years, and yet had not felt the urge to legalise their affair. There had not been a

whisper in that direction, either in the cuttings she
had read or from Susie. Erin felt empty inside. Few
parallels existed between her and Olivia, yet so
what? The writing on the wall was clear—Jago was
not the marrying kind.

There was a movement in the corner of her eye,
and she looked up to glimpse a figure disappearing
below the front porch. The gas man, she decided,
and ran downstairs.

'Where have you been? I thought you were never
coming,' she said in jokey protest, opening the door.

'Hey, those are my lines,' chided a familiar
American drawl. Her visitor removed his cap,
folded a pair of sunglasses and slipped them into the
top pocket of a dark blue leather jacket. 'Have you
missed me?' he grinned, as she stood and gaped.
'Never given me a passing thought, eh?'

'Yes, yes, I have.' Her face might be as vacant as
a potato, but inside her mind was jigging. She had
planned to write on reaching Scotland and explain
why their future was doomed, but his arrival had
smashed this approach to smithereens. Now Erin
wondered how she was supposed to tell him face to
face—coolly and calmly—that she wanted what he
wasn't prepared to give ... a wedding ring? Cool
and calm was impossible. Jago's proximity had
already sent her heart banging inside her breast,
made her legs feel shaky. Strange that when
common sense demanded she push him away,
instinct told her to devour him whole. Discovering
her palms were damp, Erin wiped them on the seat

of her jeans. 'Would—would you like to come in?' she enquired, backing into the hall.

In reply he slung his suitcase inside, and before she could protest had reached for her.

'Honey, honey,' he murmured, burying his face in the dark clouds of her hair. 'You sure as hell take your time. Okay, I said to come back when you were ready, but to let two months pass without even a hint of when I can expect you—Erin! It seems like two years.'

'Does it?' Her voice was faint. She wished she had backed away further. She wished he would let her go. Also she wished he would hold her close like this for ever.

'Like two centuries. How I've managed to stay away this far is a miracle of self-control.'

His eyes wandered down to her mouth, and she knew he was about to kiss her. Erin pushed back.

'When did you arrive in England?'

'Three hours ago. I took a taxi straight from the airport,' he muttered, his eyes still on her mouth.

'Why didn't you let me know you were coming?'

He sighed, raising his gaze. 'If I had, would you have baked me a cake?' he asked drily. 'Look, toots, it was only last night that my patience finally snapped and I realised no way could I live through another day of you being on one side of the Atlantic and me on the other. I fixed myself a ticket and decided to surprise you.' Ready to enfold her in his arms once more, Jago suddenly noticed the hall's Spartan appearance. 'You've sold up? You're moving out?' he hazarded, and at her nod, hugged her tight, murmuring his delight. 'Erin, you fiend.

Now I understand. Before you joined me you
wanted to tie up all the loose ends. I should've
known Organised Annie would do the right things
in the right order.' He looked around. 'Where's that
cat of yours? Has it been sold too, or is it coming
with you to the States?'

'The cat's staying with my mother, but——' A
deep breath was required. A deep breath was taken.
'I'm not coming to the States.'

'I beg your pardon?'

'I'm not coming. I was going to write and explain.
Jago, I just—I don't think we're . . . compatible.'

His arms dropped from her. He looked as
stunned as if she had punched him in the solar
plexus.

'How d' you work that one out?' he demanded. 'I
love you and I understood you love me?'

'I do,' she said feebly.

'Well then? On an emotional level we click and
physically we have everything going for us. What
more do you want?'

Erin felt her colour rising. The 'more' was
marriage, but a complex of reasons—pride, the fear
of sounding like an accuser, a puritan—tied her
tongue.

'We—we come from different countries,' was
what she eventually mumbled.

'Agreed.'

'You grew up moving around. I grew up in one
place.'

'Agreed.'

'And—er.' The look on his face told her she was
not making much headway. 'My background was

kind of narrow, and yours was—wide.'

'Agreed. Go on.'

Where could she go? Only to the truth. 'Jago, you and Olivia were together for three years,' she stated, setting off at a cracking pace. 'The two of you were close. You appear to have been together night and day. You cared as much for her career as you did for your own. There was this depth of feeling between you, and yet . . .' The cracking pace met a bump in the road. 'I accept that for some people marriage is a meaningless formality, and don't think I'm criticising because I'm not, but for me—oh Jago,' she wailed, 'you loved Olivia and yet despite that——'

'I didn't love her,' he cut in.

'You—you didn't?' That hadn't been a bump in the road, it had been a hole. Erin felt as if she had fallen into it. 'But Susie told me how——'

'Susie doesn't know the half of it. Nobody does. Do you mind if we sit down?' he enquired. 'I guess I need to explain about Olivia, so we could be talking for quite a while. I'd prefer to do it in comfort.'

'I'm afraid there isn't any comfort, just the stairs or a window-seat.'

'Window-seat,' Jago decided, and gestured for her to lead the way. In the bedroom he plunked himself down opposite her, his back against the oak window surround, his long legs spread with his feet planted firmly on the shaggy white carpet. 'Olivia possessed what I can only describe as a fey quality,' he began. 'She was inconsistent, erratic, and for some inexplicable reason that intrigued me. I knew she was riddled with insecurities, the danger signs

were there very early on, and yet . . .' He looked out
on to the lane where the green-leaved branches of
the sycamores moved in the breeze. 'Like you were
attracted to Edward Lanham for no good reason, so
I was attracted to her. At first things were fine, then
she began to be jealous of my success. There was
nothing I could do. I was what I was. I couldn't
change the past. In time her animosity developed
until it began to poison our lives together.'

'Why didn't you end the relationship?'

'Everyone wondered that. The general opinion
was I was crazy to put up with her.' Jago gave a dry
laugh. 'What they didn't know was that I didn't
have any choice. After a while I got a little sick of
her attitude, and a lot sick of being used, so I said
that I felt we should go our separate ways,' he
explained. 'I wasn't hostile, I just said it didn't make
sense to be causing each other pain. But Olivia
wasn't having any. She started to play the Tragedy
Queen.' He let out a breath. 'If she could act one
tenth as well on stage as she does in real life, she'd
have a shelf full of Oscars. But she can't, that's the
pity of it. However, I was given the full works—the
tears, the pleas, the pathetic pose on the sofa. She
vowed I was the only man she'd ever been able to
trust, that she depended on me in total, and——' He
ran a hand through his hair. 'And when it was all
over I discovered I'd caved in. I allowed us to
hobble on. Mind you, it was hobbling. And it wasn't
long before I decided I really must make the break.
The tears were joined by heavier artillery the second
time around. Olivia made a few choice statements
like, "If you feel this way I'd be better off under a

bus" and "If you send me away, my life might as well end".'

Erin felt gooseflesh cover her arms. 'She was threatening suicide?' she asked in horror.

He nodded, his face grim. 'But it didn't stop at threatening. For a long time after that, even though I rebelled against what was emotional blackmail, I handled her with kid gloves. Then one day, it got too much. I blew my top. I said everything I'd said before, how living together was no good for either of us, in fact it was hell on earth, and that if she wasn't prepared to move out of my apartment, I was! Much to my surprise, she promised she'd be gone the next day. That night I arrived back late from the theatre and the moment I unlocked the door I could sense something was wrong. There was a silence, an eerie silence.' Jago rubbed the back of his neck. 'God, I go hot and cold now, just thinking about it. I knew Olivia had to be there and I called out. No answer. I charged around and found her in the bedroom with pill bottles strewn around, all empty. I hauled her into the bathroom, stuck my fingers down her throat and made her sick. She began to revive. When the doctor arrived I think I needed him more than she did! He took me to one side and dismissed what she'd done as attention seeking. He said she'd taken nowhere near enough pills to finish herself off, that it had just been a gesture. Some gesture! But after that I guess I became paranoid. It seemed like if I said one wrong word Olivia might throw herself off a high tower.'

'Did she try anything again?' Erin asked, in a hushed tone.

'She didn't need to. I wasn't having her ending her life because of me. We continued to hobble on, with me giving up daily prayers that either she'd strike lucky in her career or would switch herself to some other guy.'

'And then the crash intervened?'

'Yeah.' Jago turned from the window and slumped forward, clasping his hands between his knees. For a moment he was thoughtful. 'Susie and I had planned to visit Thailand together; she wanted to see the temples Ursula had raved over, I wanted to visit my birthplace. Everything was fixed, then Olivia muscled in. My sister was not pleased.'

'I can imagine!'

He gave a wry smile. 'I did my best to persuade Olivia the vacation was a family jaunt, but she went into the old sob routine, made a few oblique threats, and to cut a long story short, she came with us to Thailand. One day we hired a car and decided to visit a village where there was a market and a cultural show. At first I drove, but I'd picked up a bug, one of those twenty-four hour things, and I began to feel lousy. It ended up with Olivia driving, Susie reading the map, and me lying flat out in the back. Susie's a pathetic navigator and we took a wrong turn. She and Olivia started to bicker, I sat up, and the next thing I knew there was this pick-up truck roaring straight at us on the wrong side of the road. I crawled out of the wreckage and amazingly I was fine, cut and bruised, but that was all. Olivia was also unhurt. But Susie——' He took a snatched breath. 'She was lying there, so still. It was obvious she'd been seriously injured, but how could I get help? The next few hours were the worst in my life. The guys in the pick-up were labourers, they didn't speak any English and, given the chance, I think they'd have just scooted off. But I started to rant and rave, and I managed to get them to take me to the nearest village. It seemed to be a hundred miles away. By the time we arrived I was frantic. Nobody there spoke English either, but somehow it filtered through that an ambulance should be summoned. A shopkeeper telephoned, then had someone drive me back to the car. Olivia'd been looking after Susie, and when I arrived she promptly laid into me for leaving her alone there for so long!' He wiped a hand across his brow. 'All I could do was pin my hopes on that ambulance materialising, but it took hours to arrive and in all that time Susie never moved. I thought she was going to die. She nearly did.' Jago's face crumpled. 'Maybe if I'd been able to get help to her sooner she wouldn't be stuck in a wheelchair now,' he muttered.

Erin laid her hand on his arm. 'You don't know that,' she said gently.

'No.' When he looked at her, his eyes were wet.

'And Susie stayed in hospital in Thailand for several months?' she prompted.

He gave a noisy sniff and nodded. 'I was warned her bones might take a long time to settle. I was also warned her medical care wouldn't come cheap. Maybe they were fleecing me, I don't know, but I wasn't in any position to argue. I'd been geared up to start rehearsals for a Broadway play the following week, so I got in touch and said my return had been delayed. The response was an ultimatum, be there in a fortnight or else!'

'You really were being hanged, drawn and quartered,' she sympathised.

'With a vengeance. I needed to be in that play because it was imperative I earn money. I rang round my brothers and sisters and somehow we managed to work out a way of having someone in Bangkok with Susie for the foreseeable future. The only problem was a gap between me returning to the States and one of my sisters arriving to take over. As it was just a few days, I asked Olivia if she'd fill in.' Jago balled his fists. 'But that damn woman——'

'She wouldn't?

He shook his head. 'I accept she'd had a shock, I accept she may have had some sort of guilt hang-up, but even so. My God, that accident concentrated her mind wonderfully. She said she couldn't stay, that I couldn't expect her to stay because she wasn't family, was she? In fact, she'd known for a long time she didn't mean much to me and I most certainly did not mean much to her. I had been right, we would be much better off apart. Zoom— her bags were packed and she was boarding a plane. I stayed with Susie until my other sister arrived, then set off home.'

'To be out of work?'

'No I managed to cling on to my part in the play by the skin of my teeth.'

'So it was exit Olivia, stage left?'

'Yeah. She'd gone by the time I arrived back at my apartment. I've never heard from her since.' Jago frowned. 'She's the real reason why I stopped you writing about Susie in your profile. You see, I don't know how she'd react. If the facts were publicised and a reporter knocked on her door asking questions about how she'd been driving at the time my sister had been crippled, what would she do? Maybe she wouldn't give a damn, but maybe Olivia would go the other way, get depressed, take pills? It's enough that Susie is like she is without another life being damaged.'

'Which is why you kept the accident out of the papers?' Erin surmised.

'It wasn't difficult. Thailand isn't gossip column country.' Jago cast her a glance. 'I know I should have told you all this before, but——'

'But you don't find sharing things easy?'

He grinned. 'Isn't that becoming a fallacy? I seem to be sharing one hell of a lot with you.' He paused, his blue eyes intent. 'Isn't it time you shared something with me?'

'Like what?'

'Like the real reason for this——' he thought better, and substituted a less impolite word for the one he had been ready to use '—— tosh about you not coming to the States.'

'Oh.'

'Yes, oh.' There was the hint of a smile. 'If it's any help, I have somehow gained the impression you believe I'm anti-marriage?'

Erin felt skewered. 'Aren't you? You—you have reached the grand old age of thirty-six without tying any knots,' she protested. 'And Olivia apart, there have been other relationships, and——' Saying

exactly what she wanted to say remained a
stumbling block.

Jago helped again. 'And I've never made them
permanent? Want to know why? Maybe this is a
paradox, but it's out of respect for the institution of
marriage that I've preferred to co-habit. I happen to
believe marriage is for ever, and finding someone I
wanted to live with for ever was a problem.
However, a while back this lady author in beautiful-
ly short shorts woke me up one morning, and in no
time at all was throwing herself on top of me and
squirming around in a most unladylike fashion.
Now I knew from the start we weren't compatible.
After all, she's easy with seven-letter words, while I
use four. She's a straight-A type, while I'm lucky if I
scrape by with Cs. She says "autumn" while I say
"fall" but——' He reached for her hand, mingling
his fingers with hers. 'Will you marry me?'

He had unlocked the door to paradise and led her
inside.

'Yes, yes, *yes!*'

Even if it had been two months since they had
kissed, his mouth was just as she remembered—
warm, moist and eager. The effect it had was just as
she remembered, too. Her blood chased, her heart
thumped against his. There came that bitter-sweet
hunger, that spiralling, an ache.

'I love you, I love you, I love you.'

The words moved between them, meshing with
sighs, kisses, hugs.

'I was supposed to be going to Scotland,' Erin
remembered, after a long time.

'Scotland?' He sounded as disgusted as her

mother. 'Are you researching a Scots Edwardian?'

'No. I've found a post as a tourist guide. You see, after I left Florida——'

'And me.'

'Yes, after I left you.' She kissed his cheek. 'After I left I started thinking. I realised the best way to break the stranglehold my writing had was to give it up for a while, take a sabbatical. I completed your profile, handed the book over to Cleo, and the very next day I happened to see an advertisement for a tourist guide.'

'You never told Cleo you wanted a sabbatical,' Jago intruded.

'Not then. I phoned her last night. I wanted to have everything cut and dried, just in case she protested.'

'Did she?'

Erin laughed wryly. 'No. She said to hell with her ten per cent, she was just happy I'd got my priorities right at last, though she did think Scotland an odd direction to head for.'

'It should've been the States?' Jago suggested.

'As she noticeably inserted a long screed about how she could tell from the profile that I thought you were a wonderful man—yes, that was the general impression.'

'Do you think I'm wonderful?'

Grinning, she folded her arms and weighed him up.

'Hmm, your nose is a bit skew-whiff.'

He made a grab for her. 'I said wonderful, not perfect. Besides, if I stand sideways you can't tell my nose's off-centre. Not that I intend to spend the

rest of my life standing sideways-on to you. There
are other positions which interest me more. Like me
lying on top of you, or you lying on top of me,
or——'

'Jago!' she protested, and laughingly succumbed
to a second batch of kisses. 'How did you know I
hadn't warned Cleo I'd be taking a sabbatical?'
Erin queried, surfacing.

'Because I kept track of you through her. How
was I supposed to carry on for two months without a
single word?' he appealed.

'She never said you'd been in touch.'

'I asked her to keep quiet. The ball was in your
court,' he pointed out, 'and I didn't want to crowd
you.'

'You didn't!'

'From now on I will,' he promised.

'How can I make a graceful exit from the job in
Scotland?' she wondered vaguely, as Jago began to
kiss her again.

'Search me.'

'And how do I break it to my mother that her
grandchildren will be wearing baseball caps?'

'Search me.'

Erin slid off the window-seat and into his waiting
arms. The shaggy white carpet felt far more erotic
than any water-bed.

'And what do I do if the gas man comes to read
the meter in the next half hour?'

'Search me. You would like to, wouldn't you?' he
murmured, his mouth finding hers.

'Mmm.' She started by unbuttoning his shirt.

'I was supposed to tell you I've landed a role in a

film,' he said, helping her and thus speeding up the process. He also shucked off his leather jacket. 'And I was also supposed to say that your solution to the Susie problem worked like a dream. She and Robert have a house. It's being renovated right now, but will be ready in a couple of months when they're due to be married. After us. I was also supposed to tell you I've made enquiries and we can get a special licence. Also—oh hell,' he sighed, pressing her back on to the carpet. 'When am I ever going to find time to say all these things?'

'Search me,' Erin smiled.

Jago did.

Merry Christmas one and all.

ROMANCE

Next month's romances from Mills & Boon

Each month, you can choose from a world of variety in romance with Mills & Boon. These are the new titles to look out for next month.

THE CALL OF HOME Melinda Cross
BLIND DATE Emma Darcy
THE FOLLY OF LOVING Catherine George
RETURN MATCH Penny Jordan
PASSIONATE CHOICE Flora Kidd
A GAME OF DECEIT Sandra Marton
FANTASY WOMAN Annabel Murray
THE SECRET POOL Betty Neels
LOVE IN THE MOONLIGHT Lilian Peake
CAGE OF ICE Sally Wentworth
*****WINTER AT WHITECLIFFS** Miriam Macgregor
*****UNFINISHED BUSINESS** Nicola West

Buy them from your usual paperback stockist, or write to: Mills & Boon Reader Service, P.O. Box 236, Thornton Rd, Croydon, Surrey CR9 3RU, England.

*These two titles are available *only* from Mills & Boon Reader Service.

Mills & Boon
the rose of romance

She had everything a woman could want... except love.

Locked into a lovel[e] marriage, Danica Linds[ay] tried in vain to rekindle t[he] spark of a lost romance. S[he] turned for solace to Mich[ael] Buchanan, a gentle yet stro[ng] man, who showed h[er] friendship.

But even as their so[uls] became one, she knew s[he] was honour-bound to ob[ey] the sanctity of her marria[ge,] to stand by her husban[d's] side while he stood trial [for] espionage even though h[er] heart lay elsewhere.

WITHIN REACH
another powerful novel b[y]
Barbara Delinsky,
author of Finger Prints.

Available from October 19[ ]
Price: £2.95. **W⊕RLDWI[DE]**

YOURS FREE
an exciting
Mills & Boon Romance

Spare a few moments to answer the questions
overleaf and we will send you an exciting
Mills & Boon Romance as our
thank you.

We are always looking for new and appealing
ways to bring you the very best
in romantic fiction
and we are now interested in how many
books you purchase, where you buy
them from, and what you do with them
when you have read them.

So please help us to continue
to bring you the very best
in romantic fiction by completing
the simple questionnaire overleaf.

**Don't forget to fill in your name and address
so we know where to send your FREE BOOK.**

Please tick the appropriate boxes to indicate your answers.

1 How many Mills & Boon books have you purchased in the last six months?

1 ☐   2-6 ☐   More than 6 ☐

2 Did you buy these books new or secondhand?

New ☐   Secondhand ☐   Both ☐

3 If you bought new books, how many did you buy?

(a) 1 ☐   2-6 ☐   More than 6 ☐

(b) Where did you buy them?

Bookshop ☐	Reader Service ☐
Newsagent ☐	Other (Please state) ☐
Department store ☐	

_____

4 If you bought secondhand books how many did you buy?

(a) 1 ☐   2-6 ☐   More than 6 ☐

(b) Where did you buy them?

Market ☐	Jumble sale, fete etc. ☐
Secondhand shop ☐	Other (Please state) ☐

_____

(c) How much did you pay per book? _____

5 What do you do with your Mills & Boon books when you have read them?

Keep them ☐	Sell or exchange them ☐
Throw them away ☐	Other (Please state) ☐
Pass them to friends/relatives ☐	
Give them to jumble sales etc ☐	_____

6 What age group are you in?

Under 25 ☐   25-34 ☐   35-54 ☐   55+ ☐

POST TODAY ——————————————

Name _____

Address _____

_____

_____ Postcode _____

Thank you very much for your help. We hope that you enjoy your free book. Please send your completed questionnaire to:-

Mills & Boon Reader Survey FREEPOST,
P.O. Box 236, Croydon, Surrey. CR9 9EL
Your address details may be retained by us for
mailing you with other offers.

NO STAMP
NEEDED

SEC1

UNI

From the moment they met, Rick Dalmont had made it plain that he wanted Shanna. But Rick had 'wanted' plenty of other women in his time—and tipped them on to the rubbish heap the moment the novelty had worn off. Why should Shanna add herself to their number?

Books you will enjoy
by CAROLE MORTIMER

LIFELONG AFFAIR

Her sister's death had been a terrible blow to
Morgan—but the sadness was slightly relieved
by the fact that Glenna had given birth to a
baby and appointed Morgan as its guardian.
But the other guardian was to be Glenna's
brother-in-law Alex—and that was where
Morgan's real troubles began . . .

FANTASY GIRL

One of the reasons Natalie's modelling agency
was so successful was her biggest customer,
Thornton Cosmetics—but now its formidable
head, Adam Thornton, was threatening to
close his account unless her top model Judith
mended her ways! But how could Natalie do
anything to harm Judith?

LOVE UNSPOKEN

'You're so busy trying to do your job as well
as a man you've forgotten how to be a
woman!' Zach Reedman had thrown bitterly
at Julie—and so they had parted for good.
Yet, three years later, Zach had turned up
again, announcing that he was going to marry
the sweet, gentle Teresa Barr. Was it really
the end of everything between them now?

HEAVEN HERE ON EARTH

Mark Montgomery was a good friend of
Ryan's—nothing more—and it was in a
friendly spirit that he had offered her the use
of a cottage on his family estate in Yorkshire
for a holiday. But his overbearing older
brother Grant chose to misunderstand the
whole situation, and the holiday turned into a
very exhausting battle of wills. Could Ryan
possibly win it?

UNDYING LOVE

BY

CAROLE MORTIMER

MILLS & BOON LIMITED
15–16 BROOK'S MEWS
LONDON W1A 1DR

First published 1983
Australian copyright 1983
Philippine copyright 1983
This edition 1982

© *Carole Mortimer 1983*

ISBN 0 263 74351 9

Set in Monophoto Plantin 10 on 11 pt.
01-0983 — 52520

*Made and printed in Great Britain by
Richard Clay (The Chaucer Press) Ltd,
Bungay, Suffolk*

For
John and Matthew

CHAPTER ONE

THE first person Shanna saw when she entered her brother's spacious lounge was Rick Dalmont. And that was enough to make her want to leave again!

But she met that black-eyed gaze without blinking, nodding cool acknowledgment before turning to talk to her sister-in-law, Janice. But she knew those strange dark eyes still watched her, was always aware of Rick Dalmont's gaze on her whenever they happened to meet. And that had been all too often lately as far as she was concerned.

'I'm so glad you made it,' Janice said with some relief; she was a small blonde-haired woman, married to Shanna's brother Henry for the last ten years; their two offspring, a boy and a girl, were fast asleep upstairs.

Shanna didn't need to question her sister-in-law's feeling of relief; she knew the reason for it—Rick Dalmont. Half Spanish, half American, the black-haired, black-eyed business tycoon had made no secret of his pursuit from the moment they met two weeks ago. Until that time a young up-and-coming actress had shared his life; she had been asked to leave the night Rick met Shanna for the first time. A lot of women would have been flattered by the almost single-minded pursuit by such a man—Rick Dalmont was a very eligible bachelor—but Shanna would rather he turned his attention elsewhere. Ricardo Dalmont, to give him his full name, wasn't her type at all. His reputation with women was no secret, his method of ending those relationships was not always gentle. In fact, it was very often cruel; the women were simply replaced, without notice.

7

But that wasn't the reason for Shanna's lack of interest, she simply wasn't interested in any man at the moment. Clinically she could admire Rick Dalmont's looks, the over-long black hair, the hard tanned face, the jet-black eyes that revealed none of the man's thoughts; his mouth was a cynical twist, his tall body leanly muscled, his sexual magnetism tangible even to the immune Shanna. But as a person she disliked him intensely, disliked all that he stood for.

'For goodness' sake get him away from Henry,' Janice pleaded with her. 'This is supposed to be a party, not a business meeting,' she groaned.

'I'm sure Henry doesn't mind,' Shanna said dryly, knowing her brother's preoccupation with business. She hadn't reached the age of twenty-five without learning that of her older brother.

'He probably introduced the subject,' the other woman nodded. 'But he suddenly seems to have lost Rick's attention,' she mocked dryly.

Shanna followed Janice's amused gaze, her green eyes clashing with his black ones. She had never seen eyes like Rick Dalmont's before, so dark a brown they appeared black. That dark gaze moved slowly over her body, from the smoothness of her straight shoulder-length black hair with the feathered fringe from a centre parting, her green eyes surrounded by dark sooty lashes, the small straight nose, the bright lip-gloss on her slightly pouting lips, the slenderness of her throat, the perfection of her body in the clinging knee-length red dress, her long legs thrust into black high-heeled sandals, adding to her already considerable height.

She met that intimate gaze with a challenge of her own, and made herself return the inventory, the over-long black hair swept back from the wide intelligent forehead, the harsh features carved as if from stone, the animal elegance of the powerful body beneath the black evening suit, the material stretched over wide shoulders, tapering to a narrow waist and powerful thighs. Rick Dalmont was a magnificent specimen of manhood; and he left Shanna cold, both physically and emotionally.

And he knew it too, had known of her coldness from the beginning, and it only increased his desire for her. She should have known such a man would consider her a challenge, that he would meet that challenge head-on. If she had known of his presence here, at what was primarily a private party for a few friends of her brother's, she would have refused the invitation. That was probably the reason Henry had remained silent; her brother was well aware of her feelings in regard to his new business acquaintance.

The newness of Henry's apparent friendship with the other man bothered her somewhat. Rick Dalmont wasn't a man's man, his relationships were mainly sensual, his many business interests seeming to be his only other occupation. The Dalmont fortune had been made by Todd Dalmont, Rick's father, originally in oil, but since Rick Dalmont had taken over fifteen years ago he had diversified the family fortune, successfully, into a number of different industries. A man like Rick Dalmont would be successful at anything he set out to do, from winning the woman of his choice to getting the best deal for Dalmont Industries!

And that was what bothered her. Henry and Rick had absolutely nothing in common socially. Henry was a staid family man, very much in love with his wife, whereas Rick Dalmont had made his opinion of marriage known on more than one occasion; he approved of it for other people, but not for himself. So that only left business that Henry could have in common with the other man, and yet even that didn't seem plausible, for as far as Shanna knew Rick Dalmont had no interest in the newspaper business, and as Henry ran and owned one of England's biggest newspapers . . .

'He's coming over,' Janice whispered softly.

She had been expecting it, could sense his presence even now, was aware of the warmth of his body as he came to stand beside her, could smell the spicy aftershave that was exclusive to him, as were the cheroots he smoked.

'Shanna,' he greeted in a voice of gravel and honey. She had been surprised by that voice the first time she heard it, had never heard such a smoothly seductive voice cloaked in such husky tones, his accent softly American.

'Mr Dalmont,' she returned smoothly, knowing he found her distant behaviour amusing.

'Could I get you a drink?' he offered gruffly.

'I'm sure Henry——'

'Rick knows the way to the bar,' her brother dismissed unhelpfully.

Shanna gave a haughty inclination of her head, left with no other choice. 'Then I accept your kind offer, Mr Dalmont.'

Her arm was taken between vicelike fingers as she was steered away from Henry and Janice and through to the bar in the adjoining room. 'I wasn't being kind at all, Shanna,' Rick told her softly. 'Not unless you count to myself. You left Doug Gillies' party two evenings ago before I even had the chance to talk to you.'

She would have left this evening too if it hadn't been her brother's party. 'I'm sorry,' she said coolly, only reaching up to his shoulder despite her own considerable height.

He grinned, deep grooves in the hardness of his cheek, his eyes a deep enigmatic black. 'You aren't sorry at all,' he derided. 'But I'll let it pass for now. Dry Martini, isn't it?' he nodded towards the bar.

Shanna didn't question his knowing her preference in drinks; this man would make it his business to find out her preferences in everything! 'Thank you,' she accepted distantly.

'My pleasure,' he drawled suggestively.

Shanna ignored the innuendo, realising that this man was used to a more positive reaction from women, that her indifference to him intrigued him. She had had no choice, she either showed him her indifference or gave him what he wanted. And as he wanted her, made no secret of the fact, she had decided to show him indifference. Either way he was sure to lose interest soon, and this y there was no harm to her. She had no intention of sleeping with a man just as a means of getting him out of her life! Rick Dalmont wasn't a man who enjoyed the chase for long, she just hoped he would tire of her soon; he was making it awkward for her to go anywhere, always seeming to be where she was.

'Here,' he held the long glass out to her, somehow managing to touch her slender fingers in the process. 'Not very subtle,' he acknowledged the slight raise of her brows. 'But I figured it's the only way to touch you at all. Do you usually freeze men off the way you've been freezing me?'

He was beginning to tire, she could tell that. Until tonight Rick Dalmont had shown her of his attraction to her, but it had always been charmingly done, never a word or movement out of place. Tonight his behaviour was noticeably different; the chase was over, the feline abobout to catch his prey, any way he could. It was the time she had been dreading the most; her own polite but distant behaviour was no longer enough to repel him. She would have to be as blunt as he intended being.

She met his gaze unflinchingly, her black hair swinging back over her shoulders. 'Yes,' she answered abruptly.

The charm had gone from his face now, leaving his expression harsh, his mouth taut, his eyes narrowed. 'So I'm not the exception?' he bit out, seemingly unaware—or just unconcerned—of the people standing near them, the conversation and loud laughter doing a lot to mask this very private conversation.

'No,' she drawled, knowing the idea displeased him. Rick Dalmont was a man who arrogantly dismissed women when they displeased him; he was *never* dismissed himself. It would have been that way all his life; the Dalmont fortune had been made long before Todd took his young Spanish bride and produced Ricardo. Rick Dalmont had grown up with a gold spoon in his mouth, and the determined line of his mouth said he wasn't going to allow a mere woman to deny him something he wanted—even if it was her! For thirty-seven years nothing had been denied him, and Shanna Logan wasn't about to be the exception, not even when it was her body he wanted. 'What do you and my brother have to talk about so earnestly?' She decided attack was still the better form of defence.

Rick's mouth twisted derisively. 'He hasn't told you yet?'

'No,' she evaded.

'I wonder why?' he taunted.

She gave a careless shrug. 'I have no doubt he will, in time.'

Rick gave a haughty inclination of his head. 'In time. But will that be too late?'

'I have no idea. Will it?'

He gave a husky laugh. 'It could be,' he mocked her attempt to get information out of him.

'Then perhaps I'd better go and talk to Henry now.' She turned to leave.

Firm fingers grasped her arm, strong relentless fingers that held Shanna to his side. 'It can wait,' he dismissed abruptly. 'Maybe if you ask me nicely enough I might be persuaded to tell you.'

She eyed him coldly. 'I can get the information from Henry with much less effort.'

His breath was warm against her cheek. 'Would it be so much of an effort?'

'Yes!' she snapped—and then cursed herself for her show of anger. She had intended to show this man no emotion at all, but his manhandling of her couldn't go without retaliation of some sort. She pulled pointedly out of his grasp, knowing her arm was going to be bruised in the morning from his reluctance to release her. 'Yes, I'm afraid it would, Mr Dalmont,' she repeated coldly. 'And I hate having to make an effort of any kind.'

'Poor little rich girl,' he rasped.

Her cool green eyes openly mocked him. 'Isn't that slightly ridiculous, coming from you?'

'I worked for my place as head of Dalmont Industries from the time I could understand what stocks and shares were,' he bit out fiercely. 'My father never gave anyone anything for nothing in his life, and he wasn't about to start with me. What's your excuse?'

She had hit a raw nerve, she could tell that; Rick Dalmont would lose his temper only rarely. He had just done so very effectively. 'I don't have one,' she told him quietly. 'I'm the editor of a magazine Henry owns.'

'So he informed me,' Rick nodded abruptly. 'A cursory title, I'm sure.'

'Then don't be,' she snapped. '*Fashion Lady* may only be a women's magazine, and unimportant to a man like you, but I run it to the best of my ability.'

'And how good is that?'

She flushed at the quietly intended insult. 'Ask Henry!' her eyes flashed.

To her chagrin Rick Dalmont began to smile. 'At least this is an improvement. I've made you lose your temper with me three times in the last five minutes.'

'I think that probably makes us even,' she taunted.

'Nothing like it,' he still smiled. 'My temper has been much less controlled since I met you. But you could soon change that,' he added throatily. 'All it would take is one word from you.'

And she knew exactly what that word was! 'I haven't been using that word too often lately,' she said abruptly.

'Since your husband died.'

Shanna froze. 'What do you know about that?'

Rick shrugged. 'It's no secret that he died, is it?'

'No.' She avoided that black-eyed gaze, knowing this man could see into her soul if he wanted to. And from what she knew of him he would want to.

'Or how he died?' His eyes were narrowed now, sensing her increased hostility.

She swallowed hard. 'No.'

It had been no secret how Perry died, it had been emblazoned across the front page of every newspaper in the world. A famous ex-racing driver killed in a road accident was world-wide news.

'Or that you were in the car with him at the time?' Rick continued his prodding into her personal pain.

This time she didn't even answer him; her expression was wooden, refusing to show any emotion to this man. He would take any sign of weakness and use it to his advantage.

'Or that your marriage had already ended.'

The cruelly stated words brought a light sheen of perspiration to her brow, although her dull gaze remained fixed on one of the light-fittings on the far wall.

'That the two of you be together at all was an unusual occurrence.'

Her gaze slowly moved back to the hard face of the man standing in front of her, missing the taut enquiry of his expression, seeing only the determined cruelty of his eyes and mouth. 'If you'll excuse me, Mr Dalmont——'

'And if I won't?' Once again his fingers bruised her arm, but this time she didn't even feel the pain.

'You will.' The cold dullness of her voice made his hand drop away, and without another glance in his direction she walked away.

People rarely spoke to her of Perry, most of them respecting the fact that she must still feel her husband's loss after only six months. But Rick Dalmont had a hard cruelty about him that didn't respect anything, even a widow's grief. He had even mentioned the reports in some newspapers that her marriage to Perry had been far from happy at the end. Only an insensitive swine could have done that. Rick Dalmont would use anything to get what he wanted, including her grief for Perry.

'Shanna,' Henry touched her arm lightly. 'What have you said to Rick?' he asked anxiously. 'He looks like thunder.'

She blinked up at her brother, her elder by five years, his receding hairline adding to his air of maturity. Although right now he looked very worried.

'You haven't upset him, have you?' He kept shooting worried glances at the other man.

'Does it look like it?' she mocked. Rick Dalmont was

now leaning against the wall talking softly into the ear
of a giggly blonde.

'Rick isn't interested in Selina,' Henry dismissed.

'Oh?' She was regaining control now, wishing she
hadn't made her distress quite so obvious to Rick
Dalmont. He was a man who shouldn't be given any
advantage, and she had just given him one.

'You know he isn't,' her brother sighed.

'Do I?'

'You're too old to play coy games, Shanna,' he said
impatiently. 'The man wants you, and you know it.'

'I also know he isn't going to have me!' Her eyes
flashed deeply green.

'Shanna——'

'Henry, I think we should talk,' she watched his
flushed face warily. 'I don't like the way you've
suddenly become involved with that man.'

'That's business, Shanna——'

'But what business? When did Rick Dalmont
become interested in the world of newspaper publishing?'

'He isn't——'

'Then what business are you involved in with him?'
she frowned.

'We can't talk about it here, Shanna,' he avoided.
'This is a party. And you know Janice doesn't like
business discussed at her parties.'

She sighed. 'Tomorrow, then?'

'Sunday? Mm, come to lunch,' he added. 'Peter and
Susan will like that.'

Her expression softened at the mention of her
nephew and niece. And she had a feeling she was
being manipulated once again, and this time by her
own brother; Henry knew how fond of Peter and
Susan she was.

'We'll talk about Rick Dalmont before lunch.' She

didn't let him even think he had got away with the distraction. 'I'll come over about twelve.'

He grimaced. 'Fine.'

She smiled at his lack of enthusiasm. 'You got into this, Henry,' she drawled at his discomfort. 'Now you can explain it to me.'

'Shanna——'

She touched his cheek mockingly. 'Tomorrow, Henry. And I shall expect a full explanation.'

'But——'

'A full explanation,' she repeated determinedly.

'I'm beginning to wonder who's the eldest in this family,' he muttered before moving away to join his wife, as a couple of the guests were taking their leave.

'A good question,' drawled an amused voice from behind her, an unmistakable voice of honey and gravel. Shanna spun round, wondering just how long Rick Dalmont had been listening to her conversation with her brother.

'You really shouldn't pressurise Henry, honey,' he mocked. 'Now me, you wouldn't have to pressurise at all.'

'I told you——'

'You wouldn't even have to be persuasive,' he cut in softly. 'Let me take you home and I'll tell you all.'

She stiffened at the intimate warmth of his gaze. 'I have my car here.'

He shrugged his broad shoulders. 'Then you drive me home—I came by cab.'

'I'd rather not,' she refused distantly.

Anger flashed in the dark eyes. 'No wonder your husband turned to other women!' he rasped.

Shanna went deathly pale. 'What did you say?'

'When a man is frozen out of his own bed it's inevitable that he'll turn to other women for physical satisfaction,' he scorned.

'Are you saying that's what Perry did?'

'It's public knowledge,' he shrugged again.

'Is it?'

'Was he still sleeping with you before he died?'

'Our sleeping arrangements have nothing to do with—Oh!' she gave a painful gasp as her wrist was grasped and her arm twisted up behind her back, her body brought dangerously close to the hard-muscled flesh of Rick Dalmont. 'Let me go,' she ordered between gritted teeth.

'Smile,' he instructed curtly, his teeth showing white against his dark complexion. 'I said smile, damn it,' he bit out savagely at her lack of response to his order.

She looked about them desperately, amazed that no one could see what this man was doing to her. And then she realised that several people who had come here alone were now in rather close clinches with a man or woman they had met here tonight. Janice would be shocked to know that some of these couples whom she had only just introduced would even be in bed together later tonight.

But not Rick Dalmont and herself. And he was still hurting her, his hold on her arm brutal. 'How can I smile when you're breaking my arm?' she groaned.

He lightened his grip slightly, although the relaxation made her body curve more intimately against him. 'I'm sorry,' but he didn't look very repentant. 'Now answer my question,' he ground out.

'I've forgotten what it was,' she muttered.

'Liar!'

She blinked at the vehemence of his tone. 'I won't discuss my marriage to Perry with you!'

Rick sighed, releasing her completely at the inflexibility of her tone. 'Even in the face of danger you choose to defy me.'

'Danger?' She raised black brows.

'So cool,' he shook his head. 'It isn't natural. Your eyes speak of fire, of all you have to give a man——'

'Not you!'

'Me,' his eyes glittered furiously. 'I'm getting tired of waiting for you, Shanna——'

'What is it, Mr Dalmont?' She refused to rub her aching wrist and arm; she wouldn't show any weakness to this man, ever. 'Did you think that because I've been widowed for the last six months I would fall into your arms like an over-ripe plum? Did you think I would be so sexually frustrated that you would have no trouble at all getting me into bed with you?' Her voice rose angrily.

'Maybe you're sexually cold,' he dismissed.

'Oh, that's usually the next insult!' she scorned. 'Then I'm supposed to sleep with you just to prove that I'm not cold at all. I've been through it all before, Mr Dalmont. I must say, I'm disappointed in you—I expected more sophistication from you.'

His mouth tightened. 'Why do you have to fight me?' he asked quietly, impatiently. 'I've asked you out so many times over the last two weeks that I've lost count.'

'Then give up!'

'I want you, Shanna,' he told her forcefully, pinning her to the spot with the intensity of his gaze. 'And I never give up on something I want as badly as I want you. I've left a trail of broken people behind me who could tell you that.'

She had gone very pale, believing his threat. 'That was business——'

'Business or personal, it doesn't matter,' he shrugged. 'I always win in the end.'

She had heard of his ruthless business dealings, of the people he had ruined in his desire to add to the

Dalmont coffers, but she had never heard of this singlemindedness with a woman before. Although perhaps he had never been turned down before! 'No,' she shook her head. 'Not this time you won't,' she told him with quiet conviction.

'You loved your husband, is that it?'

She couldn't help flinching at the scorn of his tone. 'Yes,' her voice was husky, her head bent.

'You still love him?' he grated.

'Yes.'

'I don't believe it!'

Her head went back proudly, her eyes flashing. 'It's the truth,' she snapped.

'And the parties almost every night, the men who pay you attention—that's mourning him, is it?' Rick derided harshly.

'He wouldn't want me to stay at home.'

'I would!' he bit out fiercely, his eyes jet-black. 'I'd want you to lock yourself away until you died too.'

His intensity took her breath away, and she swallowed hard. 'Maybe that's what I am doing, waiting to die,' she said softly.

'At parties every night?' he scorned.

She looked at him with steady green eyes. 'Maybe I just don't want to be alone when I die.'

Rick Dalmont looked as if she had physically hit him, paling slightly beneath his olive complexion. 'Shanna . . .?'

She sighed, shaking off his hand. 'Selina seems anxious for you to return to her side,' she drawled. 'I'm sure she'll be much more—amenable than I could ever be.'

'I don't want Selina,' he rasped.

'Poor Selina,' she murmured, her cool façade back in place. 'She's very attractive.'

'She doesn't have black hair and green eyes.'

'I'm sure there are thousands of willing women who do.'

'With emphasis on the willing, hmm?' he taunted.

'Exactly.' She gave him a saccharine-sweet smile.

He shook his head. 'It's still you I want, Shanna.'

'I'm sorry.'

'I really believe you are,' he frowned at her quiet sincerity.

'Yes,' she nodded.

'I can't work you out.' Rick shook his head dazedly.

'Don't even try,' she advised. 'Just don't become involved with me——'

'I want to go to bed with you, not become involved!'

Her smile was genuine this time. 'And one precludes the other with you?'

'Yes,' he bit out tautly at her mockery.

'Goodnight, Mr Dalmont. We'll meet again?' she drawled.

'You can bet on it!'

'I'm not usually a betting woman, but I'm sure that if I were I would win that bet.'

'Little tease!' he rasped.

Her humour faded as quickly as it had begun. 'That's one thing I'm not, Mr Dalmont. I've told you bluntly to leave me alone, you've chosen not to take that advice. You would be doing us both a favour, and saving yourself a lot of time, if you gave up on me now.'

'Because you'll never give in to me?'

'No.'

He shrugged. 'I'm not *prepared* to give up on you yet. I'll be seeing you, Shanna.' He ran a fingertip lightly down her cheek, lingering against her mouth, nodding confidently before going over to Henry and Janice to take his leave.

Shanna wasn't altogether surprised at his departure

from the party; he knew there was no point in pursuing her any further tonight, not when she had made her feelings more than plain. And she didn't want to stay here any longer herself now; the verbal encounter with Rick Dalmont had opened up wounds that she knew would never get the chance to heal.

'What did you do to him?' Henry demanded when she joined him. 'I've never known Rick to leave a party at eleven o'clock before!'

She shrugged. 'There has to be a first time for everything.'

'Yes, but——'

'It may have escaped your notice,' she taunted, 'but Selina has gone too.'

'She left with Gary,' her brother dismissed. 'She gave up once Rick returned to you. She decided it's Gary's lucky night instead.'

'Bitchy!' she smiled.

Henry grimaced. 'Selina picks up a different man every time she comes here. I'll have to tell Janice not to invite her again.'

'A snob too!' Shanna mocked.

'Stop changing the subject,' he scowled. 'What did you do to make Rick leave?'

'Nothing.'

'Nothing?' Henry frowned.

'Exactly that,' she nodded. 'And I intend to continue doing nothing. Don't forget to tell Janice I'll be here for lunch tomorrow,' she reminded lightly, intending to show him she had far from forgotten the talk she wanted to have with him.

'She always cooks enough for an army,' he answered vaguely.

Her brother's air of distraction did nothing to reassure Shanna. Henry always knew what he was doing, had been a more than competent successor to their father as head of the family newspaper and magazine empire.

Poor little rich girl, Rick Dalmont had called her. He didn't know anything about her. Until her marriage to Perry four years ago, perhaps that description would have fitted her, but marriage had matured her far beyond the spoilt girl she had been at twenty-one.

She had married Perry against her father's wishes, something that had been hard to do considering her closeness to her single parent, her mother having died years ago. Her father had been completely against her marrying a man who risked his life for a living. But the marriage had been a success, and it had perhaps been Perry's constant brushes with death that had speeded the process of her maturity and cherishing of the deep love they had for each other. Whatever the reason, her father had been assured of her happiness before he died two years ago. At least she had given her beloved father that, and he had been spared the pain she was still suffering, the pain of losing Perry.

No one knew or could understand the loss she felt at Perry's death, not even those closest to her. And no one knew how she feared death for herself . . .

She breakfasted alone the next morning, as she had for the last six months, before tidying the apartment. Not that it needed much of that, one person didn't make much mess, and because she and Perry had spent most of their marriage living out of suitcases she had learnt not to have too many personal possessions, so the apartment was bare of all personal imprint.

It was a new apartment since Perry's death, the one they had used as their home-base when in London had been on the other side of town. But photographs of Perry were prominent in every room, photographs of him racing, of him winning, of the two of them together. Most of them were from before Perry's first accident, the one that had precipitated the end of his career. A serious back injury meant the end of his career as a top racing car driver six months before his death, and she knew it had been a blow Perry had never fully recovered from. Racing had been his life, his career, and for a time he had gone wild.

Damn Rick Dalmont! She knew he was the reason for the memories. What else could she do but remember when he had pointed out so forcibly that all had not been well between Perry and herself at the time of the fatal accident? But he had been right about one thing, the fault in the marriage had been hers, not Perry's. It was true that when a man couldn't find satisfaction in his own bed he turned elsewhere for solace. Perry had done just that.

None of her sleepless night showed as Janice opened the door to her shortly before twelve, her expression coolly composed, looking elegant in a dress the same green of her eyes, its long-sleeved, high-necked style more provocative than a more seductive style could be.

'I'll never know how you do it,' said a harassed-looking Janice, her blonde curls in disarray, a smudge of flour on her nose. 'You always look like a fashion-plate, and I—Well, I look what I am, I suppose, a housewife.'

'A beautiful housewife,' Shanna smiled, kissing her sister-in-law affectionately on the cheek. 'And I look this way because I go out to lunch,' she laughed.

'Hm,' Janice acknowledged wryly. 'Although that doesn't explain how you still look this way when we come to your apartment for dinner too.'

'Caterers,' she taunted dryly.

'You know you're a fantastic cook,' Janice dismissed with a sigh. 'Well, I'd better not keep you from Peter and Susan any longer. They're waiting for you in the lounge.'

The next few minutes were taken up with the ecstatic greetings of her young niece and nephew, although Shanna had time to realise that there was no sign in the spotlessly clean lounge of the smoky party of the night before.

Peter and Susan were five and six respectively, as alike as if they had been twins, both fair-haired and blue-eyed like their mother, although they had their father's height and were both inclined to be serious like Henry too. But they were lovely children, and Shanna greeted them as enthusiastically as they did her.

Henry sat back in his favourite armchair and watched them with an indulgent smile on his lips, puffing away on his favourite pipe; an affectation he believed gave him a look of distinction. It just made him more endearing to Shanna. She and Henry had always been close, despite the difference in their natures, but as the time for lunch neared and Henry still made no effort to bring up the subject of Rick Dalmont she decided to broach the subject herself.

'Henry——'

'Lunch is ready,' Janice came through to announce.

Henry gave a pleased smile as he stood up. 'Thank you, darling.'

'I'll give you thank you!' Shanna muttered as she accompanied her brother through to the dining-room. 'You won't get away so easily after lunch.'

He turned to grin at her. 'But at least then I'll have a full stomach!'

'It won't help you,' she warned.

'Maybe not, but you'll seem less fierce once I've eaten.'

'Fierce, Henry?' she spluttered. 'I've never been fierce in my life!'

He shook his head. 'Sometimes you remind me so much of Dad it's incredible.'

'Dad was a lovely old man, despite his crustiness; I can't see the resemblance at all,' Shanna smiled.

'Oh, it's there. I've seen it in your handling of Rick Dal——'

'—Mont,' she finished triumphantly. 'I'm so glad you haven't forgotten about him, Henry.'

'No,' he mumbled. 'But lunch first, hmm?'

'But no longer,' she warned. 'My patience is wearing a little thin, Henry.'

'I didn't know you had any!'

Shanna grinned at his woebegone expression, and her good humour lasted all through the delicious Sunday lunch Janice had prepared. Peter and Susan helped her with the washing-up afterwards, then she carried through a tray of tea to her brother and Janice, arching her brows at Henry as he seemed settled in front of the television.

'Henry and I will take our tea through to the study,' she announced firmly. 'Won't we, Henry?' She looked at him steadily.

'Will we?' He sighed at her stubborn expression. 'I suppose we will.' He stood up reluctantly.

'I won't keep him long, Janice,' she promised.

'Oh, I think you will,' her sister-in-law said knowingly. 'Good luck, Henry.'

'She sounded as if she thought you might need it,' Shanna questioned as she sat opposite her brother in his study.

'I might,' he nodded.

She frowned. 'Tell me, Henry,' she said quietly, 'what business do you and Rick Dalmont have?'

'You won't like it,' he warned.

'I have a feeling not,' she acknowledged heavily.

He stood up to pace the room. 'You see, the

newspaper hasn't been doing too well lately, and I needed a cash flow for a while.'

'Yes?'

'I've been trying to get this deal together with Rick for months, and when he came over to England two weeks ago it was an ideal opportunity to further the talks. We finalised the deal on Friday, that's partly what the party was about last night.'

'Yes?' Shanna was very wary now, Henry deliberately avoiding her gaze.

'Well, that's it,' he shrugged.

'No, that isn't it at all, Henry,' she refuted softly. 'You haven't told me anything I didn't already know. What's the deal you've made with Rick Dalmont? Has he come in as your partner or just with a financial loan?'

'Neither.' Henry wetted his lips nervously.

Shanna's unease began to deepen. It wasn't like Henry to be so evasive. 'Then what is the deal?'

'Look, when Dad died he left all the publishing business to me. Maybe he shouldn't have done, but you were happily married to Perry at the time, and Dad did leave you financially secure.'

'I never wanted any of the business, Henry, you know that,' she dismissed. 'You're entitled to make whatever deals you want. I just want to know where I come into it, because I do, don't I?'

'Yes,' her brother sighed heavily. 'It's *Fashion Lady*.'

'What about it?' she gasped.

Henry shrugged. 'As of Friday it belongs to Rick Dalmont. You now work for him.'

CHAPTER TWO

SHANNA's breath left her in a hiss. *Fashion Lady* now belonged to Rick Dalmont! She couldn't believe it. *Fashion Lady* had become her lifeline the last year, had given her something worthwhile to do after Perry's death six months ago. And *Fashion Lady* had continued to thrive under her control, her natural flair for what was fashionable and what would interest the fashion-conscious woman of today increasing the magazine's circulation considerably.

And now it all belonged to Rick Dalmont. 'I'll have to leave,' she said dully.

'Er——'

'Yes?' Her tone was sharp at her brother's hesitation, sensing there was more to come.

Henry looked anxious. 'Part of the deal was that you would stay on for at least a transition period.'

'And how long is that?' she frowned.

'Six months,' he revealed reluctantly.

Shanna rose slowly to her feet. 'No, Henry,' she told him coldly. 'You had no right to sign a deal like that without consulting me. Or were you asked not to?' she realised sharply.

Henry looked sheepish. 'I knew you'd never go for it——'

'*You* knew?' she accused.

'All right, both Rick and I knew.'

'Then you were both right,' she snapped. 'I could never work for him.'

'But I've signed the contracts now!'

'But *I* haven't,' she pointed out stiffly. 'You knew

28

I would never agree to it, Henry,' she shook her head. 'And your signature can't commit me to anyone.'

'You're contracted to *Fashion Lady*, regardless of who owns it.'

'Then I resign,' she snapped.

'Your contract requires three months' notice,' he reminded her.

'I rescind all right to the money owed me,' Shanna told him. 'Just give me my references.'

'I can't do that,' Henry shook his head. 'I'm no longer your employer. And if you leave now Rick would sue you and me for breach of contract.'

'Then let him!' Her eyes flashed in challenge.

'Shanna, I signed my part of the bargain in good faith.' Henry's voice lowered pleadingly. 'One breach of the contract could ruin the whole deal.'

She glared at her brother. 'Then it will have to ruin it!'

'And the *Chronicle* could go under!'

She frowned, searching her brother's face, seeing the lines of worry there, the strain he had been hiding from her. 'That bad?' she said softly.

'That bad,' he nodded grimly.

'Rick Dalmont wouldn't call off the whole deal just because I won't work for him!'

'He will,' Henry said with certainty.

'He—will?'

Her brother nodded. 'He refused to even consider signing the contract until you were included in it.'

'God,' she said shakily.

'It's normal practice for senior staff to stay on after such a negotiation,' Henry pushed his point as he sensed her confusion.

'*Nothing* about Rick Dalmont is normal,' she flashed. 'You know why he's done this, Henry. I won't go out with him, so he's forcing me to relate to him from a work point of view.'

'That's rubbish,' he dismissed abruptly. 'I told you, we've been discussing the deal for months.'

'And when did I enter into it?'

'About—Well, I——' Henry broke off, frowning.

'About two weeks ago, right? Before that I'm sure he had no interest in the staff of *Fashion Lady*,' she scorned. 'That he didn't give a damn if they stayed or went.'

'That isn't true,' her brother blustered. 'The future of the staff of *Fashion Lady* has always been high on my list of priorities.'

'*Your* priorities, Henry,' she pounced triumphantly. 'Rick Dalmont doesn't give a damn about the little people who get in his way. He told me so himself.'

'No one at *Fashion Lady* is in his way.'

'I will be. His being my boss won't make the slightest difference to how I feel about him personally. I don't like him, nothing will change that.'

'You don't have to like him, just work for him.'

'That isn't what he wants, and you know it,' Shanna sighed. 'Henry, how could you do this to me?' she groaned. 'You've seen the way he follows me, the way he never stops looking at me. I'll be handing in my notice—I have to, Henry,' she insisted as he went to protest. 'But don't worry, I'll give him his three months. With any luck he'll leave the acquisition of *Fashion Lady* to one of his hirelings.'

But she knew he wouldn't, knew this was just the opportunity Rick Dalmont had been waiting for. She wasn't conceited enough to think he had bought *Fashion Lady* just to get a hold over her, but she felt sure he would lose no opportunity in using it as such. She would have to be very careful of Ricardo Dalmont in future; he didn't play by any rules she knew, in fact he didn't play at all!

Everything seemed normal when she went in to work on Monday morning; no high-powered executive was waiting for her to tell her of her new employer. Gloria, her secretary, sat in her normal place behind her desk, handing over the mail and messages that had already come in.

But Shanna knew that she was different, that inside she was a seething mass of emotions. If Rick Dalmont thought he was going to breeze in here and take her by surprise as the new owner of the magazine then he was going to be out of luck; she intended greeting him as coolly as ever. And she didn't intend that he should have the upper hand in anything.

'Gloria,' she buzzed through to her secretary, 'get Mr Dalmont of Dalmont Industries for me. He's at the Excellence, I believe.'

'*Rick* Dalmont?'

'That's the one, Gloria,' she said lightly, releasing the intercom button. Gloria was a good secretary, and had worked for the previous editor too, but even her usually unruffled demeanour had been unnerved by the mention of Rick Dalmont. He would have that effect on most women, and as most of the staff at *Fashion Lady* were women she envisaged more than a little hero-worship once it was known he was the new boss.

'Mr Dalmont, Shanna,' Gloria announced a few minutes later.

She picked up the blue telephone on her desk that matched the blue and white décor of her executive office. The cover of *Fashion Lady* was always in blue and white, and for the most part so was Shanna's office. Blue was a colour she tended to avoid away from work.

'Mr Dalmont?'

'Shanna,' he returned throatily.

'I believe we should meet, Mr Dalmont.' Her tone was briskly businesslike as she imagined his mocking humour at the other end of the telephone.

'You've spoken to Henry?' he drawled.

She could now visualise the look of satisfaction on his smug face. 'I've spoken to him,' she acknowledged. 'Would twelve o'clock in my office be convenient?'

'Are you inviting me out to lunch, Shanna?' he taunted.

Her mouth tightened, the gleam of revenge in her eyes making them glow deeply green. 'I'm inviting you to my office at twelve o'clock,' she told him stiffly.

'I'll be there.' He rang off abruptly.

And so would she. She could sense his feeling of triumph even over the telephone, and she was determined he wouldn't know any more such feelings where she was concerned. He had won this round, and she would see that Henry didn't have to go back on his word as a business man because of her, but Ricardo Dalmont wouldn't win any more rounds over her. She was going to be one step ahead of him from now on. Ignoring him hadn't worked, being polite to him hadn't either, she would have to try and make sure she stayed that one step ahead of him in future.

She had warned Gloria to buzz through to her office when Rick Dalmont arrived, and it was exactly twelve o'clock when the single buzz alerted her. She moved smoothly to her feet, ethereally thin in the black dress, her black hair caught in at her nape, her eyes like twin jewels above her high cheekbones.

Rick Dalmont's eyes widened appreciatively as she went out to greet him, those same dark eyes narrowing at her formality.

'Please come in, Mr Dalmont,' she invited coolly, vaguely irritated by the way Gloria couldn't seem to

stop staring at the man. Admittedly he looked very
handsome in a fitted iron-grey three-piece suit and
snowy white shirt, but he was only a mere man after
all. She didn't notice the power that emanated from
the force of his body, or the shrewdness in the dark
eyes, the determination on the sensuous mouth. She
should have noticed all those things about him, but she
didn't, was blind to it all. Perhaps if she had
noticed . . .

She opened her office door for him to enter,
standing back as silence fell over the seven people
waiting inside the room, all of them looking at Rick
Dalmont with open curiosity. Rick's reaction to this
unexpected meeting with *Fashion Lady*'s heads of
department was harder to discern, and a hard mask
fell over his face as he raised dark brows at her in
acknowledgment of the first round going to her.

'We'll discuss this over lunch,' he told her softly,
a smile to his lips, only the flare of anger in his dark
eyes telling her it would be far from a pleasant
conversation.

She moved forward hastily, and silence fell over the
room where conversation had begun to buzz as Rick's
identity was realised. Her body moved gracefully
beneath the black dress, the heels on her sandals
adding to her height. 'I'm sure you all know Mr
Ricardo Dalmont,' she introduced unnecessarily,
knowing that they all realised who he was. 'What you
aren't yet aware of is that he is now our new boss.' She
turned to him with a challenging smile, the conversation behind her increasing to a roar as the information
was absorbed and disbelieved. Like her, her heads of
staff had had no idea a takeover was in the offing.
Henry had certainly played this close to the ground,
and she didn't need two guesses at whose instigation
that had been.

Rick met her challenge with an arrogant inclination of his head. 'Mrs Logan has been—premature in her announcement,' he drawled reproachfully. 'I had meant to talk to you all when Mr Blythe was present. But as I was here to take Mrs Logan out to lunch she thought I should have a few words with you before we leave.' It was his turn to give Shanna a challenging look, triumphantly so.

Shanna was so angry that she didn't hear a word he said over the next few minutes, but she could see by the pleased expressions on her colleagues' faces that they liked what he was saying. He might think he had just trapped her into having lunch with him, but he was wrong, no one forced her to do anything she didn't want to do. And she didn't want to have lunch with Rick Dalmont.

'So I can assure you all that I will make as little change in the format of *Fashion Lady* as I can,' he concluded. 'I look forward to working with you, ladies—and gentleman,' he acknowledged the single male head of department in the room with the six ladies. 'A little discrimination in reverse?' he mocked.

Joe Deane gave an appreciative laugh. 'I have no complaints.'

'I don't think I would either.' Rick looked at the women with open appreciation.

'If you've quite finished?' Shanna said icily. 'We still have a magazine to run,' she reminded him curtly.

Rick's eyes narrowed dangerously before he turned to smile at the others. 'I'm sorry I kept you so long,' he told them smoothly. 'I'm sure I'll meet you all later, individually, in the week.'

Shanna could have cringed at some of the open smiles of encouragement on some of the faces of the women she could have sworn were hardbitten career women. Was no woman immune to this man's rakish charm!

'That was not only unethical,' a cold voice of gravel and honey told her softly. 'It was also unprofessional,' Rick bit out tautly; the two of them were completely alone now, and the tension between them was almost unbearable.

'Unprofessional?' she echoed quietly. 'You don't call buying this magazine without even informing the editor unprofessional or unethical?' she demanded angrily.

He shrugged broad shoulders. 'It isn't required of me to tell you anything.'

'Not even when I'm included in the deal?' she snapped.

'As editor of the magazine, of course,' he drawled.

'Of course!'

Again he shrugged. 'It's normal practice——'

'For senior members of staff to stay on after such a negotiation,' she finished dryly. 'You coached Henry very well, Mr Dalmont, he used exactly the same argument.'

'Did it work?' He leant casually back against her desk.

'No!' she told him curtly, holding out an envelope to him. 'I'm giving you three months' notice.'

He took the envelope, putting it away in the breast pocket of his jacket. 'Can you train your replacement in that time?' he enquired coolly.

Shanna bit back her chagrin with effort; he hadn't even tried to talk her out of leaving, damn him. 'I'm sure I can,' she confirmed waspishly.

He nodded. 'I think so too.'

'You don't seem—surprised,' she couldn't prevent the words spilling out of her mouth.

'I'm not,' he shrugged. 'You're an independent lady, you don't like being manoeuvred.'

'You've learnt that much about me at least!' she snapped.

Rick moved closer, his aftershave tangy and pleasant to the senses, as was the good tobacco in the cheroots he smoked, their aroma clinging to his clothing. 'I'd like to learn a lot more about you—if you would let me.'

Her eyes flashed deeply green. 'No!' she took a step away from him. 'I've already told you, I'm not interested. Just leave me alone, Rick.'

'Rick,' he repeated softly. 'I think that's the first time you've ever called me that.' He touched her cheek with gentle fingers. 'It makes a pleasant change after the cold "Mr Dalmont" I've been used to from you.'

She had realised her slip as soon as she said his name. But she was beginning to tire of this man's constant pressure on her; she hadn't slept well the night before, and she felt as jumpy as a kitten about this man as a result of that. 'It won't happen again,' she told him stiffly.

'Won't it?' he derided confidently. 'I have a feeling it will happen a lot in future. You see, I am the new boss around here, and I like my senior *employees* to call me Rick. Let's go to lunch, hmm?' he taunted. 'I have a lot of things to discuss with you.'

'No, I——'

'Concerning the magazine,' he gave her a sideways glance.

Shanna eyed him warily. 'Is that all?'

Dark brows rose mockingly. 'I can't promise not to throw in a few personal remarks of my own, but for the most part—yes, that's all,' he mocked.

'A business lunch?'

'Exactly,' he agreed with satisfaction.

She still didn't trust this man, knew that he was capable of lying to get his own way. But for now she had to fall in with his plans, she owed him a certain amount of loyalty as the new owner of *Fashion Lady*. 'I'll just go and tell Jane I'm leaving,' she nodded coolly.

'Your assistant editor?'

He certainly didn't forget much, she had only briefly introduced him to Jane Meakins, her assistant editor, and yet he had remembered her. She didn't know why that should surprise her, she doubted many things escaped Rick Dalmont's notice. 'I shouldn't be long,' she told him abruptly. 'If you need anything I'm sure my secretary, Gloria, would be pleased to help you,' she added with veiled sarcasm.

'I won't need anything,' he drawled, making himself comfortable in the chair behind her desk.

'Trying it out for size?' she taunted.

He gave her a pitying glance. 'Editor of a women's magazine is not something I had in mind for my future!'

Shanna shot him an impatient look before leaving the room, wondering how one man could induce such violence in her; simply to be with him now made her want to fight or scream at him. And they were both destructive emotions. But also ones that made her feel vibrantly alive, something she hadn't felt for a long time. And she didn't thank Rick Dalmont for arousing such emotions now. Three months of working for him; it could be the longest three months of her life!

He was frowning when she went back into her office several minutes later, standing up ready to leave. 'Do you actually like the décor in this room?' he grimaced.

'It's very—effective.' She shrugged into her jacket with a little help from him, moving away as she realised how close he had suddenly become.

'It's disgusting,' he said bluntly, opening the door for her. 'Your predecessor had abominable taste.'

Her eyes widened as she looked at him. 'How do you know I didn't choose it?'

'You have too much style.' He smiled at her gasp. 'You're a classy lady, Shanna Logan. That's part of your attraction for me. You have style from the tip of your head to your toes.' He handed her into the black London taxi he had miraculously managed to flag down in the busy lunch-hour traffic. 'The Savoy,' he instructed the driver, getting in beside her.

She sat back, very conscious of the length of his thigh pressed against hers as he deliberately sat as close to her as he could, although there was plenty of room on the seat the other side of him. 'You'll have to change your eating habits if you're going to claim this lunch on *Fashion Lady*'s expenses,' she taunted.

His mouth twisted. 'Dalmont Enterprises can pick up the tab for this one,' he smiled. 'And get the decorators into your office first thing tomorrow, will you? It must give you nightmares!'

'Yes,' she admitted reluctantly. 'But Henry always thought it was——'

'Effective,' he echoed her description of earlier mockingly.

'Yes,' she confirmed defensively.

Rick Dalmont was obviously known at the Savoy, from the doorman to the maître d', and one of the best tables in the restaurant was made available to them. It obviously paid to have influence and notoriety; the only time she had brought one of the so-called stars here after an interview for the magazine she had had trouble getting a table at all.

'Tell me, Mr Dalmont,' she said once they had ordered their meal. 'If you knew—expected me to hand in my notice, why did you make my being editor part of the deal?' She looked at him with cool green eyes.

He sat back, satisfaction and triumph in every line of his body. 'It gives me three months with you I wouldn't otherwise have had.' He smiled at her puzzled frown. 'Making you—as editor,' he taunted. 'Part of the deal, makes you feel obliged to at least work your notice. I'm sure Henry has explained to you the pitfalls of leaving a job without references. Also it could affect the rest of the deal I have with him if you leave now. But I'm sure you know all this, otherwise you would already be walking. Wouldn't you?' he prompted confidently.

'Very clever, Mr Dalmont,' she said tautly.

His mouth quirked. 'Why do I get the impression that was an insult?'

Green eyes clashed with black. 'Because you're a very astute man, Mr Dalmont!'

He laughed softly. 'And you're a fascinating woman, Shanna,' he said without rancour. 'And the name is Rick. I told you, I like all senior members of staff to use it.'

She eyed him sceptically. 'Those poor people you assured you would make no changes to *Fashion Lady*?' she derided hardly.

His mouth tightened. 'You doubt my word?'

Shanna gave him a considering look. 'Not at all. I'm sure that "as little change in the format as you can" will mean exactly that, as little change as *you* can accept until you have the magazine exactly as *you* want it!'

His brows rose in silent appreciation of her deduction, as if he hadn't expected her to be that intelligent.

She sighed. 'I grew up in the world of business, Mr—Rick,' she amended reluctantly. 'My father built up his empire during my childhood, and because my mother died years ago he used to discuss his business with Henry and me.'

'The Stock Exchange for breakfast, hmm?'

'Yes,' she nodded.

'Sounds similar to my own childhood.'

She recoiled from any similarity between herself and this man, regretting telling him even the little she had. 'I doubt it,' she derided. 'We were rich, but not that rich.'

His eyes darkened at the barb, although luckily the arrival of their lunch prevented the biting reply he had looked about to make. 'Let's just enjoy the meal,' he suggested once their food had been served. 'I don't like to argue while I eat.'

'I can't argue with you, I work for you.'

His hand grasped hers as it lay on the table-top. 'At least give me a chance to be pleasant to you. I can assure you I don't usually get as ruthless with women as I have been with you.'

Shanna purposefully disengaged her hand from his. 'As you said, let's eat.'

He gave an impatient sigh, but as he picked up his cutlery she knew they were to at least eat in peace.

'What do you think of Jane for my replacement?' she asked as they drank their coffee, having decided it was time for the 'business' discussion he had asked for.

Rick frowned, giving the idea some thought. 'No,' finally came his blunt answer.

She held back her sharp retort with effort. When she had taken over *Fashion Lady* a year ago Henry had more or less given her complete control, to do what she felt best for the magazine, to make what decisions she felt were necessary, and without being conceited she knew that the majority of them had been the right decisions. For her to have consulted Rick Dalmont at all just now had been hard enough, to have him turn down her suggestion so emphatically was a damned insult.

'Why not?' she snapped in challenge.

He shrugged. 'I want someone with a new approach, not a staff member who still has her loyalties to you and the new projects you started.'

'Then you agree I've given *Fashion Lady* some input?' Her sarcasm was barely contained.

Rick raised dark brows at her vehemence. 'It's good to see that something can fire your interest.'

'Plenty of things do that, Mr Dalmont!'

'But not me?'

'No, not you! Now about Jane——'

'I said no,' he rasped.

'And that's the last that will be said on the subject?' she scorned.

'Yes!'

She drew in a deep controlling breath. 'Very well,' her tone was once again cold and remote, 'I'll see about advertising for a replacement.'

'It was your decision to leave, Shanna,' he reminded softly.

'And I don't regret it for a moment!' She stood up. 'If you'll excuse me, my lunch-hour was over long ago.'

Rick stood up too, putting some money down on the table to cover the bill. 'I didn't think you had noticed,' he taunted, his hand firm on her elbow as they left the restaurant together.

'I noticed,' she derided. 'But it's your time . . .'

'In that case,' his mouth tightened, 'I'd like you to spend the afternoon with me at my hotel, discussing business, of course.'

'Of course,' she said dryly. 'I have too much to do at the office, Mr Dalmont,' she refused.

'Some other time, eh?' he mocked.

'I doubt it.'

'So do I,' he grinned, suddenly looking younger. 'I

wish you would reconsider your decision to leave, Shanna. With a few changes, and your dedication,' he taunted, '*Fashion Lady* could become the top women's magazine in the country.'

'I doubt I would like your changes, Mr Dalmont.'

'Even if they are for the good of *Fashion Lady*?' His eyes were narrowed.

'In your opinion!' she scorned. 'Since when did you become an expert on publishing, Mr Dalmont?'

'Since I bought *Fashion Lady* and made it my business to be!' he snapped angrily, stopping a passing taxi to open the door for her to get inside, leaning on the open window after closing the door behind her. 'I'll be seeing you, Shanna,' he told her grimly before nodding to the driver to take her back to her office.

Shanna stared straight ahead as the taxi moved off into the heavy London traffic, knowing Rick Dalmont's last words had been in the form of a threat. She would indeed be 'seeing' him—he would make sure of that.

It wasn't until she got back to her office that she realised that, except for her asking about Jane, they hadn't discussed business at all during lunch. Rick Dalmont was more than distrustful, he was dangerous!

'What a shock!' Jane came into her office on her return. 'I had no idea *Fashion Lady* was for sale.'

Shanna grimaced. 'Neither did I until yesterday.'

Jane's eyes widened. She was a pretty woman in her early twenties, the same as Shanna, her blonde hair kept short and easily styled, her make-up light and attractive, her clothes always fashionably smart. 'Henry didn't tell you?' She sounded surprised.

'Not until it was too late.'

'Mm—well, Mr Dalmont does have the financial backing *Fashion Lady* needs.'

She frowned. 'You don't mind that he's the new boss?'

Jane shrugged. 'I know it must be difficult for you, with Henry being your brother, but a boss is a boss as far as I'm concerned. The way things are for unemployment in this country at the moment we're all lucky to have jobs at all.'

Jane's down-to-earth attitude was something she needed at the moment. They *were* all lucky to have a job, and jobs as editors didn't come along every day, she doubted she would be lucky enough to find another one, even *with* references.

It was something that bothered her as she prepared to go out later that evening. Financially she didn't need to work, both Perry and her father had left her very well off, but mentally and emotionally . . .? Heavens, she couldn't spend her days sitting around the apartment just counting the minutes away! That would only lead to thoughts of Perry, of the last traumatic months of their marriage.

Damn, she was thinking about it already! She had taken great care to fill all of her time, with work in the day, sometimes until she felt like collapsing, and with a round of parties in the evenings. She rarely gave herself time to think, let alone dwell on the past.

And tonight would be no exception! So she would be out of a job in three months, she would find something else, she would make sure she did.

She looked her usual cool and composed self later that evening when she arrived at Steven and Alice Grant's for dinner. The middle-aged couple were old friends of her father's, and her own friendship with them had continued even after his death. This evening was a celebration of their twenty-fifth wedding anniversary, and she knew Alice was pleased with the jade figurine Shanna had given her to add to her already extensive collection.

She already knew most of the other guests at the Grant house, and made a beeline for her brother as she spotted him across the room, a smiling Janice at his side.

'Going somewhere?' drawled the familiar gravel and honey voice that she was beginning to feel was haunting her.

She schooled her features to remain calm, turning slowly to face Rick Dalmont. Goodness, he was dressed to kill tonight! The black velvet jacket fitted smoothly across his powerful shoulders, the white of his shirt making his skin appear swarthier than ever, his black trousers moulded to the lean length of his long legs. His dark eyes were filled with amusement as he met and held her gaze, his black hair brushed back from its side-parting to rest low over his ears and collar. He held a drink in his hand, evidence that he had been here for some time.

'Good evening, Mr Dalmont,' she greeted softly.

He moved closer to her. 'Hello, Shanna.'

'We do seem to—keep meeting.'

'No, we don't *seem* to do anything,' he drawled. 'But then I'm sure you already knew that.'

'Steven and Alice are friends of yours?' She ignored the intimacy of his tone.

He shook his head. 'I've never met them before this evening.'

She gasped. 'You gatecrashed their party?'

His mouth quirked. 'I came with Henry and Janice.'

Shanna's mouth tightened as she shot a resentful glare at her unsuspecting brother. 'I should have known! Well, if you'll excuse me——'

'No,' his hand on her arm stopped her leaving. 'I'm still trying to be pleasant, as I tried at lunchtime,' he smiled tightly. 'But you angered me then, and you're angering me now,' he added tautly. 'What do you think I can possibly do to you here, Shanna?' He looked pointedly about the crowded room.

She blushed at the rebuke of his words, and knew she was behaving ridiculously. There were at least forty people in the room; not even Rick Dalmont would try anything here.

'Exactly,' he correctly read her thoughts. 'Although most women don't show such aversion to the thought of my wanting to make love to them.'

'I'm not most women,' she snapped.

'I agree, you aren't.' He took her hand and placed it in the crook of his arm, holding it there with his other hand. 'Which probably accounts for the way I ache for you,' he lowered his voice seductively. 'Put my plain speaking down to my Spanish ancestry,' he chuckled at her tight-lipped outrage. 'I want you very badly, Shanna.'

'You told me that the other evening,' she dismissed abruptly. 'And what you're talking about is sex, Mr Dalmont, not making love.'

'The way I would worship your body it would be making love,' he murmured against her earlobe.

'I——'

'Ah, Shanna, you found Rick,' Alice Grant, an attractive woman in her late forties, beamed at them both. 'With the rush of the Sinclairs arriving at the same time as you I completely forgot to tell you Mr Dalmont had already arrived with Henry,' she told Shanna hurriedly. 'And how silly of you to think we wouldn't have room for your—for Rick,' she corrected awkwardly. 'We've all been so worried about Shanna, Mr Dalmont,' she confided to the silently watchful man at Shanna's side. 'We all miss Perry enormously, but Shanna really is too young and lovely a woman to deny her company to some lucky man.'

Much as she liked Alice Grant, who was the nearest

thing she had to an aunt, Shanna could cheerfully have
strangled her at that moment. And this 'lucky man'
was going to be told a few home truths as soon as they
were alone! How dared he have implied to Alice that
he was her partner for this evening!

'I do consider myself very lucky, Mrs Grant,' Rick
drawled confidently. 'And I've also been very worried
about Shanna. But she has me now, don't you,
sweetheart?' He looked down at her in mocking
challenge.

Anger lit up her eyes. 'I——'

'Ah, the Daniels have arrived,' Alice sighed her
relief. 'Steven's boss,' she confided softly. 'I'll talk to
you both later,' and she hurried to be at her husband's
side as he greeted the other couple.

Shanna wrenched away from Rick Dalmont,
breathing deeply in her agitation. 'What did you tell
Alice when you arrived?' she demanded to know.

He met her gaze with bland innocence. 'That you
were working late and would meet me here as soon as
you could get away.'

'You—I—And Henry went along with that?' she
gasped indignantly.

'Why not?' he shrugged. 'I told him the same thing
when I spoke to him on the telephone and he told me
you were all going to a dinner party this evening.'

'You arrogant—My God, I can't believe this!' she
shook her head. 'You have the cheek of the devil!'

He nodded. 'Some people have even claimed we're
related,' he said with amusement. 'But I doubt Alice
would understand if you tried to explain the true facts
to her. She's a romantic lady, and she thinks that by
seeing me you're finally getting your life back together
after your husband's death. Don't ruin her evening,
will you?' he mocked.

'What about mine?' she bit out.

'Yours is already ruined,' he shrugged dismissively. 'Look, I'll be on my best behaviour, okay?'

'That isn't good enough! I don't——'

'Behave yourself!' Rick rasped as Henry and Janice walked over to join them. 'Save your insults for when we're alone and stop behaving like a child! Just think of this as an exercise in employer/employee relations.'

'I don't want any sort of "relations" with you,' she snapped.

He gave her a mocking smile before turning to charm her brother and Janice. The last thing she needed was an example of his lethal charm at work, and she was too angry to notice the curious looks her brother kept shooting her. And she didn't *want* to feel angry either, didn't want to feel anything for this man, not even dislike.

'By the way, Henry,' Rick gave Shanna a sideways glance, 'Shanna has already introduced me to some of the staff at *Fashion Lady*.'

Henry frowned his puzzlement. 'She has?'

'Mm,' Rick nodded. 'Only casually, of course, on our way out to lunch.'

Henry looked even more puzzled. And well he might after her vehement avowal of dislike of Rick Dalmont over the weekend. To all intents and purposes she had already lunched with him today, and now she was spending the evening with him too!

Rick's arm moved about her waist, pulling her close against his side. 'And how could I resist your sister when she asked me out so persuasively?' he added throatily.

'*Shanna* invited *you* out to lunch?' Henry was astounded—and unable to hide it.

Before Shanna could defend any such misconception dinner was announced, and to her chagrin Alice had put Rick Dalmont next to her at the table. His smile of triumph was enough to make her ignore him throughout the meal, although this only seemed to amuse him. Trying to reject this man was like hitting her head against a brick wall, and she just didn't know what to do next. How pleased he would be if he even knew he was succeeding that far!

'I like your friends,' he told her as they circulated after the meal, his hand on her arm refusing to be shaken off as she would have gone alone to speak to Henry and Janice.

'They like you too,' she muttered, knowing he had been at his most pleasant as they spoke to the people she knew at this dinner party, his hold on her enough claim of possession for him at the moment. In this lazily charming mood it would be difficult for anyone to dislike him, but she knew the other side of him too well to be fooled for a moment; when thwarted this man was lethal. 'I think I'd like to leave now,' she said tightly.

'What a good idea,' he nodded. 'Let's go and make our excuses.'

'You don't have to leave with me,' she faced him.

He quirked one dark brow. 'Now wouldn't it look a little odd if you left and I stayed?'

'That didn't seem to bother you earlier when you arrived without me!'

'Ah, but I had a good excuse for that.' He looked at her mockingly.

'All right,' she agreed tightly. 'We'll leave together.'

'Could I have a word with Henry before we go?'

'Why not?' Her voice was taut, her nerves at breaking point. 'You seem to do everything else you want to!'

Rick laughed softly. 'I'm glad you realise it.'

'*Almost* everything,' she amended hardly.

His chuckle deepened. 'Let's go and see Henry,' he prompted lightly.

Her brother was looking very pleased with himself when they joined his group, and Shanna didn't need two guesses as to the reason for that; he believed she had decided to accept Rick Dalmont after all. She could have told him she intended leaving Rick Dalmont as soon as they were out of Steven and Alice's door, and she didn't intend being caught in this position again. So much for keeping one step ahead!—she had taken half a dozen backwards this evening.

CHAPTER THREE

'I JUST wanted to remind you that you're taking me round *Fashion Lady* tomorrow at ten,' Rick told Henry a few minutes later; the four of them were now alone.

This was news to Shanna, and she decided to listen to the rest of their conversation in case there was something else she didn't know either!

Henry frowned. 'But I thought Shanna had already——'

'Your sister just sprang a little surprise introduction for me,' Rick drawled, enjoying the cold look she gave him. The reason he had mentioned *Fashion Lady* was now becoming apparent; he hoped to embarrass her in front of Henry. 'I wasn't quite prepared for it,' he continued lazily. 'But I think I handled it okay.'

He had more than handled it okay, and he knew it! He had been so charming, so easygoing and assured, that there had been none of the uncertainty and resentment that usually initially went along with a take-over like this. Most of the staff she had spoken to had reacted with the same untroubled acceptance that Jane had.

But Rick's lazily drawled words now had aroused Henry's suspicions, and she could see him mentally adding up the situation—and arriving at the right answer!

'We'll be round at ten in the morning, Shanna,' Henry told her curtly, 'when I'll give Rick the official introduction to the staff that he deserves.'

It took a lot to anger her usually even-tempered

brother, but she could see that her method of dealing
with Rick Dalmont over his acquisition of *Fashion
Lady* had far from met with Henry's approval. It had
backfired on her anyway. Rick's arrogant assurance
was such that nothing unsettled him.

'We'll be ready,' she told her brother softly, a plea
for understanding in her eyes. He gave her an
impatient look, shaking his head in silent reproach.
She turned away, her mouth tight.

'I think I've already had the introduction to the staff
of *Fashion Lady* that Shanna thinks I deserve,' Rick
drawled tauntingly, enjoying her discomfort.

She turned blazing green eyes on him. She didn't
mind that he mocked her, and if they were alone she
would probably have given back as good as he was
giving. But as he was five years her senior, and the
only close family she had left, she valued Henry's
liking and respect for her as a businesswoman as well
as his sister. He had taken a chance on her with
Fashion Lady, a chance that had, luckily, paid off. Her
behaviour this morning might have been petty and
spiteful, but she didn't appreciate Rick telling Henry
about it; the argument between the two of them was
strictly private!

'I shall be honoured to show you round the
magazine tomorrow, Rick,' she told him coolly. 'There
really isn't any need to bother Henry.'

'I'll be there,' her brother told her grimly. 'It's only
protocol that the previous owner should introduce
the new one.' He gave her another disapproving
glare.

'Shanna wants to leave,' Rick spoke smoothly. 'So
we'll say goodbye now.'

She seethed inside all the time they were making
their farewells to Steven and Alice, wrenching out of
his grasp as soon as they were outside, the cool

evening air making her huddle down in her velvet
jacket. 'That was the most despicable, rotten——'

'I know, I know,' Rick interrupted her tirade
impatiently. 'But what you did this morning wasn't
according to the rules of the game.' He held her in
front of him, his eyes very dark in the light flowing
from the house behind them. 'I like to keep business
and pleasure completely separate, but this morning
you crossed over that line.'

'Because you'd already done so!' She was taut with
tension. 'You did so the moment you included me in
your contract with Henry.'

'I've been making the arrangements to buy *Fashion
Lady* for months.'

'And two weeks ago you suddenly decided I should
be included in it!'

His mouth tightened. 'Henry has a big mouth,' he
ground out.

'He's my brother!'

'He's also a businessman!'

Her mouth twisted with scorn. 'You may be able to
separate your priorities into such defined categories,
Mr Dalmont,' she ignored the warning narrowing of
his eyes at her formality, 'but I can't—and neither,
thank God, can Henry.'

There seemed to be a mental battle going on behind
the dark eyes, until finally Rick sighed. 'I warned you
there would be retribution for this morning, so now
we're even,' he shrugged dismissively.

'No, we are not even,' she bit out in a controlled
voice. 'I don't want to be even with you, I don't want
to be anything with you. What I did this morning you
deserved, what you've done, making me work for you,
invading my life like you did tonight, I've done
nothing to deserve.'

'You're too damned beautiful,' he rasped.

Her eyes widened. 'I have to be punished for *that*?'

'Working for me won't be a punishment!' His expression softened from anger. 'It could be very— rewarding, if you would let it be.'

Shanna drew in an angry breath. 'I believe this is sexual harassment, and I have a right to——'

'Sexual harassment!' he exploded, his eyes black his mouth grim. 'I've never had to harass a woman into bed with me!'

'Then you're giving a very good impression of it!'

Black eyes warred with green for several long tension-filled minutes, until Rick finally sighed his exasperation with her. 'I don't intend arguing out here with you,' he reasoned. 'For one thing it's too damned public, and for another it's too cold. The dampness of the weather here gets into my bones,' he grimaced. 'We can talk in the car. Which one is yours?' There were almost two dozen cars parked down the driveway.

'Mine?' she echoed sharply. 'But you——'

'I told you, I came with Henry and Janice, and I meant that literally. I took a cab to their place and drove here with them.'

'But——'

'Which is your car, Shanna?' he rasped impatiently. 'Before we both freeze to death!'

'The brown Mercedes sports car. But——'

He took the car keys out of her hand, striding purposefully over to her car to unlock the door, and sliding in behind the wheel. Shanna stood indignantly beside the car, glaring down at him as he switched on the engine.

'Well, get in,' Rick indicated the passenger door he had opened for her.

'You're in my seat,' she ground out.

He relaxed back against the leather. 'I never allow a

woman to drive me,' he drawled. 'Not since my
mother told me she always thinks out the day's menus
as she drives.'

'Well, I don't. And I——'

'No, you probably organise the layout for the
readers' letters while you drive,' he taunted. 'It's just a
question of differing values.'

Shanna knew she was occasionally guilty of letting
her mind wander as she drove, but she was sure it
wasn't a practice limited to women as Rick seemed to
imply it was! 'And you probably think of the next
woman you're going to bed!' she snapped waspishly,
getting into the car beside him, only just managing to
fasten her safety belt before he put the Mercedes in
gear and drove off.

He turned to give her a confident smile. 'You're
never far from my mind, Shanna,' he mocked.

She turned away, her mouth tight, deciding to end
the intimacy of *that* conversation. 'I don't remember
ever offering to drive you home.'

'But you aren't—I'm driving you.'

And very capably too. Perry had been a good driver,
but his skill on the race-track, his enjoyment of speed,
had occasionally spilt over during his normal driving,
and that didn't make for an enjoyable drive. Rick
Dalmont drove with ease and the minimum of effort,
instilling confidence in his passengers. But she
shouldn't have been the passenger, damn him!

'Would you mind?' A gold cigarette case appeared
in her vision, and she looked up to see Rick was
holding it out to her. 'Could you get me a cheroot
out—please?' he added in a cajoling voice as he saw
the hardening of her mouth.

She did so with little grace, watching as he put the
dark cheroot between his teeth.

'Could you light it for me too?' He handed her a

lighter that matched the cigarette case he was now sliding back into the breast pocket of his jacket.

She sat forward to click the lighter to a flame beneath the cheroot, her mouth unsmiling as she gave it back to him to put away.

'Of course I could have done it myself,' he told her conversationally a few seconds later, 'but I'm desperate enough to want you to perform any little intimate task for me.' He glanced at her sideways. 'And there's something very intimate about what you just did.'

'Really?' she drawled uninterestedly, burning inside with indignation.

'Yes,' he mocked softly. 'Admit it, Shanna, you liked me a little better tonight.'

'I'll admit nothing of the sort! You're a manoeuvring, arrogant bast——'

'Do you usually call your boss a bastard?' he rasped.

'I've only ever had one other boss, and I know for a fact that Henry is legitimate.'

'He's also given you too much freedom,' Rick snapped. 'I would hazard a guess that most of the men in your life have allowed you too much of your own way. First your father and brother, then your husband. And now there's me.'

'You certainly couldn't be accused of being indulgent!' There were two bright spots of angry colour in her cheeks.

'I can be—at the right time, in the right place,' Rick taunted. 'Now we're in the right place, I just have to persuade you it's the right time.'

He had halted the car outside one of London's quietly exclusive hotels and was already getting out from behind the wheel, coming round to open her door for her.

Shanna stood next to him on the pavement. 'If you'll just give me my car keys . . .'

'I thought we could have a drink before you leave.'

'No, thank you.' She held out her hand for the keys. Rick made a point of putting them in his trouser pocket. 'Just one drink?'

'No!' She met the challenge in his dark eyes, seeing he wasn't about to give in. 'I'll get a taxi home,' she decided tautly.

'Good idea.' He took the steps two at a time to the glass doors that led into the hotel, pausing to turn and look at her. 'I'll bring your car to the *Fashion Lady* offices in the morning when I meet Henry. Of course he could be curious as to how I come to have your car, but I'm sure I can come up with some viable explanation for that.' He was whistling tunelessly beneath his breath as he allowed the doorman to open the door for him, cheerfully nodding his thanks as he went inside.

Shanna watched him go with a feeling of a trap closing about her. Rick Dalmont was a manipulating swine, but at the moment he held all the top cards.

Her heels clicked angrily as she ran up the stairs to find the door already being held open for her; the man's expression was deadpan, telling her that he had overheard most if not all of the conversation between Rick and herself. Her head went back defensively as she saw Rick leaning against the lift door to keep it open for her.

'Relax, Shanna,' he drawled as she reached his side. 'This is a hotel, not an apartment. We can even have that drink in the lounge if you like.' He stepped into the lift, pressing the hold button as she made no effort to join him. 'The lounge and bar are upstairs,' he mocked.

She stepped in beside him silently, her face averted as she felt his taunting gaze on her.

'One drink and then you can have your keys back,'

he told her softly as the lift doors opened and he stepped out.

Shanna followed him down the carpeted corridor. The luxury of the hotel meant nothing to her; she and Perry had stayed in plenty of them during their tours of the race circuit.

Rick unlocked the door to a room, gently pushing her inside before switching on the lights. It was obviously a hotel suite and not a public lounge at all.

She turned to him accusingly. 'You said——'

'I said a lounge and a bar,' he held up his hands defensively. 'This is the lounge of my suite, and over there is the bar,' he pointed to the extensive bar in the corner of the room.

'You lied by omission,' she said tautly.

'I didn't lie at all,' he told her slowly. 'I've been honest with you from the beginning—about everything. Now, what would you like to drink?'

'Nothing. I'd like my car keys so that I can leave.' She stood in the middle of the room, the dark green velvet jacket she wore darkening her hair to the same black as her dress, her eyes a deep glowing green.

'No drink?' Rick took a step towards her.

She stood her ground, proudly erect. 'Just the keys.'

'You can have them back——' he stood only inches away from her now, his warmth reaching out to her, the tangy smell of his aftershave and the faint aroma of the cheroots he smoked discernible to her—'if you'll give me one kiss first,' he prompted softly.

'No,' she scorned.

'Then no keys,' he shrugged.

'Mr Dalmont——'

'Shanna,' he mocked.

'This is blackmail,' she snapped.

'You see what you've made me resort to,' he groaned.

'I think I'd rather get a taxi and let Henry make his own assumption about why you have my car,' she turned away.

'No!' Rick pulled her round roughly. 'No, Shanna, I can't let you go . . .' His head bent down and his mouth captured hers.

She knew that fighting him would do no good as soon as she felt the steel of his body in front of her and the strength of his arms about her. The only alternative was to limply accept the assault on her mouth by his, to offer no resistance as he probed her lips to search her mouth, drinking deeply of the warm recesses.

'Kiss me back, damn you,' he raised his head enough to rasp, a wild light of recklessness in his black eyes. 'I've got you this far, you aren't going to leave now!' His mouth claimed hers once again, ravaging her softness, desperately trying to evoke a response from her.

And she couldn't give him one, wouldn't give him one. This man was taking, he wasn't giving, and she wouldn't give to him either.

'Damn you!' he finally thrust her away from him, turning his back on her. 'Go if you want to!'

'I want to.' Shanna straightened the smoothness of her silky hair, moistening her lips, already feeling their tenderness from his onslaught. 'My keys,' she reminded him.

He thrust his hand into his pocket, throwing the keys at her. 'Drive carefully,' he muttered as she walked towards the door.

His concern stopped her in her tracks, and she looked at him dazedly. 'Rick . . .?'

He turned, taking a deep breath, running a hand through his hair and ruffling its darkness. 'I'm trying to be a good loser,' he told her ruefully. 'It just isn't a role I'm used to,' he said without conceit.

His lack of apology was enough to break the tension between them, and her mouth quirked into a smile of amusement. 'Humility certainly doesn't become you!'

'No,' he sighed. 'Neither does sexual disappointment. I need a cold shower.'

Shanna was smiling openly now. 'Does that really work?'

Rick grimaced. 'I'll know that later.'

'Having no previous experience, hmm?'

'None,' he drawled.

'No one could ever accuse you of being modest,' she taunted.

Rick shrugged. 'No one has ever wanted to.'

'You're incredible!' she gasped.

'Incredible as in amazing, or incredible as in arrogant? No, don't answer that, I can guess.' He shook his head. 'You do nothing for my ego, Shanna.'

'It doesn't sound as if your ego needs anything doing for it. There are millions of women out there,' she indicated the rest of the world. 'Go after one of them, Rick. Please!'

'I can't.'

'You can! There must be——'

'I can't, Shanna,' he repeated softly. 'My reputation is going to suffer, you know,' he added lightly as he sensed her tension rising once again. 'My ladies don't usually leave ten minutes after they arrive.'

'Maybe they weren't really ladies,' she said curtly.

'Maybe not,' he conceded. 'Come on, I'll walk down to the car with you.' He grasped her elbow, taking her to the door.

She shook her head. 'That isn't necessary.'

'My mama would never forgive me for not seeing a lady to her car,' he derided.

She shrugged acceptance, knowing that to argue with him would do no good; this man was a law unto himself. 'I didn't realise your mother was still alive,' she told him as they went down in the lift.

'Both my parents are,' he nodded. 'Dad retired fifteen years ago to spend more time with Mama. She has a heart complaint,' he frowned. 'My father is almost twenty years older then her; she was only eighteen when they got married, and yet Mama is probably going to die first. I don't think my father ever expected that.'

'I'm sorry.'

'Yes, so am I,' his voice had hardened, too intent on his own thoughts to notice how much she had paled. 'They've been in love almost forty years, I don't know what Dad will do when he's on his own.' His expression became closed as they walked across the foyer and out to her car. 'I didn't mean to bore you with my family history,' he said as he opened her door for her.

'You didn't bore me,' she said slowly.

'No?' he grimaced at her air of preoccupation. 'You're giving a good impression of it.'

'No, I——' She broke off, biting her lip. 'I'd better go,' she told him lightly. 'My new boss is coming to the office tomorrow; I have to be fresh and alert for him.'

Rick returned her smile. 'I'd rather you were soft and kittenish, maybe a little sleepy, after a night in my bed.'

He made the statement in the form of a question, and for her answer Shanna switched on the ignition. 'I'll see you in the morning, Mr Dalmont.'

'Ten o'clock—Mrs Logan,' he taunted, stepping away from the car.

Rick would have been right in his assessment of her mind not being on her driving as she went home—it was far removed from that! After the way Rick had kissed her, forced his passion on her, she had been ready to walk out of his hotel room hating him more than ever, but listening to him talking about his parents, his obvious concern for his mother, somehow made him seem less the arrogant Rick Dalmont and more Ricardo, the son of Teresa. And that could be dangerous for her, could break down all the defences she had built up this last year, the defences she needed to get her through the rest of her life.

Henry's telephone call to her office at five past nine the next morning wasn't exactly unexpected. 'What you did yesterday was childish, Shanna,' he told her crossly. 'It was also unprofessional.'

'So Rick told me,' she said dryly.

'Yes—well, he was right!' her brother regained some of his composure. 'But at least he's willing to forget about it.'

'How do you know that?' she asked in a surprised voice.

'Well, the two of you had lunch together, and you were together last night too.'

'Yes, but—Yes,' she sighed. 'Although you shouldn't read too much into that, Henry.'

'Everyone else at the party was. Rick isn't known for his consistency with women, and yet he didn't leave your side all night.'

'One evening doesn't constitute a change in his character,' she derided.

'You're hardly giving the man a chance, Shanna.'

She gave an impatient sigh. 'You could be his P.R. man, Henry,' she taunted bitterly. 'But I have no intention of giving him or any other man "a chance". Perry's only been dead six months, I thought you had more loyalty to him than that.'

'I have,' he sighed. 'I liked Perry, you know that, we

all did. It's just—things were far from smooth between
you before he died. You're still young, Shanna, you
deserve to still have a life of your own.'

'I have a life. I work. I go out——'

'Always alone,' he pointed out.

'I prefer to be alone.'

'That's my whole point——'

'And you've completely missed mine,' she snapped.
'I lost my husband only six months ago. I loved Perry
very much, Henry.'

'I know,' he acknowledged quietly. 'But the way he
treated you before he died . . .!'

'He loved me,' she insisted.

'I know that too. But there are different ways of
loving. Perry loved you while the marriage and his
career were going well. But after the first accident,
when he couldn't race any more, he treated you
abominably.'

'He was lost without his racing——'

'He had you!'

'And it wasn't enough!' she said heatedly. 'It
wouldn't be for a lot of men. I understood what he
went through, you didn't, so don't presume to judge
him on what you do know. Perry loved me, he never
stopped loving me. And I loved him. I don't want to
talk about it any more,' she added abruptly. 'And I
don't want to discuss Rick Dalmont any more either.
He wants a quick affair and I don't, that's the end of
it.'

'Shanna——'

'I mean it, Henry,' she told him in a softly
controlled voice. 'One more criticism against Perry
and you're going to find this office empty when you
arrive with Rick at ten o'clock,' she warned.

'I'm not criticising him,' her brother defended. 'I'm
trying to understand.'

And he never would, no one would, because no one
knew the whole truth about Perry's first accident, or
their six months of marriage after that. And no one
ever would!

'I'll see you and Rick at ten o'clock, Henry,' she said
curtly.

'Shanna——'

'Ten o'clock.' She rang off abruptly, lacing her
fingers together to stop her hands from shaking.

For six months she had lived without curiosity or
probing from her older brother, knowing that he
respected the privacy of the problems in her marriage
before Perry died. In just two weeks Rick Dalmont
had shaken her whole life upside down, was forcing
her out from behind the wall she had built over her
emotions. Until she met him two weeks ago she hadn't
felt love and she hadn't felt hate, she had lived her life
day after day, often wishing that Perry hadn't died
alone in that second accident, that she didn't have to
spend the rest of her life without him.

But Rick Dalmont wasn't going to let her stay
behind that wall; he had even involved Henry on his
side of the argument. Some of the foundations might
be a bit shaky, but she would soon build the wall back
up again—she had to!

No one could have faulted her manner or
appearance as she welcomed her brother and Rick into
her office at exactly ten o'clock. Her manner was
coolly polite, her dress a deep shade of burgundy,
giving an ebony sheen to her hair.

But Rick wasn't at all deterred by her coolness,
grinning at her unabashedly as he mocked, 'And are
you feeling fresh and alert this morning, Shanna?'

She looked at him with unflinching green eyes,
subconsciously wondering how he managed to look so
much more impressive in his navy suit than Henry did

in his. The two men were of a similar build, both tall
and powerfully built, but there the similarity ended;
Rick Dalmont possessed an elegance and style Henry
could never hope to achieve.

'Yes, thank you, Mr Dalmont,' she replied distantly.

One dark brow quirked mockingly. 'I think I would
still prefer you soft and kittenish,' he taunted.

'And I still prefer my own bed!'

'You should have said so,' he drawled. 'I had no
preference as to the bed we used.'

The embarrassed colour in her brother's cheeks
reached the tip of his ears, and Shanna's coolness had
turned to anger. How dared he talk to her this way in
front of Henry! One look into the black eyes told her
that he would dare more than that if he had to.

She stood up, unconsciously graceful in her
movements. 'If you're ready for the tour,' she said
pointedly.

'Any time you are,' he mocked.

'Now,' she said abruptly, moving to the door. But
Rick was there before her, holding it open for her, a
teasing quirk to his mouth. She chose to ignore it,
sweeping past him with cool disdain.

She had to admire him during the next hour, the
way that he obviously had done his homework on
publishing; all the questions he asked, of Henry and
herself, and also of the people in the different
departments who now worked for him, were very
relevant and knowledgeable. Rick Dalmont was
obviously a man who didn't ask someone to do
something if he wasn't well aware beforehand that it
could be done, even if it might be difficult. He was
like a sponge, absorbing and filing away each piece of
information he received for future reference.

'It looks good, Henry,' he told her brother when
they returned to Shanna's office for coffee. Gloria was

so agog with curiosity about their new boss when she brought in the tray, she almost walked into the door on her way out, although Rick didn't seem to notice her.

Henry nodded. 'Your lawyers did a pretty thorough job of investigating before you bought *Fashion Lady*.'

'They always do,' the other man nodded, his gaze warm as Shanna handed him his cup of coffee. 'Thanks, sweetheart.'

She stiffened at the endearment, although Henry seemed not to notice anything unusual about a boss calling an employee 'sweetheart'. It made her realise that her brother still harboured some hope that she would come to like the other man.

'Surely *Fashion Lady* is rather small for the head of Dalmont Industries to interest himself in personally?' she prompted abruptly.

Cool black eyes were turned on her. 'When *Fashion Lady* is being run as I want it to be perhaps I'll move on, but until that time it remains my prime project.'

And you along with it! his eyes seemed to say. Shanna turned away, making a point of serving her brother his coffee.

'Will you be making many changes?' Henry asked interestedly.

'Some.' The other man didn't elaborate.

'Shanna has done a good job this last year.'

'I agree,' Rick nodded.

'But?' she prompted softly.

'I don't believe I said "but".' His black eyes taunted her.

'Then you should have,' she challenged.

He gave an inclination of his head, his smile mocking her. 'Perhaps I should,' he agreed, again not elaborating any further.

'Well?' she prompted after a lengthy silence.

'Well,' he nodded, obviously enjoying himself—at her expense.

Her mouth tightened. 'Just tell me if anyone is going to lose their job in this shake-up.'

Rick met her gaze steadily. 'I don't have to tell you anything, Shanna. You'll know any management decisions along with everyone else.'

'Management?' she frowned. 'Is that just you? Or do you have an entourage you take around with you?'

His expression darkened at the scorn in her tone. 'I have an entourage,' he bit out.

Her eyes widened. 'How many?'

He shrugged. 'Half a dozen highly trained people. They'll be here next week.'

'*Here* here, or just here in London?'

Rick's mouth quirked with amusement. 'Here here—they're already in London, they have been the last two weeks or so.'

'The same amount of time as you.'

'The same as me,' he nodded. 'They go everywhere that I go.'

'Everywhere?'

'Well, almost everywhere,' he chuckled throatily. 'I like my privacy at times like everyone else.'

'I can imagine,' she drawled. 'And who do "they" consist of?'

'A couple of secretaries, two personal assistants, a lawyer, and a P.R. man. Publicity is necessary some of the time,' he grimaced, 'but I want no part of it. Jack does a good job of keeping those sort of people off my back. I have a mobile office staff, we function from wherever we happen to be at the time, usually hotel rooms. It will make a nice change to have an office for a few weeks. I'm sure my people will appreciate it.'

'But there isn't room for another seven people here,'

Shanna protested. 'We barely have room for the staff we already have. Of course, there's the executive office Henry uses when he's here . . .'

'And this one,' Rick put in softly.

Her eyes widened as his words sank in. 'This one . . .?'

'Mm,' he smiled. 'You won't mind sharing with me, will you, Shanna? It seems a pity to throw someone else out of their office for the short time we'll be here. My two assistants, Jack and Peter, can take Henry's old office, Petra and Kate can move in next door with Gloria. Did you do anything about getting someone in to change this room?' he demanded abruptly.

Shanna was too stunned by his reorganising of his private staff into her offices to do more than nod. 'I have a man coming in this afternoon to discuss it.'

'Good girl,' he said appreciatively. 'Make sure you tone it down in here. Hell, I don't have to tell you, you've lived with this the last year,' he derided.

Henry looked puzzled. 'You're having this office redecorated?'

'Yes,' Rick drawled. 'Blue and white are my least favourite colours.'

'Oh, I see,' the other man nodded. 'I've always liked this office myself, but if you don't like it . . .'

'I thought maybe a restful green or brown,' Rick answered Henry, but he was looking at Shanna.

It was an instruction, she knew that. She also knew it was going to be nearly impossible to share an office with Rick for the next three months while she worked her notice.

'Make sure it's ready for Monday,' he added curtly.

'That's too soon—'

'I don't care what it takes,' he told her grimly. 'Triple time over the weekend, a bonus, whatever. But I want it changed before I come in here Monday.'

'I'll do my best,' she said tightly.

'That's good enough for me,' he nodded, his mouth twisted derisively. 'Well, I think that's all for now, don't you, Henry? We've taken up enough of Shanna's time for one morning, we mustn't keep her from her work any longer,' he taunted.

'The magazine has never run itself,' she told him tightly.

The two men stood up. 'Come to dinner tonight, Shanna,' Henry invited softly, taking one of her hands in his in silent apology for their argument on the telephone earlier this morning. 'I'd like to talk to you.'

She squeezed his hand. 'Not tonight,' she refused softly.

He glanced over at Rick and then back to Shanna again. 'You have a prior engagement,' he realised.

'No,' she answered tautly. 'I just don't feel— sociable today. I'd like to be alone tonight.' The last was said for Rick's sake as much as Henry's.

'Everyone needs to be alone sometimes, Henry,' Rick drawled, taking the hint.

Her brother nodded. 'I'll call you tomorrow, Shanna. Maybe we can see you some time over the weekend?'

'Maybe.' She was noncommittal, as she walked to the door with them.

'I'll see you on Monday morning, Shanna,' Rick told her with satisfaction. 'Bright and early.'

'The office opens at nine o'clock,' she said stiffly.

He nodded. 'I'll be here at eight. Have a good weekend, honey. I'll be away until late Sunday evening, so I won't see you until Monday morning,' he explained.

That suited her perfectly! A weekend free of him after two weeks of having him dog her every footstep would be a welcome relief. 'Eight o'clock,' she conceded agreeably.

He gave a grin, touching her cheek with gentle fingertips. 'I can hardly wait!'

She suffered his touch for several seconds before moving back, her smile tight. 'Neither can I.'

'I bet,' he mocked.

It took her several minutes to regain her composure after Henry and Rick had left. But at least she wasn't to have Rick's tormenting presence for the next five days; it had been worth putting up with his arrogant assumption that he could touch her just for that!

But her temples ached from just that one encounter. Three months, three *long* months——

Her eyes widened as her office door softly opened, tensing as Rick closed the door behind him. She stood up warily. 'Did you forget something?'

'Yes.' He advanced further into the room.

She frowned, looking about the tidy office. Nothing looked out of place. 'You forgot to tell me something?'

'Yes.' He stood in front of her now.

She stood her ground, her mouth suddenly dry as his dark gaze roamed slowly over her face, lingering on the parted softness of her lips. 'Yes?' she prompted nervously, feeling trapped, with her desk behind her and Rick in front of her. And he knew it, that knowledge was in the confidence of his black eyes.

'Yes,' he said again softly.

He was doing this deliberately! She should have known she couldn't escape for five days that easily. 'What is it?' she asked irritably.

'This,' he groaned, his head bending before his mouth captured hers, pulling her against the hardness of his body.

But that was the only similarity to the way he had

kissed her the night before; his lips were pleading for
her response this time, tasting, cajoling, *tempting* . . .

'Put your arms around me,' he murmured against
her lips, his hands linked at the base of her spine for
closer contact with her, the hardness of his thighs
telling her what the black glow of his eyes had already
conveyed. 'I'm going to be away almost a week,
honey,' he said softly. 'Surely one little kiss isn't going
to hurt you?'

'I don't want to kiss you.' She strained away from
him.

'I know that,' he said unconcernedly. 'But I'd hate
to change my mind about going away. Now kiss me!'
he instructed fiercely.

Shanna recognised a strength and determination
more formidable than her own, giving a small sigh of
capitulation as she put her arms about his neck and
raised her face to his.

'*You* kiss *me*,' he reminded her throatily.

'I——'

'Kiss me, Shanna!' he ground out. 'And make sure I
enjoy it!'

Her eyes were stormy as she raised her mouth to his,
instantly knowing by his lack of co-operation that he
wasn't going to make this easy for her. Damn him, he
wanted a kiss—he was going to get one!

She arched her body against his, her breasts pressed
against his chest as her hips moved slowly against him,
her parted mouth moving erotically over his. With a
deep groan his arms came about her like a vice,
drawing her into him, every hard line of his body
outlined against her, hiding none of his passionate
response to her.

She pulled away, her gaze cold as she calmly
registered the high flush to his cheeks, his eyes
darkened even more with sexual excitement. 'You

enjoyed it,' she told him icily, moving away as his arms dropped from about her.

His face tightened, his eyes narrowing as he breathed angrily. 'And all you enjoyed was knowing how you arouse me!' he rasped.

She sat down behind her desk. 'You didn't ask that I enjoy anything else. But then your sort never do.' She was deliberately insulting, hating the physical strength he had exerted over her to get his own way. 'Your own pleasure is all you're interested in.'

'I've never had any complaints,' he bit out.

'I'm sure you haven't,' she derided. 'But there's more to any relationship than being able to perform in bed. I'm sure no woman ever leaves your bed dissatisfied, Mr Dalmont, but it's still only a way of giving *you* pleasure. It would damage your ego, your self-esteem, if you couldn't tell yourself the woman had enjoyed it too. It's just another form of taking,' she dismissed scornfully.

'Was your husband a taker too?' he rasped. 'Is that why you're so familiar with the "type"?'

'Perry?' she gave him a startled look. 'No, Perry was not a taker,' she told him stiffly.

'Then why did your marriage fail?'

'It didn't fail!' Her eyes blazed.

'So your idea of a successful marriage is affairs on the side?' Rick taunted harshly, a white ring of tension about his mouth.

She swallowed hard, hating him more than ever in that moment. 'I've never had an affair,' she told him dully, knowing that hadn't been what he meant at all, but still too raw to accept the truth.

'No, but your husband had plenty.' Rick felt no such reluctance. 'Maybe you aren't a giver either.'

She looked at him with dull green eyes, the fire having left her face and body. 'Maybe I'm not,' she agreed evenly.

'Shanna——'

'I apologise if I was rude to you just now,' she told him coolly. 'I had no right to say the things I did.'

'Of course you did, if you felt them. You're going cold on me again,' he realised angrily. 'I really felt as if I was getting through to you yesterday and this morning, but now the cold Shanna is back,' he said grimly. 'Is it because I mentioned your husband and his affairs?'

'Not at all,' she dismissed distantly. 'I don't think it was any secret then or now that Perry had—other women.'

Rick's eyes were narrowed to black slits. 'But it still hurts you, nonetheless.'

'Did you think it wouldn't?'

'I hoped not! It means you still love him,' he bit out harshly.

'I've told you I do,' she nodded.

'But he's *dead*, Shanna. I'm alive, and I——'

'Want me,' she finished dully. 'Yes, I know. But want and love aren't the same thing. Even if I didn't still love Perry, I could never involve myself in so selfish a relationship as wanting someone.' She shook her head. 'I can never involve myself with *you*.'

'We'll see,' he told her fiercely. 'I have three months of sharing this office with you, Shanna. And I'll break you down, you'll see.'

He wouldn't break her down, she knew that. But nevertheless, three months was a long time. It could be a lifetime for her.

CHAPTER FOUR

SHANNA had prepared herself for another confrontation with Rick on Monday morning, but it wasn't he who entered her office at five to eight, it was another man, a man she didn't know, and yet one who was startlingly familiar.

Her gaze flew to the photograph of Perry that stood on her desk, the over-long blond hair and laughing blue eyes, the firm chin and lean capable body. The man standing in the doorway could have been his double!

'I haven't disturbed you, have I?' The man frowned his puzzlement at her suddenly pale face. 'I thought you told me to come in when I knocked.'

The first thing she realised was that his voice differed drastically from Perry's; his accent was distinctly American, the Bronx by the sound of it. And his nature looked as if it might be a little more intense than Perry's too, the laughter lines beside his eyes were not as plentiful. But the physical similarity was undeniable, and she couldn't seem to stop staring at him.

'Miss Logan?' he prompted concernedly.

'*Mrs* Logan,' Rick Dalmont corrected as he walked past the other man and into the room with a confidence that bordered on arrogance. He looked at Shanna with narrowed eyes, his formal appearance in a brown three-piece suit and cream shirt doing nothing to detract from the physical awareness of her in his eyes. 'What's the matter, Shanna?' he taunted. 'Seen a ghost?'

She gasped at the cruelty in his face, and tears welled up in her eyes, her throat moving convulsively.

'Come back later, Lance,' Rick turned to growl at the other man.

'But——'

'Later!' he rasped, moving purposefully around the desk towards Shanna.

She wasn't aware of the man called Lance moving, but she knew seconds later by the soft click of the door closing that he had indeed gone. She couldn't hold back the sobs any longer, and she buried her face in her hands as the tears flowed freely.

'Shanna——'

'You knew!' she flinched as Rick's hands touched her shoulders, glaring up at him. 'You knew that man—Lance looks like Perry!'

'Almost mirror image,' he nodded, and moved away, his hands thrust into his trousers pockets, his expression brooding. 'He's one of my assistants, his name is Lance Edwards. But I didn't know seeing him would affect you this badly.'

'Didn't you?' she choked her disbelief. 'I think you knew exactly how it would affect me—and that you're cruel enough to enjoy my reaction.'

He shook his head. 'When we first met I had no idea . . . Lance has worked for me for over ten years, Shanna, and until I saw that photograph of your husband on your desk last Monday I had no idea of the likeness between the two of them——'

'Perry's photograph was always in the newspapers when he was racing.' There was still accusation in her voice.

'And after,' Rick nodded. 'But I was usually too busy looking at the beautiful *Shanna* Logan to notice what her husband looked like.'

She blinked. 'You knew what I looked like before three weeks ago?'

He nodded again. 'And wanted you. But you

were married, were the socially popular Shanna Logan.'

'And I didn't have affairs.'

'No,' he acknowledged ruefully. 'So the grapevine informed me. Shanna, about Lance——'

'That was unforgivable,' she said bitterly. 'You could at least have warned me.'

'We didn't exactly part the best of friends last week, otherwise I might have done. It really did slip my mind, sweetheart——'

'Don't!' she shuddered at the endearment. 'Please don't.'

Anger blazed from his coal-black eyes. 'I'll call you what I damn well please,' he rasped.

'I hope that gives me the same privilege,' she snapped. 'Because I think you're a——'

'I think we both know your opinion of me,' he cut in harshly. 'It doesn't need any repeating, especially from such pretty lips.' His mouth twisted ruefully. 'I was going to ask if you'd missed me the last few days, but I think I already know the answer to that.'

'Yes!' she hissed, her mind still trying to assimilate the fact that there was a man in this building who could be Perry's double. The shock of seeing Lance still made her tremble.

Rick sat on the side of her desk. 'Aren't you even interested in where I've been?'

'Not particularly.'

He shrugged. 'I'll tell you anyway. I've been home to see my parents.'

'Your mother——'

'Is fine. Thanks,' he added warmly at her show of concern. 'I just hadn't been home for a couple of months, and as I'm an only child my mother tends to worry about me. At thirty-seven it's a little ridiculous, but I like to humour her.'

Yes, she could imagine that whatever else this man was he was a good son. He would have been brought up with all the Spanish sense of family unity and closeness, wouldn't shirk his duties as a son no matter what.

But she didn't want to like anything about this man, not even his respect and love for his family. He was cruel and barbaric, and she hated everything about him.

'What do you think of the office?' she prompted tautly.

He looked at the pale green and cream painted walls, even the carpet changed from deep blue to a pastel green. 'It looks fine,' he nodded.

'Is that all you can say?' she gasped. 'The men were here until ten o'clock last night finishing off, and all you can say is that it looks fine!'

He shrugged. 'There isn't a lot else that can be said about green and cream walls,' he derided.

'You were vocal enough about the blue and white!'

'Because I didn't like it.'

'I take it that means you do like the new colour scheme?'

'Oh, I get it,' he smiled. 'Yes, I like it very much, Shanna. You did a good job.'

She stiffened at his patronising tone. 'And I wasn't seeking praise from the master like all the other simpering women who adorn your life!' she snapped.

'What a nasty little tongue you have at times, my darling.' He bent forward, his face only inches away from hers. 'Careful I don't bite it off one of these days—or nights.'

She blushed at his implied intimacy. 'I had a desk moved in for you over there, Mr Dalmont,' she pointed to the large wooden desk that had been placed in front of the other large window in the room. 'Please use it.'

'Oh, I will.' But he made no effort to move.

'Then do so now!' Shanna snapped her agitation.

'In a minute,' he dismissed. 'Lance *isn't* Perry, Shanna, just remember that,' he warned softly. 'If you have to imagine anyone as your husband I'd rather it was me—with all the privileges that go with the role.'

'You're disgusting!'

'I'm staking a claim,' he corrected grimly. 'One you would be well advised to heed.'

'No one could ever take Perry's place!'

'Not even Lance?' he taunted softly.

She stood up noisily. 'No one! Now if you'll excuse me I——' she didn't get any further, for the door was flung open noisily, and a beautiful blonde woman of about thirty stood in the doorway, the light blue dress she wore clinging lovingly to her tall voluptuous curves, her shoulder-length fair hair softly waving and very feminine, her make-up heavy without being too much. She was a very attractive woman, if a very angry one at the moment. And Shanna had never seen her before, she was sure of that.

'Rick, I refuse to work in the same office as that moron Jack!' she burst out furiously, her beautiful face twisted in anger, her body moving in natural seduction as she came further into the room.

Rick sighed and stood up. 'Jack isn't a moron, and you know it. And I wish the two of you would settle your differences away from work!'

'We don't have any differences,' the woman snapped. 'At least, none that couldn't be solved if he left.'

'Or you did,' Rick pointed out softly.

'Oh, Rick, you don't mean that!' She moved up close to him, touching his cheeks with caressing fingers. 'What would you do without little old me?'

'I'd have harmony among my personal staff,' he

said derisively, removing her hand to hold her at arm's length. 'I don't believe you've met Shanna Logan,' he drawled, knowing very well that the two women had never met before. 'Shanna, this is my other personal assistant, Cindy Matthews. Cindy, this is the editor of *Fashion Lady*, Shanna Logan,' he introduced smoothly.

For some reason it had never occurred to her that Rick's second assistant would be a woman. She didn't know why it hadn't, women could definitely go as far in business nowadays as men, and Rick Dalmont would like women about him at all times. The intimacy with which Cindy Matthews treated him seemed to imply that their relationship didn't always exist just on a business level. That definitely didn't surprise her!

The other woman was looking at her with equally speculative blue eyes. 'You aren't what I was expecting,' she said bluntly. Another American! Shanna had a feeling that all Rick's personal staff would be.

She gave a smile; the other woman's directness appealed to her. 'I could say the same about you,' she drawled derisively.

Cindy returned the smile. 'You were expecting a man, huh?'

'Yes,' she admitted.

'So was I when she came for her interview,' Rick revealed dryly. 'She signed all her correspondence with my New York office C. Matthews. I was a little surprised when a woman turned up.'

'Admit it was more than a little,' Cindy taunted.

'All right,' he laughed. 'I was more than a little surprised, I was astounded.'

'He doesn't like women working for him,' Cindy confided to Shanna.

'Really?' she taunted. 'Now that does surprise me.'

'I think he finds them a distraction.'

'Then how did you get the job?' Shanna joined in the teasing, liking the fact that Rick was on the receiving end of the mockery for a change; she doubted it happened very often!

'Her qualifications were too good to pass up,' Rick drawled. 'Thirty-eight, twenty-four, thirty-four.' He laughed at Cindy's look of outrage. 'I'm right, aren't I?'

'You're the expert,' Cindy nodded. 'Now what are you going to do about my working conditions?'

'You know the rules, Cindy,' his own humour faded. 'You share with the boys as usual.'

'But you know how strained things are between Jack and me,' she pouted.'

'I also know why,' he said grimly. 'I warned you about involvements like that in the beginning. It doesn't work in a close working relationship like the one we have.'

Shanna instantly revised her opinion of Rick being emotionally involved with the other woman, he wouldn't make one rule for his employees and another one for himself. If he disapproved of relationships between his employees then he wouldn't indulge in them himself either. Then why make her the exception? Because he had known from the first that she would never stay on and work for him!

'Perhaps Miss Matthews——'

'Cindy,' the other woman invited.

'Shanna,' she returned. 'Perhaps you would like to share an office with Jane Meakins, the assistant editor? I'm sure she wouldn't mind, and——'

'But I would,' Rick rasped. 'Cindy made her bed, and now she'll have to lie on it.'

'But not with Jack,' Cindy snapped.

He shrugged. 'I seem to recall you weren't saying that a week or so ago.'

'You're an unfeeling swine!' Cindy turned on her heel and slammed out of the room.

Shanna felt dismayed to have witnessed such a scene, knowing that Rick wasn't going to thank her for her interference either. She had only been trying to help, and—She gave him a sharp look as he began to chuckle.

'Don't look so worried,' he mocked lightly.

'But Cindy——'

'Knows damn well that she'll be sharing with Jane by tomorrow,' he mused.

'But you told her——'

'It's a little game Cindy and I play; I win the first round, but she always wins the battle. It's been that way ever since she came to work for me three years ago.' He shook his head. 'I think she lets me think I've won to save my pride.' He sighed. 'I guess I'd better go and talk to Jane. Unless you would prefer to do it?' he arched dark brows.

'No, thanks,' Shanna refused dryly. 'I wouldn't want to spoil your—game.'

'Shanna——'

'Besides,' she added mockingly, 'I have a feeling Jane would just love you to go into her office and see her. It will start her week off perfectly.'

His eyes were narrowed. 'What's that supposed to mean?'

'You must know that all the female staff on the magazine are half in love with you already,' she scorned, having heard nothing but speculation and admiration for Rick Dalmont for the remainder of the previous week.

'All except its editor!'

She nodded coolly. 'Don't feel too bad about that, Rick. You can't win them all.'

'I don't want them all,' he paused at the door, 'I want you. And I'm going to have you,' he told her confidently.

She glared at the closed door after he had left. He wasn't going to 'get' her at all—no one was. She took two tablets out of her handbag, swallowing them down, wondering if her nervous system was going to be able to take working with Rick.

She almost choked on the tablets as Gloria came into her office, her hand shaking as she put the glass of water down. 'Doesn't anyone knock any more?' she snapped irritably. 'People have been walking in and out of this office today as if it was a railway station!'

'Sorry,' Gloria said without remorse. 'I just arrived, and—Did I hear Rick Dalmont say he *wants* you?' Her eyes were wide with speculation.

Shanna drew in an angry breath, thinking fast. It was one thing for her to know Rick's intent, quite another for the whole of the staff of *Fashion Lady* to know it too. 'You only heard part of the conversation, Gloria,' she told her secretary calmly. 'You may as well know that I've handed in my resignation at *Fashion Lady*. Mr Dalmont was merely—merely trying to talk me out of it.'

'And did he?' Gloria gasped.

'No.'

'You're really leaving?' the other girl frowned.

'Yes.'

'But that's terrible! What is it, don't you like Mr Dalmont?' she asked avidly.

Much as she liked Gloria and valued her services as her secretary, she also knew the other girl was an incurable gossip. The fact that she was leaving *Fashion Lady* would be broadcast over the whole building by lunchtime, but she wanted no speculation as to the reason she was leaving. It was no one's business but her own.

'I like him very much,' she lied. 'I just have the offer of another, more interesting job.'

'Where?' Gloria asked interestedly.

'It's all a little delicate at the moment, Gloria,' she invented. 'I'd rather not talk about it yet.'

'Oh,' the other girl looked crestfallen. 'Well, we'll be sorry to see you go.'

'Yes.' Shanna held back her smile, sure that every female member of staff would prefer to see Rick Dalmont walking about the building than her. A month after she had gone these people would have trouble remembering her face. She couldn't blame them for that, the new owner was more important than old management.

She was hard at work when Rick came back to the office fifteen minutes later. She didn't look up, she didn't need to, she just knew it was him as if by instinct.

'Do you mind?'

She looked up slowly. 'Mind?' she frowned, her concentration on a fashion layout broken.

'If I smoke.' He held up a cheroot. He was seated behind his own desk, a huge file opened in front of him.

'No, go ahead,' she nodded, bending back to her work.

'Some people don't like the aroma.'

'Really?' He was surrounded by smoke when she glanced up at him this time.

'Mm, I suppose if you don't smoke yourself it can be unpleasant.'

'Yes,' she answered vaguely.

'Personally, I've always found the——'

'Rick, if we're to share this office you'll have to get on with your work and I'll have to do mine,' she told him in a carefully controlled voice. 'I don't mind if you smoke, I don't mind what you do, I just want to get on with checking this layout—Amy is waiting for it.'

His eyes narrowed through the smoke. 'I meant what I said earlier, Shanna,' he said softly. 'Lance may look like Perry, but he isn't him. And I'll never stand for you going out with him.'

'I have no desire to go out with him. As *I* told *you* earlier, no man could ever take Perry's place.'

'*This* man is going to,' Rick bit out grimly.

'I thought you didn't like to get involved,' she taunted.

'I don't. Three months will be long enough for me.'

'More than long enough for me.' She stood up. 'I have to go and see Amy in Fashion. I'll see you later.'

His mouth twisted. 'I don't intend going anywhere.'

Shanna swept past his desk and out of the room, her head high as she made her way to the Fashion Department, spending over an hour with Amy Roberts going over the latest fashion layout. She knew she was being more thorough than usual, malingering, not wanting to return to her own office. And this was only the first day!

'Hey, Shanna.'

She turned at the sound of that lighthearted voice, smiling as she recognised Cindy Matthews. 'Hello,' she returned softly.

Cindy walked down the corridor to join her, a friendly grin on her face. 'I just wanted to apologise for this morning.' She shrugged. 'Rick and I like to rile each other, but I guess I forgot we weren't alone.'

'It's all right—Rick explained.'

'I'll bet he did!' the other woman grimaced. 'He's a fantastic guy to work for, and most of the time we get on great together. But he really is mad about Jack and me.'

'You were friends?'

'A bit more than that,' Cindy admitted ruefully. 'It was a stupid thing to do, Rick told me the rules, but I couldn't resist the big ape.'

'Rick?' she taunted.

'Jack,' the other woman laughed. 'You could never call Rick an ape. He has style, from the top of his head to the tip of his toes.'

'And Jack doesn't?' she teased, reaffirming the fact that she liked this woman, liked her friendliness and her blunt way of speaking.

Cindy pulled a face. 'Oh, he has style—too much of it. He can't resist any pretty face that comes along. He was making a play for one of the secretaries here the last time I saw him.'

Shanna had the impression that the lighthearted words hid a wealth of pain. No matter how lightly Cindy dismissed Rick's P.R. man she liked him much more than she was willing to admit, maybe even loved him. She couldn't understand how any man could resist Cindy; she was beautiful, intelligent and witty. What more could any man want?

'But enough about Jack,' Cindy brushed him aside as if he weren't important. 'I really am sorry about this morning.'

'I told you, it doesn't matter,' Shanna assured her. 'Has Rick told you yet that you'll be sharing with Jane as from tomorrow?'

Cindy grinned. 'Not yet, but I guessed it. He'll just keep me waiting a while before he tells me.'

'Another part of the game?' she mocked.

'I suppose it is,' Cindy answered slowly. 'A game, I mean. But then most of life is, isn't it?'

'There seem to be more losers than winners.'

'Hey, that's cynical!' Cindy frowned.

Shanna shrugged. 'It's also the truth.' She gave a regretful smile. 'I'd better be getting back.'

'No, come along and meet the gang.' Cindy put a hand on her arm. 'They're all dying to meet the first women ever to——' she broke off, biting down on her bottom lip.

Shanna raised dark brows. 'Ever to what?' she prompted softly.

The other woman grimaced. 'Me and my big mouth!'

'Ever to what?' Shanna repeated firmly.

Cindy sighed. 'Rick has been pretty impossible since he met you. We all figured it's because you turned him down.'

'How do you know his mood has been because of me? It could be some other woman——'

'No way,' Cindy shook her head confidently. 'He went to a party, met you, threw that bozo out of the hotel—Sorry,' she added ruefully. 'The bozo was Anna Kalder—the actress. At least, she thinks she is. She had cotton-wool between her ears. I don't know where Rick gets them from. All his women are beautiful, but a bit lacking in brains, you know.'

'Maybe he prefers them that way,' Shanna dismissed coolly, not at all interested in Rick Dalmont's 'women'.

'You disprove that idea,' Cindy grinned. 'A woman with brains and beauty at last!'

She returned the smile wryly. 'Too much brains to get involved with a man like Rick.'

'Mm, that's what we figured,' the other woman replied seriously. 'But he hasn't given up, has he? You have to admire his singlemindedness.'

'Believe me, Cindy,' she scorned, 'I don't have to admire anything about him—and I don't.'

Cindy whistled through her teeth. 'You just have to come and meet the others, they'll never believe it if I tell them.'

'Tell them what?' Shanna managed to ask as she was half dragged down the corridor.

'That you've managed to resist Rick this long because you really *don't* like him. He's had other women play hard to get,' she shrugged. 'But that's all it was—pretence. You're the genuine article.'

'I may be,' Shanna admitted. 'But I don't intend broadcasting the fact.'

'You won't have to.' Cindy stopped triumphantly outside the executive office Henry had always used in the past. 'Just to listen to you is enough.'

'Cindy——'

'Just come and meet everyone,' she persuaded. 'Rick should have introduced us all by now.' She grinned. 'You'll have to excuse him, sexual tension makes him forget his manners!'

She had opened her mouth to give a sharp retort when the office door opened unexpectedly, and the words froze on her lips as she gazed up at Lance Edwards, unable to believe even now how like Perry he was. She had persuaded herself the last two hours that she had blown the likeness up out of all proportion in her mind. But she hadn't—oh, she hadn't!

'Mrs Logan?' he frowned as she stared at him wordlessly.

'*Mrs?*' Cindy echoed in disbelief. 'Hey, you aren't married, are you?' she gasped.

'Widowed,' Shanna managed between stiff lips.

'Thank God for that,' the other woman sighed. 'Oh, not that your husband is dead,' she added hastily. 'I just thought for a moment that Rick had broken all his own rules and gone for a married woman.'

'Why don't you shut up, Cindy,' a man drawled from inside the room, 'before you stick your foot in your mouth any further.'

She turned blazing blue eyes on the man. 'Mind your own damned business!' she snapped. 'How was I supposed to know Shanna was married?'

'By making a few enquiries before you jumped in with both feet,' he taunted, tall and dark, very good-looking in an obviously muscular way, turning a seductive smile in Shanna's direction. 'You'll have to excuse Cindy, she never stops to think before she speaks.'

'Just because I don't nose into other people's lives——'

'It's my job to nose,' he returned tautly. 'And when I have to I hush up whatever Rick says I should.'

Shanna had listened to the exchange with growing awareness that this must be Rick's P.R. man Jack. 'And what did he tell you to hush up about me?' she asked tartly.

'I——'

'The whole thing,' Lance answered for the other man. 'Rick is very newsworthy, but he's deliberately kept your name out of the newspapers.'

She turned shadowed green eyes on the blond man. 'Why?'

'To protect you——'

'I don't need protecting,' she said sharply. 'And even if I did I wouldn't ask it of a man like Rick Dalmont.' She became aware of the sudden silence in the room once she had finished, and turned slowly to find Rick standing in the corridor behind her. 'Perhaps you would like to explain,' she said tautly.

'Gladly,' he nodded, his expression cold. 'If I knew what it was I had to explain.'

Nothing ever shook this man's confidence! Her mouth tightened angrily. 'Why everyone seems to assume that I'm your latest conquest,' she snapped. 'Someone whose name you're keeping out of the papers in connection with yours. Can you tell me why everyone thinks that?' she demanded.

'Do they?' he taunted.

'Obviously!'

'Perhaps we could talk about this later, Shanna,' he bit out softly, aware of their stunned audience even if she wasn't. 'In the privacy of your office.'

Did the others notice the slight emphasis on the word privacy? She certainly did, realising just what she had done. Her antipathy towards Rick should have been kept between the four walls of her office, not displayed in front of these people who had respected and worked for him for years. 'I'm sorry,' she said stiltedly. 'I—Excuse me,' and she turned and fled, ignoring Rick as he called her name.

She was behaving like a fool today, had decided to act so cool, and instead she had been stupid. Stupid, stupid, *stupid*! Rick certainly wouldn't let her get away with that, her excuse that seeing Lance Edwards this morning had unnerved her wouldn't make any difference to a man as hard as Rick Dalmont. And seeing Lance Edwards, his likeness to Perry *was* no excuse for her rudeness to Rick just now, rather she should be thanking him for keeping his interest in her *out* of the newspapers!

'Hey, are you all right?'

She looked up from her desk to find Cindy had followed her back to her office, coming in to close the door behind her.

'Rick sent me after you,' she explained gently as she came to stand at Shanna's side, her hand resting lightly on her shoulder in silent comfort.

Shanna swallowed hard. 'Rick did?'

Cindy smiled. 'Don't worry about what happened just now. Rick can take it. Believe me, this will all blow over in a few days.'

'Rick doesn't appear to me to be the forgiving type,' she grimaced.

Cindy shook her head. 'He cares about you, Shanna——'

'No! No, he doesn't. He——'

'Yes, Shanna,' Cindy insisted firmly. 'I should have guessed from the beginning, we all should. He doesn't usually give a damn about the publicity his lady-loves get when they're with him, and neither do they. But he's tried to keep you out of it from the be-ginning——'

'Because I'm not one of his lady-loves!'

'I know that,' Cindy sighed. 'We all know that—now. But I think we half guessed it already. He was only trying to help you, Shanna, to protect you.'

'But Shanna doesn't need protecting.' The man himself walked in, lacking none of the confidence that was a fundamental part of him. 'Do you, honey?' he derided.

Cindy looked away uncomfortably—an emotion Shanna felt sure was alien to the other woman. 'I—er—I'll get back to my office.'

'You do that,' Rick drawled pleasantly.

'To answer your question,' Shanna snapped once they were alone, 'I can take care of myself, from the press or anyone else.'

'And if you don't always need to?'

'Even then,' she nodded coolly. 'However,' she sighed, 'I do owe you an apology for any embar-rassment I may have caused you just now. I forgot where I was for a moment.'

He raised dark brows. 'Apology accepted.'

'But unexpected,' she derided.

'Yes.'

She gave an unwilling smile at his bluntness. 'I don't mind admitting when I'm wrong.'

'Then have dinner with me tonight.'

'Implying that I've been wrong to refuse you in the past?' she mocked.

Rick grinned, his good humour seemingly restored. 'You learn fast, Shanna.'

'So my college professors always told me,' she nodded. 'They also taught us a sense of self-preservation, so if you don't mind I'll refuse your invitation to dinner.'

'Self-preservation?' he echoed softly. 'You make it sound as if you aren't as immune to me as you would like to be.'

She flushed, realising she should never give this man an advantage of any kind, not even a verbal one. 'It's just a figure of speech,' she dismissed abruptly.

'Nothing personal, huh?'

'Nothing,' she bit out. 'Rick, would you rather I moved next door with Gloria and your two secretaries come in here? I'm sure it can't be very convenient for you this way.'

'Maybe not,' he shrugged. 'But it sure is a hell of a lot more interesting. You won't change your mind about dinner?'

'No.'

'I'll see you later, then. I have a luncheon appointment in half an hour,' he explained. 'A failing airline I might be able to bail out.'

Her eyes widened. 'Don't you ever stop acquiring new businesses?'

'Nope,' he shrugged. 'I've found no viable substitute to that challenge yet. Maybe when I do I'll work and play a little slower.' He moved swiftly around her desk and kissed her hard on the mouth, a gleam of satisfaction in his eyes as he raised his head at her lack of resistance. 'You see, you're getting used to my kissing you. Pretty soon you'll be so used to it you won't even look surprised.'

'I doubt it,' she said tautly, indignation burning within her at his audacity.

'You will.' He straightened, moving to the door. 'By the way, I'm taking Lance with me, so don't get the idea that you can sneak back to his office once I've gone.'

She stiffened at his insinuating tone. 'I don't *sneak* anywhere in this building, Mr Dalmont. Until a few days ago, I ran it! As for going to that particular office again, Cindy thought I should be introduced to the rest of your staff, something you apparently didn't think of.'

He scowled at her intended rebuke. 'I've had other things on my mind.'

'Cindy had an idea about that too,' she taunted.

'I'll just bet she did!' His scowl deepened. 'That young woman is getting too big for her pants—trousers,' he amended in a slow drawl. 'Pants are men's shorts over here, aren't they?'

'I'm sure you know that they are.'

'Just checking.' His humour seemed to be back intact. 'I'll do the introductions when I—when Lance and I,' he corrected pointedly, 'get back from lunch. In the meantime, perhaps you could try and rub off a little of that frosty disdain you have in such abundance on Cindy. She really knows how to pick the wrong men. Jack is a great P.R. man, but as far as permanent relationships go he's no good,' he shook his head ruefully. 'Cindy's got to a stage in her life when she needs to settle down with one man, get married, have kids. Although don't tell her I told you that,' he grimaced. 'She thinks she's the original career woman.'

'There's nothing wrong in a woman having a career——'

'Not when that's what she wants, no,' he agreed. 'But Cindy's gone past that now, she needs more than a career alone can give her.'

'She can't have marriage and a career?' Shanna derided.

'She could,' he nodded, completely serious now, 'if she didn't want kids too. But there's a lot of maternal instinct inside Cindy just bursting to come out.'

'Are any of your personal staff married?' Shanna queried mildly.

'They wouldn't be any good to me if they were,' he answered instantly.

'That's an arrogant assumption——'

'It's a sensible one,' he corrected. 'No man—or woman—can give me his best when he—or she,' he derided again, 'is just longing to get back to his or her spouse. I know damn well I wouldn't be able to.'

'And if you ever marry?'

'My wife will travel with me, of course,' he stated with arrogance.

'The same couldn't apply to your staff?'

'We're a work force, not a marriage guidance council! Which reminds me, I want to talk to you about the magazine's problem page when I get back.'

Shanna frowned. 'But we don't have one.'

He nodded. 'That's what I want to talk to you about. See you later, sweetheart.'

She glared at the closed door, for once the endearment not bothering her. Only Rick Dalmont could make such an enigmatic statement and then walk out. *Fashion Lady* had never had a problem page, had never needed one. And yet she had a feeling they were going to get one.

CHAPTER FIVE

RICK was too busy to discuss anything when he got back late that afternoon. Talks on the airline had apparently progressed a further stage, and Rick was spending most of what was left of the afternoon with his lawyer, Peter Lacey, going through contract suggestions.

It was like watching a tornado at work. The two men pored over papers on Rick's desk, although Rick was definitely the more quickwitted of the two, showing he wasn't just a figurehead to Dalmont Industries but a very active member of it.

Just to watch and listen to his decisive and intricate dealings with the airline made Shanna feel tired, and it was with more than her usual relief that she packed up for the day. Her nape ached, her head throbbed, and what she needed most was a relaxing shower and a quiet dinner.

'Tired?'

She looked up to find Rick watching her unconscious kneading of her nape, his eyes narrowed. She instantly removed her hand. He hadn't paid any attention to her all afternoon and now he had to catch her in a moment of weakness! 'Of course not,' she denied stiltedly. 'I've just been bent over these layouts all afternoon.'

'Neck ache?' he persisted.

'Only a little,' she admitted grudgingly. 'Nothing a hot shower won't cure.'

He quirked dark brows, looking as immaculate and unruffled as he had first thing this morning. 'Sounds interesting,' he drawled.

Shanna pulled on the jacket of her navy blue suit, the crisp white blouse she wore underneath adding to her look of cool competance. 'There's nothing interesting about my taking a hot shower, Rick,' she told him briskly as she walked to the door. 'Goodnight,' and she swept from the room before he could come back with any smart retort. He seemed to have one for every occasion!

But her tiredness was a tangible thing, and instead of taking her shower after she had undressed and put on her robe she fell asleep on the bed. She hadn't meant to, she was invited to a friend's party this evening, and yet a short lie-down turned into a deep sleep that was only interrupted by the insistent ringing of the doorbell. By the time she had pulled herself up from the blankets of sleep that cocooned her the doorbell had stopped ringing, and she dropped back weakly against the pillows, shaking from the suddenness with which she had been woken.

'Shanna!' Rick rasped worriedly as he came striding into the room, sitting on the side of the bed as she struggled to sit up, grasping her shoulders painfully as she swayed weakly. 'What the hell is it?' he demanded, shaking her. 'Shanna, speak to me! Are you on something?' he grated roughly.

'On something?' She pushed her dark hair back out of her eyes. 'What—No,' she groaned in denial. 'No, of course not. I was tired, you know I was. I—What are you doing here?' She was coming fully awake now. 'How did you get in?'

'Your lock isn't very strong——'

'You broke in?' she gasped.

'No, I didn't *break* in,' he dismissed impatiently, standing up to thrust his hands into his trouser pockets, navy blue trousers that clung to the lean length of his thighs and legs, a lighter blue shirt fitting tautly over his chest and stomach. 'I told you, that lock is too fragile. A credit card and a little skill and I was in within seconds.'

'You broke in!' she accused.

'And what was I supposed to do?' He glared down at her, his eyes black. 'I could hear water running and no one answered the door when I rang. I knew you were tired, despite your denial earlier—you could have fallen asleep in the bath and drowned for all I knew!'

Only one thing he said made any sense to Shanna— or rather it *didn't* make sense. 'Water running?' she frowned her puzzlement.

'Yes. Can't you hear it?'

She could now, now that he had pointed it out. But where was it coming from? She didn't remember— 'The shower . . .' she realised weakly.

Rick gave her an impatient glance before striding into the adjoining bathroom, and the sound of the water spray stopped seconds later. When he came back seconds later he just stood looking down at her.

Shanna moistened her lips, then straightened her robe, checking that the belt was fastened securely before she stood up, conscious of her nakedness beneath the green silky material even if Rick wasn't. Although she had a feeling he was more than aware of it as his gaze never left her as she moved about the room.

'You were asleep.' He was finally the one to speak. 'What was the shower doing on?'

Once again she moistened her lips with the tip of her tongue. 'I was going to take a shower, and then I—then I decided to take a nap first and shower later. I—I must have forgotten to turn off the water.' She omitted the most important part, about how weary she

had suddenly felt after undressing, how she hadn't had
the strength to step beneath the water she had been
running, how she just had to lie down. She didn't tell
Rick any of that, and she didn't intend telling anyone
else of the feelings of weakness that had been
increasing lately, how sometimes she couldn't even get
out of bed in the morning. It was no one's business
but her own, she owed no explanations to anyone.

'Do you often—forget to do things like that?'

'I—Sometimes,' she dismissed lightly.

'It doesn't sound like the Shanna Logan I know.'

She shrugged. 'I'm not at work now, Rick. I'm
allowed to forget things in my own home. I was just
waking up when you rang the doorbell. I would have
been there to answer it——'

'But you couldn't get up,' Rick frowned. 'Are you
always this tired when you get home from work?'

No, sometimes she was even tireder! 'No, of course
not,' she snapped. 'Look, instead of questioning me
would you mind telling me what you're doing here?'

'Dinner,' he stated bluntly.

She flushed angrily. 'But I told you——'

'That you wouldn't have dinner with me.'

'Will you stop putting words into my mouth and listen
to me!' she snapped. 'I'm capable of speaking for myself.'

'I've noticed,' he drawled. 'But as you wouldn't
have dinner with me I decided to come and have
dinner with you.'

'I'm not going out to dinner, either with you or
without you.'

'Now you're the one who isn't listening. I said I've
come to have dinner *with* you.' He took his hands out
of his pockets. 'Which is precisely what I intend
doing. While you dress I'll get dinner.'

'Rick!' she stopped him at the door. 'Rick, I'm
going out.'

Love, romance, intrigue...all are captured for you by Mills & Boon's top-selling authors.

TAKE TWO EXCITING BOOKS FREE EVERY MONTH

A Sensational Offer from
largest publishe
JOIN OUR READE
TAKE TWO BOOKS

Every month we publish twelve brand new Romances – wonderful books by the world's biggest names in romantic fiction – letting you escape into a world of fascinating relationships, exotic locations and heart-stopping excitement. Thousands of readers worldwide already find that Mills & Boon Romances have them spellbound from the very first page to the last loving embrace.

And now, by becoming a member of the Mills & Boon Reader Service for just one year, you can receive *all twelve* books hot off the presses each month – *but you only pay for ten.*

That's right – *two books free every month for twelve months.* And as a member of the Reader

Service, your monthly parcel of books will b delivered direct to your door, postage and packing free. And just look at these other exclusive benefits:

🌹 **THE NEWEST ROMANCES** – reserve the printers for you each month and delivered direct to your door by Mills Boon.

🌹 **POSTAGE AND PACKING FREE** – un other book clubs, we pay all the extras You only pay the same as you would the shops.

🌹 **14 DAY FREE TRIAL PERIOD** – you c return your first parcel of books withi fortnight and owe nothing.

WIPE AWAY THE TEARS — atricia Lake

MAKEBELIEVE MARRIAGE — Flora Kidd

BURNING OBSESSION — Carole Mortimer

Two New Books FREE EVERY MONTH

Mills & Boon - the World's f Romantic Fiction.

ERVICE AND REE EVERY MONTH!

FREE MONTHLY NEWSLETTER – keeps you up-to-date with new books and book bargains.

SPECIAL OFFERS, recipes, patterns and competitions. This year our lucky winners are spending a fortnight in Barbados.

EXCLUSIVE BARGAIN BOOK OFFERS – available only to subscribers.

HELPFUL, FRIENDLY SERVICE from the girls at Mills & Boon. You can ring us any time on 01-684 2141.

have nothing to lose, and a whole world of romance to gain. Just fill in and the coupon today.

Mills & Boon Reader Service,
PO Box 236,
Croydon,
Surrey CR9 3RU.

REE BOOKS CERTIFICATE

o: Mills & Boon Reader Service, FREEPOST, PO Box 236, Thornton Road, Croydon, Surrey CR9 9EL.

'ES! Please enrol me in the Mills & Boon Reader Service for 12 months and send me all TWELVE latest romances every month. ch month I will pay only £9.50 – the cost of just TEN books – plus TWO OOKS FREE. Postage and packing is completely free. I understand that this ecial offer applies only for a full year's membership. If I decide not to bscribe I can return my first parcel of twelve books within 14 days and I will ve nothing. I am over 18 years of age.

ease write in BLOCK CAPITALS

ame _____

ddress _____

_____ Post Code _____

gnature _____ **9R3P**

e offer per household. Offer applies in UK only – overseas send for details. If price changes are necessary you will be notified.

END NO MONEY – TAKE NO RISKS. NO STAMP NEEDED

For you from Mills & Boon:

* The very latest titles delivered hot from the presses to your door each month, postage and packing free.

* FREE monthly newsletter.

A parcel of brand new romances – deliver direct to your door every month.

Simply fill in your name and address on the FREE BOOKS Certificate over leaf and post it today. You don't need a stamp. We will then send you the TWELVE latest Mills & Boon Romances – but you only pay for TEN.

That's *two books Free* – every month!

'Not before you've eaten,' he shook his head. 'Then if you still want to go out I'll take you. Didn't you eat lunch, is that why you look so washed out?'

She drew in an angry breath. 'You certainly know how to flatter a woman!'

'You look terrible, Shanna——'

'I don't have my make-up on,' she snapped. 'Can I help it if you don't like the naked me?'

'Oh, I like the naked you, Shanna,' he took a threatening step towards her. 'What I can see I like very much.' His long sensitive hands framed each side of her face. 'I just don't like to see the shadows under these beautiful green eyes.' His thumbtips smoothed the dark circles beneath her eyes. 'And you're so pale. Sweetheart, you don't look well,' he frowned.

'I'm always pale when I wake up,' she excused herself abruptly. 'Just give me a few minutes and I'll put on my make-up and get dressed. I'll look fine then. But I don't have anything in for dinner, Rick, nothing I could give you anyway.'

'I brought it with me,' he dismissed. 'Hotels are okay when I'm away on business, but I get a little tired of restaurant food. I went shopping for steak and salad, cheesecake, wine, and——'

'*You* did?' she looked at him in disbelief. 'You went shopping in a supermarket?'

His mouth twisted. 'You can't see me doing that, eh?'

'No,' she answered truthfully.

'To tell you the truth, I've never done it before,' he shook his head. 'It was like a jungle.'

'I'm sure you're the first millionaire they ever had in their shop.' She couldn't help her humour.

'Shanna, let me cook you dinner,' his voice was husky. 'Then if you aren't still pale I'll take you wherever you want to go.'

'And stay with me,' she realised dryly.

'Of course,' he drawled. 'Privilege of the cook.'

Shanna stepped away from him, relieved when he made no effort to stop her. 'I only have your word for it that you can cook. You're right, I did miss lunch, and I need a good dinner, not a burnt offering,' she mocked him.

'Just wait and see,' he warned. 'You'll want me to cook for you again.'

'Not if you break in I won't.' She began to brush her hair. 'Do you realise I could have you arrested?'

'But you won't,' he said confidently.

'I'm still thinking about it!' His manner angered her.

'In that case,' he stepped over the frivolous green mule slippers she had taken off before lying down on the bed, coming determinedly towards her, 'I'd rather it was for something more interesting than opening that feeble lock.'

'Rick——'

'Shanna,' he taunted, taking the brush out of her hand before pulling her hard against him. 'You have the sexiest body I've ever seen,' he murmured throatily. 'Or touched. Or wanted. You're driving me insane, sweetheart,' he groaned before his mouth possessed hers.

She told herself afterwards that her defences had been down after her sleep, that she wasn't properly awake. Whatever her excuse, she responded to Rick Dalmont with an abandonment that later made her blush with shame.

But right now there was no thought for anything but Rick's mouth moving druggingly over hers, the heat of his body pressed against her, his hands roaming freely over her slender curves.

'God, how I've waited for this,' he groaned into her

throat, his mouth moving slowly down to the hollows at its base, his tongue tasting every silken inch.

Shanna trembled against him, the first sexual excitement she had known in a long time ripping through her body in a red-hot ache, and she made no demur when he swung her up in his arms to place her on the pale green silk bedspread, curving his lean length against her side as he continued to kiss her on the mouth.

His hands moved with deft movements to the single tie-fastening of her robe, untying the simple knot, parting the silky material to reveal her nakedness. 'Oh, God . . .' he murmured shakily, his own body leaping with desire as one of his hands moved tentatively up to cup her breast, his thumb moving with sure arousal over the deep red tip. With a groan his head lowered and his lips caught the nipple in pleasure-giving movements, his tongue soft and then hard in circular movements.

Shanna arched against him, a moan escaping her throat as he bit down erotically on the hardened nipple, sucking it deeper into his mouth, tugging gently. Her breathing was ragged as he continued to caress the other breast, the other nipple now caught between thumb and finger as he squeezed with just enough pressure to make her shudder with desire.

She was lost in a haze of passion and need as he parted her legs to move between her thighs, the roughness of his clothing abrasively pleasure-giving as he moved down her body with slow kisses of discovery and desire, lingering over her navel before moving down to the mound of her womanhood.

Shanna whimpered softly as she felt his lips and tongue there, shaking so badly now she was almost out of control, her breath coming in sobbing gasps.

Rick moved up beside her, frowning his concern.

'I'm not hurting you?' he asked gently, smoothing back her hair.

She swallowed hard, shaking her head. 'I just—It's been too long—It's too much for me!' she moistened her dry lips with the tip of her tongue. 'I'm not sure I'm ready for this.'

His eyes darkened even more, a deep enigmatic black as he gazed down at her for long timeless seconds. 'Then we'll wait until you are ready.' He spoke huskily, swinging his legs off the bed to stand up. 'You're looking pale again anyway. I think I should feed you, not make love to you.' He leant over to touch her cheek with a gentleness that brought tears to her eyes. 'Dinner in ten minutes,' he said briskly. 'Is that long enough for you to dress? If not, just stay as you are.'

She couldn't do that, they both knew that. Whatever had happened just now she had no control over it, knew that Rick had been the one in control from start to finish, and to stay in this robe would be an invitation to more of the same.

Ten minutes later she was dressed in a severe black dress, its high collar and loose style giving her a look of cool sophistication rather than flattering the perfection of her body, her make-up erasing the pale and tired appearance she had had when she woke up. Rick was in the kitchen when she joined him, and she withstood his searching gaze with cool challenge, determined not to blush or show embarrassment at the intimate discovery he had made of her body. Not in front of him anyway! Later, when she was alone, it would be a different matter.

'Can I do anything to help you?' she queried distantly.

Rick's mouth twisted. 'No, thanks, I'm over it now,' he taunted.

He was being deliberately provocative, and her mouth tightened. 'Dinner smells delicious.' She refused to be drawn into an intimate conversation with him, intending showing him that nothing had changed between them because of a few moments of weakness in his arms.

'Then let's hope it is,' he nodded, and turned back to the steaks.

'You didn't answer my question,' she prompted.

'What was it?' he derided.

'Would you like me to do anything?'

'Several things,' he drawled. 'But all of them are out of the question at the moment; the meal is almost ready.'

'If you're going to be rude I'll leave you to it!' she snapped, turning to walk out of the room.

Rick caught up with her in two strides, jerking her round to face him. His eyes glittered down at her. 'Don't try and pretend that what we just shared together didn't happen,' he grated. 'It happened, Shanna,' he told her grimly. 'I know, because I still ache for you in my gut!'

'Rick——'

'I let you go this time, Shanna, but next time I won't. You understand me?' He shook her slightly.

She swallowed hard. 'I understand.'

'As long as you do.' He thrust her away from him and returned to the grilling steaks.

They ate in silence, neither of them in the mood to break it. Shanna was too full of self-recrimination, and Rick, she felt sure, was kicking himself for turning down this golden opportunity he had had to make love to her. She was determined there wouldn't be a 'next time'.

'You're a very good cook,' she told him once they had cleared away.

'Thanks,' he nodded abruptly, enjoying one of his cheroots after their meal.

'Where did you learn to cook like that?'

'University. Shanna——'

'Which university did you go to?' she asked quickly.

'What the hell does that matter?' he rasped.

'I was just interested——'

'You were just avoiding my conversation, is what you were doing,' he bit out grimly, stubbing the cheroot out in the glass ashtray. 'I'm not going to be put back in that ice-box, Shanna,' he told her tautly. 'I made love to you an hour ago, and I'm not going to let either of us forget it.'

'It was a mistake——'

'It was beautiful,' he corrected harshly. 'It was better with you than with any other woman I've ever known.'

Her mouth twisted. 'That line is far from original, Rick,' she derided. 'We also know it's untrue.'

'Damn you, it's the truth!' he told her savagely, sitting forward. 'I'm not dealing in lines here, I'm dealing in sanity—*mine*. If you want to drive me out of my mind just keep saying no.'

'I intend to!'

'And I'll just keep showing you that you really mean yes! Damn it, Shanna, I know I said I wanted to take your husband's place——'

'For three months,' she scorned.

He gave an angry sigh. 'For any amount of time. I know now that isn't possible for any man, that your husband will always remain a part of you.'

'A part you aren't interested in!' Her eyes flashed.

'Not true.' He shook his head, coming down on the carpet in front of her chair and taking her hands in his. 'Tell me about him, Shanna, talk to me. Tell me what went wrong between you——'

'No!' she wrenched away from him. 'I don't intend discussing any aspect of my marriage with you, not the beginning or the end of it. I'm Perry's widow, that's all you need to know—or respect. But you don't respect widowhood, do you, Rick?' she scorned. 'You've shown that from the first.'

'I respect the living; the dead are exactly that—dead. No matter how long you show your love and loyalty to Perry, a month, a year, *ten* years, he'll still be exactly that—dead,' Rick said grimly. 'No amount of celibacy—or loneliness—can change that.'

'I remain celibate, and lonely, through choice,' she told him raggedly. 'You obviously can't be either. Why do you always have to be proving what a macho man you are?' she derided. 'And why are you afraid to be on your own occasionally?'

He was frowning darkly. 'I'm not macho, Shanna. I could be very gentle with you if you would let me close enough. And I'm often alone, people who spend a lot of their life in hotels usually are. The others, my secretaries and assistants, all go their own way when we leave the particular company we're working with at the time.'

'I've seen the "way" you go from the newspapers,' she dismissed hardly.

'You make me sound like a sex-hungry Romeo!'

She remained unflinching in the face of his anger. 'And aren't you?'

'I enjoy women, I've never made any secret of that, not since the first time when I was sixteen. But I only have a healthy sexual appetite, not the excessive one you're implying. If I were married it would be perfectly normal for me to make love to my wife three or four times a week, although I'm told that twice is the norm,' he derided. 'And it's possibly a lot higher than that when you first marry.

You would know more about that than I do?' he raised mocking brows.

Shanna flushed, her mouth tight. 'You're doing very well without any help from me.'

A grin flashed across his harsh features before he was once again serious. 'Well I, as a bachelor, do not make love three or four times a week. I haven't made love for over three weeks, now, for instance,' he added pointedly.

The blush stayed in her cheeks this time, knowing she was the reason for his abstinance; he was nothing if not singleminded, and his pursuit of her had definately been that. 'Is that a record?' she scorned.

He drew in a harsh breath. 'As a matter of fact, yes! Does that give you satisfaction?'

'Your sex life doesn't interest me.' She turned away.

Rick straightened, looking down at her. 'It doesn't interest me much at the moment either, it's non-existant!'

'Maybe that will change tonight.' Her mouth twisted at his raised brows. 'I don't mean with me. If you come to the party with me now I'm sure there'll be plenty of women there only too happy to help you with your—little problem.'

'It isn't little.' He laughed at her indignant gasp. 'And my parents could tell you that a very stubborn child grew into a dogmatic man. I don't want any of the women at the party, Shanna.'

'You haven't even seen them yet!'

'And I'm not going to. Neither are you, for that matter.'

'What do you mean?' she frowned.

'I told you I would take you wherever you wanted to go if you didn't still look pale. You do, so you aren't going anywhere, except maybe to bed.'

'You——'

'Alone,' he drawled. 'To sleep. Now.'

'You can't order me about!' she gasped indignantly. 'If I want to go out I'll damn well go!'

'Try it,' he warned softly.

'Rick, I want to go out!'

He frowned at her near-desperation. 'Are you sure you aren't the one who's frightened of being alone? Shanna, what—Hell, are you going to faint?' he moved to grasp her arms as she swayed, her face paler than ever. 'Shanna?' he hissed as she leant weakly against him. 'What's wrong with you?' he rasped. 'Do you need a doctor?'

'No,' she dismissed through stiff lips. 'I—I think you're right, I need an early night. I've been overdoing it lately.'

Rick's arm about her waist supported her into the bedroom, his frown one of deep concern. 'It's all these damned parties you keep going to,' he said angrily. 'How can you expect to function properly when you go out every night and hold down a job in the day, especially one with the responsibilities yours has?'

'You do it,' she accused weakly, sitting down on the bed.

'I've built up an immunity over the years.' He pushed her hands away to pull her dress off her shoulders. 'From what I understand you've only been behaving this way since your husband died.' He put his arms around her to release the fastening of her bra. 'Calm down,' he snapped as she flinched. 'I'm putting you to bed, not raping you.'

'But I can undress myself——'

'And I can do it with much less effort.' He talked down her protests, laying her on the bed to remove the rest of her clothes, going over to the dressing-table to search through her drawers for a nightgown and coming back with a black lacy one. 'I'll be having fantasies about you all night,' he mocked gently as he pulled the garment over her head. 'Just for a change!' He stood her up to pull back the bedclothes and tuck her comfortably beneath the crisp sheets, sitting on the side of the bed to gently touch her cheek. 'You have to slow down, Shanna. The body, your body, can only take so much before it burns itself out. Heed the warnings, sweetheart, your tiredness, your weakness. If you don't you'll kill yourself.'

Sleep wouldn't be denied once he had left, and her mental decision to go to the party once she was alone became impossible as she knew she didn't even have the strength to get out of bed. Rick could have no idea how right he was. She was killing herself, slowly but surely . . .

There were no signs of tiredness about her as she entered her office the next morning, and she returned Rick's questioning greeting with cold politeness, wanting their relationship back on the strictly impersonal.

She put her burgundy-coloured briefcase on her desk-top and took out the notes she had been working on the previous evening.

Rick stood up to come over and lean on the side of her desk. 'How do you feel today?' he asked gruffly.

She looked up at him with cool green eyes. 'Just fine, thank you. Now yesterday you mentioned something about——'

'Shanna, it won't work,' he interrupted gently. 'I told you that last night. And the fantasies I had of you during the night tell me I didn't imagine one thing that happened between us in your apartment yesterday evening. I don't have that vivid an imagination!'

She swallowed hard. 'I can't work with you if you're going to constantly remind me of one lapse I had with you. I was tired, I wasn't thinking straight. Now could we talk about this problem page you mentioned yesterday?' She looked at him steadily.

For long breathless minutes he continued to look down at her, seemingly undecided about whether or not to take her lead. Finally he shrugged. 'You don't like the idea?' He straightened, every inch the businessman in his blue tailored suit and snowy white shirt.

'What makes you say that?'

'I think it was the way you pronounced "problem page",' he derided. 'You make it sound like two dirty words.'

'And isn't it?'

'A survey shows that the majority of women turn to the problem page in magazines first.'

'Whose survey?' she asked dryly.

'Mine. Oh, not personally,' he mocked. 'I had people out on the street doing it for me.'

'Where?'

He smiled. 'Central London. Satisfied?'

She shrugged. '*Fashion Lady* has always got along very well without a problem page.'

'All those women can't be wrong, Shanna.'

'Can't they?'

'No,' he shook his head decisively.

'*Fashion Lady* has always been above such things,' she dismissed.

'Then we'll just have to drag it down to my level, won't we?' he taunted abruptly. 'Because I intend to go ahead and have a problem page in the first issue of the magazine for next year.'

Her eyes sparkled with temper. 'Then why bother to tell me you wanted to talk about it?'

'Courtesy,' he dismissed. 'You are still the editor of *Fashion Lady*.'

'Not for too much longer!'

'Mm,' he nodded thoughtfully. 'Which reminds me, did you do anything about advertising for a replacement for you?'

'I've been in touch with an agency that specialises in such things. There's a couple of women who look quite promising.'

'I want to be in on the interviews.'

'Why?' she gasped. 'Don't you trust me, is that it?' Her tone was aggressive.

'You're being childish now——'

'I want to know why you feel you have to be present at interviews for prospective employees for my job,' she glared at him. 'I think I have a right to know that.'

'You have that right,' Rick nodded abruptly. 'And I have no objection to answering you. I want to be in on those interviews because I have to work with the woman who replaces you long after you're gone.'

'And forgotten,' she said tightly.

'You're never out of my mind, Shanna,' he told her throatily. 'And you know you aren't. Look, surely you can see the sense of what I'm saying?' He quirked dark brows.

'Of course,' she nodded stiltedly. 'As soon as the interviews are arranged I'll let you know. Unless you would like to do that too . . .?'

Rick gave an impatient sigh. 'No, you carry on. I can see there's going to be no reasoning with you today.' He held up his hands in dismissal.

'None at all.' Shanna stood up. 'Now if you'll excuse me, I have some work to do.'

It wasn't until she got out of the office and was walking along the corridor that she realised she had no idea where she was going! Heavens, she had allowed Rick to make her so angry that she had walked out of her own office!

'Hi, Shanna. How are you today?'

She turned thankfully at the sound of Cindy's cheery greeting. 'I'm fine,' she smiled. 'I was looking for you, actually,' she invented. 'You never did get round to those introductions yesterday, and Rick's too busy this morning for me to bother him with it.'

'Come right this way,' Cindy said lightly, as bright and bubbly as usual. 'I know the guys are all anxious to meet you.'

'The guys' turned out to be a pretty lighthearted bunch once they lost their initial awkwardness with her. Jack was exactly as she had thought he was, a flirt, Peter was very serious and quiet, and Lance was friendly without being familiar, obviously feeling she was still an unknown quantity.

'Do you enjoy the travel your work involves?' She tried to draw him into conversation, while Cindy and Jack were doing their usual bickering, and Peter was engrossed in the same papers he and Rick had been working on so intently the day before.

Lance shrugged; the two of them were in the sitting area of the office. 'It can get a little tiring, but for the most part I enjoy it. I enjoy working with and for Rick. He's a good boss.'

'Yes,' she agreed abruptly. 'I think I made—no, I *know* I made a fool of myself yesterday,' she told him ruefully. 'Rick and I don't really get on,' she chewed on her bottom lip. 'I think we both have strong personalities, and that doesn't make for working harmony.'

'But we all thought you and he—No, I guess not,' Lance drawled ruefully. 'Not after what you said yesterday. Does that mean you might be interested in a date with one of his assistants?'

'Cindy?' she taunted, not having expected this

invitation at all. It was a sure fact that Rick wouldn't approve!

Lance grinned, glancing over to where Cindy and Jack were still arguing. 'No,' he laughed, 'I wasn't thinking of Cindy.' He turned back to her, his blue eyes suddenly intense. 'Would you have dinner with me one evening, Shanna?'

'Rick wouldn't like it,' she warned him honestly.

He grimaced. 'I'm not asking Rick.'

She smiled. 'I meant he wouldn't like the two of us going out together.'

'I realise that. But I can handle it,' Lance told her quietly.

Shanna wasn't sure anyone could handle Rick's temper when he was aroused. And she also wasn't sure she should expose Lance Edwards to that. She had no doubt he was a nice man, a handsome one too, but she could never feel anything more than liking for him, despite his likeness to Perry.

'Rick explained your reaction to seeing me yesterday,' Lance spoke again as she didn't answer him. 'The reason you seemed upset.'

She frowned. 'What did he explain?'

'That I look a little like your husband. Hey, that's okay,' he soothed as she blanched. 'It doesn't bother me that you confused me with your husband for a while. I'm sure a lot of friendships have started on less than that.'

And Rick had just made certain that there couldn't even be friendship between Lance and herself. How dared he tell this man she reminded him of her husband? She knew how he dared, knew that he had told Lance that so that the other man would believe any interest she showed him was because of his likeness to Perry. And he had succeeded, damn him!

CHAPTER SIX

'You arrogant bastard!'

Shanna had remained in the executive office another half hour after turning down Lance's dinner invitation, and no one looking at her as she laughed and joked with the others could possibly have known of the anger boiling inside her.

It all came to the fore now as Rick looked up from the work on his desk with a surprised expression. 'How dare you tell Lance anything about me?' she stormed. 'What right do you have to go around telling men I only like them because they look like my husband?' she demanded furiously as he seemed to be digesting her words, taking a cheroot out of his case and slowly lighting it. 'Answer me!'

'You've spoken to Lance?' He did so.

'Obviously!'

He nodded. 'Obviously. Although I can't believe he said anything like what you're accusing me of.'

'So you didn't tell him he looks like Perry?' she scorned.

'Of course I told him that,' he rasped impatiently. 'I had to give him some sort of explanation for the way you behaved yesterday morning. Besides, the photograph on your desk only has to be seen for him to know that anyway.'

'So you deny telling him he looks like Perry because he would then think I only like him for that reason?' asked Shanna disbelievingly.

'Do you like him?' Rick snapped.

'As a matter of fact, yes!' She had found the other

man to be intelligent and interesting, and the longer she spoke to him the less she noticed any resemblance to Perry at all.

Rick stood up. 'Then I'm glad I told him what I did. And no, I don't deny I told him for exactly the reason you're accusing me of.' His expression was harsh. 'The situation between us is already confused enough without the addition of your going out with Lance.'

'I don't find it confusing at all,' she bit out. 'I don't like you, don't want to go out with you. And if I want to go out with Lance I will!'

Rick's eyes narrowed to black slits. 'Did he ask you?'

'Yes!'

'You won't go, Shanna,' he shook his head confidently, moving towards her determinedly.

She stood her ground defiantly. 'I will if I want to.' The fact that she didn't want to was none of his business.

'No!' His arms came about her like steel bands. 'Don't even think about it,' he warned raggedly. 'If you do I'll just have to do this a few times in front of Lance.' He claimed her mouth with fierce possession, bending her body into his. 'And if that doesn't work,' his eyes glittered like black opals as he raised his head, 'I'll just have to send him back to New York.'

'You wouldn't do that?' she gasped.

He nodded grimly. 'I'd do it, Shanna—believe me. Oh, I wouldn't fire him, he's too good a man for that, I'd just send him back to my head office there.'

That would be almost as bad for Lance, she knew that. The other man was very proud of his position as Rick's personal assistant, to send him back to America, in disgrace almost, would really injure his pride.

'You really are a bastard,' she told Rick with feeling.

He nodded cool acknowledgment of the fact, his mouth tight. 'If by that you mean I stake my territory and fight off anyone who comes near my property, then yes, I'm a barbarian.'

'I'm not your property. And you don't fight clean!'

'I fight with any weapons available to me,' he shrugged.

'But a man's career——'

'Is in your hands,' he drawled coldly. 'I've told you what the consequences will be if you go out with him; you know the penalty he will pay.'

'That isn't fair!' she sighed her frustration.

'Life rarely is,' he dismissed unconcernedly. 'Why not give up and go out with me, Shanna? I'll not let any other man touch you.'

'There must be some men in London that you can't get to,' she snapped.

He smiled, holding her easily in his arms as she struggled to be free. 'If there are I'll find a way, be sure of that.' His arms tightened about her. 'You're mine, Shanna, and the sooner you accept that the better.' His smile became a mocking grin. 'You'll see, I'm much easier to handle when I'm not consumed by sexual tension. And since meeting you I've known nothing else!'

'Don't expect me to do anything about that,' she told him tautly. 'Not even to get you out of my life will I go to bed with you.'

His mouth tightened. 'Not for that reason, no. Because it wouldn't get me out of your life—the opposite, I would think. I'd want to take it all over, Shanna, all your thoughts, all your smiles, your every waking moment. I'd entwine myself in your life so much you would feel haunted by me.'

'I do now!'

'As they say in the movies, "You ain't seen nothing yet, baby",' he mocked. 'At least at the moment I allow you to go home alone.'

'Oh? And who was the man who broke into my apartment last night? I'm having a new lock put on the door today, by the way,' she told him moodily. 'I don't like the idea of you being able to walk in any time you choose to do so.'

'Honey, I've just finished explaining to you that I would never leave if I had the *choice*,' he derided. 'But I'm waiting to be invited before I stay with you.'

'You'll wait for ever!'

'I don't think so.' His mouth twisted. 'I don't have that much patience. My parents would be amazed at the change you've made in me.'

'I'm sure it's only a temporary thing,' she scorned. 'Now will you kindly let me go?'

'You know the price.'

'And you accused me of being childish!' she flared at him.

'You were being at the time.'

'As you are now!' she snapped.

Rick gave a wolfish grin. 'I'm being far from childish, Shanna, I'm being *very* adult.' He curved her body more comfortably into his. 'What's one little kiss?'

'Between friends?' she scoffed.

'I never wanted to be your friend, sweetheart. Lover sounds much more—desirable.'

'If only I found you that way—desirable, I mean.'

'I've warned you about that tongue of yours, Shanna,' he rasped.

'I would think, I've had more opportunity to bite yours off than vice versa!'

He gave a deep frown of exasperation. 'You would try the patience of a saint. And as we both know, I'm

far from being that,' he mocked her scornful look.
'You can imagine that my patience is almost non-existent. Now give me that sweet mouth of yours so
that we can get on with our work.'

'Sweet, Rick?' she derided the description.

'When it isn't spouting abuse and insulting me,' he
nodded with a taunting smile.

With a resigned shrug Shanna raised her mouth to
his; she certainly never got anywhere by fighting with
this man. Her arms moved up about his neck, fitting
into the curve of his shoulder as he deepened and
lengthened the kiss. She opened her lips to him,
allowing him to search the warm cavern of her mouth
for several seconds before she bit down, just hard
enough to prove her point.

Rick was chuckling as he raised his head, releasing
her with a light tap on the nose. 'You see, you do
know how to play, after all.'

'Not by your rules,' she shook her head.

'You won't go out with me tonight?' He looked at
her with narrowed eyes.

'No.'

'Okay,' he shrugged.

She eyed him suspiciously as he went back to sit
behind his desk. He was accepting her refusal very
calmly today—too calmly. Somehow she distrusted
him more when he was this malleable. He was up to
something, she didn't know what, but it gave her an
uneasy feeling nonetheless. But there was no way he
could interfere with her plans for tonight, she wasn't
even going to be at home if he should call.

She knew the reason for his smugness all afternoon
as soon as she walked into the lounge of Henry and
Janice's London home; Rick was the only other
apparent guest! They had worked in harmony for most
of the day, had even joked together on a couple of

occasions, and not once had he mentioned the fact that he was going to be at Henry's tonight too. And she knew damn well he had known she was going to be here, knew it by mockery in his dark eyes as he greeted her now.

'You made it okay, sweetheart,' he drawled softly, but loud enough for the other couple to hear and speculate at his intimacy. 'She's such an independent lady,' he turned to smile at Henry and Janice. 'I offered to bring her out here tonight, but she insisted on driving herself.' His arm moved about her shoulders in easy familiarity. 'Didn't I, honey?' he taunted.

He had too, she knew now that this had been where he was inviting her. How he must have been laughing at her all day, just knowing that her refusal meant nothing, that he was going to see her anyway. She had the feeling that Rick Dalmont was moving in for the kill step by stealthy step—and she was slowly running out of fight!

'Yes, Rick,' she agreed dully, and her head started to pound.

'Don't feel too bad, honey,' he grinned down at her as he sensed victory. 'You can drive me home instead; I came by cab again.'

'That seems to be a habit of yours,' she said sharply.

'Only when I know I have you to drive me home.'

She moved out of the arc of his arm, moving to kiss first Janice and then Henry on the cheek, handing to Janice the flowers that she had bought for her. 'You forgot to mention that Rick would be here tonight,' she looked at them both reproachfully.

'We thought you'd come together,' Henry dismissed.

She could guess the reason they had thought that

only too well, Rick's handiwork again. 'Is anyone else coming?' she asked brightly.

'No, it's just the four of us,' Janice smiled. 'I'll just go and check on dinner.'

'Are Peter and Susan asleep yet?' Shanna asked.

'If they are it will be the first time they ever have been before eight-thirty in the evening,' her sister-in-law laughed softly. 'I put them to bed at seven-thirty every night and they never go to sleep until at least nine o'clock,' she explained to Rick.

'They're great kids,' the doting father told him. 'But I don't know where they get their energy from.'

'Certainly not from you,' Shanna mocked her brother as he slouched in a chair.

'Could I go with you to see them?' Rick requested softly.

She turned to him in surprise. 'Wouldn't you rather stay and talk to Henry? I'm only going in to say goodnight to them.'

'Would it disturb them if I came with you?'

'Janice?' she looked questioningly at the other woman.

Her sister-in-law shrugged. 'They'll probably welcome the diversion. No offence to you, Rick,' she laughed, 'but my children welcome any excuse to evade going to sleep.'

'No offence taken,' he grinned, suddenly looking boyish. 'I used to do the same thing when I was a kid.'

'It's hardly the same thing,' Shanna dismissed derisively.

He quirked dark brows. 'Oh?'

'I'm sure your nanny always gave in to you. Janice takes care of her children herself.'

'My mother took care of me too,' he said tautly.

'Really?'

'Yes—really,' he bit out. 'She grew up in a strict

Spanish household, where the children were brought up by the family and not by strangers.'

'Why don't you take Rick upstairs with you?' Henry broke the tension. 'Otherwise dinner will be ready, and they'll both be asleep afterwards.'

'Would you like to come this way?' Shanna invited stiffly, and the two of them walked up the stairs together in silence. 'I'm sorry,' she sighed as they reached Susan's bedroom door, 'I had no right to be rude about the way you were brought up.' She put a hand to her temple. 'I just didn't expect to see you here tonight.'

'I know,' he said softly, moving her hand to replace it with his own, gently massaging her tension away. 'And I didn't tell you because I thought you would cancel.'

'I probably would have done,' she acknowledged wearily.

Rick sighed at the admission. 'Does your head ache?'

'Not really. I'm just tired.'

'Again?'

'It's been another long day,' she stiffened.

'Mm,' he nodded. 'I had no idea being an editor of a magazine like *Fashion Lady* was so time-consuming. Do you usually eat lunch at your desk?'

'Usually,' she acknowledged abruptly.

'Does Jane help you enough? It seems to me——'

'I didn't come here tonight to talk about work, Rick, but to forget about it for a few hours,' she cut in firmly. 'But just for the record, Jane does more than her fair share of the work. Now let's go and see Peter and Susan before Janice calls us down for dinner.'

As Janice had predicted, both children welcomed this diversion to going to sleep, looking angelic with their newly washed golden hair and matching blue pyjamas. Rick was surprisingly good with them, not talking down to them as some adults did, but treating them as equals. He was even prevailed upon to read them another fairy-story before they tucked them up in bed.

Shanna bent over to kiss both children goodnight, not at all surprised when Susan and Peter demanded a kiss from Rick too. He accepted this as the privilege it was, wishing them a softly spoken goodnight before joining Shanna in the hallway.

'They liked you,' she told him on the way back to the lounge.

'I liked them too,' he said gruffly. 'They're beautiful children.'

'Yes.' She smiled, feeling more relaxed with him after spending time with the children.

He frowned down at her. 'You never had children with Perry?'

She stiffened with the unexpectedness of the question. 'There never seemed to be the time.'

'Didn't he like children?'

'Very much,' she frowned. 'He always got on very well with Peter and Susan.'

'Did you plan to have children with him?'

'Yes,' she said abruptly. 'We discussed having them several times. It just—never happened.'

'I'm glad.'

She gasped. 'Why?' she breathed.

'Because I'm not sure I'm selfless enough to cope with your having another man's child;' he admitted reluctantly.

Shanna drew in a ragged breath. 'You don't have to *cope* with anything, not me or my non-existent child.'

'Don't I?' Rick looked down at her as if he were seeing her for the first time. 'I think I've underestimated you, Shanna Logan.'

She had no chance to answer him, as Janice announced dinner at that moment, and the four of them enjoyed a leisurely meal together. Rick was his usual charming self, and yet as the evening progressed she noticed he was quieter than usual, his conversation lacking the usual innuendoes for her, the easy familiarity with which he normally treated her now replaced by cool politeness; even the discussion about the changes in *Fashion Lady* was conducted in a businesslike way.

'So Shanna finally got her way about that,' said Henry when Rick told him of the introduction of a problem page.

'Did she?' Rick returned noncommittally, his gaze narrowed on her flushed and guilty face.

'She suggested it herself at the beginning of the year,' her brother explained guilelessly. 'But I thought that *Fashion Lady* didn't need one, that it——'

'Got along okay without it,' Rick finished in a slow drawl.

'Exactly,' Henry nodded, warming to his subject, not noticing the way Shanna was cringing as he progressed. 'Shanna even had a survey taken, to see how the public felt about it.'

'Really?' Rick drawled, looking at Shanna with enigmatic eyes. 'Where did you do your survey, Shanna?'

She looked back at him in stubborn silence, wishing she could have foreseen this conversation and averted it. It was true, she had put forward the idea of a problem page to Henry several months ago, and had done the same research on it then that Rick seemed to have done now—and Henry had turned it down without thought. It hadn't been part of his policy.

'Shanna?' he prompted now. 'Rick was talking to you.'

'Sorry,' she blinked. 'What was the question?' she delayed.

'Where did you do your survey?' Rick answered her this time.

'Central London,' she murmured.

'Sorry?' he quirked dark brows.

'Central London,' she said more strongly. 'It showed that the majority of the women we asked turn to the problem page first,' she told him before he asked.

'I see,' he nodded.

Shanna was relieved when Henry changed the subject, although she doubted she had heard the last of it from Rick. Strangely enough he was silent on the drive back to his hotel, so she decided to tackle the problem herself.

'The arguments I used today against the problem page were Henry's,' she told him quietly, driving him this time, with no protest from him, something she was sure he hadn't noticed, since he seemed preoccupied with thoughts of his own. 'The ones he used against me, I mean,' she added.

'So I gathered,' Rick said dryly. 'But you're really in favour of the idea?'

'Yes.'

'Then maybe you wouldn't mind interviewing some applicants for that job too? I was going to ask Cindy, but . . .' he shrugged dismissively.

'Would you like to be present?' she mocked.

'Not this time,' he shook his head. 'Just make sure she has the qualifications to deal with any letters that might come her way. Some of the answers I've read in other magazines—in the course of my research, of course——'

'Of course,' she drawled.

'Well, you don't think I read them through choice?'

he scorned. 'The mess people seem to make of their lives . . .! Still, they seem to help some people, and that's what matters. But some of the replies I've read in other magazines have been enough to make the person concerned go out and throw themselves off the nearest bridge!'

'I'll make sure that she—or he—is highly qualified,' she nodded agreement. 'It wouldn't do the magazine's reputation any good if someone sued us.'

'It wouldn't do the person any good either if they were dead!'

'No,' she sighed.

Rick lapsed into silence again, resting his head back against the leather upholstery.

'Tired?' Shanna prompted softly.

'No.' He didn't even open his eyes.

'Would you like to come to my apartment for a nightcap?' she heard herself offer, then her breath constricted in her throat as she realised what she had said. She didn't want Rick in her home, so why on earth had she invited him there? What on earth was *wrong* with her! 'A—a coffee or something?' she added awkwardly.

Cool black eyes stared at her in the gloom of the car; Rick's thoughts were as enigmatic as his expression. 'Coffee last thing at night keeps me awake—or do you want that?'

She gasped. 'I——'

'Forget it, Shanna,' he rasped. 'I didn't mean to say that. And I'll take a rain-check on the coffee. Thanks anyway.'

It wasn't the answer she had been expecting, she had thought Rick would jump at the chance to spend a little more time with her, especially alone at her home. What game was he playing now? Because his behaviour had to be part of the game, his game. What was it, the 'play uninterested' routine to irk her interest in him? Because if that was the case he was going to be out of luck once again; nothing would irk her interest in the playboy he was.

She dropped him off at his hotel, acknowledging his terse goodnight with a cheery one of her own. If he thought to disconcert her with his sudden coldness he was going to be disappointed!

Rick didn't act as if he were trying to do anything to her the rest of the week, ignoring her existence most of the time, almost snapping her head off at others. When the two women came for the interviews for her job on Friday she had no idea what to expect from him; his mood was volcanic.

'The first one was too young,' he dismissed. 'The second one was too involved in her marriage.'

'*Too involved in her marriage?*' Shanna echoed incredulously. 'How can anyone be too involved in a marriage?'

'She was,' he stated flatly. 'The editor of *Fashion Lady* has to put the magazine first.'

'Then why wasn't Stephanie Simms suitable?' she frowned. 'I know she was a little young, but I was only twenty-four when I took over.'

'You had inside help.'

Her mouth tightened at the insult. 'Henry wouldn't have given me the job if he didn't consider me capable. And as for Leslie Adams, I was married, and it didn't affect my efficiency.'

'You can't give the job to both of them.' Rick sat behind his own desk, and the room was filled with smoke from his cheroots; he had been smoking a lot of them lately, she noticed.

'I don't want to do that,' she said impatiently. 'I'm just pointing out that your reasons for turning them down are invalid, as both of them were applicable to me a year ago. The magazine hasn't suffered at my hands.'

'Granted,' he nodded. 'But I stand by my opinion of Leslie Adams. Did you see the way she hesitated when I asked if she intended having children?'

'Well, it was a personal question——'

'It was a valid one from any prospective employer. I believe Mrs Adams does intend having children, no matter what she said to the contrary, and I think she intends having them soon.'

'Then why bother to try for this job?' Shanna derided.

'Why not?' he shrugged. 'It would be something to tell her children when they're grown up.'

'I think you're being unfair to her. And Stephanie Simms' age shouldn't be a black mark against her either. Someone has to give her her chance.'

'Maybe when she's older,' he dismissed callously.

'Her qualifications are excellent.' Shanna had no idea why she was defending the other girl so heatedly. It was true that Stephanie Simms did have excellent qualifications, and equally good references from her last two employers, but she hadn't really liked the other girl, finding her efforts to flirt with Rick too obvious.

'I noticed,' he drawled, his thoughts obviously running along the same lines, his smile mocking. 'Miss Simms should go far.'

'But not here?'

'No.'

'I'm sure if you called her she would be pleased to convince you otherwise,' she said waspishly.

'No doubt.'

Her mouth tightened at his calm acceptance of the other woman's attraction to him. 'You don't sound surprised,' she snapped.

Rick shrugged his broad shoulders beneath the grey fitted jacket and snowy white shirt. 'I don't believe she made any secret of her method of getting to the top.'

'Then maybe you should give her a call.'

'Maybe I will,' he nodded, his eyes narrowed.

'That should be nice for you!'

'It probably would be. Now can we get back to the subject of your replacement?'

'Of course,' she answered abruptly. 'Maybe it would be better if you chose her yourself? If the decision had been left to me I would have taken on Leslie Adams.'

'So might I—if I hadn't already found someone.'

'Already found——?' Shanna stood up angrily and went over to stand in front of his desk, leaning over it as she glared down at him. 'You already have someone, and yet you still put those two women through a needless interview, acted as it they really had a chance of getting the job?' She was breathing hard in her agitation.

'You misunderstood me,' he told her calmly, lighting yet another cheroot. 'I didn't say I had already given the job to someone——'

'You mean it isn't a little surprise for one of your women?' she scorned.

He surveyed her coolly through the smoke. 'Not many of my "women" would be interested in this sort of work, Shanna.'

'How nice for them!'

'Perhaps,' he said without interest. 'And it wasn't until I saw our only two qualified applicants that I considered a third alternative.'

'Yes?'

'Cindy.'

'Cindy?' she echoed in a bewildered voice, her anger fading. Cindy?

'Yes.' Rick stood up, moving around the desk to

pace the room. 'The idea has been bouncing around in my head for a week now. She's capable of it, with training from you, and I think it could be what she needs to take her mind off Jack.'

Shanna had sat down on the edge of the desk in surprise. Cindy? It had never occurred to her to even consider the other woman. Cindy knew the world of business, had a superb sense of fashion herself, had been very interested in the running of the magazine the last week; Shanna had spent hours with the other women explaining different aspects of running the magazine. Yes, she had no doubt Cindy could do the job, that she would be very good at it. But would she want it? She voiced her doubts to Rick.

'It's what I think she needs,' he said arrogantly.

'Another way of getting her to settle down?' she scorned.

'She's hardly likely to find the right man moving around the world with me,' he replied seriously. 'I'm convinced the only reason she got involved with Jack was because he happened to be available at the time. Here in London she might have a chance of finding the right man for her.'

'Why don't *you* marry her, then you can both be happy!'

'I don't appreciate your humour, Shanna,' he bit out grimly.

'I suppose to you marriage must seem amusing,' she said bitterly.

He stubbed his cheroot out in the ashtray with vicious movements. 'It doesn't seem amusing at all!' he told her savagely. 'Not at all!' He strode across the room and slammed out of the door.

The door opened again a few seconds later, and Petra, one of Rick's secretaries, looked in at Shanna anxiously. 'Is everything all right? Rick looked a little—explosive,' she grimaced; she was a pretty girl in her early twenties, another American, as Shanna had thought she would be.

'Rick never looks a *little* explosive,' Shanna derided shakily. 'He was very much so. And I'm fine, thanks.'

'Sure?'

'Yes,' she smiled, not sure at all. She hadn't expected Rick to slam out like that, had never known him react so strongly to one of her taunts before. But then he had been acting strangely all week; he was not the Rick Dalmont she thought she knew at all.

He didn't come back to the office for the rest of the afternoon, and as he had made no definite decision about offering Cindy the job as *editor* Shanna didn't mention it to the other woman when she came to the office late afternoon. No doubt it was something Rick would rather discuss with his assistant in private.

She went to a party that evening, and also one on Saturday evening, but as on the last four nights she saw nothing of Rick. He had suddenly stopped haunting her every movement, and was no longer there every time she looked round. The natural assumption to make was that he had found another woman to chase, that he had probably caught her, and that he had finally lost interest in her, Shanna.

The photograph of him in the Sunday newspapers walking into *the* club of the moment on Friday evening, with *the* model of the moment, Carrie, seemed to confirm that. Strange, she wasn't as relieved by his change of attention as she had thought she would be . . .

CHAPTER SEVEN

THERE wasn't much evidence of the new woman in his life doing much to improve Rick's temper when he came in on Monday morning, sending out cutting barbs to everyone he came into contact with, from Shanna to the innocuous Peter Lacey.

'I see the boss is back on form,' Cindy said dryly as she joined Shanna in her office for a sandwich lunch—after having made sure Rick had already left the office for his own lunch!

'Mm?' Shanna replied vaguely, preoccupied with her own thoughts.

'Here,' Cindy turned the pages on the newspaper Shanna had been reading so that she could see the photograph of Rick with an Italian film star, the dark-haired beauty clinging to his arm in open adoration. 'She isn't the same one he was photographed with on Friday.' She raised her brows pointedly.

'Or the one he went to lunch with just now,' Shanna said quietly.

Cindy's brows went even higher. 'He had a woman call for him here?'

'Yes.' She didn't elaborate on the fact that it had unsettled her to see the way the red-haired woman threw herself into Rick's arms, her pouting mouth clinging to his provocatively as he stood up to greet her. Shanna had recognised the woman as a television announcer, known for her glamour as much as her brains. And she obviously knew Rick intimately.

'Then he is back on form,' Cindy grimaced. 'I suppose it was too good to last. It's usually like this,' she explained at Shanna's questioning look. 'But this time I thought—Well, it's made a nice change not to keep falling over his women,' she amended awkwardly.

'It's all right, Cindy,' Shanna smiled. 'I had no doubt that Rick's interest in me would be fleeting. It only lasted as long as it did because to him I was the unobtainable. You see now why I wasn't obtainable. The last thing I need is an affair!'

'Why not?'

'Why?' she frowned. 'Because—well, because——'

'Rick's usually very good with his ladies, and as you aren't into permanent relationships either . . .'

Shanna had become good friends with Cindy over the last week, really liked the other woman, and she knew the liking was reciprocated. She had talked openly with Cindy, told her of her reluctance ever to marry again. 'I'm not "into" any sort of relationship, Cindy, you know that,' she said impatiently. 'Least of all becoming one of Rick Dalmont's numerous "ladies".'

'No one is asking,' rasped his gravel and honey voice as he came forcefully into the room, looking at them both coldly as they blushed guiltily. 'I don't care to have my private life discussed at some lunchtime gossip,' he snapped icily. 'What goes on in my life outside of this office is my affair,' he continued abruptly, 'and no one else's. Do you understand?'

'Yes,' Cindy mumbled, for once having no cheeky come-back.

He turned cold black eyes on Shanna. 'Both of you?' he prompted with soft menace.

She resented being treated like a child. He might intimidate Cindy, but he didn't frighten her, not in the least. 'You overheard a private conversation between Cindy and myself, not gossip——'

'A conversation about my personal life,' he bit out grimly.

'But not gossip,' she insisted.

'I disagree. Cindy, don't you have some work to do?' he glared at her in challenge.

They all knew that Cindy had at least another twenty minutes of her lunch-break left, and yet the other woman nodded, collecting up her things and leaving without a backward glance, just relieved to have got off so lightly.

'You're a bullying——' Shanna began.

'I'm in no mood for your insults today, Shanna,' he rasped dismissively. 'One more word and you're going to find your employment terminated right now!'

She stiffened, her own anger rising to meet his. 'Nothing would please me more!'

'I'm aware of that.' His mouth twisted. 'Which is precisely the reason I want you to get out of here now.'

'My pleasure!' She picked up her bag in preparation to leave.

'Only this office, Shanna,' he warned softly. 'Don't leave the building.'

She looked ready to explode. No one, *no one* had ever spoken to her in this way before. 'You wanted me to leave, so I'm leaving——'

'Not the building, Shanna,' he repeated, a smile to his lips now, the anger having faded to be replaced by taunting humour. 'I believe you've been looking for another job?' he added softly.

She wasn't deceived by his mild tone; she recognised the threat behind the words—and resented them. 'You wouldn't dare——'

'Wouldn't dare what?' he taunted.

'There's no way you could stop me getting another job,' she told him with haughty disdain.

'No? There's the question of your references. I believe prospective employers are very big on that sort of thing over here?'

'You wouldn't . . .?'

'If you leave now I can only assume that you've broken your contract, that you quit. I don't believe I have to give you references in the circumstances.'

She swallowed hard, hating him in that moment. 'You bastard!' she snapped coldly.

He gave a cool inclination of his head. 'Repetitious, but said from the heart. Now get out of here,' he ordered harshly.

'Didn't it work out?' she scorned as she reached the door. 'Your lunchtime bedmate?' she explained at his look of query.

Rick's mouth quirked. 'Samantha is very—accommodating.' He sat down. 'Ask Cindy to come and see me, will you?'

Shanna held in her gasp of indignation with effort. Who did he think he was talking to! She was the editor here, not some messenger girl. She wouldn't run his errands for him——

'Something wrong?' He arched mocking brows at her as she still stood in the doorway.

'Not a damned thing!' She slammed out of the room with suppressed violence. She wouldn't let him force her into leaving by ordering her around!

Lord, what a ridiculous situation! A couple of weeks ago she would have liked nothing better than to be able to just walk out of here, and now that Rick had challenged her to do just that she couldn't do it. He knew she needed his references, damn him, that no one would employ her, even as an errand girl, without her references. And only she knew how badly she needed a job, how she needed to keep busy all the time.

Rick pushed her to her limits over the next few days, making her run needless messages for him, talking to her in cold clipped tones when he bothered to talk to her at all, waiting for her to answer the telephone whenever it rang, whether it was on her desk or his. The atmosphere was so tense and uncomfortable that by Wednesday evening Shanna was at breaking point. The telephone rang on Rick's desk just as she was pulling on her jacket to leave, and by the sixth ring she knew he had no intention of answering it.

She snatched up the receiver, her hand over the mouthpiece. 'What did your last servant die of, Rick?' she snapped.

'It certainly wasn't kindness,' he drawled unconcernedly.

'I can vouch for that! Rick Dalmont's office,' she cooed sweetly into the receiver, glaring at Rick with dislike at the same time.

'Rick, please,' purred a throaty voice.

'It's for you.' Shanna thrust the receiver at him. 'And that's the last call I take from one of your women!' She seemed to have been doing nothing else the last three days!

'Jealous, Shanna?' he mocked, eyeing her challengingly.

'Go to hell!'

'I'm more likely to know heaven in Delia's arms,' he taunted. 'It is Delia, isn't it?'

'She didn't give a name,' Shanna bit out scornfully.

'Hello,' he spoke into the mouthpiece, his black gaze never leaving Shanna as she walked proudly over to the door. 'Yes, Delia,' there was mockery in his gaze now.

'Goodnight—Mr Dalmont,' Shanna told him curtly.

'Shanna?' he stopped her, his hand over the mouthpiece.

She stiffened. 'Yes?'

'You should try it some time,' he drawled. 'It does wonders for tension.'

She could feel the hot colour entering her cheeks. 'Maybe when you get your mind out of the bedroom, Mr Dalmont, you'll realise there's more to life than bedding as many women as you can!' She watched in amazement as he slowly put the receiver down and stood up to come towards her threateningly. 'I— Delia—She——'

'She'll call back,' he said grimly.

'How nice to be so confident!' she scorned, to hide her real nervousness.

'You should be less so,' he told her harshly, his fingers biting into her arm. 'My mind isn't in the bedroom at the moment, Shanna,' he rasped. 'It's envisaging how much pleasure I would get from putting my hands around that pretty little neck of yours and squeezing until no more sharp barbs could come from those delectable lips.'

She swallowed hard, looking up at him with wide eyes. 'I—I——'

'Frightened, Shanna?' he taunted hardly. 'So you damn well should be!' He flung her away from him with little regard for the fact that she struck her hip painfully on the door-handle. 'Go home, Shanna,' he added almost wearily.

'Rick——'

'I have a telephone call to make,' he bit out.

'Delia?'

'Who else?' he taunted, already dialling the number, turning his back on her as he sat on the side of his desk. 'Delia? Sorry, baby, my—assistant cut us off. Yes, it is hard to get qualified help nowadays,' he answered with humour. 'Now, about tonight——'

Shanna had heard enough, quietly closing the door

behind her as she left, leaning weakly back against it. It had been a strain working with Rick the last three days, with his desire turning to a need to punish. She wasn't sure how much more she could take.

It took all her will power to get out of bed and go to her office the next morning, dreading another day of Rick's unwarranted cruelty. She had even stopped going out in the evenings now so that she had enough strength to spar with him during the day. Even so, this constant battle of wills was sapping her strength, and she could feel the danger signals closing in on her.

Rick's desk was empty when she got in promptly at nine o'clock, and as he was usually in long before her this was surprising. There was no briefcase or papers on the desk to tell her he had even been in at all.

Cindy came into the office at nine-fifteen, her usual good humour not having suffered from Rick's temper this week. That was the one consolation to Shanna— Rick's bad temper wasn't directed only at her, although working with him as closely as she did she seemed to get the brunt of it.

'I don't think he's in yet,' she told the other woman with a smile.

'I know,' Cindy nodded. 'Did Rick tell you he's suggested I be editor here once you've left?' she came straight to the point in her usual straightforward manner.

'Yes.' Shanna's smile didn't waver. 'He said you're going to think about it.'

'I am,' the other girl frowned. 'I'm not sure I'm cut out to stay in one place.'

'Rick thinks you are.'

'And what do you think?'

'I think you are too,' Shanna nodded. 'We've worked together on a couple of things since you've been here, and I think you have a feel for this job. Besides, Rick will be here to help you for a while.'

'You don't mind?'

She stiffened. 'What Rick does is nothing to do with me.'

'I didn't mean that part,' Cindy chided. 'I meant, do you mind my being offered your job?'

'But it isn't my job—I resigned.'

'You don't regret it?'

'Not at all,' Shanna replied truthfully, knowing she couldn't continue working for Rick.

'Because of Rick?' Cindy guessed.

'Partly——'

'Mainly,' the other woman corrected.

'Perhaps,' she admitted.

'He's been such a bear lately,' Cindy frowned. 'I don't know what's wrong with him.'

'Well, it certainly isn't frustration any more,' Shanna derided. 'But it looks as if I shall be spared his temper today,' she looked pointedly at his empty desk. 'Delia must have proved as interesting as he thought she would.'

'And who is Delia?' Cindy frowned.

'The woman he was seeing last night.'

'Oh, her,' Cindy dismissed callously. 'I don't think she was interesting at all—he was back at the hotel by ten-thirty.'

That surprised her, she had been sure, by the way Rick spoke to Delia on the telephone, that he had intended it to be an all-night date. 'Are you sure he was alone?'

'Very much so,' Cindy said dryly. 'And in a lousy mood too. He had us all running around in circles last night about this airline deal.'

Shanna knew that Rick was going through with the acquisition of the airline, had gathered that much from conversations of his she had overheard. But she couldn't imagine what he could do to further its progress at eleven o'clock at night! She said as much to Cindy.

'Like I said,' Cindy grimaced, 'we were running about in circles. No one was available that time of night.'

'He must have been turned down,' Shanna taunted.

'By never-say-no Delia?' Cindy mocked. 'You've got to be kidding! If anyone said no it was Rick. He probably started to feel ill last night and wasn't in the mood.'

'Ill?' Shanna repeated in a puzzled voice.

'Oh, damn,' Cindy said impatiently. 'I came in here to tell you Rick won't be in today because he's sick and then I got sidetracked.'

Shanna shook her head, wondering at the sudden fear that clutched at her. 'What's wrong with him?'

'The doctor says——'

'Doctor?' she echoed sharply. 'He's bad enough to need a doctor?'

'Hey, calm down,' Cindy soothed. 'He only has the 'flu, not the Black Death!'

''Flu?' Shanna repeated with some relief. 'What did the doctor say?' She refused to question herself about her concern for a man she was supposed to hate.

'Bed rest and plenty of fluids.'

'And Rick meekly agreed?' She somehow couldn't envisage him doing that.

'Not meekly, no,' Cindy laughed. 'But as he's feeling too weak to get out of bed he didn't have much choice.'

'And the fluids?'

Cindy shrugged. 'The hotel will provide them.'

Shanna frowned. 'He's on his own?'

'Well, he didn't call for Delia or one of the other women he's seen this week, if that's what you mean,' Cindy derided.

She sighed. 'Do you think he's well enough to be left on his own?'

'Well, after he told us all to get out I'm sure as hell not going to volunteer to stay with him. He's more unbearable than usual!'

Shanna telephoned Rick's hotel once Cindy had left, only to be told that 'Mr Dalmont is not taking any calls'. Sleep would be the best thing for him, she decided, if he felt as ill as Cindy had implied he did—and yet as the day progressed she couldn't help worrying if he were all right. A hotel suite wasn't the best place to feel ill, and no one else seemed particularly concerned about him; all his personal staff were at work at the magazine as usual. She didn't doubt Cindy's word that Rick had told them to leave him alone—he would be impossible when weakened by illness!—but she wasn't sure it was good for him. What if he collapsed? What if the 'flu turned to something more serious?

It was no good telling herself that she had no need to worry about someone who treated her as badly as Rick did—she *was* worried, and there was nothing she could do about it.

Just as there was nothing she could do when she found she had driven to Rick's hotel that evening after she finished work. She convinced herself that as she was here she might as well go in and see how he was.

There was no answer to her knock on his suite door, but when she tried the door-handle it opened. All was quiet inside; the lounge was tidy enough, as was the first bedroom she tried. The second bedroom was a different matter! Crumpled tissues littered the floor and bedside cabinet, an empty jug and glass stood on top of the latter, clothes were scattered on the floor around the bed, as if Rick had only just managed to undress before collapsing on the bed. And it was there that he lay, the bedclothes lying badly crumpled about him, the dark growth of a day's beard very noticeable against the other pallor of his face, his eyes were closed, his breathing ragged and irregular.

He looked terrible, much worse than she had envisaged, and whether he wanted her here or not—and she was sure he didn't!—she wasn't leaving until she was sure he should be left alone. He didn't even look as if he were conscious!

'Rick?'

Heavy lids were instantly raised, cool black eyes glittering feveredly at her in recognition. 'What the hell are you doing here?' he bit out savagely, all the honey gone from his voice, only the gravel remaining.

'Nice welcome,' she said lightly, making some effort to straighten the bedclothes. 'These sheets are damp!' she frowned down at him.

'What did you expect?' he groaned weakly as he made an effort to sit up, dropping back against the pillows, his hair clinging damply to his forehead. 'I'm sweating like a——'

'I can see that,' she cut him off before he became crudely blunt. 'Well, you can't lie in damp sheets,' she told him briskly, picking up the telephone to begin dialling.

'What are you doing?' Rick glared at her, but he didn't have enough strength to do more than that.

'Calling for fresh sheets. What did you have in the jug?'

'Lime-juice. But——'

'Room service?' Shanna said haughtily as someone came on the line. For the next few minutes she gave instructions as to what she wanted sent up to Rick's suite, allowing no time for them to question her authority in turning their hotel upsidedown. After all,

if Rick could afford to stay in a suite like this then he
deserved the best service available too!

'Very efficient, Mrs Logan,' Rick drawled as she
rang off. 'Except that I have no intention of getting
out of this bed.'

'You——' she broke off her angry tirade as she saw the
lack of real fight in him, the way he lay back weakly
against the pillows, almost as white as the bed-linen
itself. 'You'll feel better afterwards, Rick,' she soothed,
and sat on the side of the bed, noticing how clammy his
skin looked. 'Have you had your temperature taken?'
she frowned, touching his forehead with the back of
her hand, surprised at how hot he felt.

'A hundred and one,' he growled, his throat
obviously troubling him too as he began to cough.
'God . . .!' he groaned weakly when he could catch
his breath.

'Indeed,' she said dryly, standing up as a knock
sounded on the door. 'I won't be long,' she promised,
opening the door to admit an army of hotel staff as
they brought in the things she had requested. 'Thank
you,' she said warmly once everything had been
deposited in the lounge.

'Will that be all for Mr Dalmont, madam?' One of
the men lingered as the others left.

'Could you get this filled out?' she asked sweetly,
handing him the prescription she had found amongst
the clutter on Rick's cabinet. 'Mr Dalmont needs the
medication as soon as possible.' She gave the man a
glowing smile, handing him a large tip.

He glanced down at the money in his hand, his eyes
widening appreciatively. 'Thank you, madam. I'll see
to it myself.'

She had thought he might—no doubt he would
expect another healthy tip when he brought the
medication up to the suite too!

'Why didn't you get the prescription filled out?' she demanded of Rick as she took the fresh juice into his bedroom.

He opened his eyes with a weary sigh. 'Why do you keep doing that?' He put a hand up to his temple as it obviously ached. 'I feel like I want to die, and every time I fall asleep you come in and wake me up! Why don't you get the hell out of here and leave me alone?' he rasped.

'Maybe you would feel better if you'd taken the medicine the doctor prescribed for you,' Shanna told him without sympathy, beginning to strip the blankets from the bed.

Rick made a grab for them as his bare chest was revealed. 'There was no one to get it for me, and I didn't fancy struggling down to the chemists myself,' he taunted.

'According to Cindy you threw everyone out,' she said in a preoccupied voice, continuing to strip the bed.

'I didn't want anyone fussing around me,' he glowered at her, clutching at the sheet as she would have removed that too. 'Will you just stop what you're doing and——'

'Rick, don't be such a baby,' she sighed. 'I'm only——'

'I don't have any clothes on, for God's sake!' he rasped, glaring at her furiously, his face pale with the effort it cost him to move at all.

She hesitated for only a fraction of a second before she pulled off the last sheet, throwing it to one side. 'You think that bothers me?' she dismissed with only the slightest tremor in her voice. 'You aren't the first naked man I've ever seen,' she said the words confidently enough, and yet she couldn't quite bring herself to look at him, very conscious of his deeply tanned body lying on the snowy white sheet, of the blatant masculinity of that body.

'I'm aware of that,' he said icily. 'And ordinarily I wouldn't mind your seeing me,' he taunted as she blushed. 'But at the moment sex is the last thing on my mind!'

'It never even entered mine!' She turned back to him from folding the sheet, and her breath caught in her throat as she forced herself to look down at him dispassionately. He had a truly magnificent body, lean and muscled, covered with a fine dark hair that grew in wiry abundance over his chest and down over the flat planes of his stomach.

'I'm cold,' he muttered as she made no further move, mesmerised by the male beauty of him.

'I'm sorry.' She was galvanised into action, hoping he didn't notice her blushes in his own discomfort. 'Do you have a robe?'

'In the bathroom,' he nodded. 'But——'

She didn't wait to hear any more of his objections, but went to get the silky black robe. It smelt of his aftershave and the cheroots he smoked, and for a moment she was tempted to bury her face in its silkiness. Then she berated herself for her stupidity. She wasn't interested in this man, she *wasn't*!

She had hardened herself against the intimacy of the situation by the time she got back to the bedroom, and helped him into the robe and into a chair while she stripped off what remained of the bedclothes and began to remake it with fresh linen.

Rick lay back against the chair. 'You didn't have to do this,' he muttered ungratefully.

'And who else would do it?' She glanced round at him, hurrying in her task as she saw how much paler he had gone now that he was out of bed. 'Does Delia intend coming round later?'

'Heaven forbid!' he scowled.

'That's what I thought,' she said dryly. 'Now can you just sit there while I give you a wash and shave— or do you want to get back into bed while I do it?' She turned from making the bed.

'I'm going back to bed. And you *aren't* washing and shaving me anywhere!'

'Like to bet on it?' she mocked.

Rick glared at her belligerently. 'You think I'd let you anywhere near me with a razor?'

Shanna smiled. 'You are taking a risk, I'll admit that, especially after your nastiness the last few days. But I'm quite good with a man's razor, I used to shave Perry all the time after his first accident when he was confined to bed for a couple of months.'

'I'm sure he loved that!' Rick scorned.

A shutter came down over her expression. 'No, he hated it,' she said dully. 'But it did make him feel better, and it will you too.' She went into the lounge to get the bowl she had requested, hating herself for letting anything Rick said get to her.

It wasn't too difficult to find his shaving things, and armed with a bowl of warm water, his toiletries and towels, she went back into the bedroom. Rick had somehow managed to get himself from the chair back into the bed, lying sideways across it where he had fallen, and he now felt too ill to move.

A knock on the door took her out into the hallway briefly, to take the medicine from the effusive porter before hurrying back to Rick. He had to start taking the medication he had been given, and now.

Blazing black eyes glared at her as she gently shook him awake. 'Will you stop doing that!' he snapped. 'I want to sleep, damn you!'

'I know that, and in a minute you can. Take this.' She handed him the small plastic cup that came with the medicine, the correct dosage poured into it. She stood over him while he swallowed it down, knowing by the grimace he gave afterwards that it tasted as awful as it smelt. 'Now help me get you up the bed and on to the pillows. I don't think you should be lying flat like that,' she frowned as he collapsed back into his prone position.

'I didn't intend lying flat,' he scowled as with her help he moved up the bed. 'I just seemed to—to fall that way.' Once again he closed his eyes.

Shanna knew exactly how weak and helpless he was feeling. 'Flu sounded innocuous enough, when really it knocked you for six—even someone as capable and self-sufficient as Rick Dalmont! How he must hate her seeing him like this!

His eyes flew open as he felt her untying the belt on his robe. 'I thought I told you I'm not in the mood,' he sneered nastily.

'You did,' she confirmed briskly, determined not to fight with him any more; she would be taking an unfair advantage of him if she did, he was obviously in no condition to fight anyone. 'Don't be difficult, Rick, please. I'm taking your robe off so that I can wash you.'

'I don't need—Oh, to hell with it, woman, do what you please! You know damn well I can't stop you.'

She finally managed to get the robe off him, and the blanket bath she gave him was as efficient as any trained nurse could have done, knowing that despite his denial of needing the wash it was making him feel better. He was even helping her a little towards the end.

'Something else you learnt when Perry was ill?' he taunted as she pulled the bedclothes back over his nakedness.

'Yes.' She didn't rise to the taunt.

'What a devoted wife you were!'

'Yes.'

He gave an angry sigh. 'You can leave now.'

She knew he hoped to anger her by his dismissive tone, but she could be as stubborn as he when she had to be. 'Not until I've shaved you.'

'I——'

'You look like an escaped convict at the moment,' she spoke over his objection. 'I pity the poor women who wake up beside you in the mornings,' she added cheerfully.

Rick scowled at her. 'I usually shave morning and night, last night I didn't feel like it.'

'The shave or the woman?' she mocked, ducking into the bathroom before he could come back with an angry retort.

'Either,' he replied grimly when she came back with his razor. 'Be careful with that, won't you?' he shuddered as she came towards him.

Shanna laughed at how really worried he looked. 'Don't worry, you'll still be as handsome, even with only one ear!'

'Thanks!'

'Mm,' she smiled. 'But while I think about it, it isn't wise to leave your suite door open,' she told him sternly. 'Anyone could have walked in.'

'Anyone did,' he growled.

She moved the razor over the hardness of his jaw firmly but with care, making sure there wasn't even one little nick in the skin that he could complain about.

He didn't complain at all when she had finished; he didn't say a word—because he had fallen asleep! So much for wondering if she was going to cut his throat.

Shanna stood back to survey her handiwork. Rick certainly looked a lot better than when she had arrived an hour earlier, with his hair neatly combed, his face freshly shaved, and the sweat bathed from his body, his bed newly made. He also seemed to be breathing easier, although she had a feeling the medicine might have a lot to do with that. She made sure the lime-juice was in easy reach for him when he woke up, he was sure to feel thirsty then.

She was just in the process of pulling on her jacket ready to leave when the door opened unannounced and Cindy stood transfixed in the doorway.

'Shanna!' she finally managed, slowly.

'Er—Hello.' Shanna moistened her lips awkwardly. 'I called round to see how Rick was, and then I——'

'Hey, you don't have to explain yourself to me,' Cindy dismissed lightly, closing the door behind her. 'I just came to see how he is myself, but I'm sure he preferred you to be his ministering angel.'

'Not so you'd notice,' she grimaced. 'He's asleep now, though. Look, Cindy, this isn't the way it seems. Rick and I——'

'It's none of my business,' the other woman assured her. 'How is he?'

'Not too good, but he wouldn't thank any of us for staying with him. I think I've left everything he needs within reaching distance. Cindy, about——'

'Please, no explanations. It's none of my business, remember?'

'But——'

'Look, you get on home, I'll keep a check on him tonight. You look tired yourself,' Cindy frowned.

She was tired, very much so. She also had the feeling that Cindy had gained completely the wrong impression about her being here in Rick's suite. And she wasn't giving her the chance to explain herself either.

CHAPTER EIGHT

SHE told herself over and over again that her feelings of anxiety for Rick were not necessary, that he had plenty of other people available to worry over him. And yet did he? He wouldn't allow anyone close to him, and although he was friends with the members of his entourage, he wasn't emotionally close to them, and the same could be said for his women, even the ones he had been seeing this last week.

Consequently she found herself worrying about him constantly during the night, telling herself she would feel the same about anyone who felt ill and was so far away from home. She even called the hotel again towards midnight, only to be told that Mr Dalmont still wasn't taking calls. After Cindy's erroneous assumption of earlier she was loath to call the other woman for fear of furthering her wrong impression any more.

She was up early and in the office long before everyone else, and yet she couldn't concentrate on her work. She kept seeing Rick as he had been yesterday when she arrived at his hotel, and somehow that thought disturbed her.

When Cindy came into her office just after nine she was ready to pack up and go to the hotel and see Rick. What Cindy had to tell her didn't change that decision, it just confirmed it.

'He threw us all out again,' Cindy grimaced. 'He threw me out last night too.'

Just because Rick had told her to go it didn't mean Cindy had had to do just that! But she didn't say anything reproachful to the other woman. 'How did he look?' she asked instead.

'Not quite as awful as yesterday—but almost. I've decided to give this job a try, by the way,' Cindy added thoughtfully.

'That's nice,' Shanna replied in a preoccupied voice.

Cindy shrugged. 'I might as well. It's pure hell working with Jack since we broke up.'

'I'm sure you'll be a success,' Shanna smiled vaguely.

'Let's hope so' Cindy walked back to the door. 'Rick doesn't bet on losers.'

Shanna tidied her desk as soon as she was alone, locking up to go and tell Gloria she was leaving for the morning at least, not sure whether she would be back in at all today. Gloria raised questioning brows, but Shanna didn't feel like satisfying that curiosity. She didn't even like admitting to herself that she was going to Rick's hotel to see for herself exactly how he was.

Once again the suite door opened when she tried the handle, and she was frowning as she walked into the bedroom. Rick was asleep, the room was in almost as much chaos as yesterday. She began to quietly clear up the mess.

'Shanna.'

She turned with a start to find Rick looking at her, his eyes still fevered and bloodshot. 'I—I thought you were asleep.' She ran one of her hands nervously down her skirt-covered thigh.

He shook his head, wincing as the movement obviously hurt him. 'I was just resting,' his voice was still pure gravel. 'I didn't hear you come in.'

'You left the door open again.'

'It's easier for people to get in that way,' he shrugged.

'I agree,' she said dryly. 'Including thieves. Only a

wealthy man would be staying in a suite like this, and that open door is an invitation someone isn't going to refuse.'

'I know—you. Come to give me another blanket bath, Shanna?' he teased.

He obviously felt slightly better than yesterday, he hadn't even been up to his mocking humour then. But she could see he was still far from well. 'That depends.' She checked the bedclothes; they were damp again. 'Has this jug been refilled since last night?' It stood empty on his bedside cabinet again.

'No. Depends on what, Shanna?' he prompted softly.

'Things. Why didn't you call down for more juice?' she demanded sternly. 'The telephone is just here. Rest and lots of fluids, the doctor told you.'

'You've been talking to Cindy,' he grimaced. 'And this is a hotel, not a hospital.'

'Exactly,' she said with satisfaction, opening his wardrobe to pull out a suitcase and beginning to pack some of his shirts into it.

'What are you doing?' he frowned as she took underwear out of the dressing-table drawers and put them in the suitcase too.

She turned to face him. 'This *is* a hotel, not the place for someone who feels ill. There's no one to care for you here. You're coming home with me.' She looked at him with challenge.

'And you'll take care of me?'

'Yes!'

'Sounds good,' he said softly. 'Although you'll have to help me get dressed.'

'Help is what you're going to get a lot of the next couple of days,' she told him, just relieved he wasn't arguing with her; she had expected him to!

'I take it you have a spare bedroom?' he drawled as she helped him into his clothes.

Shanna smiled. 'You'll soon be back to normal! And yes, I have a spare room. You don't think I want your germs, do you?'

'No,' he sighed. 'You've made it clear you don't want anything I have to give.'

She gave him a sharp look at how bitterly he spoke the words, but he was looking too ill by this time for her to pursue the argument.

It wasn't easy getting him down to her car, but somehow she managed it, leaving him there to go back up and collect his things, leaving instructions for the room to be cleaned. He certainly didn't want to come back to that mess!

Her apartment was almost as impersonal as the hotel suite they had just left, but at least she could make Rick more comfortable there, would only be in the next bedroom at night if he should need anything. She felt better just knowing he was there, she hoped he felt the same way.

'I'll have to go back to the office for a few hours,' she told him after she had organised his lunch of a little hot soup and dry bread, having comfortably settled him in the single bed in her spare room. 'After all, I have to earn the money you pay me,' she added teasingly.

'If you weren't leaving I'd give you a rise. Maybe I'll give you a bonus anyway,' Rick added thoughtfully. 'No one has ever done anything like this for me before.'

'Maybe you just didn't give them the chance to.' Her tone was brittle in her embarrassment. 'You aren't the easiest of men to be kind to, Rick.'

'Now don't spoil it!' his mouth quirked.

'I won't,' she grinned. 'And the only bonus I need is for you to get well again and go back to your hotel.'

'I suppose I deserved that,' he sighed. 'I'll be fine now, if you want to go.'

'In other words, get back to work,' she derided.

'I wish I felt well enough to offer you an alternative, but unfortunately, I don't,' he said with genuine regret.

For the first time she realised what a problem he was going to be once he started to feel better. Oh well, she mentally shrugged, she would handle that when the time came. 'You're sure you have everything?' she hesitated at the bedroom door. 'Nothing else I can get you before I leave?'

'Nothing, thanks. You're a very thoughtful nurse,' he smiled, suddenly looking boyish. 'I didn't wait for ever, did I, Shanna?'

'Sorry?' she frowned her puzzlement, wondering if he were delirious and perhaps she shouldn't go and leave him on his own after all.

'How many days ago was it you told me I would wait for ever to be invited to stay at your home?' he mocked.

Her mouth set at the taunt. 'I could always change my mind and get you a taxi back to your hotel,' she warned.

'You could,' he nodded. 'But you won't.' He lay back with a sigh of contentment after this confident statement, his eyes closed. One lid was raised as he sensed her presence still in the room. 'Changed your mind about leaving?'

'No,' she snapped. 'I'm just wondering if you aren't already back on the way to recovery.'

'Do I look it?' he derided.

No, he didn't, he still looked ill. 'I'll get your dinner as soon as I get home,' she didn't answer him. 'Try and get some sleep while I'm gone.'

'I'm trying.'

'Ungrateful swine!' she muttered on her way out.

She sought out Cindy when she got back to the

office, and found the other woman in the canteen having her afternoon break.

'A shot of caffeine to keep me going until the end of the day.' She sipped her black coffee.

Shanna sat down opposite her, but got no drink for herself, having wasted enough of the day already. 'I just wanted to let you know that Rick is with me, in case you go to his suite and get worried because he isn't there.'

'Rick—is—with—you?' Cindy repeated disbelievingly. 'You mean at your home?'

Shanna swallowed hard, knowing how damning this must seem after yesterday. 'I couldn't just leave him in the hotel,' she tried to explain. 'It was so impersonal, and he looked so awful. I went to the hotel this morning and took him back to my apartment.'

'So that's where you were.' Cindy's frown cleared. 'Gloria was very evasive as to where you'd gone when I asked her.'

'That's because she didn't know.' Shanna's smile was tight. 'It isn't something I want broadcast,' she gave Cindy an expressive look. ' 'Flu doesn't usually last very long, another couple of days and Rick will be well enough to come back to the hotel. I'd rather no rumours started—erroneous rumours, of us cohabiting.' She was aware of how pompous she sounded, but she couldn't impress on Cindy enough how innocent Rick being at her apartment was.

'You can rely on me,' Cindy grinned. 'I may put my foot in my mouth every time I open it, but I certainly know when to keep it closed. Although the others are going to be curious as to where the boss has gone, and some of them couldn't keep a secret if their life depended on it,' she grimaced.

Shanna sighed, realising the embarrassing position her 'good deed for the day' had put her in. 'What was

I supposed to do,' she said moodily, 'leave him there alone to suffer?'

Cindy held up her hands defensively. 'Hey, I haven't said a word!'

'But everyone else is going to!' groaned Shanna. 'There's no way I can keep something like this to myself, is there?'

'Well . . .'

'Always supposing Rick wants to keep it quiet,' she frowned. 'I wouldn't put it past him to have all his calls transferred to my apartment,' she grimaced. 'I should have just left him there to suffer in his own sweat,' she muttered.

Cindy shook her head. 'You don't have it in you to be that unfeeling. When I first heard that Rick was getting the run-around from a frosty lady called Shanna Logan I thought you must be a snobby bitch who thought herself too good for him.'

'And?' Shanna taunted, interested in spite of herself.

'No snobby bitch, just a lady who's been hurt in the past and doesn't intend to be again. Rick doesn't have a very good record in long-lasting relationships,' Cindy shrugged.

Shanna's laugh was completely lacking in humour. 'Whatever gave you the impression I've been hurt?'

'I'm an expert on relationships that go wrong,' Cindy said ruefully. 'I recognise the signs.'

Shanna shook her head. 'You're wrong this time,' her voice was sharp. 'My marriage was just about as perfect as I could have wished for.'

The other girl gave her a searching look, seeming to give a mental shrug. 'I have to get back to work,' she stood up. 'Rick may be ill, but he'll still expect all the work to be done when he gets back on his feet. Give him my love, won't you?' She raised a hand in parting, her head back as she walked past Jack making his way to their table.

Now Shanna understood the other woman's abrupt departure; nowadays Cindy avoided Jack wherever possible.

Jack sat down opposite her, giving her his usual leering smile. 'Cindy got herself a new boy-friend?' he drawled.

Shanna frowned, not liking this man at all, finding him too familiar for her tastes. 'Sorry?' she blinked.

'I overheard her tell you to give her love to someone,' he shrugged. 'I assumed it was a new boy-friend.'

'Not at all.' She got to her feet, deciding she might as well tell the 'town-crier' as have smutty rumours running through the building. The last thing she wanted was snide sniggers behind her and Rick's backs. 'She was asking me to give Rick her love when I see him—he's staying at my apartment at the moment,' she announced tautly. 'Any message *you* would like me to give him?'

Jack looked taken aback by her blasé attitude, although he recovered well. 'Not that I can think of, although you might tell him he's a lucky devil,' he added suggestively.

She nodded coolly. 'I'll tell him.'

'No! I mean—I was only joking, Shanna.' He looked less than confident that either she or Rick would appreciate his humour.

'I understand that, Mr Priest,' she said with sweet insincerity. 'Let's hope Rick sees it the same way, hmm?' she taunted.

'There's no need to tell him,' Jack blustered. 'I didn't mean anything by it,' he muttered.

'I'm sure you didn't,' she continued in the same saccharine voice. 'As I'm sure you'll correct anyone else who gains the impression that Rick is staying with me for any other reason than his illness?'

He gave her a speculative look, but agreed readily enough. She had the feeling that there was one man who was still unconvinced as to the innocence of Rick's stay with her, but that he would slam into anyone else who dared to suggest it was more than that. Jack Priest might be a womaniser and a flirt, but he knew that it wouldn't be wise to antagonise a boss like Rick Dalmont, especially when he had no idea of just how deep her involvement with Rick was. For the moment she had an ally, albeit a reluctant one.

Rick was asleep when she looked quietly into his room later that evening. He had been asleep since her arrival home an hour earlier, and she had been careful not to wake him, knowing that the sleep would help him as much, if not more, than any dinner she could give him.

She ate her dinner alone, her usual salad and cold meat, tidying away neatly afterwards. The apartment was as cold and stark as usual, although tonight there was a difference. She was very conscious of Rick in the spare bedroom.

She switched the television on softly, beginning to doze in the chair, once again feeling the tiredness that seemed to be increasing of late.

'Shanna?'

She was instantly awake, turning to find Rick standing in the bedroom doorway, swaying slightly on his feet, although he had had the forethought to pull on his robe first! 'You shouldn't be out of bed,' she stood up, pushing down her own feelings of weakness.

He leant against the doorframe, very pale, a gaunt look to his face. 'I called out to you,' he told her gruffly. 'You didn't hear me. You were so white just now, Shanna. I thought you—Do you always sleep so deeply?' he frowned.

'Yes.' Her answer was abrupt as she reached his side. 'Now go back to bed.'

'I need to go to the bathroom.'

She helped him through to the other room, sitting down in a chair to wait for him, feeling too tired to stand any longer. Thank goodness it was the weekend tomorrow and she could have a lie-in, although with Rick about the place it didn't look like being a restful time.

She prepared him a late dinner once he was back in his room, watching over him as he managed to eat a little of the omelette, making sure he drank the fresh orange-juice she had given him with it.

'I'm going to bed now,' she told him a little after nine.

'Bed?' he blinked, his jaw clean-shaven, having shaved and washed while he was in the bathroom, applying a tangy aftershave to his jaw too. 'But it's early.'

'And I'm tired,' she said flatly.

'No party tonight?'

'Not while I have a guest, no,' she answered stiffly.

He looked at her with dark mocking eyes. 'Guests are usually—entertained.'

He was recovering fast, she could tell that, his humour and outspoken comments coming more frequently this evening. 'You want entertainment?' her eyes gleamed vengefully.

His brows rose. 'Yes.'

'Right.' She left the room, coming back a few minutes later. 'Your entertainment,' she said triumphantly.

Rick looked blankly at the portable television set she had placed on the dressing-table, then he turned angry black eyes on her. 'What the hell do you mean by bringing that in here——'

'You wanted entertainment,' she shrugged. 'There it is.' She grinned at him. 'Isn't television what you had in mind, Rick?'

He scowled. 'If I thought I could catch you I'd get out of this bed and give you the beating you deserve. How dare you carry that heavy thing in here? You could have injured yourself!'

It was slowly dawning on her that his anger was directed at the fact that she had carried the television in here, not because he had been given that as his entertainment. 'It's portable——'

'What does that mean?' he dismissed scathingly. 'Just that it has a handle on the top of it to transport it by! It doesn't make it weigh any less.'

'Rick——'

'Don't ever do anything like that again!' he was glaring at her now. 'Not even to get in a low-blow at me.'

She flushed at the rebuke. 'Do you want the television on or not? I'm going to bed.'

'Not,' he snapped. 'Television happens to be my least favourite form of entertainment.'

'I can guess what tops the list!'

'I doubt it,' he drawled. 'Women are a necessary part of my life, Shanna, as I've already admitted, but they aren't a really enjoyable part. They demand too much and give too little in return.'

'Then what do you enjoy?' she asked, interested in spite of herself.

He lay back against the pillows. 'I have a ranch in Montana, in the mountains, right alongside my parents' place. Some day I'm going to retire there like my dad did.'

She could see how the thought pleased him. 'Why

not now?' she frowned. 'Surely you're wealthy enough not to keep on with this merry-go-round?'

'Yes,' he said without conceit. 'And I can't deny I like being there, but at the moment there's nothing to hold me. I have someone to run the ranch for me, and the house is too big for one man. Maybe when I have a wife and children . . .' he shrugged.

Her eyes widened. 'You intend marrying?' He had never given that impression.

'One day,' he nodded.

'And having children?'

'They usually come along with the wife,' he smiled ruefully.

'Yes,' she said flatly. 'Well, if you need anything, just call me,' she added briskly.

'Would you hear me?' he derided her heavy sleeping.

She grimaced. 'Probably not.'

'That's what I thought. Okay, Shanna I'll see you in the morning. I like coffee with my breakfast, by the way.'

'Because it wakes you up,' she drawled.

'You remembered,' he grinned.

'I remember a lot of things about you, Rick Dalmont,' she warned. 'And most of them are bad.'

His husky laugh followed her from the room, although her own smile faded as soon as she closed her bedroom door; the talk of wives and families was upsetting her.

She awoke to the sound of china rattling against china, opening her eyes to find Rick standing next to her bed, fully dressed today in faded close-fitting denims and a black silk shirt, a tray of tea and biscuits in his hand.

Shanna sat up with a start, pushing the dark hair from her face, feeling strangely vulnerable without her make-up, the sheet pulled up to her chin as she looked at him questioningly.

'It's after ten,' he explained gently, putting the tray down. 'I was awake at seven.' He sat on the side of the bed, frowning his concern. 'I'm beginning to wonder who should be looking after who.'

She sipped her tea. 'You're obviously feeling better,' she said briskly.

'A little,' he conceded. 'Although my small burst of energy seems to have tired me. But at least I felt refreshed when I woke up, you look more tired today than you did last night.'

'That often happens,' she dismissed. 'It's just the tiredness catching up with me. I'll be fine once I've showered and eaten breakfast.'

'I'm not so sure——'

'No one asked you to be,' she told him waspishly. 'Now get out of my bedroom—I don't remember telling you you could just walk in here any time you felt like it?'

He raised mocking brows. 'Does that mean you don't want the tea?' he taunted.

'Get out of here,' she sighed wearily.

To her surprise he went without further argument, the apartment in silence now, so she assumed he had gone back to his own room. The tea and biscuits were very welcome, although she had no intention of telling Rick that; she didn't want him to make a habit of coming into her bedroom. What was she thinking of— of course he wouldn't make a habit of it, he was leaving as soon as he was feeling better!

He was back in bed by the time she was up and dressed, asleep by the look of him, and from the mess he had left in the kitchen he had prepared himself some eggs for breakfast.

She took no risk of him causing that much havoc

again in her kitchen by preparing a late dinner for him when he woke up, the two of them eating it in the kitchen.

'I hope you don't mind,' Rick looked across the table at her as they lingered over the strong coffee he had made for them. 'I used your telephone to call Cindy this morning.'

'Feel free,' she invited lightly.

'She said you'd already explained.'

'I did,' she nodded. 'I also told your P.R. man to watch what he thinks, let alone what he says!'

Rick smiled. 'I imagine Jack has been suitably put in his place.'

'Very suitably,' she confirmed tightly.

'Just what did you tell Cindy?' he mused.

She shrugged. 'The truth.'

'You do a lot for my ego,' he grimaced.

'I didn't realise you would want people to believe you were here for any other reason than the real one?'

'I guess not,' he shrugged. 'It was a good meal, Shanna,' he complimented.

'Thank you.' Shanna stood up to clear away. 'Shouldn't you go back to bed now?'

'Another invitation, Shanna?'

She turned to find him standing very close to her, closer than she had realised, and she recoiled back as she almost touched him. 'Would you please go back to bed?' she said tautly. 'I just have to tidy up here and then I'm going to bed myself.'

Rick looked down at her for long timeless minutes, half a dozen different emotions flickering in his eyes, all of them too fleeting to be analysed. Finally he nodded. 'I'll see you in the morning.'

'Er—Rick,' she stopped him at the door, 'I think you should leave tomorrow,' she told him as he slowly turned.

He seemed about to argue, then he shrugged. 'All right. Late tomorrow. I suppose it must have been forty-eight-hour 'flu, huh?'

'I suppose,' she agreed softly, just wishing he would go, leave her alone.

He nodded. 'Tomorrow.'

'Yes,' and she turned away.

She knew he had gone, could sense it, her fingers clutching on to the work unit in front of her. It was a strange feeling having Rick here, knowing there was someone else in her home. It wasn't an unpleasant feeling, just a forgotten one. Rick's manner today was definitely that of a predatory male as he regained his strength. She had become used to her privacy, she wasn't sure she liked having to check the bathroom was free before she went in there, having to be careful she was always fully dressed. Just having Rick here at all made her feel uncomfortable.

It was even worse the next day. The tension built up inside her as the day progressed, just longing for the time Rick said he was leaving. He seemed in no hurry to do so.

He prowled around the lounge after dinner, stopping to pick up a photograph of Perry that stood on the side table. 'Good likeness,' he muttered.

'Very good.' Shanna moved to take the photograph out of his hand.

'I've noticed a lot of them about the apartment,' he persisted in spite of her pale face.

'Why not?' she said sharply. 'Perry was my husband.'

'Was,' Rick agreed grimly. 'But he's dead.'

She drew in a ragged breath. 'Isn't it time you left? It's getting late.'

His mouth tightened, his hands now thrust into the pockets of his denims, the blue shirt stretched tautly across his chest. 'You can't wait for me to leave, can you?' he bit out angrily. 'Well, okay, I'll go! I'll get my things and be out of your hair in a couple of minutes. Will that satisfy you?'

She didn't answer him, but stood still clutching on to the photograph of Perry, holding it protectively in front of her. The bedroom door slammed behind Rick and she could hear him moving about the room as he threw his things in his suitcase.

The tears flowed down her cheeks, as she looked down at Perry's photograph. He had been so young, so full of life, and now he was dead, dead, *dead* . . .

She stiffened as the bedroom door opened, knowing that Rick was leaving, that after today he might never be back. And she suddenly knew the reason for her tension all day, knew that she didn't want him to go.

'I'm going now,' he said softly, the anger having left his voice at least. 'Thanks for taking care of me. I—Shanna?' he frowned as she turned, the tears still wet on her cheeks.

'I——' her voice came out as a shaky croak, and she swallowed convulsively. 'Rick, don't—don't go.' She licked the tears from her lips, looking at him pleadingly. 'Please don't go!'

'Hey, of course not, if you don't want me to.' He pulled her into his arms, holding her gently.

She clung to him unashamedly, needing his warmth, his strength. 'I'm so frightened at times,' she quivered against him. 'So frightened of being alone,' she admitted the accusation he had once levelled at her.

'We all are, honey,' he murmured into her silky hair.

'Even you?' she trembled.

'Even me,' he nodded. 'Now do you want to watch television, or let me beat you at Monopoly again?' he teased her with the fact that he had beaten her at the game twice this afternoon. 'You just name it and we'll do it,' he told her indulgently.

She looked up at him with unwavering green eyes. 'Make love to me, Rick.'

His breath seemed to catch in his throat, looking at her as if he couldn't quite believe what he had just heard. 'Shanna——'

'I need you, Rick,' she admitted softly. 'I need to feel wanted, loved. Would you please make love to me?'

He drew in a ragged breath. 'You're sure this is what you want? You aren't going to hate me—afterwards?'

She could never hate this man, she knew that now, knew that the thought of him leaving tonight filled her with despair, that she had come to rely on him, to need him, that she had done the one thing she had sworn would never happen again—she had fallen in love, and with Rick Dalmont.

'No,' she moved easily back into his arms, giving herself to him in that moment. 'I won't ever hate you.'

CHAPTER NINE

AFTERWARDS she lay cradled in his arms, the tears of ecstasy she had cried as he possessed her dry on her cheeks now, the even tenor of Rick's breathing beneath her telling her that he had already fallen asleep.

It had been beautiful between them; Rick had taken her with a mixture of tenderness and passion that had her crying out his name as wave after wave of pleasure flowed between them as if it would never stop.

And when it had stopped the closeness had still been there, Rick telling her over and over again how beautiful she was.

Her arms tightened about him now, this man she had discovered she loved. She had no delusions that she meant any more to him than the dozens of other women he had made love to and forgotten, but she was glad she had known him, that they had become lovers. And when the time came for her to be forgotten by him she would let him go without reproach. He would never know of her love for him, never know of the happiness he had given her when she had thought only loneliness remained.

Finally she drifted off to sleep herself, although she was conscious of Rick's possessive hold on her all night, as if he thought she might leave him if he didn't hold her tightly.

He was already awake when the alarm clock went off at seven, reaching over her to switch it off, bending over her sleep-drugged face as she opened her eyes. 'Good morning,' he greeted throatily, almost uncertainly.

She knew the reason for the emotion, knew he doubted her reaction to their lovemaking of last night. She smiled up at him sleepily. 'Good morning, Rick. You're very nice to wake up to,' she told him huskily.

'I am?' Still he hesitated.

'Do you doubt it?'

'I doubt a lot of things where you're concerned,' he admitted with a self-derisive smile. 'For a moment when I woke up this morning I thought I'd dreamt the whole thing, that I was still delirious from the 'flu and had imagined you. Then I felt you curved against me and I knew it was all true. Shanna, I wouldn't have stayed last night if you hadn't wanted me to. Oh, I wanted to stay, but I was through forcing myself on you.'

'And now?'

'Now I want to make love to you again,' he admitted softly.

She smiled up at him. 'I thought you'd never ask!'

He bent his head, his mouth moving against hers questioningly, as if he were still wary of the change in her. 'Shanna, what changed your mind?' He looked down at her with coal-black eyes.

'Didn't you know, it's a woman's prerogative?' she teased. 'And what changed yours? After we had dinner with Janice and Henry last week I thought you'd decided to give up on me. You didn't show the same reluctance last night.'

'I "gave up on you", as you put it, because you'd made it plain that you would do anything to thwart me, even down to denying you had had an idea similar to mine. It seemed obvious that you really disliked me, that I could go on chasing after you for ever and not get anywhere. I'm not a masochist, Shanna, I'll only hit my head against a wall for so long, then I decide the pain isn't worth it.'

'I'm really sorry about the problem page—I was being childish.' She shook her head. 'You bring out the worst in me, for some reason, and I oppose you even when I don't really want to. I've liked all the new ideas you've brought into the magazine, including Cindy as the new editor. She's going to accept, by the way.'

'Good,' he nodded his satisfaction. 'I'm sure she'll make a good job of it.'

'So am I.'

Rick's eyes darkened. 'You could still change your mind——'

'I don't want to.' The last thing she wanted was to be anywhere near Rick in six months' or a year's time. No, an affair now, an affair that ended when he became bored with her, was much more agreeable to her. She wanted to be well away from Rick when the weakness became a final blackness.

'Sure?' His gaze probed.

'Very,' she smiled up at him, dispelling the impression of vulnerability she had acquired the last few minutes. 'Now do you usually have lengthy conversations with your women at this time of the morning?' she mocked.

'No,' he laughed throatily. 'Most of my "women" are still asleep at this time of the morning.'

'Ah, but they don't have jobs to go to.'

His hand gently caressed her pale cheek. 'We could take the day off, Shanna. Do something crazy like go for a boat-trip in the park.'

'In the winter?' she teased.

'Well, I said it was crazy!'

'It's also impossible—you can't get boats out in the winter. There isn't the trade, you know,' she added mockingly. 'Besides, Mr Dalmont, haven't you taken enough time off lately without playing truant for the day?'

'Slave-driver!'

'Someone has to keep you in line.' She threw back the bedclothes. 'Now as we seem to have *wasted* all this time talking, would you like to use the bathroom first or shall I?'

Rick pinned her back to the bed, his hands on her shoulders, one of his legs thrown casually across hers. 'I want *you* before I do anything else.'

'So you're a morning man,' she derided.

'And an afternoon one. And an evening one too,' he grinned.

'In other words, you're insatiable?' Her arms curved about his neck.

'At the moment, yes.'

None of last night had been a dream for either of them, if anything their lovemaking was more explosive than ever.

It was after eight when they finally got out of bed, only time left for them both to have a quick shower and drive to work.

Rick held out his hands for her car keys. 'I was in a state of delirium when I let you drive me from the hotel,' he mocked as he got in behind the wheel.

Shanna sat next to him in the passenger seat. 'And when I drove you back from Henry's?' she taunted.

His expression became bland as he shrugged. 'You aren't a bad driver, Shanna. And you don't cook well enough to be planning the day's menus as you go along.'

'Just for that you can cook dinner tonight!'

He gave her a searching look. 'I'm invited?'

'Yes.'

'I can stay tonight?'

'Yes.'

His throat moved convulsively. 'Can I move in with you?'

'If you'd like to,' she nodded.

'I'd like to,' he confirmed huskily.

'And I'd like you to too,' she said briskly. 'So that's settled.'

'Shanna——'

'No questions, no post-mortems,' she pleaded. 'Let's just enjoy what we have for the moment.'

'Is that what you really want?' His eyes were narrowed.

'Yes,' she answered abruptly, knowing it was the only answer she could give.

'Okay,' he sighed.

If she didn't know better she would have said it wasn't what Rick wanted at all. But she did know better, and she was determined to show him that she wanted no more from him than any of his other women had expected, that the affair was as casual to her as it was to him.

The atmosphere in their shared office was so much lighter today, and she knew that everyone who came in to see one or both of them was aware of the subtle difference in their relationship. At first she felt some discomfort, never having been in this position before, not used to being thought of as any man's mistress. But the open seduction in Rick's eyes whenever he looked at her more than made up for it, the smiles they shared were warm and intimate.

'God, what a day!' he groaned into her hair when they reached his suite to pick up some more of his things.

'I quite enjoyed it.' She sounded puzzled.

'It was too damned long,' he growled against her throat. 'And I'm sure that half the people who came in to see us today only did it out of curiosity.'

Shanna laughed softly as he scowled. 'I didn't mind.'

'I did,' he muttered. 'Every time I decided I just had to kiss you someone came in.'

'We're alone now,' she encouraged, feeling the excitement of being in his arms, the moist warmth of his lips against her throat.

He didn't need any further encouragement, removing her clothes with infinite enjoyment, allowing her to do the same to him, then the huge double bed welcomed the weight of their bodies.

'Shanna darling . . .!' Rick cried as pleasure enveloped his body, shuddering with the delight of possessing her once again. 'I've been longing to do that all day,' he chucked against her breast. 'You have a very sexy body, sweetheart, and seeing you walk about all day has been torture for my self-control.'

Shanna was totally exhausted, too weak even to speak, unable to stop the waves of sleep that swept over her, and Rick's voice reached her as if from a distance, a great distance.

It was dark when she woke up, and Rick was no longer beside her in the bed. It took her several minutes to wake up enough to get up and go in search of him, pulling on one of his shirts over her nakedness, her own clothes still scattered about the lounge where Rick had thrown them.

He sat in one of the comfortable armchairs drinking what looked like whisky, staring off into space, although there were some open papers on the table in front of him. Shanna moved to put her arms about him from behind, kissing him on the mouth as he turned his head sideways, tasting the whisky on his lips.

'Mm,' he groaned his satisfaction a few seconds later. 'And how is my Sleeping Beauty?' He pulled her round so that she sat across his knees, her arms still about his neck.

'Awake,' she murmured against his chin, nibbling lightly.

'Just,' he nodded as she stifled a yawn. 'Why don't you get dressed and we'll have dinner sent up? We may as well stay here tonight, it's already late.'

'How late?' she frowned.

'After nine. By the time we've eaten——'

'We can eat at the flat,' she insisted.

'Not if I'm cooking,' Rick shook his head. 'Let's eat here, sweetheart. I'm sure neither of us is in the mood to cook tonight.'

Shanna wasn't even sure she was in the mood to eat, let alone cook, but she didn't want to spend the night in his hotel room. She struggled to sit up, but his arms remained firm about her. 'Rick, please let me go. I want to shower and dress.'

'You still look tired.' He touched the dark shadows beneath her eyes.

She forced a tight smile to her lips. 'Can I help it if you're a demanding lover?'

'Can I help it if you're so damned beautiful I can't keep my hands off you?' he smiled.

'And can I help it if I can't resist you?' she joined in the teasing.

'You managed to do just that until yesterday,' he grimaced.

'When I couldn't resist the Dalmont charm any longer,' she taunted.

'I should have got 'flu earlier,' he grinned. 'I never realised you had the nursing instinct in you.'

'Well, now you know,' she mocked, swinging away from him. 'Rick, I don't want to stay here. I don't want to be just another Anna Kalder.'

'Anna?' he frowned. 'You know about her?'

'I know she was your mistress for a few weeks. But then so have a lot of women been.' She couldn't keep

the bitterness out of her voice, try as she might. 'I
won't be kept at your hotel like all those other women.
If you care anything for me at all please let's go to my
apartment.'

'Shanna——'

'*Please*, Rick,' she looked at him with pleading eyes.

'Okay, okay,' he sighed. 'But could we just eat
first—I'm starved! We could eat in the restaurant
downstairs if you would prefer it.'

'That won't be necessary—up here will be fine. But
I want to leave straight afterwards.' She went back to
the bedroom and into the shower, feeling refreshed
under the cool spray, regretting her argument with
Rick but still determined she wouldn't become just
another of his women, moving in here with him until
he threw her out. When it came time for someone to
leave it wasn't going to be her!

She was dressed when Rick came into the bedroom,
unable to meet his gaze as she retouched her make-up.

'Honey, I'm sorry.' His arms came about her from
behind, pulling her back against him. 'But surely you
know you're different, special? And no, I don't tell all
my women that,' he said dryly. 'You really are special.
And if I've upset you I'm sorry. I didn't realise you
felt this way about staying here. We'll go back to your
apartment now.'

'What about dinner?' She looked at him with wide
eyes.

'We'll eat when we get to the apartment—if we feel
hungry.' The look in his eyes told her food wasn't
what he had on his mind for when they reached her
home.

It had been strange having Rick about the apartment
during his illness, but it was even stranger looking
across the room at him and knowing by the look in his

eyes that soon they would be in bed together, their bodies entwined as they made love.

The knowledge that she could arouse Rick that easily gave her a glow of satisfaction, and she knew that not even on her honeymoon with Perry had she spent so much time in a man's arms, feeling cherished and needed. Rick held nothing back, completely honest in his desire for her, and as the days passed, as three weeks passed, she began to wonder when he was going to tire of her. His affairs never lasted long—he wasn't usually in one place long enough to maintain them!—and yet he gave no indication of wanting to leave her. It was then that Shanna really began to worry, to know that she might have to be the one who ended their relationship. She had envisaged a brief affair with Rick, and hadn't wanted any more than that.

He brought her breakfast in bed on their fourth Saturday together, sitting in the chair and watching her indulgently as she ate the scrambled eggs and toast he had prepared for her. 'I could quite get used to this.' He sat back with a lazy stretch of satisfaction.

Shanna looked up from drinking her coffee, hoping the love she felt for this man didn't glow in her eyes, but very much afraid that it did. 'To what?' she asked softly.

There had been a lot of gentleness and pleasure between them the last three weeks, and even working together in the day hadn't diminished Rick's consideration for her. Everyone at the magazine was aware of their changed status now, and the curiosity about them faded somewhat as their relationship continued to flourish.

'Domesticity,' he smiled. 'It feels good to wake up in the morning and feel you beside me. I even enjoy spoiling you with breakfast in bed occasionally. And I more than enjoy our nights together,' he teased.

So did she. It seemed as if Rick only had to touch her for her to be trembling with desire, and not a night had passed without that desire flaming between them at least once. Sometimes their lovemaking would take them through until dawn, when they would finally sleep satiated in each other's arms. It was at these times that her body felt so drained of strength she felt as if she might never wake up, and although Rick occasionally mentioned her tiredness he didn't pursue the subject.

'How about you?' he prompted softly.

She shrugged. 'I've enjoyed our time together too. But it can't last, can it?' Her tone was light, her eyes unblinking as she saw his face darken with displeasure.

'Why can't it?' he demanded.

She sat back against the pillows with a sigh. 'How long do your affairs usually last?'

'This is diff——'

'How long, Rick? What was the longest relationship you ever had?'

'Shanna——'

'Please, Rick, this is important!'

His mouth tightened. 'I think—six weeks,' he muttered.

'And we've already been together three and a half weeks,' she pointed out.

'That has noth—Damn!' he rasped as the ringing of the telephone interrupted him. 'I'll get it,' he told her as she went to get out of bed, her nakedness in front of him something she no longer felt embarrassed about.

She let him go; most of the calls to her flat lately had been for him anyway. She could hear him talking on the telephone for several seconds, and then he came back to the bedroom.

'It's for you,' he told her flatly. 'Henry,' he murmured as she reached the door.

Shanna hesitated only fractionally, before pulling on her robe to go and talk to her brother. She had seen nothing of Henry the last few weeks, although she had spoken to him several times on the telephone. As far as she was aware, he knew nothing of Rick staying here. Although that might not be true now!

'Hello, Henry,' she greeted calmly.

'Shanna? Is everything all right? Rick said you were in bed.' Her brother's concern could be clearly heard.

'I was,' she said dryly. 'He'd just given me my breakfast.'

There was silence at the other end of the line for several long seconds. 'He's there rather early, isn't he?' Henry sounded confused.

'Not really, he was here rather late.'

'Shanna . . .? Is it true, then, is he living with you?' her brother demanded. 'There's been talk, but I couldn't believe it.'

'Believe it,' she said dully. 'Rick's been staying here for almost a month.'

'Shanna!' Henry sounded deeply shocked.

She sighed. 'You were the one who thought I should go out with him,' she reminded him.

'But I didn't mean you to set up house with him!'

'I haven't set up house with him,' she snapped. 'I'm not living with him either. Both those terms imply a sort of permanence to the relationship, and we all know there's nothing permanent about this.'

Henry gave a deep sigh. 'You're twenty-five years old, old enough to know your own mind, but I can't help but be surprised about this affair with Rick.'

'I know,' she sympathised gently. 'And I'm sorry.'

'Don't apologise, Shanna, it's really none of my business. Actually, I telephoned to ask you over for

dinner one evening—we haven't seen you for weeks.
You'd better bring Rick with you, I suppose,' he
added grudgingly.

'I'll sort out an evening and get back to you,' she
promised. 'Give my love to Janice and the children.'

'Shanna!' he stopped her ringing off.

'Yes?' she was wary now.

'Take care, won't you?'

Her mouth twisted. 'Yes, Henry, I'll take care. And
I'll call you soon.' She turned from ringing off to find
Rick scowling across the room at her.

'What did he mean by that last remark?' he rasped.
'Does he think I'm irresponsible enough to get you
pregnant?'

'Rick——'

'Because I wouldn't do that to you.'

'I know that,' she soothed him, going over to lightly
touch his arm. 'Rick, he's my brother, he's naturally
concerned for me. I'm sure he didn't mean anything
by what he said just now.'

'I should damn well hope not!' His arms came about
her. 'How would it look if you were pregnant when I
introduce you to my parents?'

Shanna stiffened, pulling back to look up at him.
'Your parents?' she repeated softly.

He grimaced. 'Sweetheart, I didn't want to tell you
like this, but it doesn't look as if I have any choice.
There've been some problems in the States that I have
to go back and sort out. I thought you could come
with me, meet my parents at the same time.'

'No!' She moved out of his arms, standing some
distance away from him. 'I have no intention of going
to America as your mistress.'

His expression darkened. 'Who said anything about
a mistress?' His eyes were narrowed to black slits. 'I
may be thirty-seven years old, but my father would

bodily throw me out of the house if I introduced one of my mistresses to my mother. I want to take you to them as my wife, Shanna. I was trying to ask you to marry me when Henry called just now.'

Marriage. It wasn't a word she associated with Rick, it wasn't something she had even thought of in connection with him, and she couldn't think of it now either.

'Shanna?' He sounded anxious as she didn't answer him. 'Honey, this wasn't the way I had it planned, just blurting it out like this, but I love you, and I want to marry you. I don't like the impression your brother has of our relationship, I don't like anyone thinking that about you, but at the time it was all you would accept. Honey, please answer me, will you marry me?'

Shanna swallowed hard at the ragged pain in his voice, wishing with all her heart and soul that she could throw herself into his arms and never have to leave. 'I—I can't,' she turned away. 'I can't, Rick!'

Pain flickered across his face, his eyes were darker than ever. 'I know something about your first marriage has made you wary of that sort of commitment, but whatever it was, it doesn't apply to us. God, I'm not even asking that you love me in return, all I want is for you to let me love *you*, take care of you.'

She chewed on her bottom lip to stop it trembling, overwhelmed by the wealth of love Rick was showing her. She hadn't believed he was capable of loving like this, and yet she couldn't doubt him, could see it all in his face, in his eyes. And she loved him *so much* in return.

'Cindy once told me,' she moistened her lips nervously, 'she told me you don't bet on losers. I'm a loser, Rick. I'd be no good for you.'

'I'm sure Cindy wasn't referring to you when she spoke about losers. And I happen to think you're very good for me. I want you for my wife, Shanna,' he repeated firmly.

'I can't!' she repeated raggedly.

'Why the hell not?' he rasped, not used to opposition in anything. 'You would never want for anything as my wife, and I can't continue living like this. I moved in here with you because you made it plain you wouldn't accept marriage then, but I have to leave next week, and I don't intend going without you.'

'You'll have to,' she said dully.

'No——'

'Yes!' she told him forcefully. 'Can't you understand, I don't *want* to marry you!'

His breathing was harsh and ragged as he looked at her as if he had never seen her before. 'What's that supposed to mean? You don't love me? What?'

'Work it out, Rick,' she sighed wearily, wishing he would just go away and stop torturing her.

'I'm okay for an affair, to go to bed with, but you don't want to marry me, is that it?' he bit out tautly. 'Answer me, damn you!' he moved to shake her roughly.

'Yes!' she cried. 'Yes, that's it exactly.' Her hair swung about her face where he shook her.

'*God!*' He pushed her away from him with an agonised groan; he was very pale, almost grey beneath his tan. 'I'll come back for my things later,' he spoke almost dazedly. 'I just have to get away from you.' He shook his head, pulling on his jacket, suddenly looking up at her with pained eyes. 'Why do I get the impression that this scene is exactly what you wanted?' he groaned. 'That you planned for me to walk out this way?'

Shanna paled at how astute he was. She had known of his intelligence, his quicksilver method of making decisions, but she hadn't realised he had come to know her this well, that he would guess exactly what she had been trying to do. She *did* want him to walk out; she knew it had to be his decision to walk away.

'Shanna, what are you hiding from me?' He was in command of himself again, had her pinned to the spot with his sharp gaze.

Nevertheless, she couldn't meet that gaze, and she looked anywhere but at him. 'You're imagining things,' she dismissed lightly. 'Why should I want to hide anything from you? We've had fun together, now it's over. Do you always take the end of an affair this seriously?' she mocked.

'An affair, no. But when the woman I love, the woman who has been my lover, who has seemed as if she cares for me a little in return, turns down a proposal of marriage in the cruel way you've done, then I know something is wrong. Why do you want me to hate you, Shanna?' he asked shrewdly. 'Why are you pushing me out of your life like this?'

'You're imagining things——'

'No!' his fist landed violently on the coffee table, although he didn't even flinch at the pain it must have caused. 'I'm not imagining a thing. Why is it imperative I get out of your life, and in a hurry?'

'Perhaps so that someone else can take your place!' she snapped.

He gave a tight smile. 'Careful, Shanna, your desperation is starting to show. I'm not going,' he told her hardly. 'Not until I have the truth from you. I know you're hiding something from—God!' he rushed forward to catch her as she swayed and fell. 'Shanna!' He looked down at her waxen features as he lay her down on the sofa, rubbing her numbed hands as consciousness faded and swam for several minutes.

As she watched the concern in his face turn to fear,

horror, she knew he had discovered her secret. It had always been a possibility, of course, one that she had tried to avoid him realising by trying to avoid *him*. But being with him these last weeks virtually twenty-four hours a day she had exposed her every weakness, and the truth now was in Rick's eyes.

'How long?' he croaked. 'How long have you known?'

She swallowed hard. 'Just over a year.'

'Perry knew?'

'Yes,' she confirmed with bitterness.

Rick was breathing heavily, swallowing convulsively, a nerve jumping erratically in his jaw. 'Can anything be done?'

'I don't know,' she said dully.

'God, you don't mean——'

'That I'm dying?' she finished flatly. 'I think so. Yes, I think I'm dying, Rick.' She touched the rigidness of his jaw as he seemed to flinch.

CHAPTER TEN

IT had come as much as a shock to her a year ago as it did to Rick now. Old people, people who had lived their lives, had had their children, their grandchildren, had heart complaints, not people of twenty-four! It had been just over a year ago when the doctor had told her of the defect, of the operations she had needed then to right the wrong. She had never had that operation, and the increasing weakness she felt lately seemed to say it might already be too late.

The possibility that Rick would realise had always been there, the shock of knowing his mother had a similar problem had told her that. He had grown up with the knowledge that his mother was ill, had known all her symptoms, although until this moment his desire for Shanna had blinded him to her own weakness being of a similar kind.

But he knew now; the full knowledge of it was in the pained blackness of his eyes. She hadn't meant for him to love her, had never dreamt that he would; she had believed she would just be another affair to him before he moved on. If she had even guessed his feelings for her could develop into something serious she would never have become involved with him. But it was too late for that now, too late for her to stop him loving her. She had caused him this pain, and there was nothing she could do about it.

'You *think* you are?' He shook her now, his expression intent. 'But you don't know for certain?'

She moistened her dry lips with the tip of her

tongue. 'Not for certain, no. But I've been feeling so weak lately, the tiredness has been more intense.'

Rick seemed to be thinking fast, each problem thought out quickly in his mind and dealt with. 'Do you have a doctor? Someone who's been dealing with your case?'

'Well, yes. But——'

'Who is he? What's his telephone number? Shanna!' he prompted hardly as she seemed dazed.

'I—He—It's in my bag,' she told him abruptly. 'But I haven't seen him for months.'

'Why the hell not?' he rasped, frantically throwing everything out of her bag on to the table, picking up a bottle of pills to frown at them for several seconds before once again searching through the papers he had taken out of her bag. 'Is this it?' He held up a card.

'Yes.' She swallowed hard, her expression turning to one of alarm as he began to dial the doctor's number. 'Rick, you can't call him now—it's a Saturday!'

He gave her a look that said he didn't care if it was three o'clock on a Sunday morning; he was calling the doctor. 'A damned recording,' he muttered a few seconds later, grabbing a pen off the table where it had been tipped out of her bag, scribbling down another number as it was obviously recited to him. 'Go and get dressed, Shanna,' he ordered as he re-dialled. 'I want to be able to leave as soon as possible after I've made this call. You—Sweetheart!' he groaned as she buried her face in her hands, crying uncontrollably. He slammed the receiver down to go to her, taking her in his arms, holding her tightly against him. 'I love you, Shanna. I love you,' he murmured the words over and over again until she stopped crying.

'I'm sorry,' she shuddered back to control. 'It's just that—You reacted so differently from Perry. He—

hated the thought of my being ill, of something inside me being wrong.'

Rick's arms tightened. 'Tell me about it, Shanna. Tell me what happened a year ago.'

She lay heavily against his chest, clinging to him but unable to look at him. 'We wanted children,' she wiped her cheek dry with the back of her hand. 'We'd been trying for some time, and so we—we both had medicals. Just general things, because Perry hated all things medical. He'd had so many accidents during the course of his career that he'd grown to hate the sight and smell of hospitals. The doctor found no reason why we couldn't have children, but he did find—he did find——' she stopped talking as her voice shook uncontrollably. 'He said I needed an operation, that if I didn't have it I would die——'

'Then why the hell didn't you have it?' Rick rasped.

'I couldn't have gone through it without Perry's support, and—well, as soon as he heard the result of the medicals he went out and crashed in a race. He injured his back and could no longer compete in races. He hated me to be anywhere near him, he began to resent me—blamed me for his accident. We had been so happy until then, but my health and his accident seemed to change everything. He—he—You know the rest!' she shuddered.

'Other women?'

'Yes,' she sighed. 'And drink. He was drunk when we had the accident that killed him. I wanted to drive, but he said he didn't want a—a cripple driving him, that I'd probably kill him. He was completely drunk when he drove into the brick wall. I don't know how it was kept out of the newspapers, and at the time I was past caring. Perry was dead, and they told me at the hospital then that my operation was imperative.'

'And?'

'And I just wanted to die!'

'You told me that two weeks after we met,' Rick frowned. 'But I couldn't believe you really meant it.'

'I meant it. I welcomed death, the idea of it. I loved Perry, and my illness repulsed him, made him hate me. I even went to work at *Fashion Lady* in the hope of showing him I could carry on a normal life, that nothing had changed.' She gave a bitter laugh. 'Even that backfired on me! After the first accident he had to give up his career, and the thought of his wife going out to work made him feel inadequate.'

'But you still loved him.'

'Yes!' she trembled.

'And now?'

'Now?' she blinked up at him.

'I've just told you I love you, Shanna,' he rasped. 'And if you think another man's inadequacies are going to rob me of *my* chance of a wife and children then you're mistaken!' His expression was harsh. 'Perry may have been the man you loved, but he was weak—*I'm* not. I want you to live, and you're *going* to.'

'But——'

'You're going to, Shanna,' he told her with conviction. 'One day I'm going to watch as you put *our* children to bed and kiss them goodnight. That was the night I realised I loved you, you know. I watched you laughing with Peter and Susan, watched your gentleness with them, and I knew that I wanted it to be our children, that I loved you. It was the biggest shock of my life,' he said self-derisively. 'Especially as you felt no reluctance to show me how little I meant to you.'

'I——'

'Yes?' he prompted sharply.

Shanna shook her head, biting her bottom lip. 'Nothing.'

He gave her a piercing look. 'You had me trapped, Shanna, and I didn't like the feeling,' he continued with a sigh. 'Hence Samantha, Carrie, Delia, and all the others,' he said grimly. 'All those beautiful women, and I didn't make love to any of them!'

'You didn't?' she gasped.

'No,' he admitted ruefully. 'I just felt more trapped than ever, just wanted to be with my woman with the jet-black hair and flashing green eyes. And although you said you didn't care for me it was you who looked after me when I had 'flu.'

'I would have done the same for anyone,' she blushed.

'Jack?' he taunted.

'No,' she admitted with a laugh. 'Not Jack.' She knew Rick was waiting for some kind of admission from her of her love for him, but she couldn't give it to him. If she were to die—and God knows she so much wanted to live now!—then it wouldn't be fair to burden him with her love. Maybe if she were to live . . . But that could still only be a possibility.

'I should have realised you were ill.' He spoke almost to himself. 'There was the night I had to break into your apartment because you'd fallen asleep, and then the excessive tiredness you felt from working, the way you sleep so heavily. I wondered if you took sleeping pills at first, but there didn't seem to be any evidence of them, so I dismissed that. I never even suspected the truth . . .!'

'You weren't supposed to,' she told him quietly. 'I wish you didn't know now.'

'Well, I'm damn glad I do!' He sat up straight, putting her firmly away from him. 'I'm not going to let you die, Shanna. You're going to live, for *me*. Do you have any idea how lucky you were to even be given the chance of an operation? My mother isn't so lucky, or you can bet she would have had it by now.'

She flushed her guilt, knowing the truth of his words. She had been a coward all this time.

'I can't understand why Henry hasn't—My God, he doesn't know, does he?' Rick breathed slowly as the colour increased in her cheeks. 'Of course he doesn't,' he spoke softly to himself. 'If he did he would never have let you strain yourself by working at *Fashion Lady*. And he would have insisted that you have surgery. You didn't tell your own brother, Shanna?' he demanded incredulously.

She turned away from the recrimination in his eyes. 'I didn't see the point of upsetting him.'

'You would rather he just found you dead one day, eh?' Rick rasped angrily. 'God, woman, you deserve a beating!' he snapped as she paled. 'Can you imagine what that would have done to Henry?'

'I didn't want to worry him . . .' she said weakly.

'Just contribute to your death by giving you a job! Hell, Shanna, if I didn't love you so much I'd beat you myself!' He stood up in forceful movements. 'Now go and get yourself dressed while I call the doctor.'

'He won't see me on a Saturday,' she shook her head as he pulled her to her feet.

'He will,' Rick said grimly. 'And if he won't then I'll find someone else who will.'

Shanna went into the bedroom to dress, feeling a certain amount of relief that Rick knew the truth, that she had been able to at last tell someone about the last six months with Perry, to explain his behaviour if not excuse it. Rick's strength had been what she had needed to go through with the operation a year ago, a strength Perry had been unable to give her despite their love for each other. When she had woken up in hospital six months ago to be told that her husband was dead, and that her own operation was urgent, she hadn't even *wanted* to live, had wanted to die.

And now—now she wanted to live, wanted to be Rick's wife, to give him the children he wanted. It had been strange the way she had never given Perry a child, despite trying for months, although the doctor had told her the body was a strange thing, that it compensated for its own weaknesses. *If* she had become pregnant, then having the baby would probably have killed her.

'He'll see us in twenty minutes,' Rick told her when she rejoined him, having dressed in casual black trousers and a bottle green blouse.

She gulped. 'He will?'

'Yes.' Rick's expression was grim.

'But——'

'I'll be right by your side all the time, Shanna,' he told her gently. 'Even if there's only a slim chance you realise we have to take it, don't you?' He held her gaze with his.

We. Yes, they were a couple now; she realised they had become so the first time she gave herself to him.

'I won't let you down, Shanna,' he told her gruffly. 'Just live for me, darling.'

She couldn't answer him, didn't speak at all on the drive to see the doctor, although her eyes widened as they drove to a residential part of London.

'I managed to find the doctor at his home.' Even Rick looked a little bashful at this intrusion. 'Once I'd explained the situation to him he said he would see us here.'

Her nervousness wasn't helped by the fact that Rick refused to leave her side even once the doctor began his examination, and she felt very conscious of his black-eyed gaze on her all the time Dr Hunt did his examination.

Finally the doctor stepped back, a tall grey-haired man in his early fifties, his casual dress pointing to this being his day off. 'You can get dressed now,' he told her. 'Well, you've reduced your chances considerably by waiting like this,' he continued bluntly. 'Although that isn't to say there's no chance,' he added hastily at Rick's groan of protest.

'How much of one is there?' Shanna asked softly, gripping Rick's hand tightly.

'Hard to say,' he frowned.

'When can you operate?' Rick demanded.

The doctor's brows rose. 'Are you a relative of Mrs Logan's?'

'Her fiancé,' he bit out arrogantly, squeezing her hand reassuringly.

Dr Hunt was frowning as he turned back to Shanna. 'But your husband . . .?'

'He died,' Rick told him tersely. 'When can you operate?' he persisted.

'That would depend——'

'On what?' Once again Rick was demanding.

'On Mrs Logan's general health at the moment, on her own will to live, and on when the operation can be scheduled.'

'Her health is fine,' Rick told him arrogantly. 'No worse than anyone else's who expects to die at any moment,' he added bitterly. 'And she'll live for me,' he stated imperiously. 'So when can you schedule the operation?'

The doctor looked disconcerted by the arrogance of this man, although he recognised a lot of it as being because of his deep love for the woman at his side. 'I——'

'Tomorrow?' Rick prompted.

'Well, no, not that soon. But——'

'How soon?' Rick's voice was taut.

'Rick, calm down,' Shanna soothed him. 'Give the doctor a chance to speak!'

He bit back his impatience with effort. 'Sorry,' he muttered to the other man.

'That's perfectly all right,' the doctor accepted. 'In your position I would feel the same way. And I agree with you that no more time should be lost. I may be able to arrange something for the end of the week——'

'Make that definite, doctor, and we'll leave you to your day off,' Rick put in eagerly.

The other man gave a resigned shrug. 'All right, the end of the week. But Mrs Logan must have complete rest until then,' he added sternly. 'And we'll want her in a couple of days before the operation for more thorough tests.

'She'll be there,' Rick told him. 'And so will I!'

It was strange, but for the last three days neither of them had talked too much about the impending operation. Oh, they calmly discussed the arrangements for her admission, and Rick drove her in himself, although Henry had wanted to come too. Her brother had had to be told, and Rick had been the one to do the telling. Henry was calm by the time he came to see Shanna, although tears glistened in his eyes. Rick had persuaded him that it would be less traumatic for her if they went to the hospital alone, and on this, her last night at home before going to hospital, Henry and Janice had brought the children over to visit for an hour, although the cheerful youngsters could have no idea of the gravity of the occasion.

And now she lay in the strength of Rick's arms, needing more than just this physical closeness, needing so much more. She began to caress his body, instantly feeling desire surge through him.

'No!' he stopped the movement of her hands.

88   UNDYING LOVE

Sweetheart, the doctor said complete rest,' he groaned
in the darkness of her bedroom.

And Rick had kept to that instruction to the letter;
he had stayed with her day and night, the trip to
America forgotten. Lance was despatched in his place,
and Rick made sure she did nothing more strenuous
than lift a cup to her lips, holding her with platonic
comfort every night. 'We may never have the chance
again,' she reminded him softly.

'Don't!' he choked. 'God, don't say that!' He buried
his face in her hair.

Shanna could feel the heat of his tears on her cheek,
and her arms tightened about him. 'Make love to me,
Rick,' she requested boldly as she had once before.
'Let me go into this knowing how much you love me.'

They made love slowly, savouring each moment as
if it really would have to last them a lifetime. And even
when passion had been spent they remained as one,
staying together like that as Shanna slept in Rick's
arms, and Rick slowly, painfully, watched the black of
night turn into dawn's morning light, his hold on her
never wavering, as if he were willing her to live.

Shanna liked hospitals no more than Perry had,
despite being in a private room, and the days passed
slowly until the morning of the operation. To her
surprise she woke to find Rick sitting in the chair next
to her bed, his haggard expression and unshaven jaw
pointing to his having been there for some time.

She frowned her concern as she sat up.
'Darling . . .?'

'If you die, Shanna,' he told her raggedly, not
moving, 'you'll be killing me too.'

'No!' she cried her horror.

'Yes,' he insisted grimly. 'So you fight to live for
me—and our children.'

'Rick, even after the operation—if I survive,' she

added softly, 'I won't be able to have children for some time.'

'I know that,' his eyes glittered. 'And I don't care if we have any or not. But I know they're important to you, so we will have some eventually. But not for some time—I'll want you all to myself to begin with. I'm having the ranch prepared for us, and my mother is organising the wedding for when we arrive.'

'Rick——'

'Don't think negative!' he rasped, pale beneath his dark complexion. 'I refuse to. I couldn't sleep last night,' he told her softly. 'So I did some walking instead,' he explained away his unshaven jaw. 'I saw this in a store window,' he took the ring-box out of his coat pocket, 'and I knew I had to have it for you. I had the jeweller out of bed at the crack of dawn.' He opened the box, taking out the ring and slipping it on to the third finger of her left hand. 'I want you to wear this until I can put it on your finger legally.'

It was a wedding ring, a slender gold band that fitted her finger perfectly. 'It's beautiful, Rick, but——'

'I've had it inscribed inside,' he told her huskily. 'It says "I love you, R."'

Her eyes widened. 'You made the jeweller do that this morning too? The poor man will probably never be the same again!'

'Probably,' he acknowledged unconcernedly.

'It's a beautiful ring, Rick.' She touched it lovingly. 'And thank you for the inscription. But I can't wear it during the operation.'

'You can,' he nodded. 'I already checked, and wedding rings are allowed. They put some sort of tape over it, I think.'

'But we aren't married,' she laughed.

His gaze was intent, a fire burning in the dark

depths of his eyes. 'We are in every way that matters,' he said gruffly. 'And I want some part of me with you all the time.'

Shanna swallowed convulsively. 'I'll wear the ring. Did you see the lovely flowers Cindy bought me yesterday?' she attempted to lighten the tension between them. 'How is she doing at the magazine?' she asked as he made no response to the flowers.

'Fine,' he dismissed.

'Have you been in to work at all?'

'No.' He held on tightly to the hand wearing his ring. 'I can't concentrate. I can't seem to do anything without you!'

She wanted to comfort him, to help him, but there was nothing she could do or say to make this easier for him.

A nurse came into the room at that moment, coming to a halt as she saw Rick sitting beside the bed. 'I'm afraid I'll have to ask you to leave now, Mr Dalmont,' she said briskly as she came in. 'I have to prepare Mrs Logan for theatre.'

Rick seemed to blanch, his eyes looking bloodshot and haunted. 'Could you just give us a few minutes alone? I—We won't be long.'

The nurse nodded slowly. 'A few minutes.' She gave an understanding smile before leaving.

Rick's hand tightened convulsively about Shanna's. 'Am I doing the right thing by pressurising you into this operation?' he groaned raggedly. 'Am I being selfish? Would it be better to take what time we do have and be thankful for it?'

She touched his face with loving fingers, knowing that she *could* help him—by telling the truth. 'I want more than that, Rick,' she gave him a serene smile. 'I love you, and I want to spend all my life with you, not just a few months. If anyone was being selfish it was

me, by not being honest about my feelings. I thought I
would save you pain, but that was wrong of me. I'll
live, Rick, and it will be because we love each other,
because we want a lifetime, not a short time together
and then loneliness. Do you understand, darling? I'm
doing this for *both of us*.'

'Shanna . . .!' His lips claimed hers in drugging
intensity.

'I love you,' she clung to him fiercely. 'I love you so
much.'

'That's all I needed to know.' He was smiling as he
gently touched her lips with his. 'I'll be sitting right
here when you wake up. And I'll be beside you for the
rest of our lives.'

And he was, through all the years of their life
together, as they watched their children grow up
bathed in the knowledge of their parents' undying love
for each other.

How to join in a whole new world of romance

It's very easy to subscribe to the Mills & Boon Reader Service. As a regular reader, you can enjoy a whole range of special benefits. Bargain offers. Big cash savings. Your own free Reader Service newsletter, packed with knitting patterns, recipes, competitions, and exclusive book offers.

We send you the very latest titles each month, postage and packing free – no hidden extra charges. There's absolutely no commitment – you receive books for only as long as you want.

We'll send you details. Simply send the coupon – or drop us a line for details about the Mills & Boon Reader Service Subscription Scheme.
Post to: Mills & Boon Reader Service, P.O. Box 236, Thornton Road, Croydon, Surrey CR9 3RU, England.
*Please note: READERS IN SOUTH AFRICA please write to: Mills & Boon Reader Service of Southern Africa, Private Bag X3010, Randburg 2125, S. Africa.

Please send me details of the Mills & Boon Subscription Scheme.
NAME (Mrs/Miss) _____ EP3
ADDRESS _____
_____
COUNTY/COUNTRY_____ POST/ZIP CODE_____
BLOCK LETTERS, PLEASE

Mills & Boon
the rose of romance